D0396075

"A page-turner with a clever surprise ending."—G.M. Malliet, Agatha Award-winning author of the St. Just and Max Tudor mystery series

"[A] haunting tale of two murders … This is more than a mystery. It is a plush journey into cultural time and place."—Jill Florence Lackey, PhD, author of *Milwaukee's Old South Side* and *American Ethnic Practices in the Twenty-First Century*

HERITAGE OF DARKNESS

"Chloe's fourth … provides a little mystery, a little romance, and a little more information about Norwegian folk art and tales."—*Kirkus Reviews*

THE LIGHT KEEPER'S LEGACY

"Chloe's third combines a good mystery with some interesting historical information on a niche subject."—*Kirkus Reviews*

"Framed by the history of lighthouses and their keepers and the story of fishery disputes through time, the multiple plots move easily across the intertwined past and present."—*Booklist Online*

"A haunted island makes for fun escape reading. Ernst's third amateur sleuth cozy is just the ticket for lighthouse fans and genealogy buffs. Deftly flipping back and forth in time in alternating chapters, the author builds up two mystery cases and cleverly weaves them back together."—*Library Journal*

"While the mystery elements of this books are very good, what really elevates it are the historical tidbits of the real-life Pottawatomie Lighthouse and the surrounding fishing village."—*Mystery Scene*

"Once again in *The Light Keeper's Legacy* Kathleen Ernst wraps history with mystery in a fresh and compelling read. I ignored food so

I could finish this third Chloe Ellefson mystery quickly. I marvel at Kathleen's ability to deepen her series characters while deftly introducing us to a new setting and unique people on an island off the Wisconsin coast. In the fashion of Barbara Kingsolver, Kathleen weaves contemporary conflicts of commercial fishing, environmentalists, sport fisherman and law enforcement into a web of similar conflicts in the 1880s and the two women on neighboring islands still speaking to Chloe that their stories may be remembered. It takes a skilled writer to move back and forth 100 years apart, make us care for the characters in both centuries, give us particular details of lighthouse life and early Wisconsin, not forget Chloe's love interest and have us cheering at the end. A rich and satisfying third novel that makes me ask what all avid readers will: When's the next one! Well done, Kathleen!"—Jane Kirkpatrick, *New York Times* bestselling author

THE HEIRLOOM MURDERS

"Chloe is an appealing character, and Ernst's depiction of work at a living museum lends authenticity and a sense of place to the involving plot."—*St. Paul Pioneer Press*

"Greed, passion, skill, and luck all figure in this surprise-filled outing."—*Publishers Weekly*

"Interesting, well-drawn characters and a complicated plot make this a very satisfying read."—*Mystery Reader*

"Entertainment and edification."—*Mystery Scene*

OLD WORLD MURDER

"*Old World Murder* is strongest in its charming local color and genuine love for Wisconsin's rolling hills, pastures, and woodlands … a delightful distraction for an evening or two."—*New York Journal of Books*

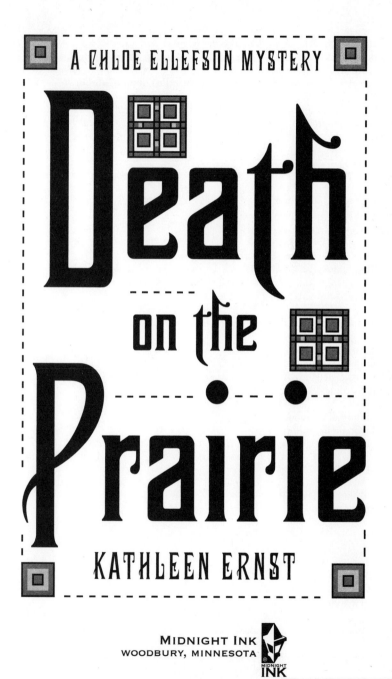

A CHLOE ELLEFSON MYSTERY

Death
on the
Prairie

KATHLEEN ERNST

MIDNIGHT INK
WOODBURY, MINNESOTA

FIRST EDITION
First Printing, 2015

Book format by Bob Gaul
Cover design by Kevin R. Brown
Cover illustration by Charlie Griak
Editing by Nicole Nugent
Interior map by Llewellyn Art Department
Photos on pages 329–334:
    #1–5, 7–9 and 11–12 © Kathleen Ernst, #6 © kenfoster.us,
    #10 © Barbara Ernst

Midnight Ink, an imprint of Llewellyn Worldwide Ltd.

Library of Congress Cataloging-in-Publication Data
Ernst, Kathleen, 1959–
  Death on the prairie: a Chloe Ellefson mystery/Kathleen Ernst.—First edition.
    pages; cm.—(A Chloe Ellefson mystery; #6)
  ISBN 978-0-7387-4470-4
1. Women museum curators—Fiction. 2. Murder—Investigation—Fiction. I. Title.
PS3605.R77D43 2015
813'.6—dc23
                        2015021840

Midnight Ink
Llewellyn Worldwide Ltd.
2143 Wooddale Drive
Woodbury, MN 55125-2989
www.midnightinkbooks.com

Printed in the United States of America

DEDICATION
For Barbara

The first book in Laura Ingalls Wilder's Little House series, *Little House in the Big Woods,* was published in 1932. The loosely auto-biographical novels depict Laura from childhood to young womanhood. Her family's joys, sorrows, and travels on the frontier of Yankee-Euro settlement have been eagerly read by millions of children. I was one of them. Years later, when working as an interpreter and curator in the historic sites world, I was delighted to discover that mentioning the Little House books often created a common bond with visitors. When I reread the series as an adult, I discovered new layers to the stories. The books are popular around the world, and have never gone out of print.

Thanks to the work, vision, and generosity of many, fans of Laura Ingalls Wilder can visit museums and historic sites where she once lived in Wisconsin, Iowa, Minnesota, South Dakota, Kansas, and Missouri. This story provides only a glimpse of the sites' histories; in most cases I made choices to help readers visualize places that may be familiar now. To learn more about the featured historic places and museums, visit:

Laura Ingalls Wilder Wayside and Museum, Pepin, WI
   http://www.lauraingallspepin.com

Laura Ingalls Wilder Park and Museum, Burr Oak, IA
   http://www.lauraingallswilder.us

Laura Ingalls Wilder Museum, Ingalls Dugout Site, Wilder
   Pageant, Walnut Grove, MN
   http://www.walnutgrove.org

Laura Ingalls Wilder Historic Homes, De Smet, SD
   http://www.discoverlaura.org

Little House on the Prairie Museum, Independence, KS
   http://www.littlehouseontheprairiemuseum.com

Laura Ingalls Wilder Historic Home & Museum, Mansfield, MO
   http://www.lauraingallswilderhome.com

Laura Ingalls Wilder fans will enjoy several sites that I was unable to include:

Wilder Homestead, Malone, NY
   http://www.almanzowilderfarm.com

Spring Valley Methodist Church Museum, Spring Valley, MN
   http://www.springvalleymnmuseum.org/wilderwilder.html

Ingalls Homestead, De Smet, SD (a hands-on, re-created experience
   on the land once homesteaded by the Ingalls family)
   http://www.ingallshomestead.com

You'll find photographs of some of the artifacts and places mentioned in the story on pages 329-334.

You can also find many more photographs, maps, and other resources on my website, *www.kathleenernst.com.*

CAST OF CHARACTERS

Chloe Ellefson—curator of collections, Old World Wisconsin

Kari Ellefson Anderson—Chloe's older sister

Trygve, Astrid & Anja Anderson—Kari's husband and daughters

Miss Lila—longtime family friend

Roelke McKenna—officer, Village of Eagle Police Department

Libby—Roelke's cousin

Chief Naborski—chief, Village of Eagle Police Department

Marie—clerk, Village of Eagle Police Department

Crystal—young Eagle resident

Mrs. Enright—social worker

Angelica & Travis—mother and infant, Eagle residents

Con Malloy—sergeant, Milwaukee Police Department

Frank McArdle—detective, Kingsbury County

Nika—intern, Old World Wisconsin

Ralph Petty—director, Old World Wisconsin

Skeet Deardorff—officer, Village of Eagle Police Department

Tony Colin—airport mechanic

Spider—bartender

Peggy—friend of Roelke McKenna's

Babs—real estate agent

Historic Sites' Representatives

Norma Epps—Laura Ingalls Wilder Memorial Society, Pepin, WI

Marianne Schiller—The Laura Ingalls Wilder Park
& Museum, Burr Oak, IA

David Rice—The Laura Ingalls Wilder Museum
and Tourist Center, Walnut Grove, MN

Edna Jo Poffenwiler—Laura Ingalls Wilder
Memorial Society, De Smet, SD

Lucille Unger—Little House on the Prairie Museum,
Independence, KS

Carmelina Biancardi—Laura Ingalls Wilder Historic
Home & Museum, Mansfield, MO

Travelers—Laura Land Tours

Alta Allerbee—tour leader

Hazel & Wilbur Voss

Bill & Frances Whelan

Henrietta Beauchamps

Leonard Devich

Additional Travelers: Jayne Rifenberg, Haruka Minari,
and Kimball Dexheimer

Little House Characters

Caroline & Charles Ingalls—Ma and Pa

Mary Ingalls—oldest daughter

Laura Ingalls Wilder—second daughter, author

Carrie & Grace Ingalls—third and fourth daughters

Almanzo Wilder—Laura's husband

Cap Garland—friend of Laura and Almanzo

Nellie Oleson—fictional composite character, Laura's nemesis

Rose Wilder Lane—Laura and Almanzo's daughter

BOOKS BY LAURA INGALLS WILDER

Little House in the Big Woods—Pepin, Wisconsin

Farmer Boy—New York; depicts the
boyhood of Laura's husband, Almanzo

Little House on the Prairie—Independence, Kansas

On the Banks of Plum Creek—Walnut Grove, Minnesota

By the Shores of Silver Lake—De Smet, South Dakota

The Long Winter—De Smet, South Dakota

Little Town on the Prairie—De Smet, South Dakota

These Happy Golden Years—De Smet, South Dakota

The First Four Years—De Smet, South Dakota,
published posthumously in 1971

*All of the above were published by HarperCollins, beginning in 1932. Books are listed in order of publication, which matches the chronological order of Laura's life. Burr Oak, Spring Valley, and Mansfield are not featured in the Little House series.

*Laura Ingalls Wilder, Farm Journalist: Writings From the
Ozarks.* Edited by Stephen W. Hines. University of Missouri
Press, 2008.—A collection of articles written before Laura
turned to fiction.

Pioneer Girl: The Annotated Autobiography. Edited by Pamela
Smith Hill. South Dakota State Historical Society, 2014.—
Laura's previously unpublished memoir.

CHLOE AND KARI'S ROAD TRIP

Pepin, Wisconsin
Burr Oak, Iowa
Walnut Grove, Minnesota
De Smet, South Dakota
Independence, Kansas
Mansfield, Missouri

They had playhouses under the two big oak trees in front of the house.
Mary's playhouse was under Mary's tree, and Laura's playhouse was
under Laura's tree.　　　　　Little House in the Big Woods

ONE

"THIS QUILT BELONGED TO *who*?" Chloe Ellefson's voice squeaked on the last word. "Did you say... Laura Ingalls Wilder?"

"*Whom*, dear," Miss Lila said. "Yes. This quilt belonged to Laura Ingalls Wilder."

Chloe reached toward the folded quilt that had been deposited with far too little ceremony on her desk. Her fingers stopped short. Instead she grabbed a ballpoint pen lying a foot away, terrified that ink might inexplicably geyser forth, and tossed it onto the floor.

Miss Lila's forehead wrinkled. "Are you alright, dear?"

"I need gloves. And acid-free tissue. And..." Chloe sank back in her chair and regarded her guest. "What... how... Are you sure? Laura?"

"Gracious, Chloe." Miss Lila's voice held the faint rebuke that can only come from long years of acquaintance.

Which was to be expected, Chloe thought. Miss Lila Gillespie had lived next to her parents' house in Stoughton, Wisconsin, forever. She always wore dresses and heavy stockings that bunched around her

1

ankles. She'd carried the same black pocketbook for as long as Chloe could remember. She was quite thin, with the posture of a broomstick. But a plump and generous heart beat beneath the starched shell. Miss Lila was the go-to grandma for every child on the block.

"Sorry," Chloe managed. "It's just that … well, lots of people contact me about donating heirlooms, but no one's offered an artifact that belonged to Laura."

Miss Lila smiled. "I remember reading *Little House in the Big Woods* to you and your sister. I don't know who enjoyed it more, you or Kari."

"Me," Chloe assured her, although Kari had loved it too. Seeing Miss Lila evoked memories of chocolate cookies and delicate china, gleaming old furniture scented with Lemon Pledge, stories read aloud as snow drifted past windows framed with long lace curtains.

"And now your mother tells me that you've been invited to give a speech about that book …? What an honor."

"Well, it's not *that* big a deal," Chloe said. "In grad school I wrote a paper arguing that although *Little House in the Big Woods* is a novel, the historical processes Laura described—churning butter, butchering, maple sugaring—were authentic, and thus acceptable as partial documentation for historic sites' programming. Somebody mentioned it to somebody else, and I got invited to talk at a gathering of Little House fans in a couple of weeks. The symposium will be in De Smet, South Dakota, where several of the later books are set."

"You must be excited!"

"Actually, I haven't had a lot of time to think about it." Like, none. Chloe planned to blow the dust from her original paper and pretty much wing it from there. "Anyway, how come you never told me about this quilt?"

"I inherited it from a cousin several years ago. I showed it to Kari, but you were living out of the country at the time."

Chloe regarded the quilt. She'd worked in the historic sites biz for over a decade and had served as collections curator at the huge outdoor ethnic museum called Old World Wisconsin for almost a year. She'd held hundreds of treasures in her gloved hands—some fragile as cobwebs, some folk art treasures worth thousands of dollars, some the only surviving scrap left to honor an unknown woman's life. But still, there'd been nothing like this.

Based on the fabrics, Chloe guestimated that the quilt had been made during the period covered in the Little House books. Maybe 1883, she thought—exactly one hundred years ago. Maybe Laura had wrapped herself in this very quilt during one of the prairie blizzards she'd described so vividly. The notion brought a lump to Chloe's throat, and she felt ridiculously emotional.

Geez, get a grip, she told herself. She imagined getting all dewy-eyed at the next Collections Committee meeting, while her boss looked on with contempt. That was a scene to be avoided.

At least no one else is here to see me reduced to a stuttering fangirl, Chloe thought. Miss Lila had presented herself without warning at Education House—the small home that the state purchased when almost six hundred acres within a state forest had been set aside to establish the sprawling historic site. It was after five, and the curators of research and interpretation had gone home.

Chloe tried to transform back into the oh-so-professional curator she generally aspired to be. "Tell me everything you know about this quilt." She retrieved her pen and grabbed a notebook.

Miss Lila folded her hands. "My cousin Inez gave me a few heirlooms, including Laura's quilt, before she passed away. Like me,

Inez had no children. I've enjoyed having the quilt, but I'm eighty-eight. This quilt deserves a permanent home."

"How did your cousin come to have it? Is there any documentation specific to Laura?"

Miss Lila waved a dismissive hand. "Nothing in writing, but it's come down in family lore. Inez's husband was descended from one of Caroline Quiner's sisters."

Chloe nodded. Caroline Quiner was Laura's mother, AKA Ma, who later married Charles Ingalls, AKA Pa.

"Caroline was born near Milwaukee, but Laura was born in Pepin, Wisconsin."

Everyone knew that. Chloe's mind danced ahead to a question she hardly dared articulate. "Did Laura ... actually ... *make* the quilt?"

"Inez used the word *own*."

"Oh." Bummer.

"Laura visited Pepin after she and Almanzo Wilder married," Miss Lila added, "and gave the quilt to a relative."

"Really? I would have figured she had her hands full out in South Dakota after she got married."

"That doesn't mean she didn't visit her old home at some point."

"No," Chloe allowed, but strands of caution were weaving through her excitement. This quilt might, or might not, have belonged to the famous author. Research might, or might not, answer that question. But she couldn't present the proposed donation to her colleagues as a sure-thing Laura artifact without more to go on.

Then, with a further sinking heart, she thought of something else. "Have you considered offering the quilt to one of the Laura sites and museums?"

"I have. Last year I wrote to someone at each historic site that preserves one of Laura's homes. The trouble is, they're *all* interested."

"Ah." No surprise there. Even without verifying that Laura had owned the quilt, just knowing that it *might* have been owned by her, and had passed down through a branch of the family, would have tickled any Lauraphile's fancy.

"I didn't know which site should receive the quilt, so I just put the problem out of my mind," Miss Lila confessed. "Then your mother stopped by this morning to ask if I needed any daylilies, and she mentioned your invitation to speak. And I thought, Well, there is the answer! Laura was born in Wisconsin, and I knew you'd take good care of the quilt, so I concluded that it should come here instead."

Chloe nibbled her lower lip. A curator's personal artifact lust was not acceptable rationale for accepting a donation. Besides, all of Old World's restored homes and farmsteads were furnished to reflect the actual family that had once lived there. Interpreters in period clothing used those specific stories to help visitors gain insight into the larger experience of the Yankees and Europeans who had flooded the state in the 1800s. If Old World Wisconsin did acquire Miss Lila's quilt, it might be displayed during some special event, but it could not be exhibited and interpreted as Laura's on a daily basis.

The trouble was, Chloe really wanted her site to acquire the quilt. She wanted to be able to look at it whenever she wished. Maybe even touch it with a non-gloved finger from time to time. If she was having a bad day.

Then a mental image of herself creeping into storage—like an art thief who hung Rembrandts and van Goghs on the walls of an armored room hidden behind bookshelves—popped into mind. And so begins a descent to the curatorial dark side, she thought.

Reluctantly, she faced facts. "As the owner, you can offer the quilt to any historic site or museum you choose. But I think it might be wise to reconsider donating it to one of the Laura Ingalls Wilder sites."

"Well, I did have one other idea," Miss Lila said. "Maybe each Laura Ingalls Wilder site deserves something. I could cut the quilt into pieces, and—"

"*No!*" Chloe's toes curled in horror. "I'm sorry, I didn't mean to yell, but I *strongly* advise against that. Wherever the quilt ends up, it should stay intact."

Miss Lila's gaze held a hint of shrewd amusement. "Then please, dear. Which site should get the quilt? I trust your professional opinion."

I think I just got played, Chloe thought. But how could she care, when a quilt that might have once graced Laura's bed was involved? "Do you have contact information for the historic sites? The names of people who responded to your original inquiries?"

"Of course." Miss Lila pulled a paper from her pocketbook. "Here you are."

Chloe accepted the page. "Even if your final choice is to offer it to Old World Wisconsin, I don't have the authority to accept it myself. All potential donations are discussed at curatorial meetings, and the next one won't take place for over a month. But that buys us some time."

"Time for what, dear?"

"With your permission, I'll contact each site and discuss your proposed donation. I can get a sense of their storage facilities, whether the quilt would be put on display . . . that sort of thing."

"Lovely." Miss Lila beamed. "I will leave the quilt in your capable hands."

Oh-boy-oh-boy-oh-boy! Chloe thought with giddy glee, before summoning her grown-up voice. "Since the quilt is not yet officially a proposed donation to Old World, I'm not sure that I should—"

"I'm sure," Miss Lila said firmly. "What was that you were saying about acid-free tissue . . . ?"

Played again, Chloe thought, but she didn't care about that either. Technically she could not provide expensive curatorial supplies to stabilize an artifact that had not been legally transferred to Old World Wisconsin, but she *still* didn't care. "I'll package the quilt properly," she promised. "And I'll let you know what I discover after talking with people at the sites."

Miss Lila looked thoughtful. "Each site will send a representative to the symposium, don't you think? Take the quilt to South Dakota so they can see it for themselves."

Chloe leaned back in her chair, picturing herself creeping along dirt roads all the way to De Smet, desperate to avoid a fiery collision. And what if she encountered a trunk-piercing hailstorm? Or a tornado? "I don't think I should travel with the quilt, Miss Lila. That would make me very nervous."

"Nonsense."

"But—"

"Chloe." Miss Lila leaned forward. "I want you to learn what you can about this quilt, and choose its permanent home."

Who could say no? "All right," Chloe conceded. "But before you go, I need you to sign a loan form." She knew she'd have a nervous breakdown if anything happened to the quilt, but at least she could avoid a lawsuit against her employer by dotting and crossing the legal i's and t's. She fetched the necessary form, filled out the basics, and handed it over.

"If it makes you feel better." Miss Lila signed with a flourish that suggested schooling in the Palmer Method of handwriting. "There you are."

Chloe walked her to the door. Before leaving, Miss Lila paused and put one hand to Chloe's cheek. "Thank you, my dear. This is important, and I trust you."

"I'll do my very best," Chloe promised humbly.

After Miss Lila left, Chloe spent a good five minutes staring at the quilt. And such a lovely quilt it was! The pretty blocks were stitched largely in soft reds and browns and tans. Through the magic of geometry, simple squares and triangles had been transformed into a complex design.

Something quivered beneath Chloe's ribs, as if one of her heart-strings had been plucked. She slowly opened her bottom desk drawer and pulled out a hardcover book. *Little House in the Big Woods.* The dust jacket was tattered, but Garth Williams's painting of young Laura hugging her rag doll Charlotte still charmed. Chloe remembered how overwhelmed she had been on her first day at Old World Wisconsin. She hadn't been in good emotional shape then; hadn't been sure she could survive the probation period mandated for state service professionals. She'd brought this book to work as a talisman, and had kept it close ever since.

Only another true Little House–lover could understand what the books had meant to her as a child. It wasn't just that she and Kari had "played Laura and Mary." Or that Chloe had turned a back yard bower into a private playhouse she called Laura Land—soft grass and green leaves magically transformed into a log cabin. Laura's adventures had captivated. Laura's struggles had inspired. Laura had been a faithful friend when no one else understood. Laura's stories had sparked Chloe's interest in history, her hobbies, her career and professional passions.

This book led me here, Chloe thought, contemplating her surroundings. Ed House was old and worn. She had only a corner of what had once been a small living room to call her own, with a battered wooden desk and an even more battered metal filing cabinet. But the house was nestled into the forest, overlooking a gloriously swampy lake—a "kettle pond," in the parlance of those familiar with the glacier-carved landscape. Beyond the pond was the historic site proper, with dozens of historic structures that had been moved from all over the state and restored to function as working farms and a crossroads village. Chloe hadn't been sure about coming to work here a year ago, but she'd long since fallen in love with this special place.

Chloe considered the contact information for the historic sites that Miss Lila had provided. Pepin, Wisconsin; Walnut Grove, Minnesota; Independence, Kansas; De Smet, South Dakota—all familiar names from the Little House books. She knew nothing about Burr Oak, Iowa, or Mansfield, Missouri.

Then Chloe dug through a file drawer until she found the packet of symposium materials. It had arrived during the height of site-opening, and she hadn't even peeked inside the envelope. She ripped the manila open now. The top page held a banner headline: *Are you **Looking For Laura?** Join us in De Smet!*

A tantalizing idea presented itself. Chloe tapped the book as she toyed with the possibility. She couldn't.

Could she?

Yes, she could. It was the first week of May. Old World Wisconsin had only been open for a few days, but *her* big push had come in April, when she'd had to ready all of the farms and shops and homes for the open season, and help train the incoming interpreters. She'd been working sixty-hour weeks for a couple of months. She was exhausted. Her boss had already approved time off for her trip to South Dakota, and he would probably approve of more. As long as he didn't have to pay for it, site director Ralph Petty was big on professional collaboration with other sites. God only knew what trouble he'd make for her while she was gone, but she'd worry about that later.

Chloe called Information and got her sister's number. She began to dial ... and slammed down the receiver after the third digit. She paced the room for a moment. Stopped to gaze upon the quilt. Paced some more.

"Okay," she muttered finally. "Nothing ventured, nothing gained."

She dialed the complete number. Kari picked up on the third ring. "Chloe?" she asked, sounding startled. Then her voice changed. "Oh God. What's wrong?"

Chloe made a mental note to call her sister more often. "Nothing is wrong. I was just wondering ... How'd you like to take a road trip?"

———

After one last admiring glance, Chloe cocooned the quilt with professional care and tucked it away. She made photocopies of the loan form and Miss Lila's letters from the historic sites—one set to keep with the quilt, one set to file. *I should have asked for more family information too,* Chloe thought with chagrin. She'd been so darn bedazzled that she hadn't even written down Cousin Inez's full name.

Then she locked up and drove to Palmyra, a small village about halfway between Old World Wisconsin and her own rented farmhouse in La Grange. She was unbuckling her seat belt when a familiar truck pulled in beside her. Roelke McKenna emerged, still in uniform after a shift as patrolman with the Eagle Police Department. He smiled the special smile reserved only for her—part seductive, part protective—that always provoked a tingle in Chloe's nether regions. His long kiss only intensified the shiveryness.

"Hey," she said when she could, a bit breathless.

"Are you game for a drive before supper?"

"Um ... sure." Chloe eyed him. Something was up.

Although they'd been a couple for a while now, they were still figuring each other out. Roelke could be intense, hard-wired, focused like a laser. Being Roelke McKenna's ladyfriend was not always easy. But I had easy once, Chloe thought, remembering a long-term relationship with a fellow museum junkie which had ended in colossal failure. Now, she wanted to be with Roelke.

As they pulled out of the lot she told him about Miss Lila's visit. "So without warning here was this quilt, just plopped on my desk, and she's telling me that it belonged to Laura Ingalls Wilder." Chloe's eyes filled with tears.

"Hey, are you okay?"

"I—of course, I just … I really loved the Little House books when I was a kid. Whenever I felt bad about something, I could disappear into Laura Land. You know?" She darted him a sideways glance. If Roelke teased her, she'd get out of the truck and walk home.

"I felt that way when I read Huck Finn," he said thoughtfully. "I was right out there on the Mississippi."

"You," Chloe said humbly, "are the best boyfriend ever." She wasn't big on the word *boyfriend*, but Roelke liked it.

He smiled. "So, what are these books about?"

How to answer that in less than an hour? "Well … they're about growing up in a pioneer family. Laura was born in Wisconsin in the 1860s. My favorite book is the first one, *Little House in the Big Woods*. The Ingalls family moved around a lot before ending up in South Dakota. Fans in each of the places Laura lived have created some kind of museum or historic site for readers to visit. I decided that if I'm going as far as South Dakota anyway, I might as well visit every homesite."

"With such a valuable antique in the car?"

"Yes. No biggie." Chloe didn't need Roelke's cop brain to spend time on that. "The sites have planned special events before and after the symposium for people making the pilgrimage. It should be interesting."

"So … where exactly are you going?"

"First stop is Pepin, Wisconsin," Chloe said. "Then on to Iowa, Minnesota, South Dakota, Kansas, and finally Missouri."

Roelke whistled. "Holy toboggans."

"That route doesn't match the stories' chronology, but it makes the most sense geographically."

"That's a lotta miles."

"It is. Which is why I invited my sister to come with."

His eyebrows rose. "Yeah?"

"Kari and I shared the books. Laura's closest sibling was her older sister, Mary. When Kari and I played Little House, she was always Mary and I was always Laura. In the books, Mary was annoyingly perfect. She went blind when she was a teenager, and even then she never complained. Laura was much more fun. Anyway, later they had two other sisters, Carrie and Grace."

"Well, hunh."

"Kari and I talked for years about visiting all the Laura Ingalls Wilder homesites, but it never happened. I didn't really expect her to agree to the trip on such short notice, not with two kids at home and a farm to help run. But she said yes."

"How come I've never met Kari?" Roelke lifted two fingers in a driver's wave as they passed another pickup. They were driving through farm country. Imperturbable Holsteins watched them pass. Fields glowed emerald green with infant alfalfa.

"She's busy," Chloe said vaguely. "And … we're not really close."

"Why not?"

She kicked off her sandals, slid down on the seat, and propped her bare toes on the dashboard. "Kari's one of those people who does everything well. I was a year behind her in high school, and I got really tired of hearing how good she was at algebra and softball and Norwegian folk dancing. She never gave our parents anything to worry about."

"And you did? Let's hear some tales!"

"Perhaps another time. Let's just say that Kari was a hard act to follow."

"But now you're going to spend a week in the car with her?"

Chloe gazed out the window. "I know what you're thinking. My last attempt at family bonding turned into a debacle." A trip with Roelke and her mom last December had *not* gone smoothly.

He paused. "No, you're right. I bet you two will have a blast."

The words were right, but something else lurked behind them. "Roelke, have you gotten your guitar out yet?" she asked. Roelke had once taken great pleasure in the band he'd formed with several cop friends. One was his best friend, who'd died in February. Roelke had lost a creative outlet as well as a friend.

He winced. "Where did *that* come from?"

"Sorry, that sounded abrupt." Her cheeks grew warm. "Charles Ingalls, Laura's pa, played the fiddle. I guess remembering the books made me think about it. It may be that the longer you stay away from music, the harder it will be to get going again."

"I'm not ready to play music again."

Okay, Chloe thought, message received. She sat up straight again as he braked gently and pulled over in front of a tired old farm. "Oh—hey! I know where we are."

"The old Roelke place. When my mom left my dad, she brought me and Patrick here." Patrick was Roelke's brother.

Chloe looked across the weeds to a two-story farmhouse built with cream city bricks—formed from the distinctive light yellow clay found near Milwaukee. The property was bordered on two sides by cornfields, and the Kettle Moraine State Forest embraced the others.

And in front, a real estate agency's sign hung from a post. "It's for sale," she observed.

"Yeah. I drove by one day last week and saw the sign."

Chloe regarded Roelke. Dark hair, strong jaw, straight shoulders, thumb tapping the steering wheel—all familiar. But he also seemed... uncertain, maybe. Something which was not part of the command presence he'd mastered so very well. "You're not..." She paused to rephrase what she'd been about to say. "Are you thinking of buying the farm?"

"It wouldn't make any sense. The guy who bought the place after my grandfather died just rented out the fields, so God knows what condition the house is in. And I don't want to be a farmer."

Chloe tried to figure out what he needed. "But that's not what I asked," she said finally. "From what you've told me, this was a good place for you when you were younger."

"It was." The thumb tapping increased. "What do you think of it?"

"Well, it's a beautiful old house," she said honestly, although she wasn't sure if he was asking what she thought of the farm or the idea of owning it. "Being by the forest is a bonus."

"The farm property actually includes a stretch of the woods. There used to be some springs back there."

"Really? I've read about trainloads of city people visiting Eagle and Palmyra to 'take the waters' at some ritzy hotel or another, back before the water tables dropped and most of the springs dried up..." Her sentence trailed away as she realized that Roelke probably wasn't interested in historical trivia right now. "So, is buying the place a possibility?" It was hard to imagine that a twenty-nine-year-old cop could even consider buying a farm, no matter how decrepit the house.

"I don't even know what they're asking."

"Maybe you should call and get the information."

"Maybe I will."

A meadowlark's song drifted through the window, but Roelke's ambivalence muted the sweet spring day. Chloe unbuckled, scooched over, and put her head on his shoulder. She couldn't picture Roelke living on a farm. Still, it was clear that this place mattered to him. Maybe her trip had popped up at a good time. Her absence would give Roelke space to think through what that For Sale sign truly meant for him.

And maybe the road trip with Kari, Chloe thought, will help me figure out why thinking about Laura Ingalls Wilder—and seeing the quilt—reduced me to tears.

Once upon a time, sixty years ago, a little girl lived in the Big Woods of Wisconsin, in a little gray house made of logs.

The great, dark trees of the Big Woods stood all around the house, and beyond them were other trees and beyond them were more trees ... There were no houses. There were no roads. There were no people. There were only trees and the wild animals who had their homes among them.
                                             Little House in the Big Woods

TWO

"WANT TO STAY OVER?" Roelke asked as they finished washing dinner dishes in his apartment.

"I can't." Chloe gave the last plate a swipe. "I didn't get family information about the quilt from Miss Lila, and it's bugging me. I'm going to drive down to Stoughton."

"Can't you just call?"

"I could, but I'm hoping Miss Lila has something in writing from her cousin that I can borrow and photocopy. I can say hey to my parents at the same time."

"Want some company?"

Chloe kissed him. "I would love some company."

Roelke drove, with Chloe's palm resting on his thigh. The terrain was mostly rural and the evening was lovely. They made most of the hour-long trip in peaceful silence. Her mind was swirling with images of Laura and quilt squares as Roelke turned into her parents' neighborhood.

He broke her reverie. "Chloe?" His voice held an unexpected note of tension. "Does Miss Lila live on the near side of your parents' house, or the far side?"

She glanced at him. "Far side. Why?"

His jaw muscles tightened. She followed his gaze down the street ... to the police cars. And the ambulance.

Chloe's skin prickled. "Pull over. Pull *over*!" She was out of the truck before Roelke had cut the engine.

Her parents stood in their front yard with a police officer. Chloe ran to join them. "What's going on?"

Dad shook his head. And Mom ... Mom was crying. Mom *never* cried.

"What *happened*?" Chloe demanded. Roelke caught up and squeezed her shoulder. She shifted so she could feel him solid behind her.

"It's Lila," Mom managed. "When I went to check on her this evening, I found ..." Fresh tears welled.

"What did you find, Marit?" Roelke asked in his steady cop voice.

Mom swallowed visibly. "She was on the floor in her bedroom."

"The window was open." Dad looked stricken. "So was Miss Lila's jewelry box—"

"What—about—Miss—*Lila*?" Chloe demanded.

"Oh Chloe." Mom put a hand on Chloe's arm. The affectionate gesture was so unusual that Chloe's core temperature plunged another few degrees. "Lila is dead."

Chloe heard a faint stirring in the atmosphere as her childhood, summoned when Miss Lila had walked into her office, receded again. "But…but I saw her just a few hours ago!" She looked at Roelke, as if he might somehow turn back the clock and *fix* this.

"I am so sorry," he said. His eyes were dark and troubled, and they left no room for debate.

———

Two weeks later, when she saw her sister pull into the driveway, Chloe carried her suitcase outside. She studied the AMC Rambler. "You sure this beast is up to the trip?" she asked as Kari emerged.

"Trygve says so. But we can still switch to your car if you want."

"No," Chloe said quickly. Kari and her husband had purchased the sedan new fourteen years earlier because they wanted a Wisconsin-built car. It was one of the cheapest vehicles available and had over sixty thousand miles on it, but Tryg was meticulous about maintenance. The Rambler was surely more reliable than Chloe's rust bucket Pinto.

Besides, if a massive oak tree happened to blow over and crash on the trunk, the quilt would be safer in the Rambler than in the back of her own hatchback.

With infinite care, Chloe nestled the gray archival box holding Laura's quilt into the huge trunk. "I still can't believe that Miss Lila is dead."

"I *know*."

Chloe tried to gulp down the lump in her throat. "Let's go." She slammed the trunk.

The sisters settled in for the four-hour drive to Pepin. It would be easier to deal with Miss Lila's death, Chloe thought, if the cops had caught the SOB responsible. Miss Lila had died of a blow to the head. The cops believed she'd walked in on a robbery-in-progress.

Kari checked traffic before turning onto a county highway. "You're doing the right thing. With the quilt, I mean."

This is important, and I trust you. "I want to honor Miss Lila's request," Chloe said. And thank God I got that loan form signed, she added silently. She'd also sent photos and a description to a New York appraisal company that specialized in textiles, so if something *did* happen to the quilt, Old World Wisconsin had proof of value. Chloe tried to shake off visions of destruction. "My first goal is to see which site might make the best home for Miss Lila's quilt."

"There are other goals?"

"I hope to corroborate the family's claim that Laura did once actually own the quilt."

"You think that's possible? To *prove* she owned it, I mean."

"Who knows?" Chloe shrugged. "Maybe Laura mentioned the quilt in a letter. Maybe we can find a scrap of identical fabric in a quilt in one of the homesites' collections."

"I haven't read the Little House books for years," Kari confessed. "But I remember Laura and Mary sewing quilt blocks."

"In *By the Banks of Plum Creek* Mary was sewing Nine Patch blocks, but Laura was making what she called a Bear's Track quilt. It included bias seams, and she noted that her blocks were harder to construct than Mary's." Chloe smiled, vicariously celebrating Laura's triumph. In the early Little House books, Mary usually excelled at whatever task presented itself.

"Did you find a name for the pattern in Miss Lila's quilt?" Kari was a quilter, so her interest was genuine.

"I did some digging." Chloe tried to sound offhand. "The oldest reference I can find calls the pattern Bear Paw, but later sources call it Bear Track." Either name would fit the pattern of Miss Lila's quilt. Each block was constructed of squares and triangles arranged to present four repeating motifs that did indeed suggest bear tracks or paws.

"*Really*? Oh my God, Chloe! Do you suppose there's any chance that…" Kari summoned the courage to finish her thought. "I can't help hoping we'll discover that Laura actually *made* the quilt Miss Lila owned."

Instead of shouting, *I know! Me too!* Chloe forced herself to say, "That's not likely."

"Why not? It could be the quilt Laura wrote about making as a child."

"Not necessarily. There are lots of different patterns with names like Bear Claw and Bear Track and Bear Boogie—"

"You made that one up."

"Yes, but my point is valid. We have no way of knowing what pattern Laura used for her childhood quilt. Back then patterns weren't named according to some kind of national standard or something. Women called blocks whatever they wished. I have nothing to indicate that Miss Lila's quilt could actually be the Bear Track quilt Laura mentioned in *Plum Creek*."

"But nothing to prove it isn't, right? The fabric fits the time period?"

"It does," Chloe allowed. "We'll see what the lady we're meeting with has to say." The Laura Ingalls Wilder Memorial Society, which managed both the homesite and a museum in the town of Pepin, was an all-volunteer organization. Chloe had made an appointment to show Miss Lila's quilt to the board member responsible for collections. And that person, she knew, would likely shoot gaping holes in the notion that Miss Lila might actually have come to own Laura Ingalls Wilder's childhood quilt.

But Chloe couldn't quite silence the voice in her head whispering, *Maybe … just maybe …*

Kari had never left her two daughters for more than a weekend before. After she stopped twice that morning to call home, Chloe started to wonder if this trip was a bad idea after all. They planned to be gone for ten days.

Then Chloe took the wheel. Kari pulled out a quilting project, and the handwork seemed to calm her anxiety. They left the interstate and stopped at the Norske Nook in Osseo, and Kari's mood lifted even more as they valiantly attacked towering wedges of sour cream-raspberry and cream cheese-maple-raisin pie. The drive west toward the Mississippi River was gorgeous. By the time they hit Pepin, just a few miles from the Ingalls family's homesite, the mood was much improved. Kari and I may not have much in common now, Chloe thought, but we'll always have Laura and Mary.

"Almost there," Kari said as they turned northwest.

Chloe flashed to their back seat days. "You sound just like Mom."

"We're about to walk the same ground Laura and Mary actually walked. What can I say? I'm eager to get there."

Chloe smiled. Their visit to the museum in town was scheduled for later that day. She and Kari had planned their visit to the actual homesite to coincide with the first public program leading up to the *Looking For Laura* symposium. She was eager too.

"Why do you suppose Mom and Dad never brought us here?" Kari asked.

"Because Laura wasn't Norwegian?"

"Oh, they aren't that narrow." After a moment Kari amended, "Well…maybe Mom is, sometimes." She pointed ahead. "There it is!"

Chloe felt a puppy's tail happy wiggle inside when she saw a sign for the Laura Ingalls Wilder Wayside. She pulled into the small lot and parked.

Then the inner happy wiggle subsided. "But…where are the woods?" she asked. The Wayside was a grassy picnic area, with a replica cabin representing the home were Laura was born. The few saplings sprinkled through the grounds were too young to provide shade. Picnic tables were scattered about, most occupied by other Laura sojourners wearing sunglasses and hats.

"Evidently the Big Woods have become the Big Cornfields." Kari's voice was hollow.

They sat in silence for a few minutes, as if hoping their dismay might miraculously transform farmland to old-growth forest. I should have anticipated this, Chloe thought. In the rush of preparing for the impromptu Laura tour, she'd gathered state maps and calculated mileage. She'd talked with her friend Dellyn about kitty-sitting, and her intern Nika about site-sitting, and her colleague Byron about training the next incoming batch of interpreters. Spare moments had been spent reacquainting herself with the talk she was to present at the *Looking For Laura* symposium. There had been no time to acknowledge that in all likelihood, the 1983 version of the *Little House in the Big Woods* cabin would not equate well with the charming Garth Williams illustrations lodged so firmly in her psyche.

Finally Kari sighed. "We're way early for the program. We might as well have lunch and look around."

As they climbed from the car, Chloe tried to adjust her attitude. "At least it's not urban sprawl. This is still the *place*. And place has a lot of power to—"

"Help!" a woman shrieked. "Somebody, please—*help him*!"

Chloe and Kari exchanged an alarmed glance and ran toward a growing huddle of horrified picnickers. When Chloe slid between a couple of onlookers she saw a young man—maybe thirty?—curled on the ground. He wore blue jeans and a yellow t-shirt, and had a sleek swimmer's physique, but the image of good health ended there. His arms were clenched tight over his belly. Horrible retching noises rasped the silence.

"I'll run to the farmhouse across the road and call an ambulance," Kari said, and took off.

Oh God, Chloe thought, as she dropped to her knees.

A pretty woman with Asian features crouched on the man's other side, wringing her hands. "I don't know what to do! Are you a doctor?"

"No." Chloe felt desperately, horribly inadequate. "What happened?"

"I don't know! I was sitting over there"—the other woman pointed to an empty lawn chair nearby—"and he was eating lunch. Then he just sort of fell over."

Chloe put a hand on the man's forehead. His skin was damp with sweat and blotched with hives. "Sir? Can you tell me what happened?"

He managed only a harsh, inarticulate wheeze in response. His brown eyes were wide open, imploring.

"Check his pockets for an epinephrine pen or kit," Chloe ordered the other woman. "I think it's anaphylaxis—some kind of allergic reaction." She began searching his arms for a telltale wheal or tiny bee stinger left in the skin. "Does anybody have some ice?" she called. "And a pen knife? Even a credit card." If she could find the damn stinger, she needed to scrape it off as fast as possible.

The man made a horrid choking sound. Then his muscles eased. He slipped from consciousness.

A heavy sensation settled in Chloe's chest. Her basic first-aid training was no match for a closing airway. She didn't see any signs of a bee sting on either arm. She switched to his ankles, shoving down crew socks, shoving up jeans as far as possible. No stinger.

23

"There's nothing in his pockets!" the other woman moaned.

Just breathe, Chloe begged the man silently. She pressed one palm against his chest and felt a racing heartbeat. This was bad, bad, bad. If she was right about anaphylaxis, this guy needed a shot of epinephrine, *fast*.

Minutes ticked by like centuries. The Asian woman began to weep. Parents pulled their kids away. Then, at the same moment, two distinct sounds reached Chloe's ears: The blessed wail of an approaching siren, and the terrifying underlying silence as the man stopped struggling for air.

———

Chloe rubbed her forehead. "I can't believe it."

She and Kari sat beside one of the token saplings in the picnic area. The EMTs had removed the young man's body. They hadn't *said* he was dead, but Chloe knew he was. A police officer had questioned Chloe, and the Asian woman too. Then the squad car had followed the ambulance. The other woman, clearly shaken, had spontaneously hugged Chloe before stowing her lawn chair in a blue VW and driving away.

Now Chloe felt numb and sad and jittery all at once. "He was so *young*. My age, maybe." Chloe had recently turned thirty-three, and that was too young to die in a picnic grove.

She blew out a long breath. "Here's what I don't get: there's no food here to purchase. Whatever he ate, he brought with him."

"If he was allergic to something, surely he'd be very careful about it."

Chloe watched a bee buzzing around a patch of clover. She heard again the choking sounds as the man tried to speak. Most of all she remembered the fear in his eyes. She had never felt so help-less. "I need pastry."

"After pie? What *I* could use is a drink." Kari's eyes were troubled, and the faint smatter of freckles stood out against unusually pale skin.

Chloe had been so focused on her own shock that she hadn't noticed Kari's. "Hey, are you okay?"

"It's just that … First Miss Lila, now this."

"I don't have booze or pastry, but we can at least eat some chocolate. Swiss, of course." Chloe dug into her tote bag and produced a bar.

Kari tried to smile. "You're a chocolate snob."

"I am." Living in Switzerland for several years while working at an open-air museum had spoiled her. Chloe broke the bar in half and nibbled slowly, willing inner calm.

A station wagon pulled into the Wayside lot, spilling parents and two little girls wearing Laura-wannabe calico sunbonnets. The girls raced toward the cabin. "Mom! It's *Laura's* house!"

"They remind me of you," Kari said. "Somewhere I have a snap-shot of you wearing a sunbonnet with your footie pajamas."

Chloe shrugged without remorse. As a child, she hadn't just wanted to emulate Laura; sometimes she *was* Laura. She'd worn a sunbonnet with her footie pajamas because—despite eating SpaghettiOs, doing homework, or taking a bath—she was still in the Big Woods.

"Just remember," she said, "I have one of you and Trygve dressed like Ma and Pa Ingalls for Halloween."

Kari had married her high school sweetheart the year they both graduated from the UW—her with a teaching degree, Trygve with a degree in Ag Science. They'd promptly settled into dairy farming and soon produced their beautiful girls, Anja and Astrid.

During those same years Chloe had gotten a graduate degree in museum studies, moved to Switzerland, and moved back to the US.

She'd descended into clinical depression's black well and made the painful crawl back to daylight. She'd almost gotten fired and lived on the edge of broke.

Chloe had seen her sister only infrequently since moving back to Wisconsin, usually at noisy family gatherings. She and Kari, who'd been close as little girls, had found little to talk about as adults. But in this clearing, Chloe finally felt the years and the distance peeling away.

———

Kari, who inexplicably didn't consider even Swiss chocolate an adequate meal, claimed a table. Chloe fetched their picnic basket from the car. "You set up," she said. "I'm going to take a peek at the cabin. It's only going to get more crowded as we get closer to the program."

"Sure." Kari folded a napkin and placed it on the tablecloth.

Chloe slid her hands into her pockets and wandered toward the replica cabin. The two little girls were playing tag. That could have been me and Kari twenty-five years ago, Chloe thought. Their joyful laughter flowed into the raw places inside her.

She paused in front of the cabin, closed her eyes, breathed deep. Sometimes she could perceive strong emotions that lingered through time. She couldn't predict it. She couldn't manufacture it. The sensations came most often in old buildings, and a replica did not qualify. Still, this was the *place*—the place where Laura Elizabeth Wilder was born in 1867, and where she experienced the changing seasons with such visceral clarity that she was able to write about them decades later. Chloe tried to open herself to whatever Laura might have left behind in this place.

Nothing came.

She opened her eyes just in time to duck an errant Frisbee before it slammed into her temple. "Sorry!" a boy called, racing to reclaim the neon green disc.

This might be the place, but any Ingalls layer had evidently been plowed up, paved over, and lost long ago.

Chloe tried to swallow her disappointment. Well, she consoled herself, this is just the first stop. This trip would provide more opportunities to look for Laura.

A plump gray-haired woman emerged from the cabin. She wore blue polyester pants and a sweatshirt that said *I Love Laura*. She offered Chloe a tremulous smile that said, *I think you understand why I'm here.*

Chloe smiled back. Instead of grieving, she should be grateful to the volunteers who managed to preserve this ground and build a replica cabin, right *here*. The Big Woods may be gone, she thought, but we pilgrims have a place to visit anyway.

———

The Wayside was growing more crowded by the time Chloe and Kari finished their lunch. A work crew set up rows of folding chairs beneath an awning, and the parking lot filled.

"I'll take the stuff back to the car," Chloe offered. She stashed the picnic basket and grabbed another Swiss chocolate bar from the cooler. She liked having one on hand.

A mini school bus pulled off the highway and parked on the verge with a hydraulic wheeze. The bus door opened, and perhaps a dozen people stepped off and eagerly headed for the clearing—half to the cabin, the other half to the restrooms. All but two of the travelers were female, which wasn't really surprising. What was surprising was the bus itself. *Alta's Laura Land Tours* was emblazoned on the bus in big red letters. Here and there were icons dear to any Laura fan: cabin, butter churn, fiddle, rag doll, etc., etc. The artist had created a collage to rival the Partridge Family's bus.

The woman who had organized the symposium and invited Chloe to speak was named Alta Allerbee. There can't be too many Altas in attendance, Chloe thought, so—

"Because we are leaving *now!*" a man snarled nearby.

"But Wilbur," a woman protested, "the program hasn't started yet."

Chloe recognized the lady who'd visited the cabin with such awed delight earlier. Shame on you, Wilbur, Chloe scolded silently. Quit being such a buzzkill.

Wilbur remained determined to kill any hint of buzz. "We've already been here for an hour."

"I was talking to a volunteer inside—"

"You've seen the damn cabin," he snapped. "You ate your damn lunch. For God's sake, Hazel, get in the car!"

Chloe walked over to join them. "Hi!" she said with her biggest, brightest smile. "Would you like some chocolate? You'd be doing me a favor, really. It's just going to melt." She held out the bar, still sealed in its wrapper.

Wilbur's expression suggested that she'd offered fried roaches. Behind bifocals, his eyes narrowed. His mouth was a tight twist. Close-clipped gray hair circled the top of his head, which was bald. Chloe hoped he'd applied sunscreen; a scalp burn would not help his disposition.

"It's Swiss," she added cheerfully.

Hazel accepted the bar, looking flustered. "That's—why—you're very kind."

"So," Chloe said conversationally, "are you folks just visiting Pepin, or are you doing a bigger tour?"

Hazel looked wide-eyed from Wilbur to this chocolate-bearing stranger.

"Get in the car, Hazel," Wilbur said. He'd been smoking a cigar and hurled it to the ground inches from her feet.

Chloe frowned. What was this guy's problem? "Maybe you should lighten up."

"Maybe you should mind your own damn business!"

Walk away, Chloe told herself. While a stare-down with Wilbur might make *her* feel better, it would probably not help Hazel. She raised her hands in surrender. "Sorry. Just trying to be friendly."

As Chloe turned, a lone woman wearing a long dress of purple calico and matching sunbonnet stepped from the *Laura Land Tours* bus. Maybe that was Alta Allerbee.

Chloe dug another chocolate bar from the cooler, ate a few bites to cleanse Wilbur's vibes, and tucked it safely away again. Then she walked to the school bus. The bonneted lady stood beside it with her back to the Wayside. Her outfit could be classified as "old-timey," rather than specific to the *Little House in the Big Woods* period, but Chloe didn't care. Alta Allerbee was all about helping others find a beloved author, and therefore worthy of great respect and affection.

As Chloe approached, she realized that the woman was talking to someone else—someone hidden from view by the bus's nose. Chloe paused a respectful distance away. She was watching a tiger swallowtail butterfly by the side of the road when the bonneted lady's voice rose.

"Please don't do that!" she begged. "You'll ruin *everything*!"

[Almanzo's father said:] "A farmer depends on himself, and the land and the weather. If you're a farmer, you raise what you eat, you raise what you wear, and you keep warm with wood out of your own timber. You work hard, but you work as you please, and no man can tell you to go or come. You'll be free and independent, son, on a farm."   Farmer Boy

THREE

ROELKE PARKED HIS TRUCK in front of the familiar old farmhouse. He'd made an appointment with the real estate agent, but he wanted a solo visit before everything got all official.

He'd been paying rent for a decade and was ready to stop flushing that money down the toilet every month. But he was a long way from knowing if buying the family farm would bring him financial independence or hang around his neck like an anvil.

He crossed the yard slowly, fighting the urge to weed the overgrown flowerbeds along the front porch. In his grandma's day there wouldn't have been a dandelion in sight. As he approached the front steps he frowned at a rotting board. In his granddad's day there wouldn't have been so much as a loose nail.

The back farmyard was equally forlorn. The guy renting the fields was keeping the barn intact, but the henhouse and corncrib were derelict. The first Roelke immigrants' original one-room log cabin had been converted to a garden shed before he was born, but the roof was missing some shingles. The old smokehouse had tumbled in altogether.

A lonesome ache bloomed in Roelke's chest. The stillness was almost spooky … yet he felt as if he could *almost* hear his granddad's old Farmall B firing up, and sheets flapping on the clothesline, and his mother singing while sprinkling feed for the Rhode Island Reds clucking around her feet. If he stood here long enough, maybe Patrick would come racing down the driveway on his bike, late for chores; or maybe his grandma would call him in for gingersnaps and milk.

I am probably six kinds of stupid to even be here, he thought. He didn't need to hear a lot of psychobabble to understand that he cared about this place because as a kid, his best times had been here, right here. That did not mean he should try to buy the property.

A sandhill crane's distant call drifted through the lazy afternoon. Shielding his eyes, Roelke spotted a pair of the gangly-graceful birds overhead. Chloe loved cranes. He wished she was here to see them. He wished she was here, period. He wanted to talk over all this farm stuff with her. In person.

Roelke checked the time and headed back toward the road. He was on his lunch break, and he'd be late for work if he stood here any longer. Enough thinking about old times. And enough missing Chloe too, for the moment. She'd worked her butt off getting Old World Wisconsin ready to open for the season. He'd have plenty of time to talk with her about the farm when she got back. In the meantime, he just wanted her to have fun.

———

Chloe frowned. What the hell? It was going to be very hard to have fun on this trip if this kept up. She'd just reluctantly left Wilbur snarling at sweet Hazel. Now a woman in prairie clothes was pleading for something she wanted or needed. It was a sunny May afternoon at the Laura Ingalls Wilder Wayside. Snarling and pleading were extremely inappropriate.

She turned and walked away from the bus. Wilbur and Hazel's car was gone, which was a shame, since Hazel had so badly wanted to stay for the program. Chloe unlocked Kari's car and rummaged in the cooler again. I clearly did not bring enough chocolate, she thought, snapping off two more squares for immediate sustenance. Maybe Pepin had a good bakery.

Across the Wayside, the chairs beneath the awning were beginning to fill. Chloe walked over and stood at the back, scanning the crowd for her sister. Finally she spotted Kari at the end of a line snaking around the ladies' room. She'll find me, Chloe thought, and grabbed two empty chairs on the aisle.

In the next chair sat a woman dressed in a prim navy blue suit, nylons, and high-heeled pumps. Everyone loves Laura, Chloe thought, as she smiled at her neighbor. "Hi."

"Hello." The woman was a bit older than Chloe, with intelligent eyes, a pert nose, and brown hair captured into a sleek chignon. "You must be a *Little House in the Big Woods* fan."

"I am, although"—Chloe made a *look around* gesture—"aren't we all? It's amazing how Laura's books touched so many people."

"You do know that Laura didn't write the Little House books, don't you?" Miss Chignon asked.

Chloe blinked. "Um … yes, she did."

"No, she didn't."

"Yes—she—*did*."

"Well, aren't you adorable." Miss Chignon's smile could not possibly have been any more condescending. "Actually—"

"Hey," Kari said breathlessly, sliding into place on Chloe's other side. "Thanks for grabbing seats."

Chloe gratefully turned her back on Miss Chignon's lunacy. It took self control to keep from cocking her head toward the woman and circling one finger in the childhood signal for "cuckoo."

Fortunately, a woman with short-cropped gray hair stepped to the podium and called briskly for attention. "I'm Norma Epps," she said. "On behalf of the Laura Ingalls Wilder Memorial Society, welcome to the birthplace of our favorite author."

Chloe leaned closer to her sister. "That's the lady we're meeting at the museum later."

"Laura's earliest memories were of falling to sleep as a little girl here in the Big Woods, listening to Pa play his fiddle." Norma smiled at the crowd. "A lot has changed in Pepin since Laura was a child. She once wrote, 'Now is now. It can never be a long time ago.'"

We can only wish, Chloe thought wistfully.

"But whenever I read one of Laura's books," Norma continued, "it *is* a long time ago. Now, Laura lived here until 1868, when the family moved—as you all know—to Kansas. In 1871, after Pa decided to leave Kansas, the family moved back here, staying for another two years."

Chloe frowned. The books hadn't said they were here twice.

"The Ingalls family moved west for good after that," Norma continued, "but we do know that Laura returned for a visit after she was married."

Kari elbowed Chloe's ribs. Chloe nodded. Miss Lila had been right about Laura's return to Pepin as an adult.

Norma gave a short talk about Laura's childhood. "Volunteers will be here all afternoon," she concluded. "Children can begin sewing their very own Nine Patch quilt block! And I urge you all to visit the Laura Ingalls Wilder Museum in town as well. Now, before we adjourn, I want to introduce a dear friend, Alta Allerbee."

The woman who made her way to the podium was indeed wearing familiar purple calico. When she turned to face the crowd, Chloe glimpsed shockingly red hair beneath the sunbonnet. "Hello!" Alta called. "I am coordinating both the special bus tour of Laura Land *and* the *Looking For Laura* symposium in De Smet."

Alta looked and sounded happy. Chloe eyed her thoughtfully. Had she imagined the angst in the snippet of conversation she'd overheard? Or were there two women in purple calico dresses and bonnets wandering around the Wayside?

"There's still time to register for the symposium, which will gather Laura scholars and fans for two days of sharing," Alta was saying. "I have a few empty seats on the bus, and you're welcome to caravan along in your own vehicles too. We have special activities planned for each Laura homesite, including a director's tour in Burr Oak and the annual pageant in Walnut Grove. We'll reach our final stop, Mansfield, Missouri, in time for the Wilder Heritage Festival. And staff there have *two* special treats in line for us. I'll leave brochures on the table. Thanks."

People began sidling out of the narrow rows of chairs. "Come on," Chloe said to Kari. "I want to introduce myself to Alta."

They swam upstream to the podium. When she noticed Chloe, Alta looked distinctly startled. Chloe had no idea why, but she trotted out her cheerful smile again, and introduced herself.

"Oh—you're one of my speakers!" Alta looked from Chloe to Kari and back again.

Now I get it, Chloe thought. Alta was sorting them out. Most people needed only a quick glance to peg the Ellefson girls as sisters, and many assumed they were twins. In contrast with Chloe's hip-length braid, Kari's cornsilk hair was cut to shoulder length. Bearing two children had broadened her hips, and fifteen years of work in the milking parlor and hay field had broadened her hands. But their eyes, their facial structure—those were still the same.

"This is my sister, Kari Anderson," Chloe said. "She's coming to the symposium too."

"*Looking For Laura* is going to be great fun," Alta said. "And—oh! Here's another speaker." She beckoned to none other than Miss Chignon.

Chloe frowned. What? *She* was a speaker? What kind of symposium was this, anyway?

"We meet again." Miss Chignon offered a cool hand and cold smile. "Jayne Rifenberg. That's Jayne with a Y."

Chloe didn't give a sugared fig how Jayne-with-a-Y spelled her name. "Chloe Ellefson. I'm presenting about the authenticity of historical processes described in *Little House in the Big Woods*."

"And *I'm* presenting the results of my research into the authorship of the Little House books," Jayne said.

"Which will be *fascinating*, I'm sure," Chloe lied. Jayne could cite sources until the heifers hopped home. Nothing could convince Chloe that anyone but Laura had written the Little House books.

Alta watched Jayne totter away in her black pumps. "Her paper is going to stir up controversy," she murmured. Then she smiled at Chloe. "Yours, I'm sure, will be a big hit."

"I'm amazed that you're leading a bus tour and organizing the symposium at the same time," Chloe said. "You must feel overwhelmed."

"I'm an elementary school librarian," Alta said with a determined smile. "'Overwhelmed' is my middle name."

Back in the sunshine, Chloe and Kari watched a cloud of little girls descend on the volunteers who'd armed themselves with calico fabric, stacks of photocopied quilt square patterns, scissors, needles, and thread. Kari nodded toward a girl with blond braids who was tracing a cardboard square with fierce concentration. "Remember when we made our first Nine Patch doll quilts?"

"Of course." Chloe still had hers.

"Sometimes I think I'd go insane if I didn't quilt."

Chloe shot a look at her sister. "Really?"

"Oh, that came out wrong. But I do love it."

"The quilts I saw at your house last Thanksgiving were beautiful," Chloe said honestly.

"Thanks." Kari cocked her head toward the car. "We should head to the museum."

Chloe turned away from the table—and promptly bumped into someone. "Pardon me!"

"I'm so sorry," the bumpee said at the same time.

Chloe was surprised to recognize Hazel, last seen being chastised by Wilbur in the parking lot. "You're still here! I thought you were, um, leaving."

"So did my husband," Hazel admitted. "But it means *so* much to be here—I love Laura's books to death, you see—and I just couldn't bear driving off so fast. So I took a deep breath and asked myself WWLD, and—"

"WWLD?" Kari asked.

"What Would Laura Do." Hazel's patient tone suggested that she was repeating the alphabet to a particularly slow toddler. "That always helps me sort through difficult moments."

"Ah," Kari said.

"Wilbur said he'd leave me here if I didn't get in the car. When I didn't, he threw my suitcase on the ground and drove away. I knew he'd be back for me, but I—I've called his bluff." Hazel sounded half triumphant and half incredulous. "I saw that tour bus parked by the side of the road, and marched over to find out what that was all about. The tour leader said she had room. Since Wilbur is obviously miserable, he can go home to Peoria! I've been dreaming about this trip ever since I saw the notice for the *Looking For Laura* symposium. Now I can enjoy it, without listening to Wilbur complain every step of the way."

"Good for you," Chloe said. She introduced herself and Kari.

"I'm Hazel Voss. And these are some of my new friends…" She beckoned to three people nearby.

Chloe shook hands with Bill and Frances Whelan, a pleasant sixty-ish couple from International Falls, and Henrietta Beauchamps, a seventy-ish North Dakotan with round black-rimmed glasses, short gray hair, a broad smile, and a bag of yarn over one arm. "I used to teach American Lit to college students," Henrietta said. "I've reread the entire Little House series every year since the books were published. I wait until February, when I need a pick-me-up."

Finally, Chloe thought, I am meeting kindred souls.

They left Hazel and her fellow travelers wandering the Wayside. "I overheard Hazel's husband chewing her out in the parking lot earlier," Chloe murmured. "He was quite the jerk. I'm surprised she found the courage to stand up to him."

"Good for Hazel," Kari said. They'd reached the car, and she unlocked the door. "Sometimes a wife's gotta do what a wife's gotta do."

Before Chloe could respond, her sister had slid onto the seat and slammed the door.

Chloe was taking the quilt box out of the car trunk fifteen minutes later as Norma Epps pulled into the private lot behind the Laura Ingalls Wilder Museum in Pepin. "You must be Chloe," she said.

"And this is my sister, Kari." Chloe braced the box on one hip and slammed the trunk. "It was kind of you to meet us during a special event."

"I'm glad to, but—Lord, what a day." Norma shook her head. "It started at seven thirty a.m. when I went out to open the cabin and found a grandma with two sobbing girls. Some little darling had left a Charlotte doll impaled on a grilling fork in front of the door."

I would have been upset too, Chloe thought.

"Two volunteers were no-shows," Norma was saying. "But worst of all, we had a medical emergency at the Wayside earlier."

"We were there," Chloe said soberly.

"Do you know what happened?" Kari asked. "Or who it was?"

"I'm afraid not." Norma was digging through her purse. "I was on an ice run—we're serving lemonade out at the cabin—so I only heard about it later." She finally extracted a key ring. "Here we go." She led the way toward the back door.

"I appreciate you meeting us here, too," Chloe said. "Obviously, I didn't want to spread a fragile quilt out on a picnic table. And I don't want to telegraph the fact that we're traveling with something so precious."

"My pleasure," Norma assured them. "I'm eager to see..." She frowned. "Hmm."

"Something wrong?" Chloe asked.

"The door is unlocked. I know I locked it when I went out earlier."

Chloe felt a twinge of unease. "Maybe you should call the police."

"Oh, no," Norma said briskly. "I'm sure that one of the other volunteers forgot to turn the little thingie. People have been running in and out all day."

Chloe wasn't sure, and Kari didn't look convinced either. But Norma opened the door and led them inside. Not my museum, Chloe thought. Not my call.

Norma led them into an office cluttered with the usual behind-the-scenes detritus: binders on shelves, files and an electric typewriter and framed family photos on a desk, cartons holding gift shop souvenirs on the floor. One long table was covered with a clean sheet. Chloe put down the box, pulled on the white cotton gloves she'd brought, and placed Miss Lila's quilt on the table.

"Oh, that's *quite* nice." Norma clasped her hands behind her back and leaned closer.

The day after Miss Lila died, Chloe had funneled some of her grief into a close inspection of the quilt: measuring, scrutinizing, taking written notes and photographs. "It smelled a bit musty," she told Norma, "but a couple of hours outside in the sun—sandwiched between two thick cotton sheets, of course—took care of that. There are no sign of recent stress lines from folds."

"Miss Lila kept the quilt flat on the guest room bed," Kari said.

"I do see some fading," Norma mused, gesturing toward one end.

"Especially the browns and blacks," Chloe agreed. "At some point the quilt was folded and left out with that portion exposed to the light." Whether from sunlight or fluorescent bulbs, ultraviolet rays brought death and destruction to textiles.

"I don't see any other signs of damage, though," Norma said.

Chloe unfolded the quilt and found a particular corner. "Just here…there's a small area where the binding fabric has disintegrated. It looks as if someone spilled a few drops of bleach or something."

"Still, all in all, it's in very good condition," Norma said. "None of the dyes used have eaten at the cloth. I don't suppose you found initials or a date thoughtfully stitched somewhere … ?"

"I wish! All I have to go on is the fabric. This madder palette was—"

"Madder palette?" Kari asked.

"For a long time, the red found in fabrics came from madder root," Chloe explained. "Right before the Civil War, someone figured out how to make a synthetic alizarin dye. Alizarin is what makes madder red."

"It was a huge advancement," Norma agreed. "This combination—lots of brown and tan, black, orange, deep red—remained popular through the 1860s and into the 1870s."

Chloe exchanged a quick look with Kari, and knew they were thinking the same thing. The color scheme in Miss Lila's quilt was popular when Laura was a child making her Bear Track quilt. But despite her own hopes, Chloe felt compelled to add, "But since women kept scraps for years and salvaged fabrics from old clothes, a quilt made with 1850s fabrics might actually have been constructed decades later."

"Quilts are one of our particular passions here in Pepin," Norma said. "Laura mentioned quilts over seventy times in the books."

"According to oral tradition, Laura owned this quilt."

Excitement flickered in the older woman's eyes. "Rose's lone heir gave us two family quilts. As I'm sure you know, Rose was Laura's only child, and Rose had no surviving children herself."

"Of course," Chloe murmured, although she really didn't know diddly about Rose.

"Laura owned at least one of our quilts. That one is quite plain, nothing like this one—"

Score! Chloe thought, feeling smug on Miss Lila's behalf.

"—but we don't know if Laura *made* it. We know even less about the second one—just that Rose owned it before she died."

"Are you familiar with this pattern?" Kari gestured to Miss Lila's quilt. "The oldest reference Chloe found lists it as Bear Paw, but other sources call it Bear Track."

"In *By the Banks of Plum Creek*," Chloe added, trying very hard to sound offhand, "Laura was making a Bear Track quilt."

"We couldn't help wondering if this was the same pattern," Kari added.

"Unfortunately, of course, we'll never be able to say." Norma looked from Kari to Chloe. "You do know that almost all of Laura's belongings were destroyed in a house fire soon after her marriage to Almanzo Wilder. Laura was quite clear about how little was saved. This quilt couldn't possibly be the one Laura mentioned in *Plum Creek*."

"Of course not." Chloe flapped a hand in a gesture that, she hoped, completely hid her disappointment. She didn't remember reading about a house fire, and the notion—and its implications for Laura artifacts—made her heartsick.

"If Laura liked that Bear Track pattern, maybe she made more than one over the years," Kari suggested. "Perhaps she made this one as an adult to remind her of her childhood quilt."

"It's hard to imagine that Laura would have felt able to give away something as valuable as a quilt, when she had so little," Norma mused. "But still . . . it is possible."

Possible is good, Chloe thought. She could work with possible. Emotionally, she really needed to leave room for the possibility that although Miss Lila's quilt was not the Bear Track quilt Laura made as a child, it had indeed been owned—and possibly made as an adult—by Laura.

Norma stepped back. "So. Because of the fire, we know that your quilt certainly does not date to Laura's childhood here in Pepin. But Pepin is the only homesite with a special focus on quilts in educational programming. We'd be honored to accept the quilt for permanent display in the museum."

"As I explained on the phone, the owner has passed away," Chloe said. "I will honor her wish to show the quilt to staff at each homesite. Then I'll have to see what her will stipulates."

"May we see the other two family quilts?" Kari asked.

"Of course." Norma headed for the door, then paused. "Chloe? I can lock the door while we step out to the museum."

Once Miss Lila's quilt was secure, Chloe followed the others to one of the exhibit rooms. The first quilt was displayed inside a glass case. It was quite plain—white squares set apart by blue sashing—and was thoughtfully displayed with the letter of donation from the executor of Rose's will.

"And here's the other." Norma gestured to a quilt composed of pieced blocks sewn into stripes, the stripes interposed with strips of green calico. It was a simple pattern, with each pieced block composed of four triangles.

"The green is different," Kari said, "but the pieced squares are largely in that madder color palette."

Chloe leaned closer. "If we can find a fabric match linking Miss Lila's quilt to one documented to Laura, it would provide evidence to support the family story."

Norma fetched gloves and held the quilt up so Chloe and Kari could get a better look. "I don't see any duplicates," Kari concluded reluctantly.

"I don't either." Chloe sighed. "And this quilt is tied, and not actually quilted like Miss Lila's quilt." Tying the layers of a quilt together became popular among busy women once commercial battings became available. Actual quilting—stitched lines or designs that held hand-carded wool batting in place between quilted top and plain backing—demanded much more time. Bottom line: neither quilt in the Pepin collection was similar in any way to Miss Lila's.

"Do you have any other quilts?" Kari asked. "I'm not a history expert like Chloe, but I do quilt."

"I knew it. You've got the look." Norma gestured toward another room. "We've got a lovely log cabin quilt, and another that features an unusual star, beautifully executed."

"I'll go box up Miss Lila's quilt while you look," Chloe said. Lock or no, leaving it unattended made her anxious.

Norma gave her the key. Back in the office, Chloe repackaged the quilt. She made sure to fold it in a way that smoothed out the creases caused by the previous folding, and tucked tissue between the layers for extra support. It didn't seem enough. I really should secure the box lid better, she thought. Her brain produced a mental movie of her tripping in the parking lot and dropping the box into a puddle.

Chloe leaned over Norma's desk, hoping to spot a handy roll of tape or spool of string. No luck on those counts, but she did see a desk calendar open to the current week. The left-side page featured a spectacular appliquéd quilt done in pinks and greens. Okay, Chloe thought. Norma—and Pepin—got extra points for truly holding quilts in high esteem.

Space on the right side held several notations pertinent to the day's special event at the Wayside. The last note said *Meet Chloe Ellefson re potential donation LIW quilt, 3 PM.*

Chloe's unease flickered back to life. That inked note was visible for anyone who wandered in to see. Considered with the back door that should have been locked, but wasn't … she didn't like it. Didn't like it at all.

Laura and Mary ran along the lake shore, picking up pretty pebbles
that had been rolled back and forth by the waves until they were pol-
ished smooth.

There were no pebbles like that in the Big Woods.

When she found a pretty one, Laura put it in her pocket, and there
were so many, each prettier than the last, that she filled her pocket full.

Little House in the Big Woods

FOUR

ROELKE GRABBED AN INCIDENT report and pulled out a chair when
Mrs. Walter Bainbridge walked into the Eagle Police Department.
He'd met Mrs. Bainbridge many times. "Have a seat, ma'am. How can
I help you?"

"I'm Mrs. Walter Bainbridge," she said, in case he'd forgotten that
they'd met many times. She lived behind the elementary school and
called whenever she saw, or suspected, any trouble on the grounds.

"Yes ma'am." He knew better than to ask her first name. And I'm
right on this one, he thought. Chloe didn't like it when women's
first names got swallowed by their husband's, and she insisted on
saying "birth name" instead of "maiden name." But Mrs. Bainbridge
was a widow, and evidently introducing herself as Mrs. Walter
Bainbridge made her happy. That was good enough for him.

"I'm here to report an obscene phone call." Mrs. Bainbridge sat very erect in her seat. "I was making deviled eggs to take to the church choir potluck when the phone rang. It was a man."

Roelke scribbled the pertinent details, which did not include deviled eggs. He assured Mrs. Walter Bainbridge that he would do what he could to track down the caller. She left in a cloud of indignation.

Roelke sat for a moment, toying with a small stone he kept in his pocket. Chloe had given it to him. She loved such things, and while he didn't completely get it, there was something good about having a pebble to worry in his fingers while thinking. Especially one she'd picked out for him.

He was still rolling it back and forth when the office clerk walked in. "I saw Mrs. Bainbridge outside," Marie said. "What was that about?" She put down a shopping bag and began putting coffee, Styrofoam cups, and napkins away in the cupboard. "And did you chip in to the coffee fund this month? I was three dollars short."

"I did, but here." Roelke pulled a five from his wallet and handed it over. "I'm heading out." He grabbed the car keys and left the building, feeling Marie's frown follow him. Once he'd started the squad and pulled away from the curb, he exhaled a long breath. He should have chatted with Marie. She knew more about Eagle than he would learn in a lifetime. Besides, Marie liked to be in the know. Everything went more smoothly when he remembered that.

But he was feeling restless and itchy. He'd gotten used to the pace of police work in the Village of Eagle, mostly. And God knew Eagle had its share of problems. But every once in a while days like this just got to him.

He looped through the park, crossed Main, and slowly cruised the residential streets. There weren't that many, so it didn't take long. He turned the last corner, trying to decide if he'd rather look for speeders or go back to the office and chat with Marie.

Then he saw the girl on the curb in front of a ranch house with peeling paint. The kid sat motionless, head bowed, shoulders hunched.

Roelke slowed to a stop. "Hey," he called in a low-key kind of way. "Everything okay?"

The girl looked up, glanced over her shoulder at the house, shrugged. "Yeah. I'm just waiting." She was ten, maybe eleven. Clean clothes and hair—always a good sign. But she looked weary.

"Watcha waiting for?" Roelke asked.

"My parents to stop fighting."

Damn. "What's your name?"

"Crystal."

"Do they fight a lot, Crystal?"

"I guess."

"Do they ever yell at you?"

Crystal considered. "Not much. Mostly they just scream at each other."

"Do they ever hit each other?"

"One time my mom threw a coffee mug at my dad, but she missed. The coffee made a stain on the wall, though."

Roelke stared at the house, drumming his fingers on the steering wheel. This kind of thing was dicey. He wanted to knock on the door, get the parents' attention, and explain that their asshole behavior had shoved their daughter from the house. An officer's intervention might startle them into straightening up.

Or, an officer's intervention might make them so angry that they'd double-down as soon as he drove away, maybe this time with their daughter in the verbal crosshairs.

He fished out a business card and handed it over. "Crystal, my name is Officer McKenna. Do you know where the police station is?" She nodded. "Well, if things ever get too bad, or if you just need somebody to talk to, you head for the station, okay? I may not be there, but anybody who's on duty will be happy to help you. And if nobody is there, you can call that number on the card."

Crystal studied the card before sliding it into her pocket.

Well, Roelke thought as he drove away, that exchange did nothing to brighten my mood.

All he wanted to do was make Eagle a safer place. Some shifts, though, left him feeling like his presence made exactly no difference at all.

———

After leaving the museum, Chloe and Kari checked into their nondescript motel in Pepin. Kari plopped her suitcase on one of the beds and announced, "I'm going to take a walk."

"Okay." Chloe shrugged. This road trip had a much better chance of sibling harmony if they did not pretend to be joined at the hip.

Besides, she wanted to call Roelke. If he'd gone home after his seven-to-three shift, she might be able to catch him. Once alone, she sat on the bed, dialed the operator, and asked to charge the call to her home number.

"McKenna here," he said briskly, as if on duty. Roelke had a wee bit of trouble relaxing.

"It's me."

"Hey, you." His voice was slower now, and warmer. "How was Day One of the Great Ellefson Sisters Road Trip?"

"Well," she began, and was surprised to hear a quaver in her voice, "we got to Pepin all right, but it sorta went downhill from there." She told him about the young man who died. "The EMTs said it was likely anaphylactic shock. Probably from food."

"Sounds like it," Roelke agreed. "That can come on really fast."

"But don't you think it's strange that he'd suffer a fatal food allergy in a picnic grove where no food is for sale?"

"Well," Roelke said slowly, "maybe he bought a ready-made salad at a store, and didn't realize it contained something he shouldn't eat. Or … it's possible, although less likely, that something just hit him really hard for the first time. Seafood can do that."

"I suppose."

"The cops will figure it out," Roelke said. "Listen, Chloe, I'm really sorry that happened. But I hope you can put it behind you and enjoy the rest of your trip. How was the cabin?"

"Kind of … sterile," she admitted.

"Did you sense anything? You know, when you walked around?"

Chloe blinked away sudden tears. She did love this man. She'd been reluctant to tell Roelke McKenna, fact-focused über cop, about her sporadic gift of perception. When she'd finally dredged up the courage, he'd been astonishingly unshocked by the revelation. She knew he didn't entirely understand it—hell, neither did she—but he accepted what she'd tried to explain.

She cleared her throat. "No, although I really, really wanted to."

"Maybe at one of the other places."

"Maybe. I don't know. There was a program at the site today, and I met a few of the other people going to the symposium, and … "

"And?"

"And, it wasn't all goodness and light." She told him about Wilbur and Hazel's argument.

48

Roelke gave an audible sigh. "Why did you project yourself into—"

"This Wilbur guy was a total jerk!"

"Then it was *particularly* bad that you tried to intervene. Call a cop in situations like that if there's reason to. Otherwise, walk away."

"Okay, yeah," Chloe said briefly. "Sure. Anyway, *then* I met this woman who's going to make a presentation at the symposium, something about the authorship of the books ... It was a strange afternoon. Not what I expected."

"What did you expect?"

"I guess I figured that everyone would be like me. You know, that I'd meet lots of people who loved the books."

"I'm sorry the afternoon was a little rough, but I bet things will go better tomorrow. And Chloe? Trust your instincts. You really shouldn't get involved in other peoples' problems."

"I know," Chloe mumbled, picturing Hazel's face when stupid Wilbur was tromping on her dreams. What was I supposed to do, she thought, turn my back?

"I'm serious," Roelke persisted. "Sometimes you're too nice. Don't be so Midwestern all the time."

"I won't," Chloe said, since it was easier than pointing out the absurdity of accusing someone of being 'too nice.' "So, What's new with you?"

"I made an appointment with the real estate agent who's handling the farm."

"Yikes!" She blinked. "Really? That was fast."

"You were the one who suggested it."

"I know I did. And I think it's a good idea. It's just that ... wow. You must be serious about this."

"There's no harm in looking. I don't know what shape the house is in. I don't even know how many acres are included."

Chloe found all this unsettling, but tried to hide that. "You'll always wonder if you don't get the information. I'll talk to you tomorrow, okay? I love you."

"I love you too."

Chloe hung up the phone. Roelke was overprotective, and she wasn't sure what to make of this whole farm thing, but she did feel better for talking with him. A good man loved her, and life didn't get much better than that.

A key rattled in the door, and Kari came inside. "It's cooling off," she announced. "And I'm hungry."

Chloe got up and rummaged in her suitcase for a hairbrush. "The desk clerk suggested a supper club that's..." She took several steps toward her sister, sniffing, and her jaw dropped. "Kari! You've been *smoking*!"

"I just had one cigarette. It's no big deal."

"When did you start smoking?"

"It's no big deal," Kari repeated, sounding irritated. "My college roommate smoked, and she—"

"Does Trygve know you smoke?" Chloe pictured her salt of the earth, tiller of the soil brother-in-law, who thought he was living wild if he indulged in a single Miller High Life on a hot afternoon. Then she pictured her beautiful, perfect nieces. "Geez, do your *kids* know?"

"No, and it's going to stay that way." Kari gave her a sisterly glare perfected decades earlier: *If you tell on me, you will be in big trouble.* "Look, I hardly ever smoke, but every once in a while that old longing comes back. Having that guy die in the picnic area today..." She shuddered.

"Yeah." Chloe told herself to lose the judgmental tone. After all, she'd responded to stress by running straight for a sugar fix. Sugar wasn't *quite* the same as tobacco, but she still shouldn't use it like a drug. "Okay, sorry."

"Forget about it," Kari said. "Let's go find that supper club."

———

They decided to watch the sun set from the shore of Lake Pepin. Which was not truly a lake, Chloe reminded herself, but a wide spot in the Mississippi. She sighed as they followed signs to a small public parking lot. "I'm thinking the marina wasn't here a century ago."

"Did you think it would all be wild?"

"I didn't think at all," Chloe admitted. "I just sort of assumed everything in the books was true."

"You mean about Laura coming back to Pepin as an adult? That happened after the sequence of the books. No biggie."

"I suppose," Chloe allowed. "But I didn't know the family came back here after the Kansas period." She watched a lone gull soar over the water. "I want everything to be like it was in the books."

"I don't think we can return to the stories as adults without catching an undercurrent we were oblivious to when we were kids." Kari flicked her hand at a fly. "Think about Ma. God knows she was patient with Pa. I'd have to count how many times he announced that they were moving on."

"That's part of the appeal! Pa was restless, and unlike most of us, he was mostly able to indulge that need to move on, see new sights."

"Funny how Pa was a farmer who always wanted to move on." Kari stared at the sky, streaked by the setting sun with broad strokes of peach and pink and orange. "Today, farmers are chained to one place."

Talk about undercurrents, Chloe thought. "Kari... is something bothering you?"

"No."

No my butt, Chloe thought, but let it go.

The sun had slipped below the horizon now. Pinpricks of light began to appear along the far shore, and Chloe noticed clouds starting to mass in the west. But twilight lingered at this time of year, and she didn't feel inclined to leave the beach yet. Instead, she shot a sideways glance at her sister. "You know, I didn't really expect you to come on this trip."

"We always said we'd do the Laura tour."

"But the idea hasn't come up in years. And I didn't give you a whole lot of advance notice."

Kari visored her hand and peered at the Minnesota shore. "You know what? Tomorrow will mark the first time I've crossed the state line since I was in high school."

"Seriously?"

"You went to college in West Virginia, did grad school in New York, and moved to Switzerland," Kari observed. "I went to the UW and married the farm boy I'd known since grade school."

"Well, the whole move-to-Switzerland part didn't work out so well," Chloe said, trying not to sound defensive. Trying not to *feel* defensive.

Kari spread her hands in an *I'm just sayin'* gesture. "It's safe to conclude that I was ready for a little vacation."

"Fair enough," Chloe said. She remembered what Kari had said earlier that day: *Sometimes a wife's gotta do what a wife's gotta do.* Were Kari and Trygve going through a thorny patch? Lord, Chloe thought, I sincerely hope not.

Time to change the subject. "I wish we could visit the sites in chronological order. You know, follow the path the Ingalls family followed." Unfortunately, the moves made by the Ingallses did not form a tidy circle, or even a straight line west.

"What's the deal with Burr Oak, Iowa?" Kari asked.

"Evidently the Ingalls family lived there for a while."

"How far is it?"

Chloe dusted off her hands and got to her feet. "I'll get the maps."

She smiled as she walked back to the car, picturing again young Laura so entranced by pretty pebbles that she'd overfilled her pocket. I'm with you, Laura, Chloe thought. There was nothing wrong with—

Her thought and her feet stopped simultaneously. Someone was peering in the window of Kari's car. "Hey!" she called sharply.

The shadowy figure jerked erect, whirled, and slid into a car parked nearby. It was the only other car left in the lot, actually, but in the dim light Chloe couldn't make out any details. An engine rumbled to life. The driver swerved from the lot and sped down the street. He was half a block away before he evidently realized that it would be a good idea to turn his lights on. "Nimrod," Chloe muttered.

Then she bit her lip. Maybe the guy—if it even *was* a guy— wasn't just a nimrod who got confused in the gloom about which sedan was his. Maybe he really had been looking for something in Kari's car, and waited until he was out of view to turn his lights on because he didn't want her to glimpse his license plate.

She quickly checked the car, and sagged with relief when she found all doors locked and the big gray box still secure in the trunk, wedged in beside the spare tire. She leaned against the car, considering. Kari's blue Rambler looked silver-gray in the faint light. There were a whole lot of gray or silver sedans in the world.

Or maybe, Chloe thought, what happened today and my quilt anxiety just gave me the spooks, and imagination took over.

After grabbing what she needed, Chloe double-checked the car locks and returned to her sister. Kari found Burr Oak on the map. "It's not far from Decorah, actually." Decorah, with its proud Norwegian-American heritage and a world-class museum, was a town they knew well.

Chloe watched a sailboat make its way toward the shore, sail down, running lights on, the motor a low hum. Laura had not written about Burr Oak in the Little House series, but there was a site or museum of some kind there. From Iowa they'd travel to Walnut Grove in Southwestern Minnesota. They'd be traveling parallel with Alta's Laura Land tour. Chloe remembered the anguish in Alta's voice when she'd argued with someone beside the tour bus: *Please don't do this! You'll ruin everything!*

Kari broke the silence. "I'm kind of glad we've never been to any of the Laura sites before. The whole trip is new territory."

"Just like when the Ingallses headed west."

"New horizons!"

Chloe smiled. This road trip *was* a good idea, and tomorrow would be a better day. "New horizons," she echoed. "On to Iowa."

It was a very fine hotel. But in the dining room door were several bullet holes...

Mary and I washed dishes and helped make beds and wait on tables... Ma was always tired, Pa was always busy, and there was some kind of disagreement between us and the partners in the hotel.

Pioneer Girl manuscript

FIVE

CHLOE FELT BLEARY AS she and Kari drove to Burr Oak, Iowa, early the next morning. The phone had jerked her from sleep in the night, and she'd been sure it was Roelke, or someone calling with bad news about Roelke. When she heard Kari softly singing "Puff the Magic Dragon," it had taken several groggy minutes to figure out that Astrid or Anja had called Mommy after a nightmare.

Then came thunderstorms. It rained all night. It was raining as they crossed the Mississippi and entered Iowa. It was still raining when they arrived at the hamlet of Burr Oak.

"Not auspicious," Kari muttered. A flicker of lightning cracked the sodden gray sky.

Chloe tried to pretend that the world was not soggy and dismal. "We're here. We should at least see the place." She squinted through the water pouring down the windshield. Between the wipers' frantic slaps she caught glimpses of something large and colorful down the street. "Park down by the Laura Land Tour bus."

Kari eased to a stop beside an old red brick bank building that served as visitor center. "Now what?"

"Wait here," Chloe said. "I'll see what's what."

She was dripping by the time she dashed inside, purchased tickets, and flung herself back into the car. "A tour started a few minutes ago," she reported. "It's in that white building across the street." Squinting, she made out the letters on another sign: *Masters Hotel*. To the left, a very twentieth-century bar had been built inches away from the small, unassuming structure.

They found the Laura Land Tour group crowded inside the hotel's front room. Alta, wearing a yellow slicker over today's red gingham pioneer attire, lifted a hand in greeting. Hazel Voss, who'd acquired a calico bonnet of her own, beamed when she recognized Chloe. Jayne was present as well, looking bored, her ridiculous high heels crusted with mud. Surely Jayne isn't actually bouncing down the highway in a repurposed school bus with the Laura Land hoi polloi, Chloe thought. Jayne was probably caravanning along the same route, as were Kari and Chloe, the lovely woman with Asian features from Pepin, and a few others.

"Welcome," the tour guide called. She was a petite woman wearing jeans and a Western-style blouse, maybe thirty-five, with auburn hair captured in an impressive French braid. "I'm Marianne Schiller, site director. I was just explaining that in 1876 the Ingalls family moved to Burr Oak from Walnut Grove, Minnesota, after the grasshopper plagues wiped out their crops."

Chloe nodded, wishing again that Pa Ingalls had moved his family in an easy-to-follow line. They went from Wisconsin to Kansas, she recited mentally. From Kansas to ... well, as she now knew, back to Wisconsin. From there, on to Minnesota. And from Minnesota to … well, as she now knew, here to Iowa.

"The family was destitute," Marianne was saying. "Some friends invited Pa and Ma to help them run this hotel. This is the only childhood home of Laura Ingalls Wilder still standing on its original location."

Chloe felt a frisson of anticipation.

"There was a saloon right next door," Marianne continued. "Laura and Mary were afraid of the rough men who gathered there."

"I do not remember this place," a dark-haired man with a delightful French accent said. "It was not in the television, I think?"

Jayne sniffed derisively.

Marianne smiled, ignoring Jayne. "No, neither the television series or the books included this period."

A woman raised her hand. "How long did the family live in the hotel?"

"Just a few months," Marianne said. "They moved out, and Pa tried to find carpentry work. Pa and Ma weren't happy having the girls exposed to men swearing and drinking. Also, although Burr Oak boomed in the 1850s, by the time the Ingalls family arrived there just wasn't enough business. There was another big hotel across the street where the trailer park is now. The stage stopped there first, so that hotel captured most of the travelers."

Chloe leaned toward the window, trying to conjure a big hotel where, as promised, a trailer park now stood. She was sorry she'd looked.

"And once the trains came through Iowa, bypassing Burr Oak…" The site director's voice trailed away. "Well. Let's see the rest of the building."

The hotel, built into a hill, was larger than it first appeared. The kitchen and dining area were in the lowest level. "This is where Mary and Laura helped wash dishes and wait on tables," Marianne explained.

"How old was Laura?" Chloe asked. Between the family's many moves, the episodes Laura omitted from the Little House series, and her own less-than-rudimentary math skills, she was having trouble keeping track.

"Nine," Marianne said. "And they all worked hard. Laura said that Ma was always tired and Pa was always busy."

They climbed to the top floor. The tiny bedrooms featured some lovely quilts.

"Did any of these belong to the family?" Chloe asked.

"I'm afraid not," Marianne said. "The family never returned to visit Burr Oak. But come back downstairs and I'll show you our treasure."

Marianne's treasure consisted of three beautifully embroidered handkerchiefs, carefully preserved beneath glass. "These were Laura's," she said proudly. "The museum in Mansfield gifted them to us when our site opened nine years ago."

"Ooh." Chloe reached toward the glass, almost touching it. She wanted badly to sense something of Laura. She longed to know that Laura had been okay here despite serving food and scrubbing dishes. But nothing came through.

Alta Allerbee thanked Marianne for the personal tour. "Now," Alta continued, "I've made arrangements for my group to eat an early lunch at the Black Crow tavern next door."

Alta's Laura Lookers pulled up hoods and gathered umbrellas. Chloe found herself next to the Asian woman from Pepin. "Nice to see you again," she said.

"After what happened, I almost went home," the other woman confessed. She had a jaw-length cap of glossy black hair, dark eyes, and porcelain skin. Her voice was soft, with a lovely accent Chloe hadn't noticed in the frenzy the day before, suggesting that English was her second language. "But I changed my mind. I've planned a driving tour of all the homesites, and I'm registered for *Looking For Laura*." She extended one hand. "My name is Haruka Minari."

Chloe introduced herself and Kari as they all stepped out to the porch. The steady drumbeat of raindrops was louder here, and thunder growled every few minutes. "I'm sure we can tag along with the tour group," Kari said. "Want to join us, Haruka?"

"I suspect that the tavern's menu has very few vegetarian options," Chloe said, 'very few' being a euphemism for 'absolutely none.' "You go ahead. I'm going to—"

The Black Crow's door slammed open, and none other than Wilbur Voss lurched outside. Alta, who'd been leading her crew, stumbled away from him … which caused a chain reaction that backed one poor woman into an ankle-deep puddle.

"Remember Hazel, who ditched her husband and sent him home?" Chloe asked Kari. "Evidently he didn't make it to Peoria."

"Hazel?" Wilbur hollered. He rocked on his feet, considering the raincoated people standing like statues in the downpour. "Hazel!"

Chloe flashed on Marlon Brando looking for Stella in *A Streetcar Named Desire*, and couldn't stifle a snigger. Wilbur, pudgy and bald and pretty thoroughly soaked, was no young Marlon Brando.

Hazel pushed through the knot of bewildered people. "Wilbur!" she cried. Her cotton bonnet, dark with rain, drooped over her forehead. "What on earth has come over you?"

"Come back with me, Hazel," Wilbur begged. "I sh-should never have let you go."

Chloe's amusement faded. This was embarrassing. Pathetic, really. And worrisome. Wilbur may have fallen apart when Hazel left him, but how would he react once he sobered up?

Hazel glanced over her shoulder, looking mortified. Then she shoved Wilbur toward the bar. Another patron obligingly held the door open until the Vosses disappeared inside. The other Laura Land guests exchanged glances, shrugged, and followed.

"Well, go enjoy your burger," Chloe told her sister. She suspected that Hazel's fellow travelers would keep an eye on her and intervene if Wilbur got abusive. "I'm going to see if Marianne can spare a few minutes."

Kari and Haruka plunged from the porch and splashed after the group. Before turning away, Chloe eyed a gray car parked in front of the bar, remembering the sedan that had sped from the lot the evening before, back by Lake Pepin. Now that she knew Wilbur Voss had not obligingly driven his belligerent self back to Peoria after Hazel decamped, she couldn't help wondering if it had been *his* car she'd seen in the dusk. She was obsessed with the need to keep Miss Lila's quilt safe, but... maybe she had other things to worry about. Like a controlling husband angry at a female stranger—*her*—who dared intervene when he was ordering his wife about.

Roelke was right, Chloe thought. Pushing herself into the middle of Hazel and Wilbur's argument back at the Pepin Wayside had probably only pissed Wilbur off more than he already was. And Wilbur was proving himself a man who didn't like being dissed.

Marianne emerged from the Masters Hotel with the French visitor, who was clutching a list of questions. Finally he thanked her and walked away. Marianne glanced at Chloe as she locked the door. "Sorry to keep you waiting."

"No problem. Do you get many foreign visitors?"

"More than you might expect. The TV show is huge in Europe, and the books are huge in parts of Asia. I had a lovely conversation with that Japanese woman before the tour started." She smiled. "Now, how can I help you?"

"I'm Chloe Ell—"

"The lady with the quilt!" Marianne's eyes narrowed with a professional but predatory hunger. "My office." She gestured toward the bank building across the street.

Chloe fetched the box, now swaddled with a green poncho. Then she followed Marianne inside, past the teen minding the cash register. The office was cramped, and the only desk was completely covered with files, papers, and books.

On top of one pile was a china shepherdess figurine, disconcertingly minus the head. "Oh, my," Chloe said. Ma Ingalls had carried a beloved china shepherdess from place to place.

"Don't worry," Marianne said. "It's antique, but certainly not Ma's original. It was in my inbox this morning, and I haven't had a chance to track down what happened." She waved a hand: *Enough of such minutia.* "May I see the quilt?"

Chloe put the box on the floor, removed the lid, and explained what she knew.

"Oh, my," Marianne said reverently. She leaned forward, grabbing her braid so it didn't drip onto the quilt. "I'm sure the Board would be thrilled to acquire it. Most people with Laura-related items don't think of us."

"Until very recently, I didn't even know your site existed," Chloe said apologetically.

"We get that a lot," Marianne told her. "Laura's daughter Rose came through town in 1932, searching for the hotel. A decade or two later, a couple of people wrote to Laura, asking if she really had lived here. Laura wrote back saying yes, but by then there was a lot of confusion about which building she'd lived in. The hotel had been turned into a residence, you see, and it was in pretty bad shape. But about ten years ago a few local people who loved the Little House books decided that it needed to be saved. They took out a $1,500 note and announced plans to purchase and restore the building."

"I'm glad they made it happen."

"We all are." Marianne looked back at the quilt. "Anyway, I'm sure all the sites are telling you the same thing, but ... it would be *amazing* if your friend's quilt could come here. We'd take excellent care of it."

"When the legal issues get sorted out, I'll let you know," Chloe promised. "I've also been trying to learn more about this particular pattern."

"A quilt expert is going to speak at the symposium in De Smet," Marianne said. "Didn't Alta tell you?"

"I haven't mentioned the quilt to her," Chloe explained. "Frankly, traveling with the quilt makes me nervous."

"Alta's put together a good lineup," Marianne said. "The homesites are so spread out ... I think this symposium will create a community of Laura fans."

Chloe nestled the lid back onto the quilt box, wary of any sadistic dust bunnies that might be lurking beneath Marianne's desk. "The Masters Hotel is special," she said carefully, "although I admit, some of what I learned is a bit unsettling."

Marianne leaned back in her chair, eyeing Chloe with speculation. "Are you a book person, a TV person, or a truther?"

"I ... um ... " Chloe floundered.

"Some people don't want to hear about anything Laura didn't include in the books," Marianne explained. "Some people love the Little House TV series, and don't want to hear about anything that Michael

Landon didn't include in a show. You may not know this, but in addition to starring as Pa Ingalls, Landon also wrote scripts, directed, and produced the series."

"Ah." Chloe hadn't watched the series herself, but she was familiar with it.

"And a few people want to know what Laura's life was truly like," Marianne continued.

"That would be me," Chloe said. "I'm a truther." She was a curator, after all. A history professional.

Marianne nodded. "Well, the truth is that the Burr Oak period was very painful for the family. Having to leave Walnut Grove was a bitter blow. And once Freddie died—"

"Who was Freddie?"

"Sorry. I forgot you joined the tour late. Charles Frederick—Freddie—was Laura's baby brother."

"Laura had a baby brother?" Chloe asked blankly. That was *not* in the books.

"She did. But he died while the family was staying with relatives on the way here. They buried Freddie and had to leave the grave behind when they traveled by covered wagon on to Burr Oak." Marianne toyed with a pencil. "Laura said it was a cold and miserable journey. Can you imagine? The family was devastated."

Chloe felt stunned. "How ... how do you know all this?"

"Are you familiar with the *Pioneer Girl* manuscript?"

Chloe shook her head.

"It's a biographical manuscript, never published. Only a few pages cover Burr Oak. If you'd like, I'd be happy to make photocopies for you."

"That's kind of you," Chloe said, although she wasn't sure she was ready to read the Burr Oak chapter of *Pioneer Girl.*

"Laura did have some happy memories of her time here. The birth of her youngest sister Grace was surely a joy. Still, those months were overshadowed by Freddie's death."

"I imagine so," Chloe said faintly.

"Pa was often away from home, trying to find work. The family never could get ahead financially. In the end, Pa and Ma were desperate to leave, but they didn't have enough money to pay the rent due *and* journey on. They ended up waking the girls one night, putting them in the wagon, and sneaking out of town."

Not Pa! Chloe thought. "Did he ever pay the landlord back?" she asked. It seemed important.

"Well," Marianne began, "we know that—"

An alarm shrilled, so close Chloe almost jumped from her skin.

Marianne shot to her feet. "Dear God, that's from the museum," she gasped. "There's a fire at the hotel!"

Often we heard drunken shouting and singing there, and one night the saloon caught fire.

[A man] who had been lying dead drunk for several days, came to, and took another drink to sober up. Before he had got it well swallowed, he put a cigar in his mouth and lit it. The flame of the match set fire to the whiskey fumes …   Pioneer Girl manuscript

SIX

A FIRE ENGINE WAILED down Eagle's Main Street. Roelke wished he could jump into his squad and go along. But he'd heard the call. A guy in the township had been burning brush, and started a grass fire. No injury, no immediate threat to property. No reason why that call should take precedence over the problem the lady from Child Protective Services had just dumped on his desk.

Roelke regarded the social worker sitting rigid in her chair. "You're going to take a three-day-old infant from his mother *now*?"

She held up her hands defensively. Mrs. Enright, her name was. Roelke had worked with her a couple of times. She had a helmet of gray hair, tired eyes, and a relentless will to protect children.

Roelke respected her, but he didn't like the sound of this. "If you had concerns, why did you let the mother take her baby home from the hospital?"

"Because she lied," Mrs. Enright said. "Angelica looked me in the eye and swore that Travis's father was no longer part of her life. But a nurse at the hospital saw the man visit. She didn't know it was a problem until I checked in with staff this morning. A neighbor has confirmed that the father is living in the apartment."

"Right." Roelke sighed. Angelica, who was nineteen, had never been in legal trouble. However, baby Travis's daddy had. Among other transgressions, he'd smacked around a child from an earlier relationship. He'd beaten Angelica more than once, including while she was pregnant. That's when CPS had gotten involved.

Mrs. Enright glanced at her watch. "The father should be at work for another hour. After that…"

"Let me make a couple of calls," Roelke said. He wanted backup. With an infant involved, emotions would run high.

Fifteen minutes later his colleague Skeet and an officer from Palmyra had arrived. Roelke went over the plan. "Alright," he said grimly. "Let's go."

Angelica lived in a second-story rental flat above one of Eagle's less desirable taverns, and they all trooped up the stairs. Raucous laughter echoed through the floor even at this early hour. Within the last month or so Roelke had answered a "shots fired" call at the bar too. Jesus. This was no place for a teen mother and her baby.

Roelke knocked on the door labeled B. Angelica answered. When she saw Mrs. Enright and three cops, her startled look quickly turned to alarm. Roelke pushed inside before she could slam the door, with the others on his heels.

"What are you doing?" Angelica cried. She looked like she belonged on a farm, all round face and freckles, wearing faded jeans and a t-shirt. The baby lay in a crib in a far corner. The living room was furnished with shabby castoffs, but it was tidy and clean. She's trying, Roelke thought, which made this even harder.

"Angelica," Mrs. Enright began, "we know that Travis's father has—"

"Get out!"

"You agreed not to let Travis's father near him," Mrs. Enright persisted. "Do you remember that?"

Roelke inched sideways, trying to ease his body between Angelica and the crib, but she blocked him and gathered the baby into her arms. Travis wore a green sleeper with yellow ducks printed on it.

Damn, Roelke thought. "Give Travis to me," he said quietly. "We need to take him into protective care—"

"*No.*"

Roelke took a step closer. "Just until things get sorted out." Another step.

"Fuck you!" Angelica clutched her baby tighter.

Roelke felt the call sliding toward crisis. "Don't make it harder than it already is, Angelica. I don't want to arrest you for disorderly conduct. Please don't make me do that."

Travis began to wail.

"I know you don't want anyone to hurt Travis." Roelke took another step and held out his arms. "Let me make sure that no one can—"

Angelica kicked wildly at him. "You can't have my baby!" she shrieked.

Skeet, who'd been hanging near the door with the Palmyra guy, shifted his weight. Roelke felt the other men itching to move, but he didn't signal them. Angelica had been given three days to cuddle her son, to sing to him, to touch his skin and breathe his baby scent. Roelke didn't doubt that Angelica loved Travis very much. But sometimes mothers who loved their babies did stupid things. Angelica might hurt herself or the baby rather than surrender him.

Travis cried harder, waving tiny fists. Roelke kept his voice gentle. "You're frightening Travis—"

"You can't have him!"

"—and I know you don't want to cause him more distress. We have to take him, Angelica. We have to. Just for a while."

Something inside the girl broke. Her shoulders sagged and she leaned back against the crib. Roelke cocked his head at the other officers, and they slowly flanked him.

"I can tell how much you love Travis," Roelke told Angelica. "I can tell."

"*Please* don't take him." She began to weep, but she didn't look away from Roelke as the other cops closed in. Each grasped one of her arms above the elbow. Roelke gently slid his palms between mother and child.

"Don't … "

He eased Travis away from her. The baby was warm through his sleeper, still squalling and wriggling. Roelke felt a dart of panic before he remembered that he did know how to hold an infant. "We just want to keep him safe," he said.

"I hate you," Angelica whispered.

What he saw in the girl's eyes sliced his chest like a knife. He turned his back because he had to. Mrs. Enright took Travis and hurried out the door.

"Are we done here?" Skeet asked in a low tone. What he meant was, *Are you going to cite her for disorderly?*

"We're done," Roelke said.

The officers let Angelica go. She crumpled to the floor. Roelke was last man out, and he closed the door behind him. Angelica's sobs followed him down the stairs.

In Burr Oak, the shrill keen of the museum's fire alarm was deafening. Chloe grabbed her box and followed as Marianne bolted from the office. "Call the fire department!" Marianne shouted at the shop clerk.

A second alarm kicked in to make a dissonant chord as Chloe followed the site director outside. Across the street, people scurried from the tavern. Shouts drifted through the rain. A woman shrieked. "Fire!" a man bellowed. *"Fire!"*

Blood pounded in Chloe's ears. There was a fire in the tavern *too*? Before panic could fully bloom, Chloe spotted her sister among the diners milling in the road. Most were coatless now, but the rain had faded to a sulky drizzle. Marianne unlocked the Masters Hotel door and disappeared inside.

Once she'd processed the fact that her sister was not trapped inside an inferno, Chloe quickly locked the quilt back into the car trunk and joined the refugees. She elbowed past a couple of women and grabbed her sister's arm. "Kari? What on earth happened?"

"I don't know." Kari shoved one hand through her hair. "I was washing my hands in the Ladies' when people started shouting 'Fire, fire!' One alarm went off, and then another. When I ran out of the bathroom everyone was bolting for the door."

"We heard the museum alarm kick in," Chloe shouted. She really wished that someone would turn off the damn things. "A smoke detector must have set it off." She didn't see any smoke, but the fire had evidently started at the tavern.

Her heart crawled into her throat. A fire at the Black Crow could leap to the hotel in an instant, and the only building in its original location once lived in by young Laura Ingalls Wilder would be reduced to rubble and ashes.

"Hey," Kari said, "are *you* okay?"

"Sure." Chloe blinked, banishing the image of the Masters Hotel as a crackling conflagration. "At least flames aren't shooting from the tavern roof. I don't even smell smoke. Did it start in the kitchen, do you know? Maybe a grease fire?"

"I don't know."

"Everybody's out!" a man shouted—the tavern owner, probably. Alta was circling through the group of maybe two dozen people clustered in the road—some Laura Lookers, some men who appeared to be on break from a construction site, and a few locals who'd come to investigate the ruckus. Alta pointed at her travelers one by one, silently counting.

A county sheriff's car screamed to a halt, lights pulsing. A murmur of relief rippled through the crowd. Chloe's shoulder muscles eased. Thank God.

Then Hazel shoved through the people. "I can't find Wilbur! Have you seen him?" Beneath her now-shapeless calico bonnet, Hazel's eyes were fearful.

"Come on," Chloe said, taking Hazel by the hand. "We'll help you look."

It occurred to Chloe that despite the bartender's all-out assessment, Wilbur might actually still be inside the tavern, lying unnoticed in a drunken stupor. Dear God, she thought, could Wilbur have somehow *started* the fire? He had been blotto.

A fire engine maneuvered the turn at the corner, and Chloe felt almost weak-kneed with relief. She'd leave the hard questions to the professionals, thanks very much.

"Hazel, going back inside is not an option," she said. "Kari, could you let the responders know that Wilbur is missing? He was last seen inside the tavern."

"Right." Kari took off.

Chloe wanted to get Hazel away from the others, in case there *was* cause for a wifely meltdown. "Let's check around back," she suggested. She led the older woman around the building.

And—to her astonishment, there was Wilbur. He was sitting on the grass, leaning against a convenient tree. His head rested against the trunk. His eyes were open, although he looked dazed. As they approached Chloe caught the stench of something burned. But it wasn't a woody smell. The left side of his shirt was gone, burned away. Dear God, what had the drunken fool done?

"Wilbur!" Hazel ran to her husband and crouched beside him.

Chloe started to follow, but stopped. *No.* Wilbur's burns needed care, and she had no first-aid supplies.

"Don't touch him," Chloe told Hazel. Then she raced back around the building. "Is there an EMT here?" she shouted. "I need help!"

————

Fifteen minutes later, a competent young man finished assessing the burns on Wilbur's chest. Alta had come into the back yard with Chloe, two EMTs, and a county deputy. The tour leader stood with one arm around Hazel's shoulder.

"You're going to be all right," the EMT told Wilbur, tucking spare gauze back into his kit. "We'll take you to the hospital and let a doc check you over."

"Oh, *Wilbur*," Hazel said with infinite sadness, bending over the gurney. "I'm so sorry this happened."

Wilbur looked at his wife with an expression Chloe couldn't decipher—pain, certainly, mixed with longing and regret. Did he even remember what happened? Or had the incident shocked him sober and left him too ashamed to speak?

"So, Mr. Voss," the deputy said, "how did you get burned?"

Wilbur's gaze drifted to Chloe, and raw hatred flared in his eyes. It was gone so quickly that Chloe almost thought she'd imagined it. Almost. She hugged her arms across her chest.

"You'll have to talk to him at the hospital," one of the EMTs told the deputy. The medical people hustled Wilbur into the ambulance.

The deputy approached the women. He was a stocky man, probably nearing retirement, with an air of competent calm. "Were any of you with the victim?"

Alta shook her head. "I was not."

"I wasn't either," Chloe said. "I was across the street when the sirens went off."

"I'm his wife," Hazel told him. "But I wasn't with Wilbur when the fire started either."

The deputy pulled a little notebook from his pocket and stood with pencil poised. "What can you tell me?"

Hazel's cheeks were pale, but her voice was steady. "I saw him shortly before … before it happened. He was upset with me." She told the deputy about their argument in Pepin and her decision to join the Laura Land tour. "I assumed he'd gone home! I had no idea he'd come to Burr Oak until I saw him come out of the Black Crow. He was drunk." She twisted her hands together. "It was embarrassing. I tried to talk to him in the hallway inside, but he was incoherent. So I turned my back and went into the main room, where I sat down to have lunch with my new friends." Two spots of color appeared in Hazel's cheeks, but she didn't look away.

Way to go Hazel, Chloe thought.

"We were together when the alarm went off," Alta added.

"So you don't know exactly where Mr. Voss was when the fire started?"

"No," Alta said, and Hazel shook her head.

"And you did not see where it started?"

Hazel and Alta exchanged helpless glances. "I didn't see it at all," Hazel said. "I ran outside with everyone else. Then I started to look for Wilbur."

"Do you think your husband might have started the fire?"

Hazel looked shocked. "Oh, no. He'd never do anything like that."

The deputy held her gaze. "Ma'am, are you afraid of your husband? Has he ever tried to hurt you or anyone you love?"

"No!" Hazel insisted. "He doesn't mean anything when he hollers, not really. And this, him getting drunk and making a scene—well, it's just that I've never stood up to him before."

"Do you want to go to the hospital with him, honey?" Alta asked. "I can get your suitcase from the bus."

Hazel looked toward the open doors of the ambulance, where the EMTs were making her husband as comfortable as they could. The blasted fire alarm abruptly shut off, much to Chloe's relief. The relative hush underscored the weight of Hazel's decision.

"No," she finally said. "I think I'm leaving Wilbur for good. I want to continue the tour with your group. The chance to go to *Looking For Laura* is too special to miss."

Lovely, Chloe thought. She didn't begrudge Hazel her dream trip in the rainbow-hued Laura Land bus, but the man she'd originally pegged as a grump and a bully was revealing himself as an irresponsible drunk with the capacity for disturbing behavior. Chloe didn't want Wilbur blaming *her* for his wife's defection.

The deputy looked confused. "The chance to look for Laura? Who's Laura?"

"Laura Ingalls Wilder," Alta explained. "You know, the famous children's author? I've organized a tour of her homesites, you see, and…"

And my presence here is not required, Chloe thought. She glanced at the yard next door, behind the Masters Hotel. The lawn was surprisingly spacious, shaded by trees, with a creek twisting through. Laura and Mary had played there, surely. Now firemen were tromping about, checking doors and windows. Chloe circled back to the street and found Kari alone, watching more firefighters stow gear on their truck.

"What's going on?" Chloe asked.

"I heard one of the fireman say that the tavern fire was out before they even got here," Kari reported.

"Couldn't have been much of a fire, then." Chloe thought that over, both relieved and suspicious. "But Wilbur Voss ended up with a pretty bad burn. I can't help wondering if he started it himself somehow."

"Dear God." Kari looked shocked. "One guy said something about a charred patch on the floor, but I don't know if that was in the kitchen or what."

"What about the Masters Hotel?"

"They gave it the all-clear. I don't know why the museum alarms went off too."

"They're probably tied in with the Black Crow because the buildings are so close." Chloe looked up and down the street. "Where did everybody go?"

"Alta's group is in the gift shop." Kari motioned toward the repurposed bank building. "Everyone else has left."

The ambulance inched away from the other vehicles. Alta and Hazel appeared, still deep in conversation. The truck was idling, its engine a dull rumble as firemen secured a hose and gear. The air was muggy, and although the rain had stopped, a line of clouds going vertical on the horizon suggested another wave of storms to come.

The door to the gift shop banged behind them, and Jayne-with-a-Y's strident voice gouged the afternoon: "…do know that Laura didn't actually write the Little House books, don't you?" she asked a heavyset woman. The woman trotted down the steps, clearly wanting to distance herself. Chloe felt a tightness in her chest. She knew the feeling.

"Chloe?" Kari said. "I'm getting a bad feeling about this trip."

The tightness intensified. What the *heck*? She felt more upset than the fire scare warranted, and she wasn't sure why. "I—I'm going to take a walk."

Kari hesitated, then shrugged. "I'll wait here."

Chloe walked away, faster and faster. Her vision blurred and she swiped at tears. She turned a corner, passed a couple of houses, turned another corner, kept going. She found herself on a gravel drive that ended in front of a small church on a hill, postcard-pretty with fresh white paint, arched stained-glass windows, and a cross-topped steeple. A sign on the fence beyond the church said *Burr Oak Cemetery, Est. 1854.*

Chloe pulled the gate open and slid through the gap. Her gaze automatically sought out the oldest stones—weathered and leaning, one or two marked with the brass star signifying a Civil War veteran. She spotted a very old monument near the entrance gate. The stone was blotched with gray moss and orange lichen, its inscription worn past easy deciphering. But an infant carved in marble relief told the story.

Chloe felt a wave of sorrow that seemed to emanate from the earth. Her legs buckled. I guess I'll sit, she thought, even as her knees hit the ground. She shrugged out of her jacket, spread it on the soggy grass, and lowered herself the rest of the way.

"What is going *on*?" she asked aloud. She closed her eyes, sifting through her grievances. Miss Lila was dead. Something was bugging Kari. The Big Woods were gone. Someone had died right in front of her in what had been the Ingallses' yard. A pleasant lady named Hazel had been yelled at, humiliated, and ultimately frightened by her bully-drunkard husband, who just might have managed to set fire to a tavern inches from the Masters Hotel. Laura's Little House canon had not mentioned that hotel, instead hopping over a horrid chapter in her life.

A chapter that included the birth and death of baby Charles Frederick Ingalls.

I understand, Chloe tried to tell Laura, as tears dribbled down her cheeks. She had once miscarried a child of her own. The pregnancy had not been planned, but the loss of that child had torn her apart.

Chloe swiped at her eyes. It all happened a long time ago, when she lived in Switzerland. She'd left the baby's father, moved back to the states, and tried to make peace with what had happened. And life had gotten better—much better. She'd met Roelke, a man who'd walk through fire if he thought she needed help.

… And a man who was evidently considering buying his old family farm.

What's really behind that? she wondered. Did Roelke want to settle down? What did that even mean? What kind of future did he want for himself—for them? Did he want kids?

Chloe didn't know if she wanted to settle down, much less plan for kids. She was like Laura, like Pa, right? Restless, always wondering what was over the next hill? She and Roelke had been doing just fine. Why did anything have to change?

The tightness was back in her ribs, sharper than ever. I think I'm having a panic attack, she thought. She'd never had one before. In the past she'd generally skipped panic and plunged straight into depression.

So maybe all in all, a panic attack wasn't the worst thing in the world. She concentrated on breathing evenly, and tuning in to this moment. Her butt was cold and wet, but otherwise, she was good. The cemetery was peaceful. A cardinal was singing nearby. A beautiful old oak stood sentinel at the crest of the hill. The earth smelled fresh and clean.

Without warning, something new wiggled into her consciousness and pinged her sternum. She sensed something here among the stones. Not grief, which she would have expected, but instead peace. No, more than peace...happiness. Light and airy, like a child's.

Chloe's eyes flew open. I sensed Laura! she thought, even as her mind scoffed at the notion. If she hadn't found Laura in the hotel, why would she find her in a cemetery? Laura had probably never even set foot in this cemetery. And if she had, dutifully attending the funeral of some neighbor, she wouldn't have left an intangible layer of happiness behind.

I don't care, Chloe thought stubbornly. After entering the Burr Oak Cemetery a sniveling mess, she'd somehow found a moment of grace. "Thank you," she told Laura.

Then Chloe got to her feet and picked up her jacket. She didn't feel like sniveling anymore. She felt like saying a respectful good-bye to the Masters Hotel, getting in the car with her sister, and continuing the road trip.

Ten minutes later, she rejoined Kari, who was sitting on the steps, reading *On the Banks Of Plum Creek*. "I bought a complete set of books in the gift shop," Kari said. "I thought it might be fun to read aloud in the car as we head toward each site." She paused. "That is, if you still want to keep going."

"Do you?"

"I miss my girls. And the trip has been strange so far. But . . . I don't want to go home."

"I don't either," Chloe said. The Ingallses had hit stony bottom in Burr Oak, and she had as well. "On to Minnesota."

(Laura's) chest felt all hot inside, and she wished with all her might that Mary wouldn't always be such a good little girl. But she couldn't let Mary be better than she was.   Little House on the Prairie

"Oh, Charles!" said Ma. "A dugout. We've never had to live in a dugout yet."

... "It's only till I harvest the first wheat crop," said Pa. "Then you'll have a fine house and I'll have horses and maybe even a buggy. This is great wheat country, Caroline!"   On the Banks of Plum Creek

SEVEN

"'A GOOD CROP OF wheat will bring us more money than we've ever had, Laura,'" Chloe read. "'Then we'll have horses, and new dresses, and everything you can want.' Oh!" She slapped the book closed and gazed out the window. "It's hard to read this."

"I know." Kari, who was driving, nodded fervently. "Inside I keep shouting, 'No, Pa! Don't count on the wheat crop! The grasshopper plagues are coming!'" She slowed as they approached a tiny town.

"Laura was a master at foreshadowing. And this book's theme—waiting and aching for the promised bounty—is really powerful."

"Foreshadowing?" Kari gave her a sidelong look. "Theme?"

Chloe felt herself prickle. "Just making an observation."

"Are you doing any writing these days?"

"A little."

"Back in high school, you always said you wanted to write a novel."

"Back in high school, all I really wanted to do was remind my teachers that I was not you."

Kari blinked. "What are you talking about?"

Chloe had no idea why she'd plunged into this particular pool of quicksand. "Let's just say you could be a hard act to follow. I wish I had a dollar for every teacher who told me on the first day of class that she hoped I was as good at whatever as *you* were."

"Oh, come on. It wasn't that bad."

Yes, it was, Chloe thought. "No, it wasn't," she said. "Whatever."

"Seriously," Kari said. "Name one teacher who—ooh!" She hit the brakes. "A quilt shop!"

Chloe braced herself as Kari swerved into a gravel lot. "Do you need some fabric?" Kari had completed several patchwork blocks since they'd left home, Flying Geese pattern.

"I won't know until I see what they have." Kari parked beside an unassuming building. "You know what they say: whoever dies with the most fabric wins."

Chloe didn't argue. She'd been known to enjoy a good fabric store in her time. Besides, it was nice to see Kari so upbeat.

The shop's front window was enticingly arranged with floral quilts and pots of flowers. Inside, quilts hung from the rafters for inspiration. Bolts of fabric filled shelves in every direction.

Kari looked around with lusting eyes. "Chloe, you should get some material! Pick out a few pieces you like and start a quilt."

"It's been years since I pieced a quilt," Chloe said, although some of the fabric was already calling to her like a siren's song. She tried to tie herself to the metaphorical mast before spending money she really didn't need to spend. "If I'm going to do another, I need time to plan."

"Why? We've got lots of hours in the car ahead of us, and handwork is good for the soul. Get a small square template and choose some calicoes. You can start a Nine Patch."

Chloe frowned. "But *Mary* Ingalls made Nine Patch quilts. I'm *Laura*. I should make a Bear Track."

"Oh, get over yourself. We're both grown women, and you can make whatever block you want. I only suggested a Nine Patch because bias seams will be trickier to manage, especially in the car."

A saleswoman sensed her moment to pounce. "How can I help you?"

"Do you have any reproduction fabrics?" Chloe asked.

The woman beamed. "Come with me!"

Chloe left with half a dozen fabrics, all copies of nineteenth-century printed designs. Once back in the car, she pulled the assortment from the bag. In honor of Miss Lila's quilt, she'd gone mostly for madder-reds, browns, and tans. The assortment pleased her.

Kari turned into a gas station and pulled up to the lone pump. "We're down half a tank, and besides, I want to catch my girls before a neighbor picks them up for swim lessons. Will you do the honors?"

Kari headed for the payphone mounted on the station's outside wall. As Chloe stood behind the car with nozzle in hand, she mentally arranged and rearranged her fabrics. It had been way too long since she'd made a quilt. She loved creating unique designs within traditional patterns. She loved feeling connected to the countless women who had stitched quilts over the last century or two. She loved the meditative calm that came as her own needle flowed through the cloth.

"Make sure Daddy put a clean towel in your swim bag, okay sweetie?" Kari was saying. "The towels were still in the dryer when I left."

Chloe was even starting to feel enthused about making a lowly Nine Patch, easiest of the easy patterns. Maybe I'll assemble the quilt top so the blocks are on point, Chloe thought. If she tipped her blocks 90 degrees, she'd create some nice diagonal movement and a more interesting overall pattern.

"I'm sorry I can't be there today," Kari was saying. "Is Daddy inside? Put him on, okay? I love you!"

Chloe switched the nozzle from one hand to the other. Good thing she and Kari were splitting costs, because gas had edged over a dollar a gallon.

"Did you turn in the application for the... Why *not*? We need those tax credits, Tryg! I left everything on the dining room table, and all you had to do was... What? What's wrong with the manure spreader?"

The pump finally switched off. By the time Chloe had paid the attendant, Kari was sitting in the passenger seat, ready to go. Chloe slid behind the wheel. "Everything okay at home?" she asked. She turned the key and the Rambler roared to life.

"Are things ever okay on a farm?" Kari reached for her sewing bag. "We're on the verge of missing a deadline for a program that would save us real money at tax time, and the manure spreader has gone belly-up. The Reagan administration just put forward a plan that will pay dairy farmers ten dollars per hundredweight for producing up to thirty percent less milk, and it looks like Congress is on board, but there's a fifty-cent milk tax—"

"So money is tight," Chloe said, before Kari launched into a detailed analysis of soybean futures or something.

"We need a new furnace too. Don't *ever* buy an old house, Chloe. They always need something, usually something very expensive. Right now—" Kari took a deep breath. "Sorry."

"Hey, I can barely manage my own meager finances. I don't know how you and Trygve keep everything straight."

"We'll manage. I just wish that Tryg would ... well." Kari pinched her lips into a grim line.

Chloe decided not to say anything more. She'd never seen the expression on Kari's face—taut and hard. Something was definitely off between Kari and Trygve.

"I was thinking about my Nine Patch while you were on the phone," Chloe said. "Stopping at that quilt shop was a good idea."

Kari managed to smile, and some of the tension left her shoulders. "Yeah," she said. "It was." She pulled out her thimble.

Chloe tried to go back to her own happy mental quilting as she drove, but after this last not-so-cheery conversation, she couldn't focus on handwork. *Don't ever buy an old house, Chloe...* Instead of pretty squares of red and brown, all she could see was an abandoned cream city brick farmhouse, and Roelke's wistful expression as he watched it slumber.

———

"This really is a marvelous property, Mr. McKenna," Babs said. "A marvelous opportunity. Watch your step there." She pointed to the top porch step.

"Un-hunh," Roelke said. He should have postponed this little tour. His only call that day had been *such* a downer. He wondered where Mrs. Enright had taken Travis.

Babs unlocked the front door and ushered him inside. "This entrance leads into the living room."

"Un-hunh," he said, thinking, No, it leads into the *parlor*.

"Lovely high ceilings," Babs said. "Those tall windows let in lots of sunlight. I can just see a shelf with houseplants sitting below each one. Can't you? Ferns would work well. And consider the window treatment options! Dusty rose, I'm thinking, including the valance."

"Un-hunh." Roelke had no idea what a valance was. He was pretty sure he didn't care.

"Come along into the kitchen. It's quite spacious. Plenty of room for informal dining. Display space on top of the cupboards. There's even room for a shelf of cookbooks there, near the sink." Babs pointed with obvious rapture. "It's really all quite marvelous."

Roelke couldn't manage even an affirmative grunt to honor the imaginary cookbook shelf. How had an agent like Babs ended up with this listing, anyway? She was a fifty-wishing-for-thirty woman with too-blond hair, too much makeup, too much gold jewelry, and a figure that hinted at anorexia. He assumed that anyone else considering the farm was actually, you know, a farmer. He couldn't imagine any farmer bonding with Babs.

"I've got dimensions for everything," she was saying, "but I brought a tape measure along too. You'll feel more confident if you double-check closet space yourself."

"I don't need to check closet space."

"Closet space is very important," Babs chided. "Do you have a ladyfriend?"

Roelke didn't feel like telling her that yes, he did indeed have a ladyfriend.

"Even if there isn't a lady in the picture now," she cooed, "there will be one day. And ladies care about closet space."

Roelke was pretty sure that Chloe didn't care a whole lot about closet space.

Then he realized that, thanks to Babbling Babs, he had for the first time actually pictured Chloe living in this house. He didn't want to picture that. It was too soon to picture that. He really wanted the agent to shut up.

She did not, so he just tuned her out as they continued through the house. All he needed to do was assess what the years of abandonment had done to the place.

"The laundry hook-up is in the basement, of course," Babs was saying, "but you could squeeze an apartment-sized washer up here if you wanted to."

"Un-hunh." The porch needed replacing. Every inch of the interior needed new paint. Someone had painted the hardwood floors, so those needed to be stripped. But the roof—

"The furnace is only six years old, and … "

"Un-hunh." The roof must still be sound, for he saw no evidence of water damage or critter habitation.

"There are three bedrooms upstairs—one small, one medium, and one large. Just like Goldilocks!"

"Un-hunh." I need an expert inspection, Roelke thought. But the signs of neglect weren't as bad as he'd feared.

They ended up back in the kitchen. Babs pulled a binder and several file folders from her garment bag–sized purse—he was surprised her bony shoulder had stood up to the rigors of hauling it around—and placed it on the counter. "Now, in addition to the house specs, I have all the information about the property itself. Forty acres, isn't that marvelous?"

"Un-hunh," Roelke said, although when his grandparents were farming the place, they'd owned at least double that number. But maybe there's an upside to lost acres, he thought. He'd yet to look at the actual asking price.

"The current owner has been renting the fields," Babs was saying, "but I've talked to the renter. He'd be willing to talk with you as well, give you a clear idea of yield per acre and current crop value. And of course there is some work to be done in the house."

Roelke squinted, imagining fresh paint and gleaming floors.

"But all in all, it's a *marvelous* opportunity for a young person like yourself. Are you farming now?"

"No."

"But you want to be a farmer?"

"No."

For the first time, Babs seemed to notice that she'd been doing all the talking. "Mr. McKenna, if I may ask, what do you do for a living?"

"I'm a police officer."

Her face tightened. Maybe she was wondering if this visit had been a waste of time. "Do you have any questions?"

"The price is on the sheet you gave me, right?" The one he'd folded and thrust into a back pocket.

"It is." She opened a little gold case, pulled out a business card, and handed it over. Instinctively he dug into his pocket and pulled out a card of his own for the ritual exchange. She glanced at it and tucked it away.

Then her forehead wrinkled, and she pulled the card back out. "Roelke McKenna," she said, pronouncing his first name as if it had three syllables.

"It's Rell-kee."

"As in ... Roelke Lane? As in, the old Roelke place on Roelke Lane?"

"That's it."

"I see." Her face softened. "How long has it been out of the family?"

"Almost ten years."

"It's marvelous that you're considering getting it back," she said, actually sounding sincere. She gave him a packet of papers and extended her hand. "If you decide to pursue the property, give me a call."

Back outside, Babs slid into her pricey car and drove away. Roelke tossed the information packet through the open truck window. Then he leaned against the hood and studied the farm. Something about Babs's nod of approval rattled him. *If you decide to pursue the property...* The phrase prompted a vague image of him chasing something, running faster and faster, never quite catching it.

Actually, the whole episode—coming here, walking through the empty house—had rattled him. He folded his arms, trying to figure out why. The house was definitely tired. His grandparents would be heartbroken to see the garden overgrown, the lawn gone to seed, paint peeling on the window trim. None of that was a big deal, and yet...

And *yet*, buying this place would take more than a financial commitment. If he actually bought this property, it meant he'd be sticking around for a while. Like, indefinitely. It was hard to imagine moving back into the farmhouse; even harder to imagine fixing it up and then moving on.

Okay, he told himself, one thing at a time. He didn't need to decide anything today. All he was doing was getting information. And speaking of information ... He sucked in a deep breath, blew it out slowly. Then he pulled the single sheet from his jeans pocket, unfolded it, and skimmed down to the asking price.

His eyes went wide. *Holy Mother-of-God toboggans.*

Roelke turned his back on the farm, got into his truck, and drove away.

"Five hundred dollars debt on the house!" Laura exclaimed. "Oh, I didn't know that!"

"No," Manly said. "I didn't think there was any need to bother you about that."   The First Four Years

EIGHT

THE ELLEFSON GIRLS HAD tickets for that night's performance of "Fragments of a Dream," the Wilder Pageant held just outside Walnut Grove, Minnesota. Tomorrow they'd visit the Ingalls Dugout Site and stop at the Laura Ingalls Wilder Museum in town.

Unable to find a motel room in Walnut Grove, Chloe had made a reservation in a town twenty-five miles away. They arrived in early evening. The motel was a mom-and-pop place with parking at the door. Kari dropped her suitcase inside and turned around. "I'll be back in a bit."

Chloe gave her a suspicious look.

"I'm not going out for a ciggie," Kari said defensively. "Just a walk." She shut the door decisively behind her.

"Okey-dokey," Chloe said, reaching for her bag of fabric. "Whatever."

A quick wash in the sink removed sizing from the material. She left the pieces dripping from the shower rod and went back to the bedroom to call Roelke. "Hey," she said when he answered.

"Hey. How was your day? Any better?"

She thought about her morning, studded with gems like the tavern fire and her own meltdown in the Burr Oak Cemetery. But no one had died, right? "Yes," she said firmly. "We visited a Laura site I hadn't even known existed before Miss Lila talked with me. And Kari and I are still getting along. Mostly, anyway. I've earned a gold star on the Scorecard of Sisterly Relations."

He laughed, which pleased her, because Roelke McKenna was not a man who laughed lightly. "Good," he said. "On both counts."

She began doodling on the notepad by the phone. "How was your shift?"

"Okay."

"Did you go see the farm after work? How did that go?"

"Okay."

"What kind of shape was the house in?"

"Not bad, actually. I think it could be made livable without too much work." He paused. "More than livable. Really nice."

"Seriously?" She didn't mean to sound doubtful, but the house *had* been empty for a while.

"The brickwork is solid. The roof is good. The furnace is only a few years old. All in all, I was satisfied."

"So ... you're thinking seriously about buying it?"

"I'm thinking about it."

She turned her squiggles into dollar signs and waited for him to bring up the obvious. After a few seconds passed, she jumped into the breach. "So ... it's feasible financially?"

"I don't know. I'm going to call an old friend from high school, someone who works in the banking industry. She can give me some advice."

"That sounds like a good idea."

"Yeah."

Another pause. "I hate this," she said abruptly. "I'm sorry my trip happened right when you've got this big thing going on. I—" She broke off when the door opened. Kari gave her a questioning look, and Chloe beckoned her inside.

"It's okay," Roelke was saying.

"Well, keep me posted. I love you."

"I love you too." They both hung up.

Kari sat on one of the beds. "Everything all right?"

"I guess so." Chloe swiveled around on the desk chair. "Roelke's thinking about buying his old family farm."

"He *is*?" Kari's eyebrows rose. "He wants to farm?"

"No. I think he just ... " Chloe spread her hands. "It's the family place, you know?"

"I do indeed."

The edge in Kari's voice was most disconcerting.

"Has he thought about how much his life will change if he buys the place?" Kari asked.

"He's a long way from deciding, but he seems to think it could be doable."

"Yeah, and Pa thought he'd grow rich on wheat," Kari muttered. "And look how *that* turned out. Grasshoppers, crop failures, debt, and a miserable stint in—"

"*Hey*," Chloe protested.

"I'm sorry." Kari rubbed her temples. "Really, I am."

Chloe didn't want to talk about it anymore. "I'm going to get ready to leave."

In the bathroom, Chloe stared at herself in the mirror as she redid her long braid. Truth was, she needed to think more about this farm business. She and Roelke loved each other, but they lived in their own places, they took turns paying for meals eaten out, and they had never, ever talked about money in any meaningful way.

Perhaps, Chloe thought, that's because I don't have any money to talk about. The historic sites biz was not even a little bit lucrative. She was still paying off school loans. Moving to Switzerland and back hadn't helped. After a year of steady employment at Old World Wisconsin, consciously trying to save for the inevitable day when her car heaved its last mechanical breath, she had about six hundred dollars in her savings account.

Roelke was younger than she was, but he didn't have school loans. He surely paid less in rent for his tiny apartment than she did for her farmhouse. And his parents and grandparents were all dead, so he'd probably inherited a little something along the way. Perhaps more than a little something.

If Roelke purchased the farm, was he planning to shoulder the entire financial burden? Chloe felt a stab of panic at the idea of personally taking even a sliver of financial responsibility for a farm. She remembered Charles Ingalls promising Caroline a life sparkling with pixie dust once the crops came in…

"Oh, bullshit," Chloe muttered, turning the water on full force so she could wash her face. She was spending *way* too much mental time in Laura Land. Charles and Caroline Ingalls were a married couple living in the nineteenth century, when life was very, very different. Roelke was not making a decision for her. He was making a decision for himself.

A decision that, assuming they stayed together, had major implications for them both …

She scrubbed vigorously, splashed away the soap, and toweled her cheeks dry. Then she took a deep breath. Enough worry about that for now. She and Kari had a pageant to enjoy.

———

Roelke loved Chloe, but that didn't mean he understood what she was thinking and feeling every minute. Half the time, maybe more, he really didn't have a clue. Their phone conversation left him restlessly prowling his tiny apartment.

His apartment was a walkup, tucked under the eaves of a commercial building. Pacing was difficult since he could only walk so far without banging his head against the ceiling. When he'd left his first cop job in Milwaukee, wanting to be closer to his cousin Libby, he'd rented this flat because it was cheap, convenient, and available. Whether I buy the farm or not, Roelke thought, I really do need a bigger place.

He dropped into his chair at the teensy table in the teensy kitchen and considered the bank statements spread on the Formica. He was no math whiz, but he scrupulously tracked his money. He kept his checking account balance low, with just enough in reserve to cover basic expenses. Everything else went into a special account. He'd been saving to buy a J-3 Piper Cub. Until he saw the For Sale sign in front of the Roelke farm, anyway.

Roelke stared at the figures he'd made on a yellow tablet. Deciding he could afford the farm wasn't enough. Was he willing to forget his dream of flight?

And then he had to figure out what any of this, all of this, meant for his relationship with Chloe.

Roelke picked up his pencil. None of the emotional stuff mattered if he couldn't swing the financial stuff. He didn't want to sound like a complete moron when he met with Peggy, his high school friend. He'd written the asking price of the farm on the top line of the paper. Below that he'd written the balance in his savings account. The difference between the two figures made him dizzy.

When the phone rang again he leapt up with a sense of reprieve, narrowly avoiding cracking his skull. He trotted to his living room and grabbed the receiver. "McKenna here."

"McKenna? It's Con Malloy."

"Oh!" Roelke blinked. Sergeant Con Malloy of the Milwaukee PD did not contact Roelke McKenna, his former rookie trainee, often. Like, never.

"I called to see how you were doing."

"Oh!" Roelke said again. "Okay, I guess."

"What happened was rough."

"Yeah." Roelke's throat grew tight. *What happened* referred to Roelke's best friend being killed on duty three months earlier.

"You did good work there."

He swallowed hard. *Good work* referred to Roelke tracking down the murderer, despite becoming a target himself. "Thanks."

"So," Malloy said gruffly. "The dust is settling around here. And people haven't forgotten that a beat cop from Waukesha County nailed a killer before our detectives figured it out. More than a couple of the higher-ups have wondered if you might want to come back to the MPD."

"…Oh?"

"I can't officially promise anything, but it's safe to say that you'd be fast-tracked."

Roelke tried to take that in. "Well, hunh."

"Don't tell me you haven't thought about it."

"Not for a while, actually."

"Are you even full-time out there?"

"I am, yeah."

"But that's about all you can hope for in a small village department, right? You're a damn fine cop, McKenna. And right now, in the city, you could go in just about any direction you want. What sounds good? Narcotics? Vice? Detective?"

Roelke sat down on his sofa, phone pressed to his ear, dazed. "I ... it would be hard for me to go back to Milwaukee. After what happened."

"I hear you," Malloy barked, which was as much empathy as Roelke had ever heard from the old copper. "But something good can come out of it. You'd be an idiot not to take advantage of that. You've got a golden opportunity here, McKenna, but it won't last forever."

Roelke pressed one knuckle against his forehead. "I'll think about it."

"Don't think too long."

"I appreciate the call—" Roelke began, but Malloy had already disconnected.

Roelke hung up more slowly. He planted elbows on knees and leaned over, thinking. *Right now, in the city, you could go in just about any direction you want ...*

"Damn," Roelke muttered. He'd moved to Eagle with two goals: make sure Libby and the kids were okay, and avoid screwing up at the EPD for long enough to earn full-time status. When he'd spent time in Milwaukee last February, grief and rage hadn't left room for anything besides catching his friend's killer. But now ... well, he had to admit that he did miss some things about Milwaukee.

For half a second he thought to call Rick. His hand actually twitched toward the phone before he remembered that Rick was dead.

I miss you, buddy, Roelke said silently. Malloy's call was exactly the kind of thing he would have once kicked around with his best friend.

Roelke swallowed hard. God, he wished Chloe was there. He wished he could talk to her about all this. Better still, he wished he could just lie on the sofa with her in his arms, his fingers tangled in her hair, breathing her in. Not talking. Not doing. Just being.

But Chloe wasn't there. And if he stayed in this apartment for one more minute, he just might explode.

He grabbed the telephone again and dialed a familiar number. "Libby? I called to see if you were home."

"I am, obviously," his cousin said. "Why?"

"Because I'm coming over."

————

Chloe drove as the Ellefson girls headed toward the pageant grounds. She was enjoying the rural road's rustic charm when something large and colorful appeared in the rearview mirror. "I think Alta's bus is behind us."

Kari looked over her shoulder. "That is definitely the LLT bus."

"Alta's driving like a bat outta hell," Chloe muttered. "I'm not sure why. We've got plenty of time to get to the pageant."

The bus horn blared. "Maybe they recognized our car and just want to get close enough to wave hello," Kari suggested.

"Maybe." Chloe kept an eye on the fast-approaching minibus as they went around a corner and started down a hill. As Alta continued to gain on them, she blasted the horn again.

Kari twisted around again. "What is she *doing*?"

The bus was close now—way, *way* too close. The blaring horn ratcheted Chloe's nerves tight. The Rambler had a stick shift, three-on-the-tree, and she changed gears to pick up speed. "I think something's wrong."

"Pull out of her way!"

"I—I can't!" Chloe stammered. The bus had gotten way too close. She glimpsed Alta at the wheel.

Then a grille filled the rearview mirror. Oh God, the *quilt*, Chloe moaned silently. She pushed harder on the gas, feeling herself at the edge of control.

"Pull *over*!" Kari shrieked.

Chloe jerked the wheel toward the shoulder. The bus flew past. A blur of trees replaced highway through the windshield. Kari screamed and tires squealed, but it all seemed suddenly distant. Chloe felt the ground start to give way beneath them and thought *We're going to roll…*

But they didn't. The car stopped so violently that Chloe thought her lap belt would saw her in half. She had stamped on both brake and clutch, and the engine roared in protest before dropping to a sullen idle. Dust swirled in through the open windows.

A loud, prolonged *crunch* sounded from somewhere around the bend ahead. The harsh sound of crumpling metal reverberated against a sharp series of percussive bursts exploding like gunfire.

"Are you okay?" Chloe asked Kari.

"I…I'm okay. Are you?"

Chloe tried to assess any damage. Her middle felt bruised. Her heart was still racing. Her muscles seemed to be trembling and clenched tight at the same time. Nothing worse. "Yeah."

Although the front tires still clung to the gravel shoulder, the car was tipped back to an alarming degree, facing the road with the rear wheels well down an embankment. I need to get the car back on the shoulder, Chloe thought. But when she commanded her foot to let off the brake, she discovered that it felt much better holding that pedal to the floorboard, thanks all the same. She felt a bit woozy.

But there was no time to indulge in wooziness. Chloe swallowed hard, shifted into first, eased down on the gas, and managed to maneuver the car to safety. "Come on. We need to see if everyone on the bus is okay."

When Laura saw the oxen, and Ma and Carrie on the wagon seat, she jumped up and down, swinging her sunbonnet and shouting, "They're coming! They're coming!"

"They're coming awful fast," Mary said.

Laura was still. She heard the wagon rattling loudly. Pete and Bright were coming very fast. They were running. They were running away.

On the Banks of Plum Creek

NINE

ROELKE WALKED OVER TO Libby's small ranch house and let himself in the back door. Libby was in the kitchen pulling plastic wrap from a Styrofoam tray of ground beef. A radio on the counter was tuned to NPR. Otherwise the house was suspiciously quiet. "No kids?" he asked.

"Justin's at T-ball practice and Dierdre's got a play date." Libby dumped the beef into a blue mixing bowl. She was a slim woman of medium height, with dark hair cut extra short for the summer. As a single mom she handled her two young children, an asshole of an exhusband, the household, and the demands of a career as a freelance writer pretty well. She'd honed efficiency to a fine art since her divorce, but her blunt demeanor had developed in childhood.

Now she pulled spice jars from a cabinet and began shaking this and that over the meat. "What's up?"

Roelke pulled the crumpled farm listing sheet from his pocket and smoothed it out on the counter. Her hands didn't stop moving as she looked at the paper. "Grandma and Grandpa's place is for sale?"

"Yeah."

She sprinkled pepper into the bowl, considered, sprinkled some more. Then she glanced up with a *So-o-o-o?* expression.

He waited.

Suddenly her eyes widened. "You're not thinking about buying it," she said flatly.

He looked at her.

"Oh my God."

"I'm thinking about it. That's all."

She fetched ketchup and an egg from the fridge, added them to the mixture, washed her hands, and began kneading everything together. She leaned over the listing again, and he could tell she was reading the price. Her hands went still and her mouth opened. It was still open when she slowly met his gaze. "Are you out of your mind?"

"Probably," he admitted.

Libby pressed her lips together for a moment. "Go fire up the grill, will you? Let me get the burgers on. Then we can talk."

———

Chloe and Kari trotted shaky-kneed around the bend. Alta's bus had come to a stop on the shoulder just beyond a bridge. She'd managed to slow down by scraping the right side against the bridge's low cement wall. The bus backfired over and over and *over*. But things could have been a whole lot worse, Chloe thought.

The door accordioned open. Alta stumbled out first, her face like chalk beneath red hair and a purple calico bonnet, one hand automatically clutching up her long skirt so she wouldn't trip.

Chloe reached her. "Is everybody all right?"

"Everybody's all right," Alta quavered. Her fellow travelers were climbing out now, some dazed, some chattering.

"What happened?" Kari asked.

"All of a sudden I couldn't slow down!" Alta wiped sweat from her forehead. "The gas pedal seemed stuck or something. I didn't know what to do! Finally I just—just turned off the ignition switch."

"I thought we were all going to die," Hazel Voss said, but she managed a shaky smile.

"Let's hear it for Alta!" another woman called. "Using that bridge to slow us down was brilliant!"

"That took skill," someone else agreed.

Or luck, Chloe thought. A shudder rippled down her spine as she glanced back at the bridge. If the high-profile bus had slammed into the bridge laterally, instead of maintaining a mostly forward motion, it might easily have flipped over and landed upside down in the gully below.

"Is the damage repairable?" asked Henrietta Beauchamps.

Alta looked at her minibus and cringed. The right side was horribly scraped, the assault particularly offensive against the cheerful paint job. "Oh, please," she whispered.

And suddenly Chloe flashed on her first glimpse of Alta Allerbee, pleading with someone unseen back at the Pepin Wayside: *Please don't do this! You'll ruin everything!*

Frost formed on Chloe's ribs. Dear God, she thought. Surely no one would… "Alta?" she began.

"Where's Leonard?" an elderly woman asked. "He might know something about mechanics."

"No, he stayed in town to talk to that nice curator about Charles Ingalls," another woman said. She turned to the sole male in evidence. "Bill? Can you figure out what's wrong with the bus?"

Bill took a wary step backward. "Definitely not."

"In *my* day," the first woman observed tartly, "men knew how to take care of things."

Before anyone could further lament the loss of manly knowledge, a station wagon stopped and two men jumped out. "Hey, everybody okay?" Then a blue pickup stopped in the other lane. "I'll go call for help!" a woman hollered through the window before speeding off again.

Alta sat on the ground abruptly, as if her knees had given out. Hazel eased down beside her. "Oh, honey. All you need is a hug."

This isn't the time to ask questions, Chloe thought. But Alta's troubles had just evolved from *None of my business* to *Heaven help me*. After the way the minibus had barreled down on them, it just might have been her and Kari who ended up crashing.

————

Roelke began to relax when, fifteen minutes later, he settled into a lawn chair on Libby's patio. The juicy smell of searing beef wafted from her enormous grill. The menu called for cheeseburgers, veggie kabobs, and skewered pineapple. Roelke had opted for iced tea.

Libby opened a Leinenkugel's and pushed a wedge of lime into the bottle. "Okay," she said after a long pull. "Can you even consider buying the old farm? I thought you were saving for a plane. When did you decide you wanted to be a farmer instead of a pilot?"

"I most definitely do not want to be a farmer. This isn't about Holsteins, or the so-called simple life, or going back to the land or whatever."

"What *is* it about?"

He'd been struggling to put that into words for a week now. "The farm is a good place. Remember when we were kids, and we'd all get together for Sunday dinners and holidays—"

"Please tell me you're not buying a farm so we can have Thanksgiving dinners there."

"It's a little more complicated than that."

Libby got up to check the burgers. "Look, I have great memories of that place. And I know you spent a lot more time there than I did, after things went sour with your dad—"

After Roelke's dad's alcoholism escalated and he began beating up Roelke's mom, she meant.

"—but that doesn't mean you should tie that anchor around your neck."

"I don't want to live in my stupid apartment forever."

"That was never meant to be more than temporary," Libby agreed. "But Roelke, you moving out here in the first place was supposed to be temporary. My divorce got ugly, I needed help, you were there. I'll be grateful forever. You will *always* be an important part of my life, and of the kids' lives."

Roelke tried to imagine life without *them*. Libby liked to boss him around. Justin was more than a handful. Dierdre believed she was an honest-to-God princess. Roelke loved them so much his heart hurt just to think about it.

"But I never expected you to stay in Palmyra," Libby was saying. "Buying any place out here would mean giving up on a city career for good—"

You've got a golden opportunity here, McKenna, but it won't last forever.

"—and I didn't know you'd made that decision. Have you?"

Roelke swirled ice cubes in his glass. "A lot of things have changed since I left Milwaukee. After what happened last winter, I don't know if I could handle going back there. And now that Chloe's in the picture..."

"Are you considering the farm because of Chloe?" Libby checked the burgers again. This time she propped the grill lid open and reached for a spatula. "What does she think?"

"Old places are her thing," he reminded Libby.

"But what does she think about you buying this particular old place?"

"She's off on a road trip with her sister, so we haven't had a whole lot of opportunity to discuss it."

She handed him a plate. "Is the idea that you'd both live there?"

"Well..." He reached for a napkin, avoiding her gaze. "I don't know."

"You don't *know*?"

His left knee began to bounce. "Look, I would love to live there, or anywhere, with Chloe. I've wanted us to move in together for a long time. And now we wouldn't be breaking the law." Wisconsin had only recently legalized the cohabitation of unmarried adults.

"So, why haven't you? Doesn't she want to?"

"We've never discussed it."

Libby sat back down with her own plate. "Why not?"

"Because I don't want to screw things up. We've been doing good." Really good, actually. It had taken them a while to figure out if they wanted to be together. Even *how* to be together. But they'd made the leap, and worked through some stuff, and grown closer. And sometimes he looked at Chloe and simply could not believe that this amazing, perplexing, beautiful, strong-minded woman had chosen to be with *him*.

"Oh, sweetie," Libby said softly. "Having the conversation about living together will not screw things up. I can't predict Chloe's answer, but that doesn't mean you shouldn't ask the question."

"She's traveling," he reminded Libby. "She and her sister are off visiting old houses where some famous author lived. And Chloe's giving a talk about her at one of the places."

"Who's the author?"

"Laura Ingalls Wilder."

Libby grinned. "I loved the Little House books when I was a kid!"

"You did?" He would not have guessed that. "Well, hunh." He finally sampled his cheeseburger. "This is great, by the way."

"Grass-fed beef and smoked Gouda. Anyway, I got the whole set of Little House books for Christmas when I was in fourth grade. I've still got them. In fact…" She hesitated.

"What?"

"Well, when my marriage went down the crapper, and I was trying to figure out whether the kids would be better off if Dan and I split—"

"They *are*."

"When you're in the middle of the mess, it's not so straightforward," Libby said. "But I came across my old Little House books when I was packing up, and they made me feel better about leaving."

"Really?"

"They're books about family, Roelke. And the dad—Pa—is just amazing. He could do anything, and face anything, and survive anything, and all he wants to do is provide for his family. And I thought, that's what I want for my kids. I want them to know that whatever bad things might happen, their parents love them and will take care of them. And Dan was not cutting it."

The moment felt fragile, so Roelke just nodded. Libby wasn't one to spill personal stuff easily, even with him.

"One day I'll read the books with Dierdre." Libby used a fork to pull chunks of pineapple from their skewer. "This road trip Chloe and Kari are taking sounds like a lot of fun."

Roelke tried to picture Chloe poking around old houses from here to South Dakota. He wondered if any of those places might have a job opening. The chance to become a curator at a historic site devoted to her favorite author would be pretty damn appealing. After all, she'd never said she was committed to working at Old World Wisconsin forever. She'd lived in Europe, for crying out loud. How could he expect her to—

"You okay?"

Roelke realized his knee was firing like a piston. "Sure," he said. "And you're right. I'm sure Chloe and Kari are having a blast."

———

Within half an hour, so many people had stopped by the battered bus to offer assistance that everything was under control. Several who were on their way to the pageant themselves offered rides. There was a moment of hesitation as Alta's gang considered accepting rides with strangers.

Then Hazel spoke up. "WWLD?" she asked brightly. "I want to see the pageant."

Alta's Laura Lookers divvied up with instructions to rendezvous near the ticket booth. A farmer said he could tow the minibus to a service station. "My cousin's brother-in-law is a mechanic," the man explained cheerfully. "He'll take a look."

Alta opted to stay with her bus. Chloe felt a niggle of unease about driving away, but the farmer seemed friendly, Alta was clearly unwilling to leave, and Kari had promised a ride to three of the strandees. "I'll come find you," Alta told her charges, "after I learn what's what. Meet me in the Grace aisle after the pageant."

Five minutes later Chloe and Kari headed south with Hazel Voss and Bill and Frances Whelan squeezed onto the back seat. Chloe, who'd decisively handed the car keys to her sister, swiveled sideways and made a stab at polite chitchat. "What brought you two on the tour?" she asked the Whelans.

"We're both retired teachers," Frances said. "I used the Little House books to get my second graders excited about reading."

"And she has a crush on Michael Landon," Bill Whelan added.

"Bill!" she scolded. Then she added, "Well, I must admit, Michael Landon makes a better Pa than Charles Ingalls did."

Chloe had no idea what to make of that.

"I taught fourth grade," Mr. Whelan said. "I integrated *Plum Creek* into lessons about state history."

"Have you seen any of the homesites before?" Chloe asked.

"No, and that was why I wanted to come," Mrs. Whelan said. "I'm not sure I could have talked my husband into a bus tour, though, if it hadn't been for the *Looking For Laura* symposium." She patted his knee.

"You're interested in the latest scholarship?" Chloe asked.

"Not really," he admitted affably. "I'm a collector, and half the fun of building a collection is sharing your treasures with people who appreciate them."

"What do you collect?" Kari asked.

"Anything Laura-related," Mr. Whelan said. "I have several first editions, and I'm after a full set." His genial smile suddenly held a sharkish gleam.

"A full set from each incarnation," Mrs. Whelan added dryly. "First editions from the original 1930s and early '40s printing, with illustrations by Helen Sewell and Mildred Boyle, and another set with illustrations by Garth Williams. You can see why we're touring the Midwest in a minibus instead of cruising the Greek isles."

"Ah," Chloe said sagely, with a *don'tcha know* smile of her own. Then she turned forward again. She hadn't even known that Garth Williams hadn't been the original artist. No offense to Ms. Sewell and Ms. Boyle, but in Chloe's humble opinion, Mr. Williams had been born to illustrate the Little House books.

More than that, though, she was struck by Bill Whelan's motivation for joining the LLT. I really did not think this through, she thought. Not everyone Looking For Laura was simply a longtime fan. Jayne-with-a-Y had pierced that pretty balloon with her incendiary authorship darts. Chloe didn't like Jayne any better today than she had two days earlier, and she would reject Jayne's cockamamie theories until the end of time, but the woman *had* opened Chloe's mind to the promise of a lively, thought-provoking, educational symposium in De Smet.

However, it hadn't occurred to her that some symposium attendees would be collectors. Which was pretty dumb, she realized, with a new stab of fear for the quilt bumping along in the trunk. But she had always valued artifacts because of the stories they could tell about the people who had once made them, owned them, cherished or disliked them. Sometimes she forgot that for most people, the antiques business was just that—a business. A business that was, for a lucky few, quite lucrative.

Chloe wished all over again that Miss Lila's quilt was locked in a vault somewhere. What would collectors make of a quilt once owned, and possibly even stitched, by Laura Ingalls Wilder?

"My goodness!" Mary said. "I couldn't be as mean as that Nellie Oleson."

Laura thought: I could. I could be meaner to her than she is to us, if Ma and Pa would let me.　　　　On the Banks of Plum Creek

Laura was on her feet. Her fury took possession of her, she did not try to resist it, she gave way completely.　　　　Little Town on the Prairie

TEN

"First editions are lovely," Hazel was saying thoughtfully, "but I'd love to own something that Laura actually touched. Maybe a letter she wrote. That might not be too costly...well. It would be a luxury."

Chloe glanced in the mirror as Hazel pinched her lips and looked out the side window. I doubt if she had a whole lot of discretionary cash even before deciding to leave her husband, Chloe thought. She wondered where Wilbur was. Had he sobered up and driven his sorry-ass self home? Or might he still be stalking his wife? Alta's little band had enough trouble without Wilbur Voss showing up again, drunk or sober.

When they reached the pageant grounds, the LLT folks reunited, greeting each other like shipwreck survivors. Some drifted toward the souvenir stand. The others purchased hot dogs and sodas and headed for picnic tables. "Please join us," Mrs. Whelan urged. Chloe had grabbed the picnic basket, and as everyone settled she made herself a peanut butter and honey sandwich, with a stack of Pringles on the side.

The pageant grounds were nestled on the bank of Plum Creek, which seemed auspicious. The set was more impressive than she'd expected. Rows of folding chairs marched up a hill. Best of all was the gathering crowd, mostly family groups or grandmas and moms with little girls. Many were dressed as their beloved Laura, and bonnet sales were brisk at the souvenir stand. Kids played tag and rolled down the hill, shrieking with laughter, as swallows swooped overhead.

Watching the children, Chloe made a conscious effort to squelch the last jitters from the runaway minibus episode. The LLT group got a few grumbles out of their collective system—"I love Alta to pieces, but I am not getting back on that bus without an iron guarantee that the problem is fixed," someone said—but talk quickly moved on, drifting into a dream list of museum exhibit sightings. "I wish I could see the real Charlotte," Hazel said, referring to Laura's cherished rag doll.

"Charlotte burned in the fire," said Henrietta, the former English Lit professor, her crochet hook flashing. "*I'd* like to see Ma's china shepherdess."

"One of the younger girls ended up with the shepherdess," someone else said. "Carrie, I think. I'd choose Laura's engagement ring. Surely that escaped the fire."

Chloe was trying to remember what Laura's engagement ring had looked like when someone asked the inevitable question: "What do you suppose that would be worth today?"

"A *lot*," Mr. Whelan said firmly.

Just like that, one straggling jitter did a U-turn and sped back into Chloe's psyche. And ... oh *shit*, had Hazel or the Whelans asked Kari to put anything in the trunk? In all the commotion, she hadn't noticed. The quilt was boxed, of course. But such a large box would attract attention, especially if anyone realized that the box was of archival quality.

Chloe rubbed her palms on her jeans with a wave of remorse. What was *wrong* with her? Why had she agreed to haul Miss Lila's precious quilt around the Midwest? She'd let some ill-defined yearning, professional lust, and ingrained respect for Miss Lila lead her to a foolish decision. Now her mind presented a catalog of unsettling incidents: the unlocked door to the staff-only area at the museum in Pepin, the person who might have been looking into Kari's car by Lake Pepin, a near-miss on the road this evening that could easily have caused the Ellefson sisters' vehicle to roll, maybe crash. And maybe that crash could have caused the trunk to pop open, and the big gray archival box to go flying into the arms of a blackmarket dealer who—

Wait, protested the last rational sliver of her brain. Norma Epps hadn't been concerned about the unlocked door. The person by Kari's car might simply have been confused in the dusk. *And* the most serious problems seemed aimed squarely at Alta Allerbee and her LFL posse. Chloe had never met Alta before, or Hazel and Wilbur Voss. Most telling, it was pure freaky coincidence that the gas pedal in the tour bus had gotten stuck just as Alta drove up behind Kari's Rambler. *Nobody* could have planned or predicted that.

Alta's pleas back at the Wayside echoed in Chloe's memory again: *Please don't do this…* I should have just barged in, Chloe thought, wishing like anything that she'd seen who was giving Alta trouble.

Well, there was nothing she could do about it now.

She turned to the only other man, besides Mr. Whelan, who was traveling with the LLT group. He had evidently signed up solo, and thus far he had made no effort to join the conversation.

"I'm Chloe Ellefson," she said with her most friendly smile. "You must be Leonard."

The man, who'd been slumped over his paper plate, perked up at once. He was rangy-tall, probably in his forties, and had dressed in a yellow sports coat for the event. "Yes, I'm Leonard Devich."

"Are you enjoying the tour so far?"

"No. But I needed to get to De Smet, and I didn't trust my own car to make it that far."

So even if he'd been there, Leonard likely wouldn't have known how to fix the bus, Chloe thought, remembering how poor Bill Whelan had been chastised.

"I plan to speak at the symposium," Leonard added.

"I'm speaking at the symposium too," Chloe said. "What's your topic?"

"Charles Ingalls," Leonard said enthusiastically. "My talk is based on an article I wrote called 'Pa Ingalls: The Life of a Failure.'"

"You wrote ... *what*?"

"Well, by any measuring, he was a failure—"

"No, he wasn't!"

"Yes, he was."

"No—he—*wasn't!*" And if this guy tells me I'm adorable, Chloe fumed, I will pop him in the nose.

Rather than risk missing the pageant due to assault charges, she turned her back on Leonard. "So!" she said brightly to the Whelans, who were at the next table. "Did your group visit the dugout site today?"

"We're going tomorrow morning," Mrs. Whelan said. "Eight o'clock. I can hardly wait."

Chloe turned to Kari. "Why don't we go even earlier? Like, at dawn."

"At dawn?" Kari looked skeptical. "You? Seriously?"

"Yes," Chloe said firmly. She wanted to see the site when no one else—especially the likes of idiot Leonard Devich—was around.

"Hello, all," came a cool voice behind her.

"Hello, Jayne," Mrs. Whelan said politely. No one else managed more than a nod.

Chloe didn't turn to greet her. She didn't want to visit the site when Jayne was around, either. The more she thought about it, the more she liked the idea of going at daybreak.

Hazel joined the group. "Look what I found!" She gestured Vanna-like at the new sunbonnet she wore. "It's my favorite shade of purple."

"Just what the world needs," Jayne said. "Another bonnethead."

The joy faded from Hazel's face. "Oh," she said in a tiny voice.

"Jayne!" Chloe turned her head and rose so quickly that one knee collided with the picnic table, and she smacked back down on the bench.

Before she could recover Jayne said, "Bye, all," and sauntered away.

"Let her go," Kari advised, putting a hand on Chloe's arm.

"Yes, please do," Hazel murmured. She took a deep breath and squared her shoulders. "I think Jayne is very unhappy."

Hazel is more charitable than I am, Chloe thought darkly. She would have chosen a different adjective. "I'm sure you're right," she muttered.

"That purple is perfect for your coloring, Hazel," Frances Whelan declared.

"I'm going to the men's room," Leonard Devich announced, rising. Not surprisingly, no one seemed to care.

As Leonard shambled away, Chloe looked over her shoulder to watch Jayne climb the hill toward the cheap seats—blankets and lawn chairs people had brought to the hillside. She once again looked completely out of place in a skirt and blouse and dress shoes, arms crossed stiffly, shoulders set in a rigid line.

Kari was watching too. "That was just mean. What is *up* with her?"

"I have no idea." Chloe leaned close. "But I think I've found the man of her dreams." She told Kari about Leonard and his take on Pa Ingalls.

"Has he read the books?" Kari demanded. "Charles Ingalls managed to hold his family together despite grasshopper plagues and blizzards and—and—*oh!* What a crock."

Kari's indignation made Chloe feel a little better. Still, she wished she'd never started the conversation with Leonard Devich. Laura Land, she thought with a pang, is a much more contentious place than I ever imagined.

————

Fragments of a Dream was perfectly charming. Adult Laura narrated the action, which began when the Ingalls family arrived at Walnut Grove in their covered wagon, and included a church-raising, a prairie fire, a dance number, and too many cute kids to count. Nellie Oleson, Laura's archenemy as a child, was perfectly bratty; and if her dress was a bit over the top, it served to accent her patronizing air. Chloe loved every minute.

After the actors took their final bows, Kari and Chloe joined the flow of people making their way toward the parking field, where lanes were identified by name. "The LLT gang is meeting back by the Grace aisle," Kari reminded her.

"I'm glad to help transport people back to town, if need be," Chloe muttered. "Except Leonard. He can walk."

"Maybe Jayne will give him a ride."

Chloe followed her sister's gaze and saw Jayne and Leonard standing just outside the glow of one of the pole lights in the parking lot. Jayne seemed to be doing all of the talking, and she stabbed the air in front of Leonard's chest with one long finger. Leonard stood silently, head shaking in negation of whatever point Jayne was making. "Geez," Chloe said. "What do you suppose that's all about? It's hard to imagine that Jayne would waste time arguing academic theory with Leonard."

"Who knows," Kari said. "But I'm happy to let them entertain each other. Come on. Let's see if Alta made it."

Chloe was pleased to find Alta gathering her charges—and even more so when she announced that she'd driven herself to the pageant grounds. "God bless the good people of Southwest Minnesota," Alta said fervently. "A couple of phone calls, an hour in a garage, and we're good to go. At least mechanically. I'm afraid the right side of the bus looks like it's been through a war zone."

"But what caused the problem?" one of her passengers asked. A reasonable question, Chloe thought.

"A bit of gunk or corrosion in the linkage. I know it was a frightening experience, but it was a fluke. The mechanic who checked the bus over is affiliated with Triple A, and he says it's fine now." Alta waved an arm. "I'm parked in the last row. We'll gather by the bus and head to the hotel."

"Kari?" Hazel called. "I left my bag in your car."

Chloe pulled Kari aside. "Try to keep the quilt box out of sight," Chloe muttered.

"Absolutely," Kari said emphatically, which eased Chloe's worries only a smidge.

The group dissolved as some people headed for the bus, some thanked their own erstwhile chauffeurs, and a couple scurried off to retrieve belongings. Alta, who'd lost her bonnet somewhere along the way, ran both hands through her frizzed red hair.

"You've had a rough evening," Chloe said sympathetically.

"I've had better," Alta agreed. "And I owe you and Kari a profound apology for running you off the road."

Chloe glanced around. No one was lingering within earshot. "Alta … you're comfortable with what the mechanic said? That it was a fluke and couldn't happen again?"

"Of course!" Alta said quickly.

Too quickly? Chloe wasn't sure. "I just meant … if you need help with anything … " She let the statement trail away invitingly.

Alta responded with a bland smile. "Could you handle registration at the symposium?"

Well, *that* attempt at goodwill bit me on the butt, Chloe thought. She offered a bland smile of her own. "Sure, Alta. Glad to."

———

"Let me make sure I've got this straight," Kari said the next morning as they headed back to Walnut Grove. "The Ingallses actually lived in Walnut Grove twice, right? Before and after their time in Burr Oak?"

"Right," Chloe confirmed. Considering that she'd yawned her way out of bed before the robins, she was proud of having that factoid straight. Kari had grabbed the car keys—"I'm always up at four," she'd muttered—and Chloe had graciously consented. Riding shotgun meant she could cradle her cup of dubious motel coffee with both hands.

Now they followed signs to a wooded farm drive marked with a small sign: *Welcome to the Ingalls Dugout Site, 1874. Open Until Dusk.*

This was the homesite Laura had written about in *On the Banks of Plum Creek*.

They crept down a gravel driveway, deposited the honor-system donation in the indicated box, and continued on to a small and blessedly empty parking lot. Oh my, Chloe thought as she got out of the car, this is the *place*. Prairie grasses and flowers rippled in the breeze. Birds were serenading the new day. And just ahead, lined by mature trees—

"It's Plum Creek," Kari whispered reverently.

A modern footbridge provided passage to the dugout site on the far bank. Chloe stopped midway, leaning over the rail, mesmerized by the flowing water. She imagined Laura splashing at the edge, Laura sending mean Nellie Oleson into the murky pool where leeches lurked, Laura discovering a huge crayfish.

And Chloe *felt* something too … a tiny vibration beneath her rib cage, a flush of the special joy that only children feel. Laura lingered here—the seven-year-old Laura who knew nothing yet of grasshopper plagues, crop failure, and crushing debts. Chloe was sure of it. She closed her eyes, trying to catch more of that faint—

Footsteps thumped on the wooden bridge. "Aren't you coming?" Kari called.

The resonance disappeared. Chloe jerked erect and swallowed her disappointment. "Right behind you."

She followed Kari across the bridge and up a short trail to the top of the bank. The dugout itself was long gone, but a deep depression marked the spot where it had once stood.

"I think the property owners deserve a medal," Chloe said. "No refreshment stands, no souvenir shops. Just this place."

Kari frowned. "And a bit of trash. I'll get it." She carefully stepped into the bowl-like depression and pulled a piece of paper free from the tall grasses. "I—oh God!"

"*What?*"

Kari returned to the path and held out page 103, ripped savagely from *On the Banks of Plum Creek*. In a scene where Laura almost drowned, Garth Williams had depicted her clinging to a plank as the flood-swollen creek tried to sweep her away. Someone had scrawled *DIE LAURA DIE* below the sketch in black marker.

Goosebumps rose on Chloe's skin. She stared, horrified but unable to tear her gaze away.

"Who would do such a thing?" Kari demanded.

Chloe snatched the paper and crumpled it into a ball. "Some young deviant who got bored with all things Laura." She remembered Norma mentioning a Charlotte doll impaled on a barbecue fork found at the Pepin Wayside, and the headless china shepherdess in Burr Oak. If one kid was behind the three desecrations, Chloe shuddered to contemplate his or her future.

"Probably a little girl discovered that her book was missing a page yesterday," Kari said, "and her brother got in big trouble."

Chloe wanted to dispose of the wretched thing, right now. "I'm going to go throw this away."

They walked back down the path, across the bridge. Chloe tossed the picture into a garbage can and slapped her hands against her jeans almost convulsively. "Let's go back. I'd still like to wander for a few minutes before anyone else"—she turned at the sound of an approaching vehicle—"gets here."

Damn, she added silently, sorry to have another visitor intrude on their private time on the banks of Plum Creek. She was sorrier still when the car proved to be a gray sedan, reminding her of the possible quilt-snatcher she'd seen in the dusk near Lake Pepin. And she was *incredibly* sorry to see Jayne Rifenberg behind the wheel.

Kari made an exasperated noise. "What's *she* doing here?"

Jayne parked near the Rambler and emerged. "Good morning," she said coolly. She walked toward the bridge, wobbling a little as she maneuvered the gravel lot in high heels.

"Let's give her some space," Chloe said. "Maybe she'll leave."

They settled at a picnic table with bananas, graham crackers, and a dark bar of the good Swiss stuff. A woodpecker called from the trees. The air held the dry green scent of prairie. Chloe tried to remember that joyful quiver of Laura's lingering happiness, but she kept flashing on that defiled illustration and Jayne's sneer.

"All this bad juju is starting to piss me off," Chloe muttered. "'*DIE LAURA DIE*' and some of the other things are just icky."

"That poor man dying in Pepin was beyond icky," Kari said, "and Alta's failed brakes could have gotten somebody killed. Not to mention the fire in Burr Oak."

"I wish I hadn't agreed to bring Miss Lila's quilt on this trip," Chloe said. "It makes me extra-anxious."

"Nobody knows it's in the car."

"Sure they do. Norma in Pepin and Marianne in Burr Oak know we're traveling with it. I've already made appointments with representatives at the Kansas and South Dakota and Missouri homesites. And other people at those sites probably know about it too—volunteers and staff." Chloe rolled her banana peel up in her napkin.

"But they're all museum people."

"Museum people can go rogue. And didn't Hazel leave something in the trunk during the pageant? Are you sure she didn't see the quilt box? Or maybe the Whelans?"

Kari considered, then shook her head. "I don't think anyone noticed. Honestly, there's nothing to suggest that anyone is interested in Miss Lila's quilt."

"It's just a feeling I have. I can't shake it."

"If someone *was* responsible for the Burr Oak fire and the runaway bus and the ruined doll and book page, the trouble seems aimed at Alta's tour, not at us and the quilt. And frankly, the notion of trouble aimed at Alta's tour seems a bit…out there."

"I'm serious," Chloe insisted. "Someone was threatening Alta with something back at the Pepin Wayside." She repeated what she'd overheard. "Alta sounded desperate. She was begging."

After a moment of stunned silence, Kari said, "Are you suggesting that whoever Alta was talking to fiddled with the minibus?"

"I tried to talk to her about it last night. She shut the conversation down fast, but maybe if we tell her what I overheard…"

Kari shook her head. "I don't think we should get involved."

Chloe remembered Roelke making the same point: *You really shouldn't interject yourself into other peoples' problems.* "You're probably right," she admitted. Still, there was something about the notion of someone taking aim at Alta Allerbee of Laura Land Tours that made Chloe sizzle. "But I'm going to try again anyway. They'll be here any time."

Several cars arrived, spilling girls wearing sunbonnets and boys wearing Davy Crockett–style caps. They tossed rocks into the creek and raced across the bridge and splashed each other, just as children should, while their parents snapped pictures. Promptly at eight, the battered LLT minibus rumbled down the gravel drive. Members of the tour group emerged and headed eagerly for the creek. Alta stepped down last.

"Alta?" Chloe called. "Hold up a minute."

"We shouldn't gang up on her," Kari murmured. "She'd be most likely to confide in you."

"Fine." Chloe gave Kari a *You owe me* look. "Wait here."

Alta wore pink calico today. The delicate hue only accentuated the dark circles under her eyes. "Good morning, Chloe." Her tone was polite. "Can I help you with something?"

"Forgive me, Alta, but I wanted to follow up on the conversation we had last night." Chloe scooped up her resolve. "I'm concerned about what happened to your bus."

"What happened to the bus was an *accident*." Two high spots of color appeared in Alta's cheeks.

"The thing is, the day I met you, I overheard you talking to someone—just a bit—and you sounded worried."

"I don't know what you thought you heard, but you misunderstood." Alta tugged at her sunbonnet. "Now, you must excuse me."

"Please wait. I just want to help…"

Alta, who had evidently gone deaf, hurried after her group.

Chloe plodded back to the picnic table. "Alta did not confide all of her secrets," she reported. "Or any, actually."

"We're barely acquainted with Alta. I can't really blame her for not sharing anything personal."

Chloe glowered at some letters scratched into the wooden table. She was worried about Alta … and she had no idea what to do about it.

Someone wearing a purple sunbonnet waved from the far bank. Hazel, Chloe thought. And she thought about someone who might be pure mean enough to make trouble for the Laura Land Tour.

Wilbur had already followed the tour to Burr Oak. His burn had sent him to the hospital, but physical pain would surely add a new layer of mean to Wilbur Voss.

Okay, Chloe thought. Alta may not want to talk to me … but I bet Hazel will.

The sound of raised voices came from the bridge. Jayne Rifenberg and Frances Whelan were stalking toward the parking lot, clearly annoyed with each other. " … why children would waste time on the TV programs, much less an adult," Jayne was saying as they approached.

Frances glowered. "The show introduced the Little House world to millions of—"

"Please!" Jayne snapped. "The TV series' presentation of Walnut Grove is a travesty!"

Chloe thought longingly of the one brief shining moment when she'd sensed young Laura playing in Plum Creek. "Come on," she said to Kari. "Let's go."

Nellie's nose was still held high and sniffing, her small eyes were still set close to it, and her mouth was prim and prissy.

Little House on the Prairie

ELEVEN

"Thanks for coming, Peggy," Roelke said. "Thanks a lot."

"No problem!" With a cheerful smile, Peggy slid into the corner booth at the restaurant where they'd agreed to meet for an early lunch. "I'm intrigued by your family farm project."

"I'm probably insane to even consider it."

"Actually, the timing might be good. There's a new emphasis on farmland preservation afoot. It's a real boon, especially after a decade or so of willy-nilly development."

Roelke hadn't heard anyone say "afoot" or "willy-nilly" in a long time. But that was Peggy: perky, a bit old-fashioned in language, sedate in dress. She'd had a crush on him in high school, and he'd gone out of his way to avoid her. Last summer he'd looked her up again, desperate to get some informal help understanding some financial stuff after a suspicious death. She'd recently married, and seemed blissfully happy.

Once the waitress had delivered steaming mugs of coffee and herbal tea, they got down to business. Roelke showed Peggy the papers Babs had given him. He gritted his teeth and shared his most recent bank statements, which felt much like he imagined it would feel to run naked down Main Street. They discussed and analyzed numbers that made his stomach clench like a fist. It was terrifying and overwhelming and, worst of all, confusing. Peggy, who was obviously a whole lot smarter than he was, remained patient.

And in the end, all she concluded was that he had a difficult choice on his hands. "I wish I could be more definitive," she said with an uncharacteristic sigh. "The only thing I can offer is friendly advice before you meet with a loan officer."

Loan officer. Roelke had never taken out a loan in his life. With what he hoped was a *Bless you* look, he pushed his empty mug toward the waitress approaching with coffeepot in hand.

"Don't make a decision based solely on what the bank is willing to loan you. A financial institution might approve a loan that exceeds your comfort level."

"I passed my comfort level a while back," Roelke admitted.

Peggy smiled, as if she thought he was kidding. Then she sobered and leaned back against the cushion. "Honestly, Roelke, I think you're right on the edge. Buying your grandparents' farm won't be easy. It may not be wise. But it might be possible."

Roelke realized that he'd kinda been hoping she'd take one look at his bank book and shut the whole notion down cold. Instead, Peggy took one last sip of tea and tucked her calculator into her purse.

"Thanks," he said again. "I owe you."

"Well, I've got a couple of traffic tickets pending in Lake Geneva. Could you make a call and get those dropped?"

A muscle in Roelke's jaw twitched. "No, Peggy. I could not do that."

"I was just *teasing*, silly!" Beaming, she stood and kissed his cheek. "I will let you pick up the tab, though." Still grinning, she left.

Roelke drew a deep breath, contemplating the index cards and yellow tablet pages and photocopies spread on the table. He really was enormously grateful to Peggy. For someone who didn't specialize in real estate, she had lots of good information. It was just too bad that all that good information left him not one bit closer to knowing what he should do.

———

The Laura Ingalls Wilder Museum and Tourist Center in Walnut Grove was a larger complex than Chloe had expected. In the gift shop/reception area, she told the elderly woman behind the counter that she and Kari had already visited the dugout site. "It's a special place."

"Garth Williams discovered the location while doing research," the woman said. "The farm family who owned the land kindly made the dugout site accessible to Laura fans, but the flow of visitors became overwhelming. People were knocking on their door with questions, that sort of thing. Some townspeople decided to start the museum. We began by renting an old gas station. That was only nine years ago, in 1974."

When Chloe asked to see the curator, a young man with horn-rimmed glasses and an eager smile strode into the gift shop to meet them. "David Rice," he said, pumping Chloe's hand, then Kari's. "I'm eager to see your quilt!"

There were probably a dozen people browsing for souvenirs within earshot, and Chloe fought the urge to cringe. "I'll fetch it," she said weakly.

She felt better when she and her archival gray box were ushered behind the scenes to the collections storage area. When she removed the box lid, David drew in an appreciative breath.

"We'd love to find evidence suggesting that Laura actually made this quilt," Kari said hopefully.

David considered. "This *might* be the same Bear Track pattern that Laura used as a child."

"Of course, that quilt burned in the De Smet fire," Chloe put in breezily, now that she was in the know.

"We have two quilts that belonged to Laura Ingalls Wilder," David said. "Since you want to compare fabrics, I pulled the one—a Hexagonal Star, or Rising Star—that might be comparable." Once properly gloved, he retrieved an archival box of his own and gently transferred the quilt to the table.

Chloe inspected the Star quilt carefully. Although the fabrics incorporated some blue and green, the overall impression fell into that early "madder palette" era. This quilt had likely been made with scraps, so some pieces might be ten or twenty years older than others. Time—and dyes—had, unfortunately, left a few of the star points little more than threads. Still, enough remained for Chloe to consider each contender and, reluctantly, disregard it. "I don't see any matches."

"Me either," Kari said sadly.

David carefully repackaged the quilt. "A lot of today's quilters grew up reading the Little House books. Because the Ingalls girls were working on Nine Patch and Bear Track blocks here in Walnut Grove, I've had my share of inquiries about Laura and quilts. I wish we had more to show them." He nodded toward Miss Lila's quilt. "I'd be as excited as you would to discover that Laura made that one. You said it came down through a friend's family?"

"The story is that Laura gifted this quilt to a relative during a visit back to Pepin." Chloe tried to sound offhand, as if *everyone* knew that adult-Laura had returned to Wisconsin. "Our friend's cousin's husband was descended from one of Caroline Quiner's sisters."

"Which one?"

"I don't know," Chloe admitted. "I was on my way to Miss Lila's house to get genealogical information when she … she died."

"I'm very sorry for your loss," David said. "But given our limited storage space, we must be focused with our acquisitions. With documentation of that familial connection in hand, we'd be thrilled to accept this quilt."

Chloe's initial impression—that David Rice was here to fulfill a high school internship requirement—had blown away like chaff in a prairie wind. "May I ask another question?" She paused, thinking how to best phrase it. "Traveling with the quilt makes me uneasy. Is there much of a market for this sort of thing?"

David snorted. "Lord, yes. Open market, blackmarket, you name it. There's a hierarchy. Things Laura made, like a quilt, would be right up there with specific pieces she wrote about, like Pa's fiddle or Ma's china shepherdess."

Chloe was sorry she'd asked.

"Next would be anything owned by her or someone in her family. After that would come antiques that are duplicates of things they owned. Lots of Wilder readers want to find copies of the bread plate that Laura and Almanzo ordered from Montgomery Ward, for example. It features a sheaf of wheat in the center. The original is on display in Missouri. Those plates are expensive and hard to find."

"I imagine so," Chloe said.

"Your quilt, of course, is something special. Any Bear Track quilt from the period would attract Laura fans. But with the family story actually linking the quilt to Laura, the market value would increase tenfold. If you discover that Laura actually made it? Another huge increase."

Oh, Miss Lila, Chloe thought. I'm trying to honor your wishes, but I *really* wish I wasn't roaming the prairieland with your quilt.

"So," David said, "would you like to see the museum?"

Once Chloe had the quilt locked back in the car, David led them to a cheerful red structure. "We've turned our depot into Laura exhibit space," he explained. The first room was small, but held an impressive array of cases. "This sewing basket belonged to Laura, and she crocheted this lace. And here is our other Laura quilt." He pointed to a scarlet and white quilt.

"Ooh," Kari sighed. "That Double Nine Patch-Irish Chain is striking. Did Laura make it?"

"She owned it. We don't know if she actually *made* it."

And such is the way of the Wilder world, Chloe thought. She wished Laura had labeled all of her textiles. Really, was that so much to ask?

A mom and her two daughters approached. "Do you work here?" the woman asked. "We've looked all around"—she made a broad gesture, and the girls nodded solemnly—"and we don't see any information about Mary's husband."

"Well, actually," David said, "in real life, Mary never married."

The trio looked collectively dumbfounded. "Yes, she did!" the mom said.

"I'm afraid she didn't."

"Yes—she—*did*!" the older girl protested.

Chloe couldn't help noticing that the visitors sounded—and probably looked—as indignant as *she* had felt when defending Laura and Pa against the ridiculous charges brought by the likes of Jayne-with-a-Y Rifenberg and Leonard Devich.

"In real life, Mary did not get married," David explained gently. "Just in the TV series."

Mom seemed at a loss for words. The older girl stared, open-mouthed. The younger girl, perhaps eight, looked ready to cry. Chloe and Kari stepped away, giving David the chance to reassure the guests that Mary nonetheless had a good life.

Once out of earshot, Chloe whispered, "Have you ever watched *Little House on the Prairie*?" The television series had begun in 1974, when Chloe was already working in the historic sites world. Working in her own Little House world, in a way. Besides, she didn't have a television.

"Are you kidding? It's my girls' favorite show. It was a black day in the Anderson house when the network announced that they weren't renewing it."

"And in the TV version Mary gets *married*?"

Kari looked at her with pity. "Oh, that was just the beginning."

David was still with the guests, which earned him another star in Chloe's book, so she wandered away. The exhibits were beautifully done, using artifacts, photographs, and excerpts and illustrations to link the novel with the real people found within the pages. She lingered over a panel about Mary's illness and subsequent loss of her eyesight while the family lived along Plum Creek. "Although entirely blind," the *Redwood Gazette* reported on July 31, 1879, "she is very patient and submissive."

Chloe was *very* sorry that young Mary lost her sight. But just once, she thought, I'd like to read that Mary Ingalls pitched a royal fit.

David joined them again. "Sorry about that. I like to spend time with TV people when I can. It can all be a bit startling."

Chloe remembered what Marianne at Burr Oak had said: *Some people love the Little House TV series, and don't want to hear about anything that Michael Landon didn't include in a show.* "Are a lot of people confused about the differences?"

"A fair number. Starting with the fact that Laura's *Little House on the Prairie* book was actually in Kansas, and television's *Little House on the Prairie* is set here in Minnesota. Come this way." David led them into an exhibit room devoted to the television series.

"Wow." Chloe stared at memorabilia from the show, cast photos, and a cheerful mural depicting Hollywood's version of Walnut Grove. An episode was playing on a muted television set, with Michael Landon/Pa speaking earnestly to a tearful young Melissa Gilbert/Laura.

"I've had to break up screaming matches between Charles Ingalls fans and Michael Landon fans," David admitted. "I kid you not."

Chloe remembered Jayne Rifenberg and Frances Whelan snarling at each other that morning.

"Lots of book people *loathe* the show," David said. "But we've chosen to embrace it. That series put Walnut Grove on the map. Tourism has kept my hometown from dying. And whether readers like it or not, the TV version has become part of the bigger Laura Ingalls Wilder story."

Chloe looked at a photograph of a pretty girl with blond ringlets sneering contemptuously at the camera. "Well, at least the actress conveys Nellie Oleson just the way I imagined her."

"Laura's fictional Nellie Oleson was actually a composite of three real girls," David said. "Did you know?"

"I didn't," Kari said, which saved Chloe from acknowledging that she obviously didn't know a damn thing.

"In real life, Nellie *Owens*'s parents ran the local general store. Laura also had a contentious relationship with a girl named Genevieve Masters, a spoiled brat who boasted constantly. Later, after moving to South Dakota, Laura also disliked a girl named Stella Gilbert who lived on a claim nearby."

"Considering how nastily Nellie Oleson is portrayed in the books," Kari said, "it's not surprising that Laura fictionalized the name."

David checked his watch. "I'm giving a talk about the Ingalls family's time in Walnut Grove to a special tour group in about five minutes. Feel free to join us, and Chloe? Thanks for showing me the quilt."

When they left the exhibit building, Chloe was not surprised to see Alta's travelers disembarking from their bus.

"I'd like to sit in on the talk," Kari said.

Chloe promised to catch up before settling on an empty bench by the front sidewalk. She scribbled notes about her conversation with David. Then she sat, thinking. She tried to send a message into the cosmos: *Laura, if you actually made Miss Lila's quilt, I'd really like to know. It would mean an awful lot to everybody who loves your books. So if you could maybe give me a sign, that would be great. Nothing big and flashy. Just point me in the right direction.* She waited, not expectant but open to the possibility.

Nothing.

Well, Chloe thought, I will just keep trying. And in the meantime, a little Swiss chocolate could only help.

She headed for the car, but as she passed the LLT bus, a faint noise from the interior made her pause. The bus appeared to be empty. Hesitantly she pushed the door open and stepped inside. "Hello?" No answer. She went up another step. "Anybody here?"

Midway back, Alta Allerbee slowly sat upright. The sunbonnet didn't hide her red eyes, or the tears on her cheeks.

Chloe walked back and squeezed down on the bench seat. Alta grudgingly inched over. Chloe put one arm around the older woman's shoulders and let her cry.

Several minutes passed before Alta pulled away, sniffling violently. She opened a drawstring gingham bag and fished out a tissue. "I'm sorry," she mumbled through the last small hiccupping shudders. "You must think I'm worthless."

Chloe flinched. "Dear God, Alta, I think you're amazing! You put the symposium together, and a sites tour too."

"I'm managing all that. It's a lot of work, but fun too. But ... I just went through a messy divorce."

Chloe guessed who had introduced the word 'worthless' into Alta's psyche. "I'm sorry."

"It's left me with nothing. Financially, I mean. My husband was the bookkeeper for a large landscaping company. He embezzled a lot of money from his employer. And I'm the one who figured it out and turned him in."

Oh Lord, Chloe thought.

"I'd been thinking about starting a Laura tour company for years." Alta dabbed her eyes. "I knew Little House fans would appreciate the opportunity to travel with a guide ... but it takes a lot to start even a small business. I invested in this bus, and promotional materials, and there have been up-front expenses for the symposium ... "

"I'm sure it mounted up fast."

"I was holding everything together. But you kept asking and *asking* about whether that stuck gas pedal was an accident or not—"

Chloe flushed with remorse. She had made this friendly calicoed lady cry.

"—and the accident is bad for business. The first story my guests tell back home will be about the bus going out of control on a country road. And when the symposium starts, everyone will see my beautiful bus looking like it came through a battle."

Chloe stared at the green vinyl seat in front of her, trying to find the right words. "Alta ... I can't help thinking that your husband must have been pretty angry when you turned him in. Do you feel threatened?"

Alta sighed. "Honestly, Chloe, I think you've read too many detective novels. I've had some bad luck, but nobody is trying to sabotage my tour. My ex-husband is behind bars. Even if he were clever and vindictive enough to want to harm me—and I don't believe he is—he would never do anything that might harm others."

"Okay." Chloe couldn't argue the point. But she was a long way from reassured.

Laura sighed. "I don't know how you can be so good."

"I'm not really," Mary told her. "I do try, but if you could see how rebellious and mean I feel sometimes, if you could see what I really am, inside, you wouldn't want to be like me."   Little Town on the Prairie

TWELVE

"WOULD YOU PLEASE SETTLE?" Marie asked.

Roelke turned from the window. "Me?"

"Do you see anybody else in here?" The clerk sounded exasperated. "Don't you have anything better to do than prowl around this office?"

"I can't go on patrol because the radar company guy is coming by." The officers checked their equipment all the time, but the manufacturer's rep had more sophisticated equipment. "Besides, I need to catch up on some paperwork."

Marie looked pointedly from him to the EPD patrol officers' vacant desk and back again. "What is wrong with you today?"

Everything, Roelke wanted to say. My best friend is still dead, and Chloe's off on a road trip, and my grandparents' farm is on the market, and I want to buy a plane, and Sergeant Malloy thinks I should move back to Milwaukee, and Libby says I need to ask Chloe about living together, and yesterday I had to pry an infant from his desperate mother's arms, and—

"Fine," Marie said. She rolled whatever she was typing from the machine. "I'm going to lunch."

Once Marie left he went back to prowling, which was not easy, because the office wasn't much bigger than his apartment. He'd been at work since seven that morning, and there hadn't been a single damn call. He couldn't even follow up on the obscene phone caller complaint. The asshole responsible had called someone else, spouted inappropriate things to an answering machine, and left his number on the tape for a call-back. Skeet had already arrested the idiot.

Roelke sighed. I think I *do* want to move back to Milwaukee, he thought. He'd had good days and bad days at the MPD, but he'd never been bored. Never worried that a visit from the radar guy might be the high point of his day.

Never imagined he heard an infant crying in the squad room.

Roelke pressed one thumb to his forehead. What about Libby and the kids? What about Chloe? He couldn't move back to the city … could he?

Okay. What he needed more than anything else right now was an honest-to-God cry for help from a good citizen of Eagle. He'd settle for a civil issue—maybe neighbors bickering over their lot line. It would be his pleasure to explain that they needed to call a surveyor. At least he'd get out of the office for half an hour—

The front door opened and Radar Guy walked in, carrying a black case with his tuning forks and other gizmos. "Got the car keys?" he asked, all business.

Roelke grabbed the ring. "I can come with—"

"No need." The man took the keys, smiled pleasantly, and left him alone.

———

Chloe was still standing by the gift shop, thinking about Alta, when the group streamed outside. "You missed an interesting presentation," Kari told her. "Did you know that Laura worked at a hotel here in Walnut Grove too? After the family came back from Burr Oak."

Chloe fought the urge to plug her ears and sing la-la-la. *Her* vision of Walnut Grove life included playtime and school time and family time. She honestly did not want to know that child-Laura had gone back to work in another damn hotel.

Henrietta Beauchamps looked around, hands on hips. "Where did Alta get to? We're scheduled to eat lunch at Nellie's Café."

"She said you all should go ahead without her," Chloe said. Nellie's Café was an easy walk from the museum.

Kari turned to follow the others. "You coming? Or did you want to picnic again?"

"Nellie's is fine," Chloe said absently, watching Hazel Voss plug coins into a payphone mounted outside the gift shop. "I'll be there soon."

Kari gave her a *What is up with you?* frown. Chloe pretended she didn't see it. Kari left.

Chloe settled back on her bench and fiddled with her notebook until Hazel finished her short conversation. "Oh, Chloe!" Hazel said as she turned from the phone. Her eyes were troubled, and she had a trembly look around the mouth.

"Is everything okay?" Chloe patted the seat beside her.

Hazel sat. "I don't know. I called the hospital, and they said Wilbur was released."

"It was a shock to see him in Burr Oak yesterday. Has he told you how the fire started?"

"No. I talked to him last night, but he wouldn't say much. I'm sure he was humiliated."

"Do you think he might show up again? Maybe make some kind of trouble for you or the tour?"

"He wouldn't do that."

"Well … he sorta did once already," Chloe observed.

"And made a fool of himself." Hazel watched a dragonfly flitting among flowers in a half-barrel planter. "I think he was shocked I found the courage to actually defy him back in Pepin and join Alta's tour."

And how much angrier was Wilbur when Hazel declined to even accompany him to the ER? Chloe wondered, but she didn't press the point. "Has it been bad for a long time?"

"Honestly, I'm not even sure when things got so bad."

"Things can fall apart gradually," Chloe said gently. "Over time."

"Wilbur's always had a bit of a temper," Hazel admitted. "But he has a nice side too. I don't drive, and he used to be so patient, taking me to church and the library and my Laura fan club meetings. He never complained, just sat in the back and read the newspaper."

Was that sweet? Or did Wilbur want Hazel to be dependent on him? "Mm," Chloe said noncommittally.

"And when the trucking company cut his hours and I offered to get a job, he said no wife of his was going to work. Someone your age might not understand that, but it was very sweet."

Or manipulative, Chloe thought. "Do you have children?"

Hazel's usually-sunny face filled with grief. "I got pregnant once, but I miscarried."

Words of sympathy caught in Chloe's throat. She squeezed Hazel's hand instead.

"It was a boy. Did you know that Caroline Ingalls, Laura Ingalls Wilder, and Rose Wilder Lane all had sons who died in infancy? Three generations."

This time Chloe didn't even try to answer. She and Hazel sat watching children pose for pictures in a replica covered wagon.

Finally Chloe said, "Hazel, if you need any help, some moral support or whatever, please just let me know."

"Why, thank you, dear." Hazel patted Chloe's knee. "Let's go get lunch, shall we?"

"I'll be along in a bit," Chloe promised.

Alone again, she nibbled her lower lip. Alta and Hazel had both been quick to deny any suggestion that anything but bad luck was stalking the Laura Land Tour. Alta Allerbee was a nice lady who, even now, was incapable of believing that her thieving, no-good, white-collar ex-lout could resort to violence. Hazel Voss was a nice lady who, despite yesterday's drunken debacle, believed that her bullying, no-good, and hopefully soon-to-be-ex-lout was equally incapable.

And maybe they're right, Chloe thought. Maybe the string of mishaps plaguing the LLT was just that—all coincidence and misfortune. Maybe no one knows or cares that I have a Laura quilt in the car.

But Chloe had spent a year keeping company with a cop. For better or worse, she knew that being in prison didn't stop scumbags from causing problems for people on the outside. She knew that basically nice people could, when threatened, react with violence. She knew that when defied, men like Wilbur were *more* likely to react with anger, not less.

And Alta still hadn't explained why she was pleading with someone not to "ruin everything" back at the Pepin Wayside.

Trust your instincts, Roelke insisted.

Easy for you to say, she shot back silently, but she pulled out her notebook. She listed everything that had happened—deadly, serious, and merely creepy:

- *Pepin—man dies of anaphylactic shock, door to museum left unlocked, someone maybe looking in Kari's car window that night, impaled Charlotte doll*
- *Burr Oak—fire at the Black Crow tavern, broken china shepherdess*
- *Walnut Grove—stuck gas pedal, Garth Williams illustration labeled "Die Laura Die"*

Tapping her pen against the paper, Chloe stared at the words. She couldn't decide if it amounted to something worth noting or a whole lot of nothing.

Okay, she thought, stick with the known facts. Her first obligation was to safeguard the quilt, and trouble seemed to be stalking the LLT group. Those two facts suggested that she and Kari steer very clear of Alta's merry band.

But how was she supposed to do that? The more she got to know Alta and Hazel, the more protective she felt.

———

Roelke waited until nine p.m. to call Chloe at her motel. When the desk clerk put him through, the voice sounded a bit off. "Um … Chloe?"

"No, it's Kari. Is this Roelke?"

"It is." Silence echoed in his ear for a good half-minute. "So … how's the trip going?"

"Well, okay, I guess," Kari said, which was not even a little bit reassuring. "I'll put Chloe on."

A clunk, a mutter of conversation. Then the woman he loved came on the line. "Hey."

"Hey." He stopped pacing and sank into a chair. "How was your day?"

"Pretty good. Hold on." Another bit of muffled conversation, the wham of a slamming door. "Okay, I'm back. Kari just went out for a walk. Roelke, I wanted to tell you—I think I felt an echo of Laura this morning at the homesite in Minnesota. There was this sense of—of not just happiness, but a *fun* happiness, you know? It made my breastbone tremble."

Well, *that* choice of words was distracting. Holy toboggans.

"I was on a bridge over Plum Creek, where Laura loved to play," Chloe was saying. "And I just *know* I felt a bit of that."

He struggled to lasso his libido. "I'm glad." This was real for her, and that was good enough for him. "So you found what you were looking for?"

"Well, I wouldn't go that far. There are still more homes to see—and the symposium, of course. And … this road trip is giving me the space to try and figure some stuff out."

Yellow alert. Roelke sat up straight. "Yeah? Like … what?"

"I'll let you know when I've sorted it out."

"Chloe, if—"

"Look, you're trying to make a big decision. And I get the ramifications of that decision, Roelke. If you buy the farm, you're committing to staying local. So, all of this has made me think about the same stuff."

He really did not like where this was going.

"Anyway, how are you? Did you meet with your friend?"

"I did, yeah." He drummed his thumb on the arm of the sofa. "Peggy thinks I might be able to swing the purchase. If I really wanted to."

" … Wow."

"It would be tight, though. I've got a lot to consider."

"Roelke, are you sure you're thinking about what you want from life *now*? Or are you trying to recapture some of your childhood?"

"Isn't that what you're doing?"

"I guess it is. But I'm devoting a week to it, not the indefinite future plus every penny I have in the bank."

"If I do this, it won't be a snap decision."

"Okay," she said, but she sounded doubtful.

Roelke didn't like this turn of conversation either. "Did I tell you I'm reading *Farmer Boy*?"

"You're reading *Farmer Boy*?"

"Libby had a copy. I didn't know that one of Wilder's books was about her husband's childhood."

"What do you think of it?"

"A lot of it seems to be about food. That kid could pack it away."

"There's a lot of food stuff in *Little House in the Big Woods* too. I believe Laura emphasized the culinary abundance in their childhoods to provide context for the hardships faced in adolescence."

Roelke wondered if that sentence was part of the speech Chloe was giving at the symposium. "Probably so," he agreed blithely. And then he heard himself say in a completely different tone, "I love you, you know."

"I love you too," Chloe said softly. "Good night."

Roelke replaced the receiver, scrubbed his face with his palms, and sat back. Well, that conversation mostly sucked. What, exactly, was Chloe trying to figure out? Whether she wanted to stay in Wisconsin? And what did this road trip have to do with it? Pretty much the only thing he knew about Wilder was that the woman had moved around a lot. A *whole* lot.

Well hell, Roelke thought. He was starting to wish that the old Roelke farm had never gone on the market.

————

Chloe sat on the bed, staring at the phone. She was starting to wish that the old Roelke farm had never gone on the market.

The news that Roelke could, according to his friend, buy it if he really wanted to was unsettling. Chloe realized that despite everything, some part of her had expected him to conclude that no, he really couldn't even contemplate making such a purchase.

She picked at a loose thread in her shirt. She was older than Roelke. She had a good job. If they ever did pool resources, she should have been able to hold her own. She couldn't afford to buy a shanty ten miles from nowhere. Bottom line: there clearly was a *whole* lot of disparity between Roelke's savings account and hers.

Well, that sucks, Chloe thought.

Then she told herself to grow up. She and Roelke had worked through other challenges. They could work through this. In the meantime, she had a professional task or two to check off her list.

First, she called her mother. "Is there any news about Miss Lila's death?"

"No, I'm sorry to say. The police have not caught the person responsible, or recovered any of Lila's jewelry." Mom blew out a small sigh. "She had some lovely antique pieces. When she shifted from her upstairs bedroom to the first floor a year or so ago, I helped inventory some of her belongings. At the time I suggested that she keep the jewelry in a safe deposit box, but I never followed through. If I had, maybe..."

"It's not your fault, Mom."

"Well," Mom said, clearly unconvinced. "Is there something you need?"

"Do you have access to Miss Lila's family history? I need to show how Lila was related to her cousin Inez, and how Inez links back to Laura Ingalls Wilder."

"I compiled a basic family tree for Lila years ago. I'll call her attorney. I'm sure it won't be a problem for me to retrieve the file."

Chloe provided contact information for the rest of the trip. "One of these hotels might have a fax machine," she added. "Just call first so they can switch their phone line over. Thanks, Mom. I truly appreciate it."

Five minutes after Chloe hung up, the stale smell of cigarettes followed Kari into the room. "Don't say a word," she warned, holding up one palm.

"Okay." Chloe didn't feel like arguing. "Do you need to call home? I'm done with the phone."

"I just did. From a payphone outside."

I'm guessing she talked to Trygve this time, Chloe thought. She didn't think Anja or Astrid had put that hard, flat look in her sister's eyes.

Kari sat down and pulled out her sewing. Chloe watched Kari's fingers move as she sewed two pieces together with a smooth running stitch. What was it she'd said back at the Pepin Wayside? *Sometimes I think I'd go insane if I didn't quilt.*

So, would a good sister leave Kari alone or inquire about the obvious? Chloe decided to fling herself into the breach. "Everything okay at home?"

"Just fine." Kari came to the end of her seam and knotted the thread. "So. I got to hear Roelke's voice tonight. Why haven't I ever met him?"

Chloe set up the room's ironing board. This is what I get for trying, she thought. "Well, he had to work on Thanksgiving when you had everybody over. With his work schedule it's hard to—"

"Oh, bullshit. There was no time over a four-day weekend when you two could stop by for a turkey sandwich?"

Chloe tried to ease the tension with a hint of levity. "I don't eat turkey—"

"You could have eaten birdseed for all I care!"

Okay, the hint of levity was actually a bad idea.

Kari glared. "Thanksgiving was six months ago, Chloe. In all this time, you've never had an evening free to come by for supper?"

Chloe concentrated on ironing the wrinkles from one of her repro cotton prints. Someone in the next room turned on the television, and *The Love Boat*'s theme song drifted through the wall.

Finally she drew a deep breath. "Kari, when you and Trygve started dating, everyone said 'Oh, Trygve is the *perfect* boyfriend for Kari.' When you got engaged, everyone said 'Oh, Trygve will be the *perfect* husband for Kari.' Well, no one has ever said that about Roelke and me. When I tell people I'm dating a cop, they say things like 'Seriously?' or 'Oh my!' or their eyebrows go up and they don't say anything at all." She set one piece of calico aside and reached for another.

"Don't kid yourself. Tryg isn't perfect."

Chloe ironed another piece of cloth and put it aside.

"Mom likes him," Kari said. "Roelke, I mean."

"Well…yeah, I think she does. The first time they met she served *fattigman*." The little Norwegian pastries were putzy to make, and therefore served only to the worthy. Chloe unplugged the iron and propped it upright to cool. "Look, Kari, I'm sorry. I should have introduced you to Roelke long before now. I'll fix that when we get back."

"I'd like that." Kari pulled off another length of thread from the spool. "Has he decided about buying his grandparents' farm?"

"Not yet. But he's reading *Farmer Boy*."

"You're sure he's not harboring a secret yen to be a farmer?"

"Pretty sure," Chloe said, although she was starting to wonder. Maybe Rick's murder had affected Roelke more than she even knew. Maybe she shouldn't have left him alone for so long ... but, no. She couldn't fill the hole left by Rick's death, and she knew better than to try.

"I know you've been dating Roelke for a long time," Kari said. "But let me tell you, it's impossible to really know what's going on beneath the surface. You think you know somebody, you marry them even, and then ..." She pinched her lips together.

Chloe took a deep breath. "Kari, did Trygve do ... did Trygve have ..." She couldn't shape the words. Not Trygve, nephew of the Lutheran pastor, dutiful son, president of the FFA, and captain of the baseball team in high school. Not Trygve, tiller and keeper of the family farm, treasurer of Stoughton's Sons of Norway Lodge, and by all evidence loving husband and father.

"Just don't make the mistake of believing that you ever truly know a person. That's all I'm saying." Kari stabbed her needle through the cotton. "It's a good way to get your heart broken. You wanted to know why I came on this trip? Well, now you know. I needed to get the hell out of Dodge for a while."

Shit, Chloe thought. She felt as if she'd plunged into frigid water. Kari and Tryg, Kari and Tryg ... Their life had all seemed so irritatingly perfect, with their pretty century farm and their beautiful daughters. "Do you want to talk about it?"

"No."

"Have you decided ... Are you and Tryg ..."

Kari let the sewing rest in her lap and swiped at a tear spilling down one cheek. "I think I'm going to leave Trygve. I think I have to."

Chloe's heart cracked into pieces like lake ice in spring. "But...what will happen to Anja and Astrid?" Whatever else Trygve had done, he adored his daughters.

"I don't know." Kari rubbed her temples. "God, I would do *anything* to protect them from this. Lie, cheat, steal—"

"Kari," Chloe protested.

"You don't have kids. You don't know what it's like."

Chloe opened her mouth, closed it again. If her baby had survived, would she be ready to lie, cheat, or steal to protect the child? Probably.

She got up to give her sister a hug. "I'm *so* sorry—"

Kari jerked away. "Please don't. I'll fall apart altogether if you do, and I can't afford that."

"But if there's anything I can do to help..."

"There isn't."

They got ready for bed in silence. Once the lights were out Chloe lay staring at the ceiling, wishing she'd been a better sister. Really, it had been years since anyone actually held Kari up as a shining example. I should have let that resentment crap go years ago, she thought.

The air conditioner kicked in with a noisy rattle. The mattress was hard. The sheets were scratchy. And Chloe's brain quivered with questions and worries. Whatever Trygve had done, it must have been bad.

Even if Kari decides to forgive him, Chloe thought, can I? She'd known Trygve all her life, just about. He was a big man with broad shoulders and farmer's hands, not too talkative unless he was with people he knew well. He'd glowed with apparent happiness last Thanksgiving from the head of the table. All Chloe wanted to do right now was knee him in the nuts for making Kari cry.

"Chloe?"

"Yeah?"

"I'm sorry. I've got a lot going on inside, and sometimes it comes out in a bad way. I shouldn't have dumped on you."

"I'm glad you did," Chloe said honestly.

"I'm not."

So much for sisterly bonding. Chloe rolled onto her side, back to Kari. "Don't worry about it."

The air conditioner shuddered to a halt. In the sudden silence Kari said, "So, on to South Dakota?"

"I guess so," Chloe said. "On to South Dakota."

Laura saw Mrs. Brewster standing there. Her long white flannel night-gown trailed on the floor and her black hair fell loose over her shoulders. In her upraised hand she held the butcher knife.

These Happy Golden Years

Cap Garland was strongest and quickest ... There was something about him. He was always good-natured and his grin was like a flash of light. It was like the sun coming up at dawn; it changed everything.

The Long Winter

THIRTEEN

As Kari drove to De Smet *very* early the next morning, Chloe read from *By the Shores of Silver Lake*, the first of Laura's books set in South Dakota. Tragedies—the death of baby Freddie, Mary's blindness, repeated grasshopper plagues and crop failures—had finally pushed the Ingalls family out of Minnesota for good. When Laura's beloved dog Jack died, Chloe paused to find a tissue. "I'm a bad person. I don't cry because Mary's gone blind, but the way Laura describes Jack's death..."

"I *know*."

Chloe blew her nose. Other than Jack, she liked *Silver Lake*. The Ingalls family headed west with new opportunities on the horizon, optimistic about finding a true home.

"The South Dakota books have more mature themes, don't you think?" Kari pulled out to pass a tractor. "Remember the time Laura was teaching school and boarding out, and Mrs. Brewster threatened her husband with a knife?"

That particular scene had horrified Chloe as a child. Now, she felt sorry for Mrs. Brewster. Maybe she had postpartum depression. Maybe she had too many children and not enough food. Maybe the lonely frozen prairie was simply too much.

"My favorite South Dakota book is *The Long Winter*," Kari was saying. "As a kid, I was really afraid that everyone would perish before supplies got through."

Chloe liked that book too. "Remember when Almanzo Wilder and Cap Garland rode out on the prairie looking for wheat to buy, and almost died? Without them, everyone in town would have starved."

"That was my favorite chapter," Kari agreed. "Cap was *such* a great guy."

As they neared De Smet, Chloe put the book aside in favor of soaking in the landscape. Beef cattle had replaced Minnesota's dairy herds. Pheasants darted from fields. Hawks watched from signposts. The ground was largely open and flat. It wasn't *too* hard to imagine the Ingalls family traveling through endless prairie.

Chloe had high hopes for De Smet. Laura was twelve when the family arrived in 1879, before there even *was* a De Smet. They spent their first winter in a structure surveyors had left behind. Now restored, the Surveyors' House offered one last chance to walk the floors of a home Laura had written about.

The *Looking For Laura* symposium was being held in a church's fellowship hall. Chloe and Kari reported for duty shortly before eight a.m. Some of the LLT gang were setting up folding chairs. Bill Whelan and Leonard Devich were struggling with a jammed projection screen. Henrietta Beauchamps's voice rose from the kitchen, joining a heated debate about how much coffee to make.

Looking harried, Alta pointed to a neon green plastic tub. "The registration materials are in there. We need to set out nametags, and find the file of receipts to show who's already paid, and make sure each packet has the updated symposium schedule, and—"

"The first people are here," Hazel said, craning to see out a window.

The screen clattered to the floor. "Son of a bitch!" Mr. Whelan yelled.

"Bill!" Frances Whelan appeared in the kitchen doorway, hands on hips.

"Alta?" someone called. "Did you bring creamer?"

"Oh Lord," Alta muttered.

"Kari and I will handle registration," Chloe said firmly. "Go do whatever else you need to do."

She and Kari had barely gotten organized when the first symposium guests found their way into the hall. Soon over forty people checked in. Haruka Minari, Director Marianne Schiller from Burr Oak, and Curator David Rice from Walnut Grove greeted Chloe and Kari like old friends.

Marianne slipped a sealed envelope into Chloe's hand. "Here's the Burr Oak section of Laura's autobiography I promised you."

"Thanks!" Chloe tucked it away.

The growing crowd was eclectic—book devotees, TV series enthusiasts, academic truthers, excited romantics, professors, historic sites people, and homeschoolers. The female to male ratio was about four to one. Attire ranged from shorts and t-shirts to calico prairie garb to Jayne-with-a-Y's prim pinstriped navy suit. Ages ranged from, Chloe guessed, ten to ninety. It could have made for an awkward mix, but the underlying appreciation of the Little House stories created a common bond. Chloe loved the snippets of conversation swirling around the hall:

"Have you ever tried to make Vanity Cakes?"

"I think the house Pa built in Walnut Grove was *not* across Plum Creek from the dugout, but actually on his tree claim..."

"I've always wondered what happened to Mary's organ..."

"Remember how excited Laura and Mary were when they each found a penny in their Christmas stocking?"

Chloe loved that scene too. These are my people, she thought happily. Like-minded souls.

During a brief lull she leaned toward Kari with the schedule in hand. "Look at the presentation topics! Foodways, weather during the Long Winter, the musical history portrayed in the books..." She flipped to the next day's agenda. "And...yes, here it is. 'The Quilts of Laura's Time,' by Kim Dexheimer.'" She felt twitchy with anticipation.

"You're on later this morning," Kari observed. "Aren't you nervous?"

"Not really," Chloe said absently. She'd just noticed that one name was not on the schedule.

She spotted Alta and pulled her aside. "Was Leonard Devich left off by mistake?"

"He is not presenting," Alta said. Her pioneer dress *du jour* was a brilliant blue calico, quite striking with her red hair. "Leonard sent in a proposal to speak on 'Pa Ingalls: The Life of a Failure.' The description started with Pa's inability to hold a steady job and moved on to an analysis of Pa's—and I quote—'unhealthy relationship with Laura.' A thoughtful analysis of Pa's life would have been fine, but that last bit was too much. I sent Leonard a polite 'thanks but no thanks' letter."

"You must have been thrilled when he signed up for the Laura Land Tour."

"Oh, Lordy." Alta shook her head. "Unfortunately, I couldn't afford to turn him down." She glanced at the clock over the door. "Time to get rolling."

Alta got everyone seated and introduced herself. "We have two days to soak up this good energy! In addition to the presentations here, Edna Jo Poffenwiler of De Smet's Laura Ingalls Wilder Memorial Society has made arrangements for special tours and programs." She gestured to a lovely white-haired lady, who inclined her head with a gracious smile.

Alta introduced the other site representatives, including Carmelina Biancardi, site director at Rocky Ridge Farm in Mansfield, Missouri. Carmelina was a beautiful woman about Chloe's age, thin as a model, with long black hair, large dark eyes, and a glowing smile. "Please come visit us in Missouri!" she urged everyone.

The morning opened with a well-received presentation from a woman who'd created a cookbook based on foods mentioned in the Little House books. Then Jayne Rifenberg settled her slide carousel on the projector and stepped to the podium.

Now would be a good time for the screen to collapse, Chloe thought, but it was not to be. Jayne clicked the remote and LAURA INGALLS WILDER AND THE LIE OF AUTHORSHIP appeared in heavy black letters.

Chloe leaned back and crossed her arms. She was skeptical, and she remained skeptical as Jayne walked through her rationale for concluding that Laura's daughter Rose had actually written the Little House books. That conclusion was supported with charts and graphs, discussions of syntax, and perceived Libertarian political perspectives imbedded within the narratives. Jayne peppered her talk with comments like "as you can *clearly* see, the echoed use of subjunctive clauses reflect single creator" and "this phrase *obviously* reflects the perspectivistic worldview that only Rose, who had traveled abroad, could supply."

Forty painful minutes later, Jayne finally wrapped things up. "Undoubtedly both Laura and Rose collaborated in a methodical attempt to perpetuate a lie, one in which the reading public has unknowingly participated for decades."

"What is the *matter* with that woman?" Kari whispered.

"I do not know."

When Jayne concluded with a sharp "Any questions?" there was a moment of what Chloe interpreted as gobsmacked silence.

Then Henrietta Beauchamps stood, a half-crocheted granny square still in her hands. "I've looked into this issue as well. My conclusion is that while Rose certainly provided editorial assistance, and had valuable connections within the publishing world, she did not actually write the books."

"Your conclusion is incorrect."

"No, it's really not," Henrietta said crisply. "I have examined the correspondence between Rose and Laura, and studied the manuscripts in the Rose Wilder Lane collection at the Herbert Hoover Presidential Library. Each book began with Laura writing a first draft in longhand."

"Rose dictated—"

"Rose was not living near her parents during part of the time Laura was writing the series, so she certainly did not dictate the first drafts," Henrietta said. "*And*, if you study the diary Laura kept while the Wilders moved to Missouri, when Rose was only seven years old, you'll find examples of deft characterization, vivid description, and even simple plotting. Laura was an inherently talented writer who honed her skill by writing essays for *The Missouri Ruralist* before beginning the Little House books."

Way to go Henrietta! Chloe thought. Henrietta rocked.

Jayne's smile became a little less smug, a little more annoyed. "You are incorrect!"

"Thank you, Jayne!" Alta said loudly. She hustled Jayne aside to a ripple of halfhearted applause and disapproving mumbles.

Chloe was up next. "After over a decade of experiential research at many historic sites," she began, "I've found that the actual processes *Laura* described in such detail are accurate." She beamed at Jayne, who scowled from the back of the room.

Chloe had brought illustrations of maple sugaring, butchering, butter churning, and other *Little House in the Big Woods* activities she'd helped re-create. It was fun to revisit some of the educational programs she'd developed, and her allotted time passed quickly.

"When used carefully and supplemented with additional documentation, Laura's books can help modern children bridge the gap between present and past at appropriate historic sites," she concluded. "Thank you."

Chloe took childish pleasure in the applause that followed. So many people had questions that Alta had to cut them off. "I'm sure Chloe will be happy to chat during the break," she said. "Our box lunches are waiting on tables outside in the shade."

After collecting her slides, Chloe reached the registration table just in time to see Norma Epps, whom she'd met at the museum in Pepin, signing in. "Norma, hello!" Chloe exclaimed.

Norma smiled, but it didn't reach her eyes. "I need to talk to Alta."

Kari and Chloe exchanged a *This doesn't look good* glance as Norma beckoned Alta over. Kari started to rise, but Norma waved a hand. "You might as well hear this too." She sighed. "I have information about the young man who died at the Pepin Wayside two days ago."

"Was an allergy to blame?" Chloe asked.

"Peanuts. Evidently some had been ground into a salad. It was in Tupperware, but he probably bought it at a deli."

"That's just tragic," Kari whispered.

"I'm afraid there's more," Norma said. "I'm sorry, Alta. The victim was Kim Dexheimer."

Chloe's mouth opened as she struggled to take that in. Kim Dexheimer, the quilt historian? The man she'd been unable to help at the Pepin Wayside was the very expert she'd been so eager to meet?

Alta's jaw had dropped too. "*Kim*? Kim Dexheimer was ... wasn't ... "

"His full name was Kimball Dexheimer."

"I had no idea!" Alta looked dazed. "His was one of the first proposals I received. It included photocopies of relevant articles and an impressive resume. I just assumed that Kim was a woman." A note of panic crept into her voice. "What am I going to do? People were *so* looking forward to the quilting presentation!"

Norma patted her arm consolingly. "We'll figure something out. Let's go up and have some lunch, all right? You need to eat."

They started for the door. Kari grabbed her purse, then paused. "Aren't you coming?" she asked.

"I just need a minute," Chloe said. "If they have anything vegetarian, save a sandwich for me."

Not that she had an appetite now. Kim Dexheimer had represented her best chance to learn something definitive about Miss Lila's quilt. He was not only an expert on historical quilts, he'd had a special interest in Laura. Even if I could find another expert, Chloe thought, my legal custody of the quilt is about to expire. After this road trip, the quilt would return to Miss Lila's estate.

This is important, and I trust you.

Chloe contemplated the rest of the tour with growing unease. Suddenly, "tragedy" and "quilt" shared the limelight. The very first tragedy, she thought, was Miss Lila's death only hours after she'd delivered the quilt to *me*. The police believed that the thief who'd broken into Miss Lila's house was after jewelry, but since they hadn't caught the guy, no one knew for sure.

Chloe tried to think of possible connections between Miss Lila's violent death, a quilt historian's accidental death, and the fact that she and Kari were wandering the heartland with a quilt once owned by Laura. She tried really hard, and came up with exactly … nothing. But it was unsettling anyway.

She didn't feel ready to join the others, so she straightened the tablecloth and threw away several cups. Seven people hadn't checked in yet; she tossed Wilbur Voss's nametag in the trash and placed the others in a precise row. She arranged the folders containing their symposium information in a pleasing fan. She tapped the edges of the stack of De Smet walking tour maps.

Then she picked up the folder of registration forms. They hadn't been alphabetized, which had slowed down check-in. Chloe shuffled quickly through, pulling the A's. Her sister's came first. Kari didn't use her birth name, so *Kari Anderson* was printed on the first line.

And right beside it, the date she'd registered: 3/22/1983.

Chloe was still staring at that string of digits when Kari came back inside. "Nothing veggie," she announced, "but they have a turkey-Swiss option. I think you can scrape the turkey off without…" She frowned. "What's up with you?"

Chloe placed the registration form on the table and pointed.

Kari's shoulders slumped. "Oh, shit."

"What the hell, Kari?"

"I should have told you."

"You *think*?"

"Look, I know I ... it was just that ... " Kari ran both hands through her hair.

"When I called to invite you to the symposium, why didn't you just tell me that you'd already registered?" Chloe demanded. "You let me prattle on, telling you all about this wonderful conference coming up, and you were already frickin' registered for it!"

Kari scratched at an ink mark on the tablecloth with her fingernail. "I was embarrassed."

"Why?"

"Because I hadn't invited you! Here you were reaching out, being all nice, wanting to do a sisters thing ... How could I say, 'Oh, that? I signed up for that two months ago.'"

Chloe picked up the form and stuffed it back into the folder.

"Look, when I saw the symposium announcement, all I wanted to do was get away from home for a few days," Kari said defensively. "I wasn't thinking about us way back when. It didn't occur to me to do the whole homesites tour. I just wanted to leave town. I could have flown to Vegas for all I cared, but I figured Trygve wouldn't object to something like this."

"Didn't you know I was speaking here?"

"No, why would I? Alta didn't publish the details. Mom didn't mention it. And since you never come out to the farm—"

"I already apologized for that."

"Well, I apologize for this."

"Fine, then."

"Fine."

The words had been said, but the air remained thick with tension. It belatedly occurred to Chloe that when *she'd* accepted Alta's invitation to present at the symposium, she hadn't thought to invite Kari. It had taken the nudge from Miss Lila and her quilt to pop that idea into her brain. So technically, Chloe thought grudgingly, I guess we're even.

But she didn't feel like saying so, and Laura Lookers were starting to straggle back inside. She tossed the file into the green tub, kicked it back under the table, and stomped off in search of turkey to scrape off a sandwich.

She really needed some time alone, but when she got outside, she noticed a familiar figure huddled alone at a picnic bench. Chloe grabbed a boxed lunch, hesitated, and then approached Hazel. "May I join you?"

Hazel wiped red-rimmed eyes. "Of course."

The other woman's distress took some of the edge off Chloe's grumpy mood. "What's wrong?"

"Oh…" Hazel tried to smile. "Wilbur called my hotel room this morning. He's furious with me for leaving him in the middle of the tour. He seems more worried about that than the end of our marriage."

"Maybe that's easier than accepting the fact that you've decided to leave for good."

"I was so pleased when he agreed to bring me to the symposium," Hazel said. "I thought the trip might actually be good for us. Instead…"

Chloe sighed. "I know exactly what you mean."

————

"Got a minute?" Chief Naborski asked.

"Sure." Roelke went into the chief's office and sat down. Since he hadn't solved any homicides, found any lost children, saved any puppies from a burning building, or otherwise done gold medal work for the Village of Eagle recently, he couldn't think of any good reason for a private talk.

"I wanted to know how you're doing. After what happened."

Roelke wasn't sure if he was in trouble or not. "You mean—what happened in Milwaukee?"

"Sometimes things can kick back up weeks or months later. You lost a friend in the line of duty, and at the end of it you were involved in a shooting—"

"I'm okay."

"Because there are resources, you know. People you can talk to."

Please God, anything but *that*. "I'm okay," Roelke repeated. "Although sometimes I'm not sure I make much of a difference in Eagle."

"I think you do." The chief tipped his chair back on two legs. "But I imagine that people in Milwaukee would be very happy to see you return."

Was the man a mind reader? Or had he gotten a call from the MPD? Roelke had been a full-time officer for less than a year, and he had no wish to come across as an arrogant smartass by asking about promotional opportunities. "I have not made any inquiries about that," he said carefully.

Naborski's chair banged back to the floor. Roelke started to stand, but the chief picked up an incident report form. "You took a tricky call the other day with Child Protective Services."

"Yes sir."

Chief eyed him. "Anything further on this one?"

"Mrs. Enright has the baby in foster care. Skeet and I haven't seen either parent. No calls from the neighbor about violent screaming matches either." Roelke tried to sound matter-of-fact. He didn't want to confess that he could still feel Travis's soft, warm weight in his hands as he eased the infant from his mother's arms. He rubbed his palms on his trousers.

"Good work, Officer McKenna. Just remember, my door is always open."

"Yes sir," Roelke said again, and made his escape.

But every note from the fiddle was a very little wrong. Pa's fingers were
clumsy. The music dragged and a fiddle string snapped.

"My fingers are too stiff and thick from being out in the cold so
much, I can't play," Pa spoke as if he were ashamed. He lay the fiddle
in its box.   The Long Winter

FOURTEEN

AFTER LUNCH A MAN named James, professor of music at the University of South Dakota, took the podium. "Of all the hard times Laura wrote about in the Little House books," he began, "what strikes you as the lowest moment?"

Hazel raised her hand. "When Mary went blind," she said, which made Chloe felt guilty all over again.

"When Laura's dog died," a girl suggested, which made Chloe feel a little better.

"When grasshoppers ate all their crops!" someone called.

Alta spoke up. "When Pa tried to play the fiddle during the Hard Winter, and couldn't."

"That gets my vote too," James said. "I think that moment when Pa was too cold and weak to play is a metaphor, symbolizing just how close the family came to freezing and starving to death."

A grandmotherly woman waved her hand. "In earlier books Pa's fiddle music symbolized comfort and safety. Laura even mentioned Pa playing in a letter she wrote about Burr Oak. I think she wanted people to know that despite grief and hard times, the Ingalls family had not lost hope."

Chloe felt her mood improving as the talk continued. She couldn't think of another conference where historians and stay-at-home moms, librarians and grandmothers, shared so generously and respectfully. Except for Jayne, of course, but there was always one crank in the crowd.

For a mid-afternoon break, Alta had scheduled a walking tour of De Smet. Chloe was to meet Edna Jo Poffenwiler about Miss Lila's quilt before catching the group at the Surveyors' House. "You coming with?" Chloe asked Kari coolly.

"I'm going on the tour," Kari said, just as coolly.

The Laura Ingalls Wilder Memorial Society maintained several historic structures in De Smet, with gift shop, office, and collections storage next door. Chloe whistled softly at the number of cabinets and neatly shelved archival boxes in the storage area.

"We have a collection of over twenty-five thousand objects," Edna Jo said with quiet pride. "A wonderful young man named William Anderson began working for us in the 1970s and became our director of acquisitions. He reached out to the community and facilitated donations from friends of the Wilders and Ingallses." She turned, assessing the shelves. "We have many treasures, and I try not to think about what was lost. When Carrie had to sell the Ingalls House on 3rd Street—"

"The Ingalls House?" Chloe had never heard of the Ingalls House.

"You'll see it tomorrow. It's where Laura's parents finally settled and lived their last years. Mary lived there also. Carrie had moved farther west by the time Mary died and was in such poor health

162

that she wasn't able to get back and clean out the family furnishings. So the new owners backed a pickup truck up to the house and began pitching things out a second-story window—"

"No!" The image gave Chloe a twinge of nausea.

"Fortunately, family friends saw what was going on and managed to save a few things. And our collection is still growing. You'll appreciate these." Edna Jo led Chloe to a worktable where several newspapers and handwritten letters waited for attention. "While doing restoration work in the Ingalls House recently we found these papers stuffed inside a wall."

"For insulation, do you suppose?"

"Without a doubt."

Chloe examined them with delight. "This is like a time capsule!" She squinted at a letter. The writer had filled the sheet with cramped lines of cursive, then turned the page 90 degrees and kept going. "I admire the author's thrift, but cross-written letters are difficult to decipher."

"I've got a volunteer working on the transcription." Edna smiled. "Now, I'm eager to see your quilt."

Chloe reviewed the pertinent facts as she opened her box. "I hope to link this quilt to some textile with known provenance to Laura. Even better would be evidence that Laura actually made the quilt. We know she made a Bear Track quilt as a child."

"Ah, yes." Edna Jo smiled. "I love the description in *On the Banks of Plum Creek*. 'Mary was still sewing nine-patch blocks. Now Laura started a Bear Track quilt. It was harder than a nine-patch because there were bias seams, very hard to make exactly right before Ma would let her make another, and often Laura worked for days on one short seam.'"

I am a complete Little House piker, Chloe thought. She couldn't quote word-for-word from even her beloved *Big Woods*. "I'm impressed with your recall."

"People come to De Smet from all over the world, each looking for *their* Laura," Edna Jo said. "I feel a responsibility to our visitors, and try to meet their needs. Yesterday I met a man trying to identify the location of the Brewster School where Laura taught, a developmentally disabled girl who overcame all expectations because she wanted to read the Little House books, a needlework expert who hopes to duplicate a collar Ma crocheted, and a woman who regularly talks to Laura during séances."

"Yikes."

"Besides, I'm a die-hard fan," Edna Jo confided. "Our collection does not include any quilts stitched by Laura, but the topic comes up often. Laura's daughter Rose, who spent time with Ma and Mary in the 3rd Street House as a child, wrote that her grandmother set her to sewing a Nine Patch quilt. She also said that Mary still made Nine Patch quilts. I don't know what happened to any quilts Mary made as an adult, but her childhood quilt is on display in Missouri."

"It *is*?" Chloe quivered like a hound catching a new scent.

"That will be your best bet for finding matching fabrics. Are you going on to Kansas and Missouri?"

"We'll be in Missouri for the Wilder Heritage Festival," Chloe said. "I can hardly wait to see Mary's quilt!" Not wanting to sound too giddy, she added, "I do know that finding a fabric match is a long shot. If only Laura and Almanzo's house hadn't burned down! I haven't let myself hope that my friend's quilt is actually the one Laura made as a child"—which was not true, but seemed the professional thing to say—"but I sure wish I could have seen it."

"I know." Edna Jo nodded. "That childhood quilt of Laura's almost certainly burned."

Chloe perked up. "*Almost* certainly … ?"

"Laura wrote that a neighbor managed to rescue dishes from the fire," Edna Jo said. "Nothing else was saved except a deed-box, a few work clothes, and the glass bread plate printed with the words, 'Give us this day our daily bread.' *The First Four Years*, last chapter."

"I never read that one," Chloe said. "I was in college when it came out, and too focused on coursework."

"The manuscript was found after Laura's death and not published until 1971," Edna Jo said kindly. "Anyway, based on that description, Laura's precious childhood quilt did not survive. Still, we must remind ourselves that these books are novels, sometimes shaped in the interests of telling a story."

"Right," Chloe said slowly. She'd been disappointed more than once lately to discover that Laura had fudged, embellished, or omitted facts when writing the books. It hadn't occurred to her that the phenomenon might actually work in her favor.

Edna Jo studied Miss Lila's quilt. "I've always wondered whether Laura's childhood quilt was actually a Dove in the Window pattern."

What? Laura's childhood quilt might have been a different pattern altogether? Chloe felt crushed. "Um … and why is that, exactly?"

"A passage from *These Happy Golden Years*, when Laura was packing before her marriage to Almanzo. 'Laura brought her Dove-in-the-Window quilt that she had pieced as a little girl while Mary pieced a nine-patch.' Chapter 32."

"But … "

"Since Laura got married here in De Smet, I'm especially interested in her bridal quilt. I've found two very different patterns called Dove in the Window that date to the nineteenth century, before mail order catalogs that named quilts became common." Edna Jo reached for a photocopied quilt pattern and placed it on the table. "Notice anything about this one?"

"It's very similar to the Bear Track block," Chloe said slowly. Both patterns used the exact same pieces, just arranged slightly differently.

"So in my view, Laura's quilts present more than one mystery. Was her childhood quilt and her wedding quilt one and the same? By the time Laura wrote the books, late in life, she might have simply confused the two very similar patterns."

Chloe could see where Edna Jo was going. "*Or*, did Laura create a Bear Track quilt as a very young child, and later make a different quilt using one of these different Dove in the Window patterns?"

"I had looked forward to discussing this with Kim Dexheimer, but Alta told me … well." Edna Jo sank into a nearby chair. "We'll probably never know."

Chloe's momentary buzz at the notion that Laura's quilt might actually have escaped conflagration was gone. She began tenderly refolding Miss Lila's quilt. "No," she said with profound sorrow. "We'll probably never know."

―――――

When Roelke got off work at three that afternoon he was still trying to figure out what had happened in the chief's office. Was Chief Naborski worried about him moving back to the Milwaukee PD, or about him cracking up? The question poked at him as he drove home, and he was thrilled to hear the phone ring as he stepped inside his apartment. He ran to grab it. "McKenna speaking."

"It's Dobry." Dobry Banik was a friend from Roelke's MPD days.

"Oh! So … How are you doing?"

"I'm doing okay. I was just … well, I wondered if you might like to come into the city sometime. Maybe play some music." Like Roelke and Rick, Dobry had played in The Blue Tones—an all cop band. They'd played their last gig the night Rick was killed.

Roelke ran a hand over his face. "I can't."

"Is it because I—"

"No, Dobry. We're okay. I'm just not ready to play music again." He'd given his electric bass to Goodwill, actually. He was certain that he would *never* play music again. But didn't want to say so.

Silence stretched over the line before Dobry responded. "Sure, Roelke. I get it. Give me a call if you ever just want to hang out or something, okay?"

"I will. And … Dobry? Thanks for calling." Roelke hung up and stared at the phone. After a moment he decided he *was* glad that Dobry had called. That was progress. He hoped.

He jumped when the phone rang again. "McKenna speaking."

"It's me," Chloe said. "Is this a bad time?"

"No, actually, this is good." He stretched out on the sofa. "I figured we'd talk this evening. Is everything okay?"

"Not really. I don't know. I'm just feeling kinda down."

He sat up again. "What's going on?"

"Well, I found out today that the man I watched die back in Pepin is—was—the quilt historian who was going to speak at the symposium."

"Really? A guy?" The notion was baffling. "Well, hunh."

"The point is, first Miss Lila got killed right after loaning me a Laura quilt, and then a textile historian dies on his way to give a talk about Laura and quilts. Doesn't that seem a bit spooky?"

"Spell the guy's name." Roelke wrote it down. "Listen, I'll sound out the Pepin cops about it. I can talk to the Stoughton guys too."

"Thank you. At least that eases my mind about one problem."

"What other problems need easing?"

"Oh… Kari and I had a tiff this afternoon. Sometimes it feels like one step forward and two steps back with her. It shouldn't be this hard."

Roelke tapped his pen against his knee. There was nothing he'd rather do than solve a problem for Chloe, neat and tidy, no loose ends. But on this subject, he had nothing to offer. "I'm sorry," he said finally. "Maybe tomorrow will be better."

"Maybe."

"How's De Smet?"

"Most of the symposium speakers have been great. But the site director thinks Laura might actually have made a Dove in the Window quilt at Plum Creek, not a Bear Track."

Roelke had absolutely no idea what she was talking about. "I'm sorry to hear that."

"I guess I had unrealistic hopes about this trip. Our group toured the Surveyors' House—the last original Laura house from the books. I'd been really excited about it, but nothing happened. I couldn't find any sense of Laura there."

"I'm sorry to hear that too."

"Thanks." She drew an audible breath. "Roelke… are you thinking of actually farming?"

Roelke dropped his pen. "What? Why would you even ask?"

"Because you're reading *Farmer Boy*."

"I'm reading *Farmer Boy* because I'm trying to understand something that's important to you."

"*Oh*. That's very sweet. I miss you."

"I miss you too." He hated being here with bank statements and big decisions while she was in South Dakota with quilts and antiques and other people who really liked this Wilder woman. It suddenly seemed as if the Venn diagram of their relationship had no overlap. Being together created the overlap.

"You okay?" she asked. "You've gone quiet."

"Chloe … would you like to live together?"

Now *she* went quiet.

"I was just wondering," he said.

"Is this about the farm?"

"Well, partly, I guess."

"So … you're looking for a rent check?"

"*What?*" A check from Chloe, rent or otherwise, had never crossed his mind. "No! Of course not."

She took another deep breath. "Look, do we have to discuss something like this over the phone?"

"I can't help it that you're traveling."

"What I'm *saying* is, can't this conversation wait until I get back?"

"I suppose," he said. But he didn't want to talk about it anymore. Obviously Chloe had not even thought about living together.

"Does me saying yes or no mean the difference in whether you buy the farm or not?"

He thought about that. It wasn't about the money. It was his family farm, his idea, his ultimate financial commitment and risk. But when he tried to decide if he'd be happy living in the farmhouse, fixing it up … well, he sure liked the idea of her doing that with him. The best he could offer was, "I don't know."

Silence stretched uncomfortably over the miles. Finally Chloe said, "I gotta go."

———

Chloe ended the conversation in a flood of frustration. Roelke shouldn't have asked her something so important over the phone, but her response had been inappropriate too. *I shouldn't have made that crack about the rent check,* she thought. *That's when things really went downhill.*

Chloe leaned against the phone booth, watching a rusty red Chevy putter by. She loved Roelke. She wanted to be with him. But…was she committed long-term to Old World Wisconsin? What if some juicy opportunity popped up in Wyoming or Lithuania or someplace? What if Petty found a way to fire her? What if Roelke moved into his farmhouse, and the experience turned out to be a disaster? That kind of stress could rip a relationship apart.

"We will figure things out when I get home," she muttered. Right now, she needed food. The rest of the group had gone to a restaurant for dinner. Chloe had bailed in favor of fixing a vegetarian-friendly meal from the cooler. The weather was pleasant, so she decided to picnic on the church grounds and wait for everyone else to return for the evening's activities.

But as she started across the lawn, an unexpected sparkle caught her peripheral vision. A pile of broken glass littered the sidewalk in front of the side door Alta's group had been using.

"Would it have killed you to sweep up after yourself?" Chloe grumbled to whomever. Crouching, she began to carefully pile the biggest pieces. Suddenly she stilled, staring at the wicked triangle in her fingers. This piece showed part of a sheaf of wheat created in the glass.

David Rice from Walnut Grove spoke in her memory: *Lots of Wilder readers want to find copies of the bread plate that Laura and Almanzo ordered from Montgomery Ward, for example. It features a sheaf of wheat in the center. Those plates have gotten expensive, and hard to find.*

And Edna Jo had said that the bread plate had been one of the only things saved from the fire that consumed Laura and Almanzo's home. Although this was not Laura's plate, it was of the same vintage. Few heirlooms would be more precious to a Lauraphile than this plate.

Chloe felt a chill, as if she'd been handling shards of ice instead of glass. One of the activities on tap for the night was a "bazaar" featuring tables of Laura-related items for display and, in some cases, sale. Had some collector accidentally dropped this precious plate while carrying it into the church?

She wanted to believe that sad but innocuous explanation. And she might have, if the remains of this oh-so-precious antique hadn't been left on the sidewalk for all Laura Lookers to see. And if someone hadn't left a skewered Charlotte doll at the Pepin Wayside, and a decapitated china shepherdess in Burr Oak.

And if she hadn't seen the illustration ripped from *On the Banks of Plum Creek*, with *DIE LAURA DIE* scrawled in black marker.

Laura did not know whether or not she wanted to be settled down.

By the Shores of Silver Lake

"I've been thinking," she said. "I don't want to marry a farmer. I have always said I never would."

... Manly asked, "Why don't you want to marry a farmer?" And Laura replied, "Because a farm is such a hard place for a woman."

The First Four Years

FIFTEEN

CHLOE GROANED WHEN THE alarm clock shrilled at seven the next morning. She'd been awake until almost four, thrashing about, too hot, too cold, too upset to sleep. She'd dreamed about wooden claim shanties and brick farmhouses and pretty quilts bursting into flames.

It took four swipes to silence the buzzer. When she shoved hair out of her eyes and blearily raised her head, she saw Kari's bed empty and neatly made. There was no sign of Kari.

"Lovely," Chloe muttered. Then she staggered to the shower and tried to face the day.

She caught up with her sister forty minutes later in the church hall, helping Alta and Hazel set out a continental breakfast. "You were up early," Chloe murmured, trying really hard to sound conversational. They'd barely spoken the night before.

Kari began pouring orange juice into paper cups. "I'm a dairy farmer."

You don't look like a dairy farmer, Chloe thought. Kari looked as haggard as Chloe felt.

"I've got doughnuts!" Hazel chirped, emerging from the kitchen with a platter. She looked wide-awake and happy in her knit pants and favorite I Love Laura sweatshirt and calico bonnet.

Chloe poured herself a cup of coffee and grabbed a chocolate frosted before retreating to the registration table and her de facto role as greeter. She was feeling only marginally better by the time Alta launched Day Two of the symposium.

A woman from Arizona spoke about *The First Four Years*. "Laura evidently intended this for an adult audience," the speaker explained. "However, it wasn't published until long after her death. She wrote in a letter to Rose that she'd put the project aside because those first years of marriage were just too painful."

Lovely, Chloe thought.

"After all," the speaker continued, "the original Little House books led readers toward the expected happy ending—Laura and Almanzo falling in love and together creating the home that Laura had been seeking all her life. But in real life Laura did not want to live on a farm. Almanzo talked her into trying it for a few years."

He talked her into it? Chloe thought. Great.

The speaker turned a page of her notes. "During those first years the couple experienced drought, crop failures, debt, diphtheria, and a stroke that crippled Almanzo."

This is not the talk I wanted to hear today, Chloe thought. She needed *her* Laura, the Laura of Wisconsin's Big Woods, to have found a happy ending.

"The birth of daughter Rose was followed by the death of their infant son."

Chloe wished this informative lady had stayed in Arizona.

"Eleven days later, a fire destroyed their home."

Chloe slipped from her seat, quietly got another cup of coffee, and retreated to the registration table. She'd brought her quilting supplies, and she began pinning squares together.

The extra caffeine, a completed quilt block, and a more cheerful presentation about period games left Chloe feeling capable of coherent conversation.

Haruka Minari sat next to her at lunch, which was quite pleasant. Haruka lived in Connecticut and had recently toured Mystic Seaport, a site on Chloe's want-to-see list; and when Chloe described Old World Wisconsin, Haruka said she *must* visit. The caterer had brought cheddar cheese sandwiches and mint-chip brownies, both excellent. After all that, Chloe felt lively enough to give Jayne-with-a-Y a sunny smile and chipper "How's it going?" Just to mess with her.

But she kept an eye on her sister, who remained subdued and distant. Kari had been moody since leaving home, but she'd been able to rally and enjoy the site visits and programs. Had their argument yesterday pushed things over the edge? I really need to smooth that out, Chloe thought. She had enough to worry about without bickering with Kari.

As people finished eating, Alta called for attention. "I have a sorry announcement to make," she began, and chatter faded. "The historical quilt expert who planned to speak this afternoon died a few days ago at the Pepin historical site."

Shock and concern rippled through the crowd. Haruka put down her little milk carton and stared at Chloe. "That man who died was on his way *here*?"

"I'm afraid so. He had an allergic reaction to some ground peanuts in his salad." Chloe leaned closer. "Haruka...I know you talked with the police, but did you happen to notice anything unusual before Mr. Dexheimer fell ill?"

Haruka shook her head helplessly. "I was reading in a lawn chair nearby, so I really saw very little. I did notice *her* speaking with him at one point."

Chloe followed Haruka's gaze and saw none other than Jayne. "Really? Did you hear what they were talking about?"

"No, but it seemed pleasant enough. I glanced up because I heard them laughing."

"Laughing? Are you sure it was Jayne?"

"I noticed in particular because Jayne was so dressed up. Even holding an embroidered handkerchief."

Probably monogrammed, Chloe thought, resisting the urge to roll her eyes.

"I did mention seeing them together to the police, so I'm sure they talked with Ms. Rifenberg." Haruka frowned. "Is there some problem?"

"No," Chloe said, although she wasn't at all sure. Had Jayne actually known Kimball Dexheimer? Had she recognized him as a quilt expert on the way to *Looking For Laura*? Or was it merely coincidence that their paths had crossed?

Jayne was sitting alone, and for a nanosecond Chloe considered going over and asking her. Then sanity prevailed. It was extremely unlikely that Jayne would tell her diddly about squat.

"Alta?" Leonard Devich suddenly waved his hand like an eager third grader. "You're short one speaker, and I have a talk prepared—"

"Thank you, Leonard," Alta said firmly, "but I've had requests for some downtime. In a few minutes we'll leave for our tour of the

Ingalls House on 3rd Street. After that, you'll be free until five, when we're gathering at the Ingalls homestead claim. The Memorial Society owns an acre of land that includes the cottonwood trees Pa planted for Caroline and the girls."

Once sodas were gulped and trash discarded, symposium participants traipsed to a pretty frame house on 3rd Street. Edna Jo met them on the front step. "Welcome to Pa's House!"

"I didn't know anything about this," Chloe admitted to Henrietta, who happened to be walking beside her.

"Laura never lived here, that's why," Henrietta said kindly. "She and Almanzo were already married and living on their own homestead when Pa built this house."

Inside, the group bunched up in the parlor where Ma and Pa had spent their evenings. "After Mary graduated from the school for the blind in Iowa," Edna Jo added, "she lived here as well."

All interesting, Chloe thought. But there was no point in looking for Laura in this house.

"The night before Laura and Almanzo and Rose moved to Missouri, everyone gathered in this room," Edna Jo continued. "After supper Laura asked Pa to get out his fiddle. He played almost until sunup. Laura didn't know if she'd ever see her parents or sisters again. Pa told Laura that he wanted her to have his fiddle when he died."

Chloe's throat thickened. So much for not looking for Laura here.

"When the Wilders drove away in their wagon, Laura broke down and wept," Edna Jo said softly. "She told Almanzo that she didn't think the Ingalls family would have survived if it hadn't been for Pa's fiddle."

Hazel dabbed at her eyes with a tissue. Edna Jo is darn good, Chloe thought. She remembered what the music professor had said about Pa's fiddle. She thought about Roelke, unable to play music since his best friend had been killed.

Finally Alta broke the charged silence. "Docents are here to answer additional questions. We're going to split the group in half. The first group can go upstairs, and the second can head to the kitchen, where you'll see the original cupboards that Pa built for Ma..."

When everyone else shuffled off, Chloe stayed put. Laura's heart broke in this room, she thought. The sadness evoked by Edna Jo's story lingered with her, a faint but palpable thrum. No, more than sadness. A sense of longing lingered here. She closed her eyes, tried to open herself...

"Chloe?"

Chloe's eyes flew open. "*What?*" she snapped. Then, "Oh. Sorry, Hazel."

Hazel anxiously twisted her fingers together. "You better come into the kitchen."

"Why?"

"Something's wrong with Kari."

The first thing Chloe saw in the kitchen were Pa's handmade cupboards, which were spectacular.

The second was a row of swinging exhibit boards mounted against one wall, allowing visitors to flip through. The boards were open to show a panel inoffensively titled *Friends and Neighbors*, with photos, newspaper clippings, and bits of explanatory text.

The third thing Chloe saw was her sister, sitting on the floor with legs drawn up, elbows on knees, face in her hands, weeping.

"What's the matter with her?" someone asked.

"Could you give us a minute, please?" Chloe crouched in front of Kari. "What's going on?"

"N-nothing." Kari squeezed out the word between sobs.

"Is she sick?" someone asked.

Chloe scootched sideways to better shield Kari from the audience. "I'm pretty sure that *something* is wrong."

"I just—I just…"

"Maybe you and I should go outside," Chloe suggested quietly. No response.

"Did somebody say something mean to her?" someone asked.

Chloe put her hand on Kari's arm. Kari shook it off.

"Maybe *Chloe* said something mean to her," someone said.

Chloe ground her teeth. "Kari. For the love of God—"

Kari raised her face. Her eyes were running. Her nose was running. She looked bad. "Cap—Garland—*died*," she hissed. A tear dribbled down one cheek.

"Well…yeah," Chloe said helplessly. "Since Cap helped save the day during the Long Winter, which was a hundred and two years ago, I imagine that at some point he died."

"Maybe Kari has mental problems," someone whispered, as loudly as a human could possibly whisper.

Chloe got to her feet and faced the spectators. "Look, could you please give us a little space?"

"I think that story about Laura saying goodbye to her father set Kari off," Leonard Devich said. "Research shows that Charles and Laura had a very unhealthy relationship."

Jayne Rifenberg gave him a withering glance. "Exactly what research paradigm have you embraced? You—"

"Shut *up!*" Chloe cried. She stamped her foot, which was a first, but she'd *had* it. Miss Lila was dead, and her quilt was undocumented, and the man who might have been able to document it was dead, and Roelke was pressuring her, and her own longed-for moment in the parlor with Laura had been lost because Kari, perfect Kari, was evidently having a nervous breakdown.

"*You*"—Chloe turned on Devich with an accusatory finger—"are a nutjob. And *you*"—the finger swerved toward Jayne Rifenberg—"are a bitch. And *you*"—the finger swerved again and Chloe realized too late that the next person in line was Alta, who was staring owl-eyed at the Ellefson girls—"well, you're a very nice person. But could you all *please* just give us a minute here?"

Footsteps began clomping down the staircase from the second floor—group A coming down to switch places with group B. Chloe grabbed Kari's arm, pulled her to her feet, and used the momentary chaos to tow her out the door. She didn't stop until they stood on the sidewalk. Kari's breath still came in little shuddering heaves, but she made a visible effort to pull herself together.

"Kari, *please* tell me what's going on. I'm sorry we squabbled yesterday. I just want to help."

"You can't help."

"Is this really about Trygve?" Chloe persisted. "What did he do?"

"He … I … it's just that a farm is a hard place for a woman."

"But—"

"I don't want to talk about it." Kari swiped angrily at new tears. "I just want to be alone for a while." She turned and hurried away.

"Sit down, Charles, and tell me what is wrong," Ma said quietly.
Pa sat down. "There's been a murder."

By the Shores of Silver Lake

SIXTEEN

SINCE ROELKE WAS SCHEDULED for second shift that day, he had plenty of time to make some phone calls from his apartment before heading to work. He tried the Stoughton PD first and talked his way past the clerk to one of the officers who'd responded to Marit Kallerud's frantic 911 call after finding Miss Lila. "We met on the scene the night Lila Gillespie died," Roelke said, after identifying himself and his department. "I'm hoping you can give me an update about—"

"I can't share information about an ongoing investigation."

"Of course not," Roelke said, in his best *We understand each other completely* tone. "Here's the thing. My girlfriend's parents live next door, and everybody's worried that the SOB responsible might come back. I'd sure be grateful if you can give me any reassurance I can pass on to them."

"Truth is," the man said, "we don't have a damn thing yet."

Roelke drummed an unhappy rhythm with his fingers.

"Tell the parents that we're keeping an eye on the neighborhood. They should call if they see anything suspicious."

"I'll pass that on," Roelke said. "Thanks." He hung up, scowling. He suspected that Chloe's parents already knew to call if they saw anything suspicious.

He did no better when he called the Pepin police. "Yeah, that was a sad one," the officer said.

"My girlfriend was there when it happened. She's pretty shook up. You know, wondering if there was something she could have done."

"Not a thing," the guy said with complete certainty. "Somehow the guy got a trace of ground peanuts mixed into his lunch, and he was deathly allergic. It can happen real fast."

"Yeah, it can," Roelke agreed. "So . . . nothing suspicious about the death?"

"Nah. The guy lived alone and was traveling alone. We'll never know where that salad came from."

"Okay," Roelke said. "Thanks." He hung up and scowled again. He'd really wanted to find something, some nugget of helpful information that might put Chloe's mind at ease.

He stewed for a few minutes, knee bouncing. Then he made another call. "Mrs. Enright? It's Officer McKenna, Eagle PD."

"Officer McKenna!" She sounded surprised.

"I was just wondering how baby Travis is doing."

"Well, I haven't seen him since you called yesterday," Mrs. Enright said. "But as I told you then, he's getting good care. And I'm late for a meeting."

"Let us know if we can—"

Mrs. Enright hung up.

"—be of any assistance." Roelke hung up too. He wasn't surprised. CPS workers were *always* snowed under. "Unlike me," he muttered.

Of course, if he bought the old Roelke farm, he'd be snowed under too. A lawn to mow, porch steps to repair, windows to wash, walls to paint, etc., etc., etc. Something like panic pricked his chest. What the hell was he thinking? He wanted to be busy at work, not every off-hour for the rest of his days.

Roelke exploded from the sofa and headed for the door. He'd reach the EPD early for his shift, but with any luck, there would be some bad guys that needed chasing.

———

Kari had not come back by the time Alta's tour group straggled from Pa's House. "Free time," Alta reminded everyone. "I'm going back to the motel and take a nap. If there's a crisis, I'm in room seventeen. Otherwise, I'll see you at the homestead site."

Hazel and the Whelans paused by Chloe. "Everything okay?" Hazel asked.

"Kari's had a lot on her mind." Chloe tried to sound nonchalant.

Evidently the attempt failed, because Hazel engulfed her in an embrace. "Oh, honey. All you need is a hug."

"We're going to the Loftus Store," Mrs. Whelan said. "Remember where the storekeeper tried to overcharge everyone after Almanzo and Cap Garland brought back the wheat? It's a gift shop now. Want to come?"

As worried as she was about Kari, Chloe wasn't in the mood to see anything that had to do with Cap Garland. "No, but thanks for the invite," she said. The trio wandered off.

Ten minutes later there still was no sign of Kari. The car keys were in Chloe's pocket, so her sister couldn't have gone too far. But emotionally, Kari was in a bad place—a fragile place. Chloe knew what that was like. It wasn't good.

She walked back toward De Smet's downtown and, with nothing else to go on, found the nearest tavern. The Three Pals was in the ground level of a two-story brick structure that Laura herself may have walked past, but the interior was nothing special. At the closest table, four young men who looked barely legal were eating onion rings from red plastic baskets and swilling beer. Two guys in cowboy hats were playing pool in one corner by the light of an overhead Budweiser lamp. There was only one woman in the place, and it wasn't Kari.

Chloe silently groaned and considered the age-old question of fight-or-flight. Jayne Rifenberg sat alone at a table in the far corner. She looked extremely out of place in her Wall Street attire. The glass of red wine on the table was almost empty. She sat idly flipping a coin like a bored steelworker, over and over.

Actually, Jayne didn't look bored. She looked … bereft.

Oh hell, Chloe thought. This afternoon was sucking more and more. She didn't like Jayne, but she did owe her an apology.

Chloe paused to order a glass of Zin at the bar, half-hoping that Jayne would leave. Jayne did not cooperate. Glass in hand, Chloe took a deep breath and approached. "May I join you?"

"Suit yourself." Jayne looked away, but not before Chloe saw a suspicious shine in her eyes. Tears? Oh dear God, Chloe thought. Did I actually make Jayne Rifenberg-Iceberg cry?

Jayne blinked several times and began flipping the coin—it was a penny—again.

Chloe slid into a chair across the table. "Um … a penny for your thoughts?"

"Heads or tails," Jayne murmured. "Who's going under?"

Was that a dare? A premonition? Chloe had no idea. "Look, I'm very sorry about what I said before."

Jayne's eyebrows rose very slowly, and her features settled into their usual expression of disdain.

"My sister and I have been … I've been struggling to … " Chloe sipped her wine. "My nerves snapped back there, but it had nothing to do with you. I apologize."

Jayne put the penny down on the table, reached for her glass, and downed the rest of her wine. "It doesn't matter."

"Well, it kinda does," Chloe protested. She'd forced the words out. The least Jayne could do was take delivery.

"Do you really imagine that I care what you think of me?" Jayne asked.

"I thought maybe you could use a friend. Look, you and I got off to a bad start, and—"

"And you wanted to invite me to the quilting bee? Don't bother. Your time would be better spent considering *real* academic research instead of playing dress-up at historic sites."

That jab punched one of Chloe's hot buttons really hard. She hated it when academics dissed the good work done at historic sites. She clenched her teeth, trying not to explode.

Jayne pushed her chair back, stood, and marched away.

I stand corrected, Chloe silently told Jayne's back. You are, indeed, a bitch.

And what was up with the reference to quilting bees? Had Jayne simply dredged up a vaguely historical put-down after noticing Chloe sewing earlier? Or did Jayne actually have some interest in quilts? She had been spotted talking to Kim Dexheimer. For all kinds of reasons, Chloe did not want to conclude that Jayne was a fellow quilter. She tried to put that notion aside.

As she finished her wine, she picked up the penny Jayne had left on the table. It was old. Really old—an Indian Head penny. Chloe shook her head. Only Jayne would have an antique coin to flip.

Chloe left the bar and stood on the sidewalk, considering. She was on her own in De Smet. She had maps. She had the car keys. And she was starved for solitude.

There were several places she wanted to visit. Two miles north of town, a sign along the highway marked the plot where Laura and Almanzo had tried to make a go of farming. *I'm sorry you had it so hard,* Chloe told the young couple silently. Laura Land had been a happier place before she discovered how many times Laura's heart had broken.

Chloe drove next to the De Smet Cemetery, a peaceful place on a hilltop between the town, a remnant slough, and farmland. It didn't take long to find the graves of Ma and Pa, Mary, Carrie, and Grace. Then—"*Oh.*" She stopped in front of a low stone that said simply *Baby son of A.J. Wilder.*

"Why?" she demanded softly. Why just note the father? Why was Laura's name left off the stone? The omission was exasperating, perplexing, and terribly sad. Even sadder was the fact that Laura and Almanzo had evidently not named their son.

But perhaps Laura named him in her heart. *Like I did when I miscarried,* Chloe thought. In the midst of shock and confusion, while her ex had been speaking to the medical people in *Suisse-Deutsch,* Chloe had felt an overpowering need to name the child who never came to be.

River. The word came, and it felt right. She loved rivers—loved paddling them, loved the stories they carved through rocks and mountains. When giving programs or training interpreters, she often asked people to create a simile comparing "history" to something else; the most common response was "History is like a river." She liked the connotations of timelessness and travel for her lost baby. She had wanted to think that her loss was, for the soul that might have become her child, only one brief stop on a long journey.

Chloe wiped her eyes. Moments like this made her feel farther than ever from understanding Laura. Which was sort of like looking for Kari. Sort of like trying to figure out what she, Ingrid Chloe Ellefson, wanted from her favorite author, from life in general, and from her relationship with Officer Roelke McKenna in particular. Impossible and essential.

From the cemetery she drove southwest to the general area where historians believed Laura had taught school and stayed with the Brewster family. Chloe had learned that Mrs. Brewster—she of bitter temperament and knife-brandishing fame—had actually been Mrs. *Bouchie*. I'm sorry you had such a rough time, she told Mrs. Bouchie silently, staring at a herd of beef cattle grazing on what just might possibly have once been the Bouchie homestead claim. I'm sorry you didn't have good doctors and antidepressants in your day. I get it.

After the last two stops, Chloe needed something more uplifting, so she skirted De Smet again and found the narrow dirt lane between Lakes Henry and Thompson where Almanzo had taken Laura for buggy rides. It was peaceful there, and quite easy to picture two shy people getting to know each other.

Finally she drove to the Ingalls family homestead memorial site just southeast of town, and was relieved to find no other parked vehicles, no sign of other visitors. She got out and leaned against the car, gazing at the gently rolling land, imagining the endless, treeless prairie that Laura's family had known. She could almost see grasses and wildflowers rippling toward the horizon.

She'd read the scene in *By the Shores of Silver Lake* where Pa brought home cottonwood seedlings and planted them as a windbreak around the family's claim shanty. The shanty was long gone, but five gloriously huge trees remained. A sign by the dirt road explained how the landowning family had donated an acre of land—what had been one corner of Pa's 160-acre homestead claim—to the Memorial Society. She wandered a well-worn path into the small grove. At the first tree she placed one palm against the bark, exploring its deep ridges. The afternoon was still, the endless sky was blue, and she was touching a living thing that stretched its roots all the way back to the Ingalls family's stay in this very place.

It should have been a special moment.

But as Chloe opened her senses, something made the fine hairs along her arms prickle away from the skin. She saw nothing, heard nothing. Still... *something* was wrong.

Slowly, she stepped away from the tree. The path led through the grove and on to a small monument on a rise. Chloe passed another tree. She caught a whiff of something unpleasant before a prairie breeze snatched it away.

Just beyond the next cottonwood, something motionless and dark lay crumpled among tall grasses.

Chloe crept closer. Shards of imagery presented themselves like pieces of a mosaic. A high-heeled shoe. A navy blue skirt. A chignon of brown hair. And the handle of a large knife.

Jayne Rifenberg lay sprawled on the earth, facedown. Jayne Rifenberg had been stabbed in the back.

Laura felt a warmth inside her. It was very small, but it was strong. It was steady, like a tiny light in the dark, and it burned very low but no winds could make it flicker because it would not give up.

The Long Winter

SEVENTEEN

DETECTIVE FRANK MCARDLE OF Kingsbury County was a stocky man. He wore a wrinkled fog-colored suit and an inscrutable expression. "Miss Ellefson, let's go over it again."

Chloe rubbed her eyes. She and the detective were seated at a table in one of the church's Sunday school rooms. Student artwork covered the walls. Chloe's knowledge of Genesis was fuzzy (except for the "God created heaven and earth and it was good" part, which she liked a lot), but it looked as if the destruction of Sodom and Gomorrah had been a recent topic. The kids had gotten into the flames-raining-from-the-sky thing, creating fiery landscapes with orange and yellow crayons. Most of the pictures also included a pale lump. If memory served, Lot's wife turned to a pillar of salt because she looked over her shoulder when she should have been high-tailing it out of town.

She *looked*, Chloe thought, and a wholly inappropriate bubble of laughter rose inside. It wasn't funny, not at all, but she sure wished that *she* hadn't looked at—

"Miss Ellefson?"

"Sorry." She tugged at the blue blanket one of the EMTs who'd arrived at the grove earlier had tucked shawl-like around her shoulders. An image of Linus van Pelt of Snoopy fame popped into her head. Well, that's okay, she thought. Linus may have needed a security blanket, but he was very smart. Quite the philosopher, really. He quoted Gospel in the Charlie Brown Christmas special, and—

Detective McArdle cleared his throat. "Miss Ellefson?"

"*Sorry.*" Chloe took a deep breath and walked Detective McArdle through the events one more time: She'd arrived at the homestead memorial site, she'd paused by the first tree, she'd discovered Jayne's body. "When I couldn't find a pulse I drove out to the highway, waved down a car, and begged the driver to go call for help."

Soon waves of responders had raced to the scene in billowing clouds of dust: volunteers from De Smet's Rescue Unit, the deputy sheriff who secured the cottonwood grove, and crime scene guys. Chloe had watched, as instructed, from the Rambler. Eventually an earnest young deputy had followed her back to the church, where all the *Looking For Laura* attendees were being interviewed.

"And that's all I know," Chloe concluded. "Has anyone found my sister?" It was hard to focus with Kari unaccounted for.

"I'll see." Detective McArdle left the room. One of his shoes squeaked, and Chloe bit her tongue against another impulse to laugh. Shock, her brain informed her. She clutched her blanket-shawl more closely around her shoulders.

A few minutes later the detective returned. "One of the officers did locate your sister."

Chloe sagged with relief. "Thank *God*. Where was she?"

"In a tavern. Fortunately for her, the bartender and a dozen patrons said she'd been there all afternoon."

"What do you mean, 'Fortunately for her'?"

"Your sister's movements this afternoon have now been accounted for," McArdle said calmly. "However, *your* whereabouts have not been corroborated. Which is why I'd like you to go over it again."

An amber warning light flickered in Chloe's brain. "You can't possibly think *I* had anything to do with—"

"I am simply gathering information. Tell me what happened again, but this time, start earlier in the day."

The light pulsed red. She reminded herself that she hadn't done anything wrong. "I was at the *Looking For Laura* symposium all morning. This afternoon we visited the Ingalls House on 3rd Street, and my sister Kari got a little . . . distressed. It's hard to explain."

"Try."

Chloe fought the urge to squirm. "Well, she learned something about Cap Garland, one of her favorite characters, that upset her."

Detective McArdle looked up from his notes. "She got upset about a fictional character?"

"Cap Garland was a real person."

He did not write that down. "Let's come at this another way. How would you characterize your relationship with Jayne Rifenberg?"

"We didn't have a relationship. I only met her a few days ago."

"And yet you clearly felt a deep antagonism toward Miss Rifenberg." The detective flipped back a few pages in his notebook. "Do you recall what you said to her while your group was in the Ingalls house?"

Chloe finally realized where he was going, what he already knew. Shit. "I called her a bitch."

"And why was that?"

"Because most of the time, she was one. Look, I was trying to calm my sister down, and I got frustrated and said something inappropriate. I regret that. But I did apologize to Jayne. Kari went off by herself. After a bit I went looking for her. I stopped by a bar called Three Pals, and found Jayne instead."

"And you spoke to Miss Rifenberg?"

Chloe's face flamed hot as Gomorrah while repeating her apology, which she figured she should start with. "It really wasn't a big thing," she concluded, looking over Detective McArdle's shoulder to a picture of Jesus. It was one of the really nice ones where Jesus looked completely understanding and forgiving.

"What happened then?"

"Nothing, really. She made a snippy comment about not caring what I thought. Then she told me, and I quote, 'Your time would be better spent considering *real* academic research instead of playing dress-up at historic sites.'"

"That must have made you angry."

This conversation was making her angry, but she tried hard not to show it. "I didn't appreciate the sentiment, but I let it go. She left, and that was that."

"And nothing else was said?"

Chloe thought back. "She'd been flipping a penny, and when I sat down she said, 'Heads or tails, who's going under?' I thought that was strange. Almost ominous don't you think?"

"Perplexing, perhaps." Detective McArdle's expression remained unfathomable. "Let's move on. What did you do then?"

"I went sightseeing."

"Alone?"

"Yes."

"I find that curious. You didn't look for your sister anymore after leaving Three Pals?"

"No, I didn't." She shrugged: *No biggie.* "We're on a weeklong road trip. Kari and I both just wanted some...downtime. I stopped at the memorial sign beside Highway 23, I went to the cemetery, and then I drove out into the country southwest out of town for about ten miles."

He looked up. "Why?"

It occurred to Chloe that it might not be wise to say that she'd wanted to pay respects to Mrs. Bouchie, depicted in prose so vividly as she threatened her husband with a butcher knife. "Laura taught school somewhere in that vicinity."

"So this school is still standing?"

"No. It wasn't really a schoolhouse. They just made do in a claim shanty. It's long gone."

"But you drove out there anyway. By yourself."

"Yes," she said, as calmly as possible under the circumstances. "Yes, I did."

"Did you talk to anyone while you were there?"

"No. But I parked by..." She tried to remember. "It was just beyond a white house with blue trim and a VW bus parked in the driveway. I was there for probably...I don't know, maybe fifteen minutes? Then I circled north to the Twin Lakes so I could see where Almanzo took Laura for buggy rides."

"And no one else can corroborate your movements."

That sounded spookily official. Chloe's mouth grew dry as cotton batting. Roelke says a lot of police work has to do with eliminating suspects, she reminded herself.

She really wished Roelke was with her.

"Miss Ellefson?"

192

But Roelke wasn't there. And I am not helpless, Chloe thought. Hazel's rhetorical "What would Laura do?" came to mind, and a tiny flame of strength flared inside. Without a doubt, Laura would square her shoulders and face whatever needed facing.

Chloe shrugged out of the blanket and met the detective's stare. "Somebody might have seen me at the cemetery, or noticed my car somewhere. I was driving Kari's car, a blue 1969 American Motors Rambler." She dictated the plate number.

"How would you characterize your mood?"

"My mood?"

"Your emotional state."

"My emotional state was fine."

"Are you sure?"

"Yes, I'm sure. Other than thinking about how Laura Ingalls Wilder had some extremely hard times. I saw her baby's grave. That made me sad."

Detective McArdle looked at his notebook. "Jayne Rifenberg presented at this symposium in town."

"Yes."

"And you did as well."

"Yes."

"Is it fair to say that a professional rivalry existed between the two of you?"

"No. I'm a truther, but I'm not a—"

"You're a what?"

"I'm a professional historian. But I'm not a Wilder scholar. I didn't like Ms. Rifenberg, and I thought her thesis was bogus, but it had nothing to do with me."

"And what was her thesis?"

"That Laura Ingalls Wilder didn't write the Little House books."

"And for that reason alone you disliked Miss Rifenberg?" Detective McArdle looked confused.

He obviously did not have daughters. "No," Chloe said. "I disliked Miss Rifenberg because she was unkind. She took pleasure in speaking ill of a writer many people admire. She was patronizing. She could be mean. Once she called Hazel Voss, who is a really sweet lady, a bonnethead. Although actually, I think some people consider that a badge of honor."

He closed his notebook. "Thank you for your candor, Miss Ellefson."

His assumed use of "Miss" was getting on her nerves. "Actually, it's *Ms.* Ellefson. Is it okay if I go back to the motel?"

"You may go. I may have more questions for you later."

"We're supposed to drive to Kansas tomorrow."

He hesitated. "I'll be back here by eight a.m. tomorrow. Check in with me then, and be prepared to provide your itinerary and contact information."

Chloe left the Sunday school room and almost collided with Kari, who was pacing outside. Kari pulled Chloe into a hug. "When I heard that some maniac..."

"I was the one who found her," Chloe quavered. "And I didn't know where *you* were."

After a final squeeze, they stepped apart. Chloe reached into her pocket for the car keys. "I'll drive." She hated being afraid to walk the two blocks back to the motel, but she was; and she could smell alcohol on Kari's breath. She had no wish to add a DUI to their list of troubles.

They passed Alta and Hazel. Hazel was subdued; Alta looked white-faced and stricken. This will be lousy publicity for the *Looking For Laura* symposium and the Laura Land Tours, Chloe thought. "Do you have to stay?" she asked.

"They're through with us," Alta said. "But I want to wait here until the last symposium participant has been released. Everyone's upset."

Hazel had put a protective arm over Alta's shoulders. "I'll make sure she's okay," she murmured. "And everybody else too. You girls go get some rest."

As they walked to the car Kari admitted, "There's more to Hazel than I would have guessed."

"Yes, there is."

They made the short drive to the motel in silence. Once in their room, they sank onto their beds. "God, what a day." Kari blew out a long breath. "Let's just go to sleep."

Sleep sounded blissful, but Chloe shook her head. "Hold on. You still haven't told me what happened in Pa's House."

"Oh. Right." Kari hung her head for a moment. "It's so stupid. I read that Cap Garland—the real one—was only twenty-six when he died in a threshing accident. The steam engine's boiler exploded, and he was badly scalded. It was a horrible way to die."

Chloe winced. "That's ghastly. But . . . "

"I know. It happened a long time ago." Kari got up and tried to open her suitcase. One of the zippers jammed. "I always wanted to marry Cap Garland. When we were kids, I mean."

"For real?"

"For real in Laura Land, anyway." Kari yanked on the zipper. "When we played Little House, it was so unfair."

"*What* was?" Chloe was starting to wish she'd saved this conversation for later after all.

"You were Laura, and I was Mary. Well, Laura grew up and married handsome Almanzo and got to ride behind his beautiful team of horses. Mary went blind, and didn't get to teach like she wanted, and died single." With a final tug Kari wrenched the zipper free.

195

"We were just playing," Chloe tried.

"I guess I never got over my crush on Cap." Kari reached for her nightgown. "I'm sorry I embarrassed you." She disappeared into the bathroom.

Chloe crooked one elbow over her eyes. The conversation felt unfinished, but she was too fried to wade back into that water again right now. At least she and Kari were talking again.

Right now, she wanted to rest. She wanted to forget the look of the knife she'd seen protruding from Jayne Rifenberg's back. She wanted to go to sleep in Roelke's arms.

Roelke. "Damn," she moaned, and heaved herself to her feet. Last winter, after a difficult week spent apart, she and Roelke had agreed that they would communicate when big things happened. Finding a body definitely qualified as "big" in Roelke's book.

The booth outside the motel office was well-lit and empty, thank God. Chloe tried Roelke's home number—no luck. No one answered the EPD phone either. She hung up before the call kicked over to the sheriff's department. This bought her some time to figure out how to tell Roelke what had happened without prompting him to rent a plane and fly to the scene or something. Hey, it had happened before.

As she scooped up her change, she noticed Jayne's antique penny again. She turned it over. The mint date was noted on the front: 1870. On the back, a wreath surrounded the words *One Cent*. It's so odd, Chloe thought. Did 'Who's going under' have some dark meaning she hadn't grasped?

When she let herself into the room, Kari was on the phone. "Remember, Mommy loves you very much. Good night, sweetie." She hung up.

"Did you tell them what happened?" Chloe asked, "them" being a vague term that might or might not include Trygve.

"God, no. Trygve doesn't usually read much beyond the farm reports, so I'm hoping word of a murder in South Dakota won't blip on his meter." She reached for a whiskey bottle that had appeared from somewhere, and then a clean glass. "You want a shot?"

Whiskey is not what I need right now, Chloe thought.

Then it occurred to her that tonight, perhaps a stiff belt was *exactly* what she needed.

———

The next morning, promptly at eight, Chloe presented herself back at the impromptu command center. Detective McArdle's suit was more wrinkled than ever, but he wore a clean shirt and looked wide awake. "Thanks for checking in again, Ms. Ellefson," he said cordially. "Have you thought of anything else that happened yesterday? No detail is too small."

Chloe hesitated. Despite Kari's whiskey, she'd been awake since the wee hours, trying to decide how to answer that question. "Well, there are a couple of things."

Detective McArdle picked up his notebook and pencil.

"Remember I told you about that penny Jayne was flipping? It's an Indian Head penny, minted in 1870." She produced the penny and placed it on the table. "In *Little House on the Prairie*, Laura and her sister Mary each received a new penny for Christmas. That would have been about 1870."

Detective McArdle's expression suggested that she'd just disproved his theory; that there were indeed details too small for consideration. "I'm missing the significance."

"Well, I don't know if there *is* any significance. She also said, 'Heads or tails, who's going under?'"

"Is *that* significant?"

"I have no idea. The thing is, I've seen or heard about a number of damaged artifacts or reproductions turning up at the homesites lately." She told him about the doll, the shepherdess, the *DIE LAURA DIE* scrawl, the broken bread plate.

"Is there anything else?"

"Yes," Chloe said, determined to push on regardless. "When Laura taught school near here she boarded with a local family. One night she saw the wife threaten her husband with a knife."

"Are you suggesting that a children's book has something to do with Jayne Rifenberg's murder?"

"It's an odd coincidence. You can make of it whatever you wish. So . . . is it okay if my sister and I travel?"

"You are in luck," Detective McArdle told her. "A woman who lives in that house with the blue trim you mentioned did see your car pulled over."

The air suddenly seemed thinner, easier to process through her lungs. "So I'm off the hook?"

He actually smiled. "Let's just say that you're cleared for travel."

Chloe walked with a slightly lighter step when she left the detective. She would forever be known in LIW circles as the woman who called Jayne Rifenberg a bitch hours before she was stabbed to death. But it could have been worse.

She stopped back at the gas station phone booth and called Roelke's home number. He answered on the second ring, sounding wide awake despite his late shift.

"Hey," she began. "Listen, I'm sorry our last conversation went the way it did. You just surprised me with the living together thing, that's all."

"I got that."

She paused, giving him room to say more, but he didn't seem inclined. "So," she said finally, "I do sorta have something else I need to talk to you about."

"Oh?" He sounded wary.

She told him about finding Jayne Rifenberg's body in the cottonwood grove, and about her conversations with law enforcement officials. "I did try to call you last night," she added, wanting full credit for that.

He didn't respond right away. Finally he said, "Are you coming home?"

She knew he was quivering to *tell* her to come home, and his question made her want to. "I really appreciate you asking," she said, "but I don't want to cut the trip short. The detective said that continuing the trip would be fine. There's also a quilt I really want to see in Missouri—"

"You stumbled over a body yesterday, and you still want to drive all the way to Missouri to see a quilt?"

"Yes, I do. With a stop in Kansas on the way."

After a longer pause Roelke tried again. "Let me get this straight. You found the body of a friend yesterday, but—"

"I wouldn't call her a friend." Chloe suddenly wondered about the law enforcement grapevine. Might Roelke hang up with her, call some buddy in South Dakota, and get the full scoop? "In fact... I once called her a bitch."

Roelke groaned. "Did anyone hear you call her a bitch?"

"It's possible," Chloe admitted, picturing the ring of avid onlookers crammed into the kitchen. "Anyway, my custody of Miss Lila's quilt will legally end next week, and if I don't compare her quilt with the one in Missouri now, I'll never have another chance."

"Can't you just do it with photographs?"

"No. If there's a fabric match, we'll move on to study the stitching. And Roelke...there's a chance—just a teensy chance—that Laura's childhood quilt *did* survive. If Miss Lila actually ended up with it...I can't even tell you how much that would mean."

Another silence. She pictured him standing with eyes closed, one knuckle pressed to his forehead. Then he said, "I don't like this."

"I know. I'm sorry. Listen, did you have a chance to call the Pepin or Stoughton PDs?"

"I did, but I have no new information. Mrs. Gillespie's killer is still at large. Your quilt guy's death has been ruled accidental, death due to allergic reaction."

"Thanks for checking."

"Please call me a lot, okay? Really. A *lot*."

"I promise," she said. "I love you, Officer McKenna."

"I love you too," he said, and she pretended she didn't hear his accompanying heavy sigh.

Chloe met Kari in a booth at the Oxbow Restaurant, a diner with historical photos, antique farming tools, and ribbon-embellished hay twists hanging on the wall. Kari was cradling a heavy mug of coffee. She looked hungover.

"I'm cleared for travel." Chloe slid into the booth. "And Edna Jo told me yesterday that the Nine Patch quilt Mary made as a child is on display in Mansfield."

"Really?"

"It's our best—and last—chance to look for any fabric scraps that might match a patch or two in Miss Lila's quilt. My last chance to honor Miss Lila's final request."

Kari opened a tiny creamer and dumped the contents into a steaming mug of coffee. "Do you feel safe? After what happened to Jayne?"

"The Kansas homesite is a nine-hour drive from here, and Missouri three hours beyond that. All that distance is reassuring."

The waitress arrived, topped Kari's mug, filled Chloe's, and waited expectantly. Chloe ordered juice and scrambled eggs; Kari winced and asked for toast.

"So," Chloe continued once the waitress had disappeared. "On to Kansas?"

"If you're game, I am too." Kari raised her mug. "On to Kansas."

It was time to prove up and he could not.   The First Four Years

The yellow jackets lived in a nest in the ground and Charley stepped on it by mistake. Then all the little bees in their bright yellow jackets came swarming out with their red-hot stings, and they hurt Charley so that he couldn't get away.   Little House in the Big Woods

EIGHTEEN

WHILE KARI WENT TO clear the room, Chloe paid the bill. The clerk handed her a receipt and a curling sheet of shiny fax paper. Mom had provided information about the relevant branches of Miss Lila's family tree, from Cousin Inez, Inez's husband, and back to the Quiner girls—Ma and her sisters.

Now I won't sound like a curatorial rube, Chloe thought. She called her mother from the payphone outside. "That was just what I needed, Mom."

"Thank goodness Lila loaned that quilt to you when she did," Mom said. "She spoke of donating this or that to various historical societies, but I don't know if she formalized anything else before she died."

Kari emerged from the room with suitcases in hand. Chloe held up two fingers: *Be there in two minutes.* "Did Cousin Inez pass anything else on to Miss Lila?"

"Definitely no other quilts," Mom said. "I remember a carton with bits and pieces—incomplete sewing projects, some doilies, a few pillowcases with lace trim. Nothing that looked particularly old or valuable."

"Thanks, Mom," Chloe said, "I appreciate it."

After hanging up Chloe caught Kari's eye and did the *Two more minutes thing* again. Then she stacked up all the change she had left and called Nika Austin, her part-time intern. Nika had a BA in History from Marquette, a Masters in Museum Administration from Eastern Illinois University, and field experience at both traditional museums and living history sites. She'd started work on a Ph.D., somehow managing coursework in women's studies while *still* giving Old World a few hours a week.

"So," Nika said. "You need a favor?"

Chloe winced. "Am I that predictable?"

"I don't mind. It's become a challenge."

"You haven't been stumped yet," Chloe said. "And I do need a favor. One of the symposium speakers said something rather cryptic to me yesterday, and she...um...died suddenly a couple of hours later. Might you have time to see if Jayne Rifenberg shows up in any academic journals?" She spelled the name.

"Sure. I'm going to be at the Society tomorrow anyway." The State Historical Society of Wisconsin's collection was one of the top in the nation, backed up by the rich resources at the specialized University of Wisconsin libraries nearby.

"*Thank* you. And since Miss Lila's quilt is on loan to Old World, this is actually work-related. Do it on state time."

"I will. But I won't mention it to Petty."

"Wise," Chloe agreed. She'd learned not to volunteer information to Director Ralph Petty. It always ended badly. "How are things at the site?"

"You know how busy things are with school groups right now?"

May was peak season for student visits. "Crazy-busy."

"Well, Petty brought some big donors on a personal tour and told interpreters that the kids would have to wait outside. When the German lead tried to talk to Petty he shooed her away like, and I quote, 'a rabid chicken.' It wasn't pretty."

Chloe sighed. It was offensive to show up without warning and tell interpreters that wealthy donors had priority over the children. Also, with hundreds of kids on the site, tours were scheduled *very* carefully. A few delays could cause a cascading failure. "Another Petty atrocity," she muttered. She glanced toward the car. Kari was leaning against the Rambler, arms folded, looking impatient. "I gotta go. Thanks, Nika. I'll talk to you soon."

———

Kari was at the wheel as they left De Smet. "I finally know how to picture this place," she said. "And I enjoyed the symposium. If it hadn't been for what happened to Jayne..."

"It would have been a wonderful visit." Chloe tactfully refrained from mentioning Cap Garland. "I hope the cops find Jayne's killer fast. It must have been someone she knew, don't you think? She let someone get close to her in an isolated place."

Kari grimaced. "Did it look like there had been a struggle?"

"Not that I noticed. But I was trying hard not to throw up."

"Do you think the killer actually attended *Looking For Laura*?" Kari shuddered. "Everyone was so nice."

Chloe watched a red-tailed hawk flying parallel with the road. "Everyone except Jayne."

"Chloe!"

"I'm sorry, but she was a very troubled woman." Chloe nibbled her lower lip. "I can see why Jayne came to the symposium. Some people just crave attention, and negative attention will do."

"People were pretty upset by her claims," Kari said. "They didn't attend the symposium to get whacked in the face with 'The Lie Of Authorship.'"

"Is it possible that someone who loves Laura got so torqued that they…?"

"No."

"Some people really, really bond with Laura. Or at least with the fictionalized Laura." Hazel had. Hell, Chloe thought, Kari and I have too.

"Absolutely not," Kari insisted. "Henrietta Beauchamps might have fantasized about poking Jayne with a crochet hook, but otherwise—no."

That was pretty much what Chloe had concluded too. "What I don't get is why Jayne was doing the whole homesite tour." She pictured Jayne crossing the picnic grove in Pepin, mincing about in the rain at Burr Oak, heading up the trail to the Walnut Grove dugout site.

"I don't get that either," Kari said. "Is this our exit?"

Chloe checked the directions she'd taped to the dashboard. "Yes." She waited until Kari had merged onto the new road before asking, "Was Jayne ever near our car when the trunk was open?"

"I don't *think* so," Kari said slowly. "But I couldn't swear to it."

"Something kinda weird happened yesterday afternoon." Chloe told her sister that Jayne had mentioned quilting bees in the bar. "It's probably nothing, but hearing Jayne use a quilting term was disconcerting. Maybe someone besides you, me, and the sites people is lusting after Laura's quilt."

Kari's face paled beneath her freckles.

"Watch the road," Chloe said mildly, wishing she hadn't shared that little theory. Between marital troubles and Jayne's murder, Kari was upset already. Besides, after all the angst back in De Smet, she and Kari were getting along okay today. She didn't want to spoil that.

Chloe opened their copy of *Little House on the Prairie*. "Forget about it. We're on our way to see the last site Laura wrote about." She thumbed through the first couple of pages. "Chapter One..."

They stopped an hour or so later for gas. "Tryg likes me to keep it above half," Kari said. "He's afraid I'll get stranded somewhere."

"No problem. I need to make a phone call anyway."

Chloe tried Roelke's apartment while Kari pumped the gas. She wanted to make good on her promise to call frequently. And honestly, she wouldn't mind hearing his voice more often. No luck, though, even though she knew he was working second shift today.

She squeegeed the Rambler's windows while Kari paid, and they got back on the road. "Were you trying to catch Roelke?" Kari asked. She pulled out her quilting. "Is he still thinking about buying the farm property?"

"Yes. And he asked me to move in with him."

"Oh!"

"What?"

"It's not my business."

"*What?*"

"Well, if you're going to try living together, wouldn't it be better to start in a neutral place?"

"A neutral place?"

"A place with no meaning for either of you." Kari snipped a length of thread. "If Roelke buys that farm and you move in, you will forever be living in *his* place, full of his heritage and memories. It's not easy."

Kari lived on the Anderson farm, home to Trygve's family since the 1860s. So she would know, Chloe thought.

She stifled a sigh. She was really beginning to hope that Roelke did *not* buy his grandparents' farm.

———

Roelke pulled over on Roelke Lane. "Thanks for coming with," he told Libby.

"I could tell that something was up."

"The bank approved me for a loan. But … it's a hell of a lot of money."

Libby stared pensively at their grandparents' farm. "Just because you *can* take the loan doesn't mean you *should* take the loan. Look, I get that the farmhouse is calling to you. But buying it and then living in misery because you have to pinch every penny for the rest of your life isn't the way to go."

"I know."

"Have you talked to Patrick about it?"

"Why should I talk to Patrick?" Roelke had seen his brother twice in the past four months, which was twice more than he'd seen him in a bunch of years before that. Progress.

"Because it's a family thing?"

"*You're* my family. You and the kids and Chloe." Roelke got out, slammed the door, and walked through the dandelions to the front porch. Libby followed. He sat down on the top step.

Libby cupped her hands against one of the parlor windows, trying to peer inside. "So. What are you thinking?"

"My old sergeant at the MPD thinks I should come back to Milwaukee." Roelke tugged a mullein plant from the soil. "Other than one touchy call, it's been the most boring week of my career. It's like the universe is trying to tell me something."

"You're missing the excitement?" She sat down beside him, wiping her hands on her jeans.

"I didn't think I was until all this came up." He began shredding the fuzzy leaves. "I'm not an adrenaline junkie—"

"This from the man who jumps out of planes for fun," Libby said dryly.

"For *fun*. On my days off. I didn't think I needed it at work too. But this week... Holy toboggans, it's been bad." Roelke gestured widely to encompass the farm and, eight miles or so distant, Eagle. "I swear, Libby, I have thought and thought and *thought* and it's all just so damn big and complicated I can't figure out what I'm supposed to do."

"It's not what you're *supposed* to do—"

"I don't mean that like obligation. I mean figuring out what I'm supposed to be doing with my life."

"So stop thinking."

He shot her an irritated frown.

"I'm serious," she insisted. "You've gathered information. You've thought it over. So, close your eyes, and in the next three seconds say what your gut feeling is about buying this place."

Roelke closed his eyes. He pressed one palm against the worn boards, and planted his boots, and thought about everyone in his family who'd hurried or trudged, walked or leapt up those steps. "I want to buy this place," he said, and knew with absolute conviction he was speaking truth. "I want a home. I want *this* home."

Libby pressed her shoulder against his. A blue jay called shrilly from one of the cedar trees at the edge of the yard.

A heaviness balled within Roelke's rib cage. He sat with it for a moment, feeling its shape, its weight. He wanted to buy the farm. But he could not.

"The thing is," he said, "the money stuff is too tight for comfort. I don't want to live in dread that I can't make a payment. I don't want to have to stop and analyze whether I should take Chloe out for dinner when I want to."

An odd, muffled sound squeezed from Libby's throat. It took Roelke a moment to figure out that she was trying not to cry. She pulled a tissue from her pocket. "Okay," she said finally.

"Okay."

They sat for a while longer. Roelke inhaled the scent of his family farm, and his memories, all sunshine and dust. The heaviness seeped from his chest, leaving a palpable emptiness.

"When is Chloe coming back?" Libby asked.

"A few days yet." He looked at his watch. "Right about now, Chloe and Kari should be rolling into Nebraska." He hoped they were making good time. And he hoped to God that they'd left all the trouble behind them.

But he'd been hanging around with Chloe long enough to know that trouble had a way of finding her.

———

"A whole day with no crises," Chloe said that evening as she and Kari checked into a motel room in Independence, Kansas, twelve miles north of the Little House on the Prairie Museum. "No runaway busses, no fire alarms, no ambulances." She didn't state the obvious: no deaths. They hadn't seen the Laura Land Tour bus all day, and Chloe didn't know whether to be grateful for the break or worried about Alta and Hazel. Most likely they'd turn up tomorrow at the homesite.

"I'm going to hit the pool," Kari said. "Want to come?"

"No thanks." After being cooped up in the car all day, Chloe figured they both could use some space.

After Kari left, Chloe pulled out her quilting. She'd finished several Nine Patch blocks, and now she arranged them on the bed, quite pleased. Her impulsive purchase of fabric was turning into a surprisingly lovely quilt.

From nowhere, Jayne's voice mocked in memory: *Heads or tails, who's going under?*

Shut—up! Chloe thought. I don't know what that even means!

She tried to go back to quilting, but now the whole Jayne situation nagged at her. Finally she fetched the notebook where she'd listed the trip's troubles:

- *Pepin—man dies of anaphylactic shock, door to museum left unlocked, someone maybe looking in Kari's car window that night, impaled Charlotte doll*

- *Burr Oak—fire at the Black Crow tavern, broken china shepherdess*

- *Walnut Grove—stuck gas pedal, Garth Williams illustration labeled "Die Laura Die"*

She made two grim updates:

- *Pepin—Kim Dexheimer, quilt historian, died from peanut allergy*

- *De Smet—broken wheat sheaf bread plate,*
  Jayne Rifenberg stabbed to death

Some bad stuff here, with Jayne's murder at the top of the list. It still bothered Chloe that Jayne had been *stabbed*. As she stared at her list, her heart began to flutter like a trapped moth.

She grabbed *By the Banks of Plum Creek* and scrabbled through the pages. And there it was. In Chapter 11, Ma and little Carrie had almost been killed when the oxen pulling their wagon ran away.

Since Laura hadn't written about Burr Oak, Chloe didn't know what to make of the fire...

No, wait. Laura *did* write about Burr Oak.

Chloe upended her tote bag over the bed. She snatched the sealed envelope she'd been given by Marianne Schiller, museum director in Burr Oak, and tore it open. Inside were eleven photocopied pages from *Pioneer Girl*, the unpublished autobiography Laura had written before beginning the Little House books. She skimmed them quickly, and that fluttery sensation got worse. *"Often we heard drunken shouting and singing there, and one night the saloon caught fire."*

Chloe turned to a clean page in her notebook and started a new chart.

- *Pepin: Kim Dexheimer dies of peanut allergy*

- *Burr Oak: Fire at Black Crow tavern next*
  to Masters' Hotel site, tavern fire in <u>Pioneer Girl</u>

- *Walnut Grove: Runaway minibus,*
  runaway wagon in <u>Banks of Plum Creek</u>

- *De Smet: Jayne Rifenberg stabbed with a knife,*
  Mrs. Bouchie threatened husband with knife
  in <u>These Happy Golden Years</u>

Chloe massaged her temples. Was she wading in the whacko pool? She'd left off the unlocked door and the person looking into Kari's car in Pepin, since both might have been coincidences. And for the moment she ignored the creepy artifact stuff. Still, that left two deaths and two dangerous incidents. And three of the four reflected something that had happened in one of the Little House books.

That left poor Kim Dexheimer's death in the Pepin Wayside. That must truly have been an accident, she thought. She knew *Little House in the Big Woods* well, and no one had died of a peanut allergy. Still, in frustration she got the book and thumbed through, trying to see if she'd forgotten some obscure reference to food poisoning or something.

She had not. The worst thing that happened in Big Woods was the time that Laura's naughty cousin Charley had been stung by hundreds of bees, and—

"*Shit*," she whispered. It was oblique to be sure. Charley had survived. But if the stings *had* killed Charley, he would have died of anaphylactic shock … just as Kimball Dexheimer had.

A key rattled in the door and Kari came in, flip-flops slapping, hair dripping, a beach towel wrapped over her bathing suit. Her cheeks were rosy. She looked better than she had in days. "Hey," she said, surveying the mess strewn over Chloe's bed. "You've been busy."

"Just trying to get organized," Chloe mumbled.

The phone rang. Kari grabbed the receiver. "Hello? … What's wrong, sweetie? … Oh, I see. How about if I go over the multiplication tables with you? … Of course I can. What's five times three?"

I won't tell her yet, Chloe decided, closing the notebook. Or Roelke either. She really needed to think things through before sharing her new theory with anyone. Detective McArdle had scoffed at the notion that Jayne's death could be related to a children's book written fifty years ago. She was probably wrong, all wrong.

But if she was right, some truly twisted person was shadowing her, Kari, and Alta's group on the Laura Ingalls Wilder homesite tour.

Pa hung a quilt over the door hole. The quilt was better than no door.

Little House on the Prairie

Right in Laura's ear a wolf howled. She scringed away from the wall. The wolf was on the other side of it. Laura was too scared to make a sound. The cold was not in her backbone only, it was all through her. Mary pulled the quilt over her head. Jack growled and showed his teeth at the quilt in the doorway.

Little House on the Prairie

NINETEEN

CHLOE *thought* SHE WAS okay with the idea of visiting the Little House on the Prairie Museum outside Independence, Kansas. When she and Kari got royally lost on the way to the rural site the next morning, she did wonder if the universe was sending her a message. But Kari persevered with map and directions. They finally found 3000 Road and pulled over in front of the replica Ingalls cabin, and a schoolhouse and post office that had been moved to the site.

After shutting off the engine, Chloe didn't move. "Are you sure you want to see the place?"

"Are you out of your mind? We drove almost six hundred miles to get here."

"I know! I know."

"When the Ingalls family left Wisconsin and the Big Woods, they came right *here*," Kari added.

"It's just that … *Little House on the Prairie* is my least favorite book."

"At least Nellie Oleson isn't in it. She was so mean I hated even reading about her. I remember being really upset when she showed up in the South Dakota books."

"I'd rather read about Nellie Oleson than the Ingalls family building a cabin on Osage land," Chloe said. "I know they were a product of their time, but all that stereotypical stuff about Indian people makes me uncomfortable."

"Isn't someone expecting you to show up with the quilt?"

"Yes, but—"

Kari held out her hand for the keys. After palming them she got out and slammed the door.

"O-*kay*," Chloe muttered.

Aside from one car parked by a nearby farmhouse, which served as office and gift shop, there was no sign of humanity. Chloe took the quilt box from the trunk and they started across the lawn. "Watch out for the well," she said.

Kari stopped cold. "Where?"

"I don't know. But I read that they've identified the original well Pa dug on this land." Chloe had been up half the night, skimming back through *Little House on the Prairie* in search of any plot element that might inspire someone with malicious intent. Indian attack seemed unlikely. So did fever 'n' ague. But Pa had almost died when he went down into his well to save a friend. Chloe was determined to keep that unhappy episode from echoing into the present day.

"What is wrong with you?" Kari folded her arms.

"Just keep your eyes open, that's all I'm saying."

Lucille Unger met them with a sunny smile, and waved them through the little shop to an office. Lucille was a big-boned woman with curly, shoulder-length hair that was a lovely blend of black, gray, and white. She wore an emerald-green shirt and black jeans. Her eyes had deep lines fanning from the corners, as if she'd spent a lifetime squinting over the Kansas prairies. They crinkled even more when Chloe lifted the quilt box lid.

"Oh, that's a beauty." Lucille stared reverently. Finally she sighed and lifted her gaze. "Since you were driving to Mansfield anyway I did want to see this, but I have to tell you that as much as I'd love to acquire this quilt, you should take us off the list. We don't have adequate storage or display facilities. Maybe one day, but not now. We've only been open for six years. No one knew for sure where the Ingalls actually settled until recently."

Chloe decided that she liked Lucille a lot.

"We do have a quilt on display in the cabin," Lucille added. "If I could magically conjure two Ingalls artifacts to reflect the family's year here, I'd choose Pa's fiddle and one of Ma's quilts."

"I get the fiddle," Kari said. "The scene where Pa plays in the moonlight is one of the most hopeful in the whole series. But wouldn't Ma be best represented by her china shepherdess? She only put that out when she'd decided a new place was actually a home."

"But in my mind, at least, this place was never truly a home," Lucille admitted. "Since the family settled on Osage Reserve land, the threat of being forced from their cabin—one way or another—hangs over the whole story. According to the novel, the Ingalls family lived on this land for a year before Pa discovered that it wasn't legally open for white settlement. He likely knew all along, although he wasn't alone in ignoring that inconvenient fact. And yet, the search for a home is the most prominent theme in *Little House on the Prairie*."

Chloe didn't want to think about Pa squatting on Indian land, or the family's failure to find the home they yearned for. "Back to quilts," she said. "Other than Mary's Nine Patch, none are described or named in the Kansas book, are they?"

"No. But the quilts were much more than bedcovers. Mary pulls one over her head when she's frightened. Ma settles baby Carrie on a quilt that represents safety in the vast prairie. Most poignant is that when the family moved into the cabin, one quilt served as a door. Can you imagine how Ma felt when she heard wolves howling just outside?"

Kari shook her head with empathy. "She must have been terrified."

"No door but a quilt," Chloe murmured. It wasn't difficult to imagine the dreadful, gnawing fear that must have been Caroline Ingalls's constant companion here.

"The other scene that haunts me," Lucille said, "is the one where Charles goes down the well after his friend Mr. Scott is overcome by gas."

That damn well, Chloe thought.

"If Caroline hadn't found the strength to haul Charles up after he'd tied Mr. Scott over the bucket, both men would have died."

Chloe looked out the window to the very land where Caroline Ingalls had once walked. Chloe didn't always like the Ma who emerged on the pages of *Little House on the Prairie*. Laura painted her mother as a fussbudget who ironed clothes on the wagon seat and criticized Pa and Laura for making noise when they saw bulldog Jack—who they'd thought was lost and probably dead—creeping wearily toward their campsite. Maybe, Chloe thought, I should cut Ma some slack.

Lucille checked her watch. "Have you two seen the cabin? I've got a special group due in fifteen minutes."

"Alta Allerbee's tour?" Kari asked.

"That's right. You're welcome to join us."

"Thanks," Chloe said, but she and Kari exchanged a knowing glance. If nothing else, they wanted to get the quilt box hidden back in the car before anyone else arrived.

Once that was accomplished, they left a generous donation in the special mailbox by the road in exchange for a map of the grounds, and approached the cabin. It had been built to resemble the simple structure Laura described Pa building in *Little House on the Prairie*.

"Wait," Chloe ordered.

"What *for*?" Kari's tone was exasperated.

"Just humor me." In the book Ma had been hurt by a falling log. Chloe circled the tiny cabin, but saw nothing to suggest that a saboteur had left a log poised to crash down upon an unwary visitor. "Okay. Let's go inside."

Unlike the replica in Pepin, this cabin was furnished with a mix of antiques and reproductions to represent the general era. Perhaps even furnished a little too well, Chloe thought, imagining how few possessions the family must have had at the end of their long trip from Wisconsin's Big Woods. A repro china shepherdess stood demurely on the mantel, reminding Chloe uncomfortably of the beheaded figurine in Burr Oak.

She turned her back and regarded the quilt on the bed. "I've been so focused on Bear Track patterns that I haven't given any thought to the broader meaning of quilts in the books," she confessed. This cheerful quilt had no direct connection to the Ingalls family. But it was possible that some of the scraps used to piece Miss Lila's quilt had come from a dress Caroline Ingalls had worn during her tumultuous year in Kansas.

It didn't take long to explore the site. As she and Kari stepped from the schoolhouse, a familiar rainbow-hued minibus pulled to a stop near the split-rail fence along the road. "Alta's here," Kari said unnecessarily.

Chloe waved as the tour group disembarked and followed Alta toward the farmhouse. "Do you want to join them for Lucille's presentation? We've got plenty of time." They weren't planning to visit their final stop—Mansfield, Missouri—until the next day, and it was only a three-hour drive.

"I'd like to wander a bit. We'll be headed home in a few days, and…" Kari looked wistful. "It's so peaceful here."

Chloe was tempted to grab her sister's wrist and implore her to stay in sight. Instead she said, "See you later." Kari ambled down the road and disappeared around a bend.

It was too hot for a Wisconsin Scandihoovian, but otherwise the day was gorgeous. An azure sky, dotted with cottonball clouds, stretched endless above the flat farmland. Across the road from the cabin, a prairie rippled toward the horizon. The generous people who owned the farm were clearly working to create a sense of the landscape Laura had known. Chloe longed to walk into the prairie. She'd experienced a sense of Laura's childish joy by the banks of Plum Creek, and she might be able to find that again here.

But a more pressing need thrummed in her head, so she retreated to a picnic table with her notebook. She'd been too busy searching *Little House on the Prairie* for portents of doom last night to focus on the whys. Now, Kari's stroll had given Chloe a good opportunity to organize her thoughts.

The problem was that there were *several* problems: murder, near-misses, maimed artifacts, and the possibility that someone knew she was traveling with a Laura quilt. Chloe had no idea if they were related. She had no idea which problems might be part of a plan, accidents, or even childish pranks.

She tapped her pen against the page. *Someone* had killed Jayne Rifenberg. Who? And why?

1. Someone wanting to protect Laura Ingalls Wilder's image

Jayne's assertions at *Looking For Laura* could have enraged a devoted fan. She'd even mentioned her intent to publish "The Lie Of Authorship." It was hard to imagine even the most dedicated Lauraphile thrusting a knife between Jayne's shoulder blades, but it was too early to discard any possibilities.

Who else might have been angered by Jayne's so-called conclusions? If Jayne's intent was to discredit the beloved author, anyone with a stake in Laura Land–related commerce might have felt threatened. Collectors, dealers... How far would the price of a first-edition fall if the reading public came to believe that Laura had *not* written the Little House books?

Also, all of the sites relied on tourism. And the small towns near the homesites depended on Laura fans. Cafés, motels, gas stations... all had a financial stake.

Chloe glanced up, and her gaze settled on the Laura Land Tours bus. Geez, she thought. Talk about a business dependent on Laura tourism...

But that whole line of thought made Chloe feel squirmy, so she moved on. What else could have caused such angst within the Laura community?

2. Academic rivalry

Was someone else who'd attended *Looking For Laura* working on a biography? Or—

"Hi, Chloe," someone called. Haruka Minari had paused to wave on her way to the cabin. She'd evidently just arrived—yep, her blue VW was parked out front. Chloe lifted a friendly hand before returning to her ruminations. Had someone been competing with Jayne Rifenberg for a teaching gig or something? It was possible.

3. Jayne insulted someone who snapped

That, too, was possible. Chloe remembered Hazel's hurt look when Jayne had ridiculed her for wearing a sunbonnet. And Leonard's sullen look when Jayne had argued with him after the pageant in Walnut Grove. And Frances's irritated look when Jane besmirched her beloved television series. Chloe did not believe that Hazel Voss had gone berserk in the cottonwood grove. Chloe also doubted that Frances Whelan had attacked Jayne. Leonard Devich was more of an unknown. Bottom line: Jayne had a knack for belittling people, and she'd surely wounded or infuriated others over the past few days that Chloe hadn't happened to observe. Maybe she'd tried it on the wrong person.

4. Someone discovered that Jayne was the person behind all the problems

Chloe stared at the words, pretty confident that she'd drifted into la-la land. If someone had actually concocted a diabolical plan to cause problems ranging from mild mayhem to murder at the Laura homesites, it would have to be someone who really and truly hated Laura Ingalls Wilder. Jayne Rifenberg fit that description, but it was difficult to imagine her tinkering with a minibus or somehow starting a fire in the Burr Oak tavern.

"This is pointless," Chloe muttered. There was way too much that she didn't know about Jayne. She didn't know if Jayne was affiliated with a university or college, or if Jayne was a quilter, or *any*thing.

Haruka emerged from the cabin, wandering idly, enjoying the day. Chloe walked across the grass to join her. "Haruka? I'm sorry to bother you, but I had a quick question. Did you happen to speak to Jayne Rifenberg during the symposium? Did she happen to mention anything personal, like if she was a quilter? Or anything?"

"Well... I did talk to her once," Haruka said. "After her presentation she was getting so many scathing looks that I felt sorry for her, so I tried to strike up a conversation."

Haruka's kindness made Chloe regret her own less-than-kind impulses. "What did you say?"

"I told her I appreciated the hard work she'd put into the presentation. She said 'Hmpf,' and walked away." Haruka looked chagrined. "Needless to say, I didn't try again. Why?"

"I was just curious." Chloe tried to smile. "Thanks."

Chloe went back to her picnic table brimming with frustration. What had Jayne been up to? Was she a quilter or not? Nika was on the hunt, but Chloe wanted answers right now.

Not much I can do about it, she thought, with no handy payphones or libraries in sight. She crammed her notebook back into her tote bag. She wasn't accomplishing anything.

Besides, she *really* wanted to walk in the prairie. She had a personal quest of her own, and this was her last chance to find young Laura, her best childhood friend. Kari hadn't returned, and Alta's group was still inside the farmhouse with Lucille. Chloe walked toward the road and felt her taut nerves ease. It was *so* quiet here. Peaceful, just as Kari had said.

Then Chloe passed the LLT bus, and peace—and her resolve to forget about the problems—dissolved like a puff of smoke. There *was* a way she could learn at least a bit about Jayne Rifenberg, right here, right now.

Chloe glanced about—still no one in sight. She stepped inside the bus, dropped instinctively to a crouch, and waddled duck-like toward the back where Alta had stashed her storage tubs. The familiar neon green one was even on top.

Chloe opened the tub and pawed through its contents. Yes, *there*—the file of registration forms. Shuffling through, she found Jayne's. The address was listed as Rochester, Minnesota. The emergency contact line was blank, which was sad but not shocking.

Voices drifted through the open windows as Lucille led the group outside. "Remember, Laura was only two when the Ingalls family moved here," Lucille was saying. "Laura made herself older in the book and borrowed her parents' memories to paint such vivid pictures of the Kansas year."

One more fact to collide with my understanding of Laura's life, Chloe thought, before ordering herself to focus.

Jayne's proposal was stapled to her registration form. She'd been employed as an English Literature instructor at a private Minnesota college from 1979 to 1982. Her proposal was well written, Chloe acknowledged grudgingly, and included an impressive bibliography. Jayne's unique brand of contempt hadn't emerged on the page, and Chloe couldn't fault Alta for accepting the proposal.

"Laura faced a challenge when she began writing about what she called 'Indian Territory,'" Lucille continued. "Since *Little House in the Big Woods* ended on such a note of contentment, it's difficult to understand why the Ingallses ever left Wisconsin."

Chloe reached the proposal's last page. Jayne had not included a full curriculum vitae or any personal information. If she'd published any scholarly articles about English lit in general or Laura in particular, they weren't listed.

Chloe replaced the files in the tub and snapped the lid into place. Then she crawled up the aisle. This really is idiotic, she thought. I should just—

Thud. A foot landed on the minibus's first step.

Chloe halted midcrawl, cheeks burning. Shit!

Then came another rustle of sound, and whoever had started to board stepped back outside. Alta's voice was low and weary: "What do you want now?"

Chloe held her breath, straining to hear, but she didn't catch the response.

"No, you mustn't!" Alta hissed. "We're almost—I told you before that—*God*, you'll ruin everything!"

Déjà vu, Chloe thought. She was tired of this. It was time to see who was threatening Alta, and demand some answers.

Chloe shot to her feet and plunged down the bus steps. But instead of demanding answers, she froze. Her mouth opened, but no words emerged. Her eyes went wide. Her brain stopped functioning.

The person threatening Alta was ... Kari.

Perhaps Mary felt sweet and good inside, but Laura didn't. When she looked at Mary she wanted to slap her. So she dared not look at Mary again.
Little House on the Prairie

TWENTY

THE THREE WOMEN STARED at each other. Fear flared in Kari's eyes, and in Alta's too. Chloe struggled to comprehend the incomprehensible. The air crackled as if one of the summer storms Laura had described so eloquently was about to explode. But the sky remained inexplicably blue and serene.

Finally Chloe asked, "What is going on?"

Alta and Kari exchanged an anxious look, the apparent adversaries now collaborators.

Something inside Chloe broke like a brittle twig. She glared at her sister. "What the hell is going on?"

"Oh, God," Kari said.

"It's a long story," Alta said.

"It's complicated," Kari said.

"*Very* complicated," Alta said.

Chloe's hands curled into fists. "Alta, please go away."

Alta's face crumpled. "But Chloe, you don't ... I just ... well, *we* just—"

Chloe swiveled her glare to Alta. The older woman swallowed her words, turned, and walked away. Kari twitched as if wanting to follow, but she rooted herself.

"Kari, what is this all about?" Chloe demanded.

"A quilt square."

"A quilt square?" Chloe didn't know what she'd expected, but it wasn't that. "What quilt square?"

Kari hunched her shoulders and crossed her arms. "It was part of Miss Lila's inheritance from her cousin. Laura made it."

Chloe wondered if she'd gotten sunstroke. "Laura made it?" she echoed dumbly.

"Yes."

"There's a quilt square floating around that Laura actually *made*?"

"Yes," Kari whispered miserably.

Chloe's hand twitched with an overwhelming urge to smack her sister. She turned away, walked in a tight circle, came back. "After all I've gone through trying to verify the Bear Track quilt, after all the conversations we've had on this trip, and all along you—you—*what*? Do you have this quilt square along?"

"It's in my suitcase."

"And you never happened to mention that?" Chloe's voice was rising, but she could have stopped a prairie wind more easily than corral her anger. "What the hell, Kari?" She walked away again. Alta had trudged toward the historic buildings, so Chloe went the other way, into the empty road.

"Chloe, don't," Kari pleaded.

"Don't what? Don't get mad? Have you said one thing this entire week that wasn't a lie?"

"Of course I—if you would just listen—"

"I've spent a week taking a quilt Laura owned from site to site, and all the time you have a quilt square Laura *made* in your suitcase?" Chloe did another one of those walk away, walk back moves. "How come I never heard about this square before?"

"Stop shouting and give me a chance to explain."

Chloe remembered Mom mentioning a carton of "bits and pieces," including incomplete sewing projects, that Miss Lila had inherited from her cousin in addition to the complete Bear Track quilt. "Did you steal it from Miss Lila?"

Kari seemed to have run out of words.

"Oh my God. You *did*."

"Not entirely…"

Chloe stared at Kari, absolutely flummoxed. "Were you planning to sell the quilt square? Is that what's going on?"

"It's not a whole quilt, like what you have! It's just a square, and—"

"What the hell is *wrong* with you?"

Kari abruptly advanced, one finger stabbing the air. "Maybe if you weren't so damn sanctimonious all the time—"

"I am not sanctimonious!"

"Yes, you are!"

A station wagon came around a bend, slowed, and stopped. Chloe realized only belatedly that she and Kari were blocking the road.

Then she realized, also belatedly, that Alta's travelers and Lucille were lined up along the fence, staring as the Ellefson girls paced back and forth, yelling at each other.

Then Chloe realized that she and Kari had made clear to everyone that they were traveling with a quilt Laura had possessed. And, evidently, a quilt square stitched by Laura's very own little fingers as well.

With admirable restraint, the driver of the station wagon gestured politely: *Any chance you could get out of the road?* Kari backed toward the cabin, Chloe toward the prairie. The station wagon drove on.

Kari returned to the road. "Chloe." Her tone was pleading now. "We need to sit down and talk."

"I don't want to be with you right now."

"Please, I just—"

"I don't want to even *look* at you right now." Chloe turned her back, scrambled up the berm, and walked into the prairie.

The spring growth was waist-high at best, fescue and grama grasses, vetch and wild phlox and quinine. Chloe turned diagonally and cut toward the wooded strip bordering the prairie. Her head was buzzing like a jar of cicadas.

No wonder Alta had looked startled when I introduced myself and Kari, she thought. Since Kari used Anderson as a surname, Alta hadn't known that her speaker and her partner in crime were sisters. No wonder Kari had looked stunned when Chloe confided that she'd overheard Alta pleading with someone at the Wayside. And no wonder that Kari had withdrawn when Chloe suggested that they ask Alta outright what—and who—was troubling her.

At the prairie's edge Chloe half fell, half sat on the ground beside a sympathetic old oak tree. The day was still beautiful, the prairie still lush and green. A dragonfly shimmered among the flowers. A honeybee went about its vital work on a clump of clover. In the distance Chloe could just make out the roof of the replica cabin, still evocative.

But Kari was no longer *Kari*.

My sister is a thief, Chloe thought. And a liar too. So much for sisterly bonding.

What was she was supposed to do now? Chloe doubted she could get a cab to the airport way out here. Besides, she couldn't fly with the quilt. Maybe she could rent a car in Independence. Or maybe she *should* ask Roelke to fly down…

Then she remembered that he was wrapped up with his farm thing. And she remembered asking if he was just trying to recapture a happy time in his childhood. Damn, she thought. I *am* sanctimonious. And a freakin' hypocrite too. As he'd observed, that was exactly what she'd wanted to do on this trip. Seeing Miss Lila's quilt had triggered a yearning so strong she'd been moved to tears.

Well, it couldn't be done. Her own childhood was dead and gone. If Miss Lila's death hadn't proved that, Kari's secrets and lies made it complete.

Chloe leaned back against the oak, trying to let its power seep into her. She wasn't ready to think about Kari yet. Or some mysterious quilt square made by Laura. Or whatever was going on between Kari and Alta.

So she watched the prairie grasses and flowers, rippling ever so gently as if beckoning her to come and play. She had longed for quiet time to wander this ground, to feel the earth as it baked beneath the sun, to sniff the same kinds of flowers Laura once sniffed. Instinctively she closed her eyes and tried to empty her mind of the past half hour; tried to open herself to any lingering resonance of Laura. And for just a moment, she thought she heard a faint peal of laughter.

Then she remembered that Laura was only two years old when the family moved to Kansas—not the older child depicted in the story.

Chloe settled her elbows on her knees and her chin in her hands. Laura Land was ruined. Laura wasn't the girl Chloe had thought she was. Even Pa had let her down by bringing his wife and children here. Chloe could forgive him everything else—the moves, his restlessness— but bringing his family to this place that belonged to Indian people, people his wife feared and hated, was too harsh.

I give up, Chloe thought. She didn't even want to find Laura anymore. And if she could lose her sister too, that would be just fine.

———

After concluding that his dream of buying his grandparents' farm was out of reach, Roelke had done the only thing he could think of: he'd made some calls and booked flight time in a Piper J-3 Cub.

Now he stood on the tarmac at Morey Field in Middleton—a suburb of Madison—and studied the plane. It was forty years old and a thing of beauty: egg yolk yellow with a black lightning bolt on the side, sleek and lightweight. And it was for sale.

"The Cub is the '57 Chevy of the aviation world," said Tony Colin, the airport employee who'd walked Roelke out to the plane. "Not as fast as some, but cool. A real classic. Easy to fly and maintain. And this one's a gem." He patted the plane with affection.

"I can tell." Roelke had already looked at the logbook. More importantly, he knew Tony to be a certified—and superb—mechanic. If Tony said a plane was in excellent shape, it was.

"The owner's been leasing it to pilots who want flight time in a tail-dragger," Tony said. "If you do buy it, you could continue to lease it out." He chuckled. "You know what they say. If God had intended us to fly, he would have given us lots more money."

"So true," Roelke allowed, although honestly, after considering the price tag of a forty-acre farm, the idea of buying the plane of his dreams wasn't nearly as daunting as it used to be.

He hadn't flown in a while, and it felt good to climb into the rear seat and go through the preflight checks. Tony pulled the prop with a sharp snap and Roelke let the engine warm up until the oil pressure and temp settled in the green arc. He taxied to Runway 27 to the northwest. Before taking off he made sure the flight controls were free and correct, set the pitch trim to neutral, did a run-up to 1700 RPM, and verified that the carburetor heat was set. Finally he set power to full and left the earth, climbing at a steady 55 mph.

It was glorious. Pure joy. Roelke grinned. Piloting a plane wasn't about getting somewhere. It was about seeing the world in a whole new way.

He banked left. Chloe might like this too, he thought. Funny, he'd never considered that before. Stupid, really. He'd been all caught up in whether she wanted to live with him, but having a flying companion would be good too. He'd been in a plane with her once, and they'd gone skydiving. She'd been pissed at the time, but it turned out okay. He imagined flying with her in the front seat, imagined her turning to smile at him. It could be good.

Chloe knew he dreamed of buying an airplane … but he didn't think he'd told her how important Cubs had been during World War II. How many military pilots trained in them. He'd seen photographs of Eleanor Roosevelt posing in one to promote the Civilian Pilot Trainer Program. Chloe would be interested in stuff like that.

Although a careful and attentive pilot, Roelke had planned a route that passed several airports, just in case of trouble. He navigated over Mount Horeb, turned east to Verona, eased southeast, and passed Oregon, Stoughton, and Albion. He left the window up and the door open so he could feel the wind. Cubs were designed to go low and slow, and Wisconsin's rural landscape unfurled below like an endless patchwork quilt. Some fields were still brown; others emerald with new growth. When he flew over Lake Koshkonong, the water sparkled like diamonds. The Kettle Moraine State Forest was a fresh green swath dotted with kettle ponds, bordered by farmland.

And one of those farms had been created by the first Roelkes to arrive in Wisconsin, well over a century ago.

As he approached, Roelke didn't have any trouble identifying the family place. The house and outbuildings stood like a child's play set. He dipped lower but even then the unkempt woodwork, rampant burdock, and peeling paint didn't look so bad.

My farm, he thought sadly. He could almost see himself walking the tree line with Chloe after a long day.

Then he remembered that Chloe hadn't said she wanted to live with him.

Well, he and Libby would always share memories of this place. He remembered racing her to the springs in the creek.

Something about that last image lodged in Roelke's brain. He summoned the feel of silt between his toes as the cold water bubbled up from underground in clear pools, and the sharp calls of a hawk, and the hot muddy smell of summer. But he couldn't define why any of that was important.

Roelke sighed, made one more slow circle around the old place, and then headed back toward Morey Field. He had time to go farther, but his earlier pleasure had vanished. I'll take this plane up another day, he thought.

But next time he wouldn't be so stupid as to fly over the old homeplace.

There is no comfort anywhere for anyone who dreads to go home.
Little Town on the Prairie

"What is the matter, Laura?" Pa asked.

"Oh, I don't know!" Laura said in despair. "I am so tired of every-thing. I want—I want something to happen. I want to go West. I guess I want to just play, and I know I am too old," she almost sobbed, a thing she never did.
Little Town on the Prairie

TWENTY-ONE

CHLOE FINALLY PLODDED BACK through the prairie toward the historic site.

The only vehicle parked by the road was Kari's Rambler. The LLT bus was gone, thank God. Chloe hoped she'd never have to face anyone on the tour again. Haruka had left before the Ellefson show-down, which was good, although Chloe wished she could have begged a ride from her. But Wisconsin wasn't really on the way back to Connecticut anyway.

Kari was sitting at one of the picnic tables. Her quilting bag was on the bench beside her, but her hands were folded in her lap. She seemed smaller, somehow. Diminished. She'd often been distracted on this trip, but now she just looked sort of … empty.

Chloe sat down beside her sister. For a good five or six minutes no one spoke. Finally Kari said, "I thought you might just leave."

"I considered it. But you have the car keys." Chloe grasped her elbows. "You might as well spill it, Kari. I deserve to know what's been going on. Then you can drive me to the nearest bus station so I can buy a ticket home."

Kari pulled a rolled-up bath towel from her bag and handed it over.

Chloe slowly unfurled it on her lap. A quilt block appeared—but not the Bear Track motif she'd half expected. She didn't recognize the pattern. In the square's center, three pink diamonds were pieced between white triangles. Pieces of a pink floral print and more white triangles formed the outer motif. The fabric was much newer than what was in Miss Lila's quilt, and the raw edges had been trimmed with pinking shears.

"Laura made this?" Chloe asked skeptically. She put one ungloved finger on a pink diamond, but felt . . . nothing. No connection, no faint buzz.

Kari handed her a piece of notepaper. "This came with it."

Chloe read the note, which was addressed to Miss Lila's cousin Inez.

Thank you for your lovely note of condolence after my mother passed away. I have been going through her things, and in token remembrance of your kindness, I am sending you an unfinished bit of her needlework as a memento. Although she made many beautiful quilts, this is the only block of this pattern I've found. I never saw it until after her death, and so I do not know why she stitched it but never continued. I hope you might be pleased with it.

Sincerely yours,
Rose Wilder Lane
April 2, 1957

"This was actually written by Laura's daughter," Chloe said. It was hard to take in. She'd been searching and *searching* for some tangible link between Cousin Inez and Laura Ingalls Wilder, and here it was. Chloe didn't know if she should feel good because the link was forged or even worse because it had nothing to do with Miss Lila's quilt.

Worse, she decided. She looked at Kari. "So. You stole this from Miss Lila?"

Kari took a deep breath. "While you were living in Switzerland, Miss Lila fell and broke her hip. Mom stayed with her for a while, and sometimes I'd come help out and give Mom a break. I was there when the quilt and a box of heirlooms came from Cousin Inez. Miss Lila and I went through it together. Miss Lila talked about wanting to show you the quilt. I told her I thought the single block was pretty cool too, and she said that since I liked it, she'd make sure it would come to me one day."

"Yeah?" Chloe had no idea if she could believe anything Kari said.

"Yeah," Kari said coldly. "Look, you were off in Europe. Miss Lila was grateful for my help. I don't think it occurred to her that a single block was worth anything."

Chloe made a circular gesture with her hand. "Cut to the chase."

Kari leaned over, elbows on knees. "Last winter I reached a point where I was … desperate for money. *Desperate.* I figured the quilt square that Miss Lila had promised me, with the note from Rose, might actually be worth a lot. So one day when I was visiting Miss Lila I just … sort of … took them."

"Why didn't you ask Mom and Dad for help?" Chloe demanded. "Or me? If you need money to divorce Trygve and get an apartment for you and the girls or whatever, I would have done what I could." She felt anger steaming inside all over again. "This quilt square belongs in a museum. Why would you—"

"Because I screwed up!" Kari flared. "I screwed up, okay? Things were so bad at home, and I—I was frantic."

"Why didn't you just put the girls in the car and drive to Mom and Dad's house? Or mine? I've got room."

Kari pinched her lips in a tight line and shook her head.

Chloe was *done* with her sister's silence. "Kari, what did Trygve *do*? Is he having an affair? Whatever it is, you do not have to stay with him just because you're broke—"

"Trygve hasn't done anything."

"He hasn't … what?"

"Trygve hasn't done anything wrong." Kari stared at a small hawk soaring above the prairie. "He's a good man. He loves me. He loves the girls. He works himself to the bone to provide for us, and I've never seen him so much as glance at another woman. *I'm* the one who's screwed everything up. I'm going to lose my family, and it's my own fault."

A car parked by the fence. A couple with two young sons got out. The boys raced toward the cabin. "Don't touch anything!" the man called.

Chloe watched the family go inside, then turned back to her sister. "What are you talking about?"

"I was … drowning." Kari lifted both hands, palms up, then let them fall back into her lap. "Do you remember that scene in *Little Town on the Prairie* when Laura was so housebound and restless that she talked about needing to go west? I felt just like that."

"I see."

"I know I have everything I could ever want. And I do love Trygve. But I just felt like I was dying inside. That beautiful old farmhouse seemed like a prison. Milk the cows. Pack school lunches. Scrub toilets. Cook Sunday dinners for his parents, or our parents, or both sets of parents. Milk the damn cows again, and again, and again."

"But why are you so desperate for money?"

"For starters, I've racked up almost five hundred dollars on a credit card Tryg doesn't even know exists." Kari picked up a thin stick lying near the table and snapped off the tip.

"I could have loaned you—"

"That's not the real problem. Tryg's in a bowling league, every Thursday night. I used to be in a book group the same night. His mom stays with the girls." Kari's voice was flat. "When the book group host moved away, I decided not to mention it. The idea of a night out, just for me, sounded really good."

"What did you do?"

"I went to bars." Kari snapped off another bit of the stick. "Never in Stoughton. I'd just drive for a while, and then find some tavern and go in. I'd have a drink or two and pretend I was someone else."

Chloe struggled to wrap her brain around the fact that she clearly had absolutely no idea who her sister was.

"And one night, in a particularly seedy dive called Stagger Inn, things got a little out of hand."

"Out of hand how?"

Kari shook her head. "It doesn't matter. The bottom line is, the bartender—people actually call him Spider—he took pictures of me. And now Spider is blackmailing me."

"*Blackmailing* you?"

"Yep." Kari broke what was left of the stick in half and tossed the pieces on the ground. "If I don't pay him two thousand dollars by the end of the month, he'll send the pictures to 'important people'"—she used her fingers to make air quotes—"in Stoughton."

The ramifications of that began tumbling into Chloe's mind, one after another, faster and faster. "Oh God."

"*That's* why I took the quilt square. And why I wanted to sell it."

Chloe's brain swam with images of Kari's husband and children and extended family—all longtime bastions of Stoughton's Norwegian-American and oh-so-Lutheran community—confronted with pictures of her sister "pretending to be someone else," whatever *that* meant, plastered on page one of the Stoughton *Courier* or something.

"I sent pictures of the square to an appraisal company up in New York with a copy of Rose's note," Kari was saying. "I stressed the need for confidentiality, of course. An appraiser wrote back and said that while her response was conditional, since she hadn't actually examined the quilt block, it might be worth as much as three thousand dollars."

Chloe swallowed. Three thousand dollars was a whole lot of money. Kari's old Rambler had cost less than that *new*.

The family emerged from the cabin. "Can you imagine living here in pioneer days?" the mom was saying. The boys responded by aiming index finger pistols at imaginary threats—"Pow! Pow-pow!"—as they ran toward the gift shop.

"How did Alta get involved?" Chloe asked.

"I had no idea how to go about selling the quilt square. I needed to do it quietly, for obvious reasons. I saw a notice for Alta's symposium and figured she might know of a dealer particularly interested in Laura stuff."

"That"—Chloe gestured angrily to the quilt block still on her lap—"is hardly *stuff*. It's a precious bit of material culture. Which should be wrapped in acid-free tissue, by the way, not some ratty old towel."

"So add that to the list of my sins," Kari said wearily. "Anyway, Alta wrote back and gave me a dealer's address. I wrote to the person and got a letter back saying I needed to bring the square to the symposium."

Chloe thought of the tables set out in the church hall during the symposium, where collectors and merchants had displayed or sold their wares. "Who's the dealer?"

"I don't know. My letter was signed by 'Dealer Discreet.' Evidently the person is very protective of his or her privacy."

"Gee whiz, I wonder why. Did the letter have a return address?"

"Just a post office box number in Columbus, Ohio."

"And Dealer Discreet didn't identify himself back in De Smet?"

"Nope. No one ever contacted me." Kari made a helpless gesture. "All I can figure is that they were planning to approach me at the very end, and Jayne's murder spooked him or her off."

Which also made sense, Chloe thought sourly. While some secrecy was understandable when valuable antiques were concerned, no legitimate dealer would employ these tactics. Once Jayne was murdered and cops began crawling about and questioning everyone who'd attended the symposium, Dealer Discreet no doubt hit the highway.

Something still made no sense, though. "What were you and Alta arguing about? I heard her pleading with you before I got off the bus this morning. And I'm guessing it was you I overheard talking to her by the bus back at the Pepin Wayside?" She'd thought back through her and Kari's movements that first day. While she was soothing jangled nerves with Swiss chocolate and inserting herself into Wilbur and Hazel's unhappy exchange in the parking lot, Kari'd had plenty of time to slip over to the rainbow minibus and introduce herself to Alta.

"Yes. That was me."

"Why were you threatening Alta? Because I heard her. She was frightened." Chloe folded her arms again. The mess Kari had gotten herself into was mind-boggling. The notion that she'd somehow dragged the calico-clad, just-trying-to-help-people-learn-about-Laura librarian into it was even worse.

"I didn't threaten Alta." Kari sighed. "She got upset in Pepin because I told her I'd changed my mind and didn't want to sell the quilt square after all."

"You...changed your mind?"

"After hearing you talk about Miss Lila's quilt and having time away from home to really think about things, what I'd done..." Kari shrugged with resignation. "I couldn't do it. I just couldn't let this piece of history disappear into some blackmarket dealer's hands. I figured that after the tour I'd sneak the square back into Miss Lila's house before the lawyer or whoever goes through everything."

"Well, that's good," Chloe said grudgingly. "But why did that upset Alta? She loves all things Laura!"

"I don't know. When she protested, I even confessed that I'd taken it from an elderly friend who had died. But she didn't back off. All I can tell you is that she *begged* me to go through with the deal. Even today. She thinks the dealer is going to show up at the Wilder Heritage Festival in Missouri this weekend."

Chloe fought the urge to bang her head against the table. If Kari was telling the truth now—and Chloe thought she was—that meant sweet Alta Allerbee hadn't been dragged unwittingly into this mess. Somehow, she was right in the middle of it.

Evidently Alta Allerbee, all calico and red hair and I-Love-Laura, wasn't *quite* as sweet as she appeared.

Chloe put one palm up. "Okay, you know what? I can't handle one more thing right now. Finding out what Alta is up to will have to wait. I need to think."

"What's there to think about? I know I'm screwed. There's nothing to do but go home and tell Tryg I'm being blackmailed, and why."

Blackmail, Chloe thought again. It was a tawdry, ugly, scary word. "We need to go find a payphone," she said. "Before we do anything else, I want to make a phone call."

Every morning, as soon as the dishes were washed and the beds made,
(Laura) ran out to watch Mr. Scott and Pa working at the well. The
sunshine was blistering, even the winds were hot, and the prairie
grasses were turning yellow. Mary preferred to stay in the house and
sew on her patchwork quilt. But Laura liked the fierce light and the sun
and the wind, and she couldn't stay away from the well.

Little House on the Prairie

(Almanzo) liked Cap Garland. Cap was lighthearted and merry but he
would fight his weight in wildcats. When Cap Garland had reason to
lose his temper his eyes narrowed and glittered with a look that no man
cared to stand up to. The Long Winter

TWENTY-TWO

ROELKE SPENT AN HOUR in his patrol car, zapping cars with his newly-calibrated radar gun, and he wrote three tickets before he got bored. He drove by the ranch house where he'd seen young Crystal sitting on the curb, waiting for her parents to stop fighting. No sign of her today. He drove by Mrs. Walter Bainbridge's house, which always eased her mind, and he drove through the park, which eased parents' minds.

By then he was bored again, so he circled back to the empty station. He did what he needed to do about the speeding tickets, which took about two and a half minutes. He emptied the trash and washed the coffeepot—did *anyone* else ever wash it? He really didn't think so—and tidied the cupboard.

Then he pulled out his report on Travis, the infant surrendered to Child Protective Services. He read his own summary, trying to figure out how he could have better protected Travis. That call could have gone *really* sour.

"Damn," he muttered and shoved the report back into the file. Knee bouncing double-time, he grabbed the phone and dialed a familiar number.

"Milwaukee Police Department, District Two."

"Sergeant Malloy, please. Tell him it's Roelke McKenna."

Five minutes later, after scheduling a meeting with his former sergeant for the following Tuesday, Roelke hung up again. He felt a little guilty. The guilt pissed him off.

I'm not doing anything wrong, he reminded himself. How could he know whether he wanted to return to Milwaukee without going back? He hadn't been there since he'd caught Rick's killer. Maybe he *did* belong there. Chloe wasn't real keen on cities, but he could show her things—historic places and museums and really good bakeries. Moving back to Milwaukee wouldn't end his relationship with Chloe. They just wouldn't see each other as often. If Chloe—

The phone rang, and he snatched the receiver. "Eagle Police Department, Officer McKenna speaking."

"Roelke?" Chloe said in his ear.

"Hey."

"Is this a bad time? I'm sorry to call at work, but ... "

He sat up straight. "What's wrong?"

"I'm fine," she said quickly. "But I need your advice. It's about Kari."

She talked. He listened. "Jesus," he said at last. Blackmail was nasty.

"Yeah. I feel as if I'm traveling with a stranger, you know? And…" She sighed. "It gets worse. When the whole blackmail thing came up, Kari kind of went insane. She took a quilt square that was made by Laura Ingalls Wilder from Miss Lila's house. Miss Lila had told Kari the piece would be hers one day, but still, it was stealing."

"*Jesus.*"

"I know. Kari made plans to sell it to some dealer at the symposium so she could pay off the guy blackmailing her, but then her conscience kicked in and she changed her mind. She's going to put the square back when we get home so it's there when Miss Lila's estate is settled. But this blackmail crap could destroy her life. Not to mention her family."

Roelke pressed one knuckle against his forehead. "Let me think about this. Can we talk in the morning?"

"Thank you. That would be wonderful." Relief was clear in her voice. "I think I just really needed to share all this with you."

He liked the sound of that. He liked it so much that to his own utter surprise he said, "Have you thought anymore about living together?"

"I thought we were going to talk about that when I got back."

"Yes. We were."

"Roelke, I love you. But I don't want to live together."

Damn.

"Rick's death left a big black hole in your life, Roelke, and I am profoundly sorry—"

"This has nothing to do with Rick."

"Are you sure? You've been down in this deep well of grief, and I know how terrible that is. But here's the thing, Roelke: I don't think I'm strong enough to pull you out all by myself."

This conversation had gone completely off the rails. "I—"

"We've been doing fine as we are." Chloe's voice was still rising, gathering speed. "I lived with Markus for five years, but we were in *his* country, working at *his* museum, and honestly, I didn't realize how much of myself I'd given up until it was too late."

"I—"

"And I gotta tell you, I think this dream you have about the farm is just that—a *dream*. We can't go back to our childhoods, Roelke. I can't, you can't. This whole idea of a place, some place where we can find that—there's no such thing."

The torrent of words stopped abruptly, replaced by a muffled sniffling.

Roelke closed his eyes. He'd made Chloe cry.

"I'm r-really s-sorry." The words came out all shuddery. "I am a h-horrible girlfriend."

"Chloe, no, I—"

"I'll c-call you in the morning," she quavered, and hung up the phone.

————

Chloe sank onto the tiny seat in the gas station phone booth. What was *wrong* with her? She had, all by herself, managed to make this most horrible day even worse. She'd hurt Roelke. And she'd done it on the heels of dumping her Kari problem on his strong shoulders.

Roelke would be much better off if he ditched me and found someone else, she thought miserably. Someone younger and saner, with more money in the bank.

The very worst part? What she'd said was true. He might be ready to live together, but she was not.

And really, she wasn't out of line. The whole question had only come up because of the farm. She wasn't ready to talk about merging bank accounts and buying property, and marriage and children and whatever else came with the package. She was afraid that—

Afraid? The word struck like a gong in her brain. Was fear holding her back? Fear of getting the phone call that Rick's fiancée had gotten? Or even . . . fear that Roelke, like the father of her miscarried child, might one day decide he'd be better off without *her*?

Well, screw that, Chloe thought angrily. She'd be damned if she'd live a life defined by dread and worry. She wiped her eyes, blew her nose, and slammed out of the booth. Then she got back in the car and slammed the door. "Let's go."

"Where?"

"I don't care! Just—just go somewhere."

Kari drove until they reached a Chinese place near the motel, which reminded Chloe that lunch had been nonexistent. The Ellefson sisters managed to order take-out and get back to their room without making eye contact. They picked at Governor's Chicken and Tofu Almond Ding without speaking. Finally Kari put down her plastic fork and pushed the little cardboard box away. "So, you called Roelke?"

"I did, yeah."

"What did you tell him?"

"That you were being blackmailed." Chloe speared a tiny cob of corn on her own fork. "Why, and by whom. And then I asked his advice."

Kari winced, but she nodded. "What did he say?"

"He said he needed to think about it. We're going to talk again in the morning."

Kari began folding her napkin in a manner suggesting serious knowledge of origami. "Look, I'm going to take responsibility for my behavior. I just want Trygve to hear about it from *me*."

"Okay." Chloe put the corn down. "But beyond those things, what is it that you want, Kari? I've listened to everything you've had to say, and I still don't know."

"I want to stay married to Tryg, and to raise my kids as best I can." Muscles moved in Kari's jaw. "Look, I obviously have some problems—"

"You think?" Chloe muttered.

"For Christ's sake, just stuff it," Kari snapped. "I've done some reprehensible things, but don't you *dare* judge me."

"I—"

"You *left*. You went to West Virginia, and New York, and spent summers here and there, and ended up living in Switzerland. You have no idea what my life has been like. So keep your judgmental observations to yourself."

Chloe had no idea how to respond. Finally she said, "I am sorry."

Kari threw her a suspicious look. "For what?"

"For what you're facing," Chloe said. "Sometimes things start to go wrong, and life spirals out of control, and all of a sudden you're trying to figure out what the hell happened."

"If Tryg divorces me and gets custody of Astrid and Anja, I don't know how I'll get out of bed in the morning." Tears welled in Kari's eyes. "But maybe my girls would be better off without me."

When you're not singing Anja to sleep after a nightmare, Chloe thought, or helping Astrid with multiplication tables. She sealed up her own little cardboard box of food and tossed it into the trash. She wasn't hungry.

———

Roelke pulled off the road, turned off his truck lights, and eased close to the tavern. It was 3:45 in the morning, and he was about to visit the Stagger Inn.

He studied the place with a jaundiced eye. Given the name, the bar's patrons of choice were evidently drunk before they even arrived—never a good sign. The one-story structure with glass block windows squatted in a trash-strewn gravel lot on a rural road in Dane County. It was hard to imagine Chloe's sister coming here. But he'd been a cop for a while now; it took a lot more than what he'd heard on the phone to shock him.

Bar time had come and gone, but there were still a few vehicles in the lot. Thirty minutes later two men emerged and roared off on their Harleys. A guy built like Hulk Hogan drove away in a sedan with one headlight burned out. Now just a lonely old-model Ford sat in the lot.

Roelke eased from his truck and clicked the door closed. He'd changed out of his uniform but wore his duty belt beneath a light jacket. He hoped like anything that this would be quick and easy, but he needed to be prepared for trouble. After checking that everything was in place—gun, wooden nightstick, cuffs—he strode across the lot.

The front door was still unlocked. He threw it open, hard. It banged against the left wall. He moved right so he wasn't silhouetted in the doorway.

"Hey!" A man dumping the contents of a trash can into a plastic bag straightened with a scowl. "Knock that shit off and go back the way you came."

"You the guy they call Spider?"

"What's it to you?"

Roelke sized him up in an instant: a skinny man in jeans, forty, maybe fifty, balding. Chances were good that when things got rough, Spider relied on the big guy who'd just left for muscle. Spider's blue work shirt was helpfully tucked in, and Roelke didn't see any weapons. If he had a knife, it was well hidden. Spider was too far from the pool table to grab a cue. That left the glass bottles clinking into the garbage bag, maybe a thrown chair. Should be manageable.

The room was depressing—dark paneling, beer signs, dim yellow lights, black leather bucket seats at the bar, several mounted squirrel heads. The only incongruous touch was a big teddy bear wearing a blue sweatshirt with *Grandpa* monogrammed on the front in gold thread, surveying the room from a high shelf. Even slimeballs had grandkids.

Slimeball was still scowling. "I'm closed."

"I'm not here for a drink." Roelke crossed the open space, stopping just out of reach. "I'm here for some snapshots."

"Yeah?" The man gave a tough-guy shrug. "I don't know what you're talking about."

"I'm talking about some pictures you took of a lady."

"I said, I don't know—"

"Yeah, you do."

Spider narrowed his eyes, widened his stance.

Just hand 'em over, Roelke thought with a sigh.

"Well, maybe I do got pictures," Spider agreed. "But they're mine."

Roelke leapt. One grab, one jerk, one swing, and the bartender was backed against him, caught by the crook of Roelke's right elbow across his throat. Roelke held Spider's left wrist behind his back in a position calculated to solicit cooperation.

"Listen to me," Roelke said. "You picked the wrong lady to threaten."

"Okay!"

"I don't like bullies." Roelke inched the guy's wrist a little higher. "*Okay!*"

"I can have this place shut down by tomorrow night."

"You can't—"

"The hell I can't. Underage drinking, staying open past bar time, drug deals in the parking lot, prostitution—"

"There weren't any prostitutes!"

"But here's the kicker: I'm a cop, and you're not. Who do you think my colleagues in Dane County are going to believe?"

Spider squirmed. "Okay! Okay. You can have the pictures."

"Where are they?"

"In my safe. Back office."

Roelke released the throat hold but held on to Spider's left arm as they shuffled into the back room. "Open the safe and get them out."

The safe was small, nothing special, shoved in a corner behind a metal desk. It took Spider three tries to work the combination. When the tumblers finally clicked and the door swung open, he grabbed a plain envelope and thrust it toward Roelke. "Here. Take it and get out."

"Let me see what's in there."

Spider poked a finger into the envelope and held it up. Roelke glimpsed a face that looked so much like Chloe's that rage seared his chest. This SOB might as well have threatened *her*.

Roelke grabbed the envelope and tucked it into his deep jacket pocket. "Is this all of them?"

"Yes. I *swear*."

Roelke considered. The envelope held three or four photos. Polaroids, thank God. No film, no copies. Spider was a moron.

"So go," the moron said with a last spurt of defiance. "Take them and get out."

"Just one more thing," Roelke said in a very low voice. He patted his pocket. "I will be watching you. If you lied to me tonight, if other pictures *do* exist, I'll break your leg. If I ever discover that you've tried the same trick on anyone else, I'll break your other leg. Do we understand each other?"

The man's skin grew visibly damp. "Yes."

As Roelke turned away, Spider lunged behind his desk—and came up with an empty beer bottle in his hand.

"Don't do it," Roelke advised.

Spider smashed the bottom against the edge of the desk. Glass shattered, leaving a nasty weapon in his hand.

Roelke kicked, heard the man yelp, saw the bottle go flying. Then Roelke slammed his right fist against Spider's chin. The older man went down, slumping against a wall with a look of utter surprise.

Roelke stalked out. Once in his truck he felt inside his pocket to make sure the envelope was still there. It was.

His hand hurt. The rest of him felt pretty damn good. He knew he'd gone way over a line. He hadn't wanted to. He'd hoped that command presence and bluster would do the trick. But it hadn't, and after glimpsing that face so like Chloe's in the photo, he couldn't bring himself to care.

Roelke knew that if Chief Naborski discovered what had happened tonight, a job in Milwaukee would become his *only* option. But it was extremely unlikely that Spider would report Roelke's visit. He couldn't, not without revealing his own blackmailing scheme.

Roelke started the engine and turned the truck toward home. I needed that, he thought. It was depressing but undeniable. After giving up on the old Roelke place, and the God-awful call to rescue Travis, and hearing Chloe cry on the phone, he had needed to kick some ass.

———

Chloe called Roelke at 7:30 a.m. from a payphone in the motel parking lot. "McKenna," he mumbled.

Great start, she thought. "Sorry. You're usually up by now."

"It was a short night."

"Roelke, I owe you an apology. I didn't handle things well when we talked yesterday."

"You were kind of… shrieking. I've never heard you shriek before."

"And I will do my very best to never subject you to that again. I was furious with Kari, and I ended up taking it out on you."

"You said what was on your mind."

"I'm really sorry." She didn't know how to bridge the crevasse she'd dug between them. "Can you forgive me for being so hurtful?"

His voice finally softened. "Of course."

"Thank you," Chloe said, with heartfelt gratitude. "So… do you have any thoughts about Kari's situation? How we should handle it?"

"I've got the photographs."

"You… *what?*"

"I paid a visit to the Stagger Inn. This Spider guy handed over the pictures of your sister."

"Just like that?"

"Pretty much. We had a little talk, he saw things my way."

Chloe felt weak-kneed with relief. "Roelke, I sincerely hope my family problem didn't make you do anything that—"

"I handled it," he said briefly. "Tell your sister to stop worrying. The guy swore that there weren't any others. I'm inclined to believe him. He was in way over his head."

"I don't even know what to say. You are amazing."

"Sometimes," he agreed. He sounded a little smug.

"*Thank* you."

"You're welcome. So now you can head home knowing that Kari is off the public hook."

"In a couple of days, you mean. I need to talk to Kari about what happens now, but there's one more homesite—"

"*Seriously*? After everything that's happened, aren't you ready to end this road trip?"

"Not really."

He paused. "Have the South Dakota guys caught whoever killed Ms. Rifenberg?"

Chloe watched a very small man drag a very large suitcase from his room. "I don't know. But the sad truth is that Jayne was a miserable woman who liked patronizing people, and was sometimes just mean. I suspect she pushed somebody too far."

"People who get pushed too hard can lash out," Roelke allowed. "Sometimes the last straw is something small."

"I think that's what happened."

"But people kill for revenge, greed, fear ... lots of reasons."

"I know. But I'm sure the detectives are making progress. And there's still that quilt at the Mansfield homesite that I really need to see."

An operator's voice came through the line, demanding change. Chloe pushed another quarter into the slot.

"I just wish you'd skip Missouri and come home."

"I know. I'll see how Kari feels."

"Call me when you can."

"I will. Listen, what's going on with the farm?"

"I can't afford it."

He can't afford it, Chloe thought. That was it? Done deal? Wow. The news should have given her a sense of relief. Somehow, it didn't.

"I still really want to talk with you about all this stuff, but ... "

Chloe hated hearing the frustration in his voice, hated being absent when he needed her. "I'm sorry the timing of this trip is so bad. I can't wait to talk everything through with you when I get back. And Roelke? From the bottom of my heart, thank you for getting the pictures back. I love you."

"I love you too," he said. "That's why I worry. And please, have a serious talk with Kari about coming home."

"I will," Chloe promised. Then she went back to the room.

Kari came out of the bathroom dressed in jeans, her hair wet but neatly combed. "Well?" She put one hand against the wall as if bracing herself. "Did he have any advice beyond the obvious? Tell all to law enforcement and my family?"

"He didn't offer advice," Chloe said. "He has the pictures."

Kari's eyes went wide. Her mouth slowly opened. "He... *what*?"

"Roelke went to the tavern and got the pictures. The blackmailing thing is done and over with."

Kari stared for so long that Chloe began to wonder if she'd been speaking in tongues or something. Then Kari dropped onto her bed, put her hands over her face, and began to cry.

As Chloe watched her sister crumple, something gave way inside and the last bits of anger blew away like ashes. Things would never be the same for her and Kari... but the hostility between them was done and over with too.

Chloe considered saying *I forgive you*, but she was afraid it might sound sanctimonious. Instead she fetched a box of tissues from the bathroom and sat down beside her sister. Then she put one arm around Kari's shoulders and let her cry.

Mary had always been good. Sometimes she had been so good that Laura could hardly bear it. But now she seemed different.

Little Town on the Prairie

"That's Nellie Oleson for you," said Mary. "She just wants anything that anybody else has, that's all."   These Happy Golden Years

TWENTY-THREE

"THANK YOU," KARI KEPT saying when she finally came up for air. "Really. Just—thank you."

"I didn't do much. When the time comes, thank Roelke."

"I will." Kari shoved a hand through her hair and glanced at the bedside clock. "Chloe, I called Alta while you were outside and told her we needed to talk to her. She's on her way over. Also, the front desk called. Somebody sent you a fax."

"It's probably from my intern. I'll get it later." First things first.

Alta arrived looking tired and tense, and she'd exchanged prairie garb for jeans. Chloe almost didn't recognize her.

"I dropped everyone off at an IHOP for breakfast," she began. "Are you two okay?"

Chloe didn't feel like chitchat. "You've got some explaining to do." She dropped onto the desk chair, and the others perched on a bed.

"Kari says you're upset because she changed her mind about selling Laura's quilt square. Why do you care? What's in it for you?"

"Fifteen percent of the sale price," Alta said in a low voice.

"Well, that's just lovely." Chloe popped up again, too antsy to sit.

Alta's lower lip quivered, but she held Chloe's gaze. "I'm not proud of it. But—I need money, and I was willing to play go-between in order to get it." She lifted her chin. "We haven't done anything illegal."

"My sister stole the quilt square from a friend's house," Chloe observed, "and she says you knew where it came from, so—yeah, you have. And if you are knowingly collaborating with a dealer who routinely handles stolen artifacts—"

"I don't know that," Alta protested. "I don't even know who it is."

Chloe took two steps, almost brained herself on the wall-mounted rack of hangers, and turned around again. "How did you get connected with this dealer?"

"After I began promoting the *Looking For Laura* symposium last winter, I got a letter." Alta pulled a single sheet of paper from her bag and handed it to Chloe.

> *January 11, 1983*
> *Hello,*
>
> *I am writing to offer my services to you and the people attending your conference. I specialize in the sale of book-related antiques, especially Laura Ingalls Wilder. Everything done quietly, sure to please those who want to stay out of the public eye. If you know of anyone who has something to sell or is looking for something to buy, contact me at the address below. For any sales that result, I will provide a 15% finder's fee to you.*
>
> *Sincerely yours,*
> *Dealer Discreet*

The address provided was a PO Box in St. Paul, MN. Chloe frowned. "Kari, didn't your letter from Dealer Discreet come from Columbus?"

She nodded.

"Well, either this person moved very recently, or the business is bigger than I imagined." She looked at Alta. "Didn't it strike you as suspicious that he or she wasn't willing to sign their name?"

"I figured they were just protecting their privacy."

Chloe gave her an *Oh please* look.

"All right." Alta wilted as her last bit of defiance disappeared. "Of course it struck me as suspicious. But there's nothing blatantly illegal in this letter. Maybe the guy works with very rich clients, and everything is hush-hush."

"Discreet dealers protect their *clients'* privacy, not their own. For God's sake, Alta, you're playing with fire!" Chloe tried to cork her exasperation. "Look, I know you're struggling to get Laura Land Tours off the ground. I know your husband dumped a huge financial mess on you when he went to prison. But if you get mixed up with stolen antiques—and I suspect that Dealer Discreet is not opposed to handling stolen antiques—you could end up charged as an accessory or something. You'll lose your tour business altogether!"

"I'm not trying to save my tour business," Alta said quietly. "I'm trying to get my granddaughter out of foster care."

Okay, *that* was new information. "You have a granddaughter in foster care?"

"Courtney is fourteen months old." Alta opened her wallet to show a plastic-sleeved photo of a laughing little girl. One chubby hand reached toward the camera. She had blue eyes and a trusting look that made Chloe's throat ache.

Alta regarded the snapshot. "Her mother, my younger daughter, has been in and out of rehab since she was fifteen. She's currently serving time for possession of narcotics. My husband and I were trying to gain legal custody of Courtney, but…"

Chloe finished the sentence silently: *But it got a whole lot harder when my husband was convicted of embezzlement.*

"I'm having a tough time convincing the social worker that I'll make an appropriate guardian. I started the tour business to supplement my income, and my older daughter is happy to take Courtney when I'm giving tours, so that's okay. But my next interview is just a few weeks away. I'm trying to get a bedroom fixed up, buy her some new clothes… it would make an impression. So I thought that just this once…" She slumped back in her chair. "Oh God. I've been a fool."

Someone walked by the room with a boom box blaring "Highway to Hell." Car doors slammed, an engine roared, and silence returned. Chloe tried and failed to think of something reassuring to say.

Kari asked, "What made you think that Dealer Discreet is going to be at the Wilder Heritage Festival in Missouri?"

Alta produced another piece of paper. "Because I found this slipped under my door at the De Smet motel." She held out a plain white piece of notepaper that held a single sentence, printed in black ink: *Bring the quilt square to Mansfield.*

Chloe recoiled. There was something chilling about those six innocuous words. They might as well have been snipped laboriously from magazines, with *or else* added at the end.

Kari looked troubled too. "Why do you suppose it came under your door, and not mine? Do you think Dealer Discreet is somebody on your tour?"

"It could have been anybody at the symposium, really. I announced my room number."

"Does anyone on the tour live in the Twin Cities?" Chloe asked. "Or somewhere close enough to have a St. Paul post office box?"

"My only Minnesota people are Bill and Frances Whelan, and they're in International Falls."

"Bill Whelan collects Laura antiques," Chloe murmured. "But International Falls is ... what, four hours north of the Cities? Five?"

"I'm sure it isn't Bill," Alta protested. "He's so nice!"

You barely know Bill, Chloe thought, but she didn't argue. "Jayne lived in Rochester. That's within an easy drive of the Cities, isn't it? Do you suppose she was Dealer Discreet?" Chloe felt a flicker of hope. If Jayne had been dealing in blackmarket antiques, her death erased that problem altogether. "When did that message show up?"

"I found it just before we left De Smet."

Damn. That meant somebody had slipped the note under Alta's door *after* Jayne had been killed. Chloe tried to think of other candidates. "Where does Leonard Devich live?"

"Wisconsin. Eau Claire, I think."

Which was less than two hours from St. Paul, Chloe figured. That wasn't proof of anything, of course. But Devich had projected a weird vibe from the beginning. "Is anybody on your tour from Columbus?"

Alta shook her head. "Nobody from Ohio at all."

I don't understand this, Chloe thought. Not even a little bit.

Kari looked at Chloe. "Maybe we should go home. I'll return the square to Miss Lila's house, and that will be that."

"Not necessarily," Chloe said. "Some dubious dealer now knows that you have a quilt square stitched by Laura Ingalls Wilder. And let's not forget that Jayne Rifenberg got stabbed to death in De Smet."

"There's no reason to think that Jayne's death has anything to do with the quilt square," Alta said. "I mean ... is there?"

"Not that I can think of," Chloe admitted. "She did make a comment about quilting bees that made me wonder, although she was probably just trying to insult me. But..." She hesitated, then decided to tell all. "I have been trying to find a pattern in some of the problems that seem to be dogging your tour." She summarized her theory, connecting each incident to something that happened in one of the Little House books.

Kari went owl-eyed. "That's crazy."

"Maybe," Chloe allowed. "Alta, can you think of any reason why someone would want to drive you out of business? Something to do with your husband, maybe? Was anyone else involved in the embezzlement mess?"

"I don't think so. Nobody else was arrested."

Chloe wondered again if the Kansas sunshine had baked her brain. She felt suspicious of everyone. Maybe I've been spending too much time with a cop, she thought. Which was not comforting.

Alta raked her fingers through her hair. "What do we do now?"

"We call the police," Chloe said. "This has gotten out of hand."

Alta looked from Chloe to Kari and back again. "And... what are you going to tell them? That this note came from somebody who wants the quilt square Kari took without permission from your friend's house? Maybe you *should* go home."

Kari shook her head. "No, Chloe was right. Some black market dealer knows I have the square, and they might come looking. Besides, if Chloe and I head home now, that leaves you on your own."

"I'll be all right," Alta said.

"We don't know how Dealer Discreet will react if I'm a no-show."

"The dealer can't blame me if you don't show up," Alta protested. But she looked uneasy.

260

Chloe didn't blame her. "If Dealer Discreet is dishonest and handling Laura-related antiques, I would really like to find out who it is. But as you said, on the surface the person is just offering to buy an antique. Short of producing Laura's quilt square, which I do *not* want to do, how could we even hope to get any incriminating information from this person?"

Nobody had an answer.

"Besides, even if we *did* show the square, and learn something to implicate the dealer..." Chloe looked at her sister. "Kari, that puts you back in the hot seat. Maybe we can keep Alta out of it, but if we tell the cops about this dealer, we have to explain how you got connected to him in the first place."

"Maybe not." Kari sucked in her lower lip, as she'd done since childhood when thinking hard. "I have an idea." She fetched the protective towel from her suitcase and unrolled it on the table, revealing Laura's square.

"This is the square Laura stitched?" Alta asked. "It's nothing like what I pictured when reading the books. What's the pattern?"

"Dove in the Window," Kari said.

Chloe shot her a look of surprise. "No it's not!" She remembered how startled she'd been when visiting the collections storage room in De Smet, when Edna Jo had raised an unexpected speculation: *I've always wondered whether Laura's childhood quilt was actually a Dove in the Window pattern.* But she and Kari hadn't been on speaking terms—for the first time—when she'd met with Edna Jo, so Kari hadn't heard the story.

Chloe dug out the photocopied pattern Edna Jo had given her. "*This* is Dove in the Window. It's very similar to Bear Track. See?"

Kari produced a photocopy of her own. "Well, this is also called Dove in the Window. See?"

261

Alta looked from one to the other. "I'm confused."

"It was very common for one pattern to have different names, or for one name to be linked to two or more patterns," Chloe explained. "But we're getting off track."

Kari began rolling up the towel. "I am definitely going to return the quilt square to Miss Lila's house, to be disposed of however Miss Lila's will indicates. But how about if I sew a duplicate square, and we use that to smoke out Dealer Discreet?"

"He'll know it's a fake," Chloe objected.

Kari tucked the roll into her suitcase before perching on the edge of a bed, spine erect. "Maybe, maybe not. I'm sure we can find a good fabric shop somewhere in Independence, and the pattern is simple enough. It wouldn't take long."

Alta looked hopeful. "If we can get this person to say something incriminating, I could tell the police that after I got that first letter from Dealer Discreet, I wanted to discover if his or her offer was legitimate."

"Exactly," Kari agreed. "You have to protect your customers, right?"

Chloe understood that Alta, who probably watched *Perry Mason* reruns, wanted to know Dealer Discreet wouldn't contact her again. Chloe also understood that Kari needed to atone for her temporary insanity by pulling something good from the mess. But Raymond Burr wasn't likely to show up at the homesite, and Kari had no experience dealing with bad guys. Chloe had met a few bad guys, and heard about a whole lot more. "I don't know," she said.

"It's the right thing to do," Kari insisted. "And... I really need to do this, Chloe. I need a tiny bit of redemption. I want this finished."

Chloe thought about the ramifications of leaving this unfinished. She pictured some black-masked thug driving angrily to Stoughton in search of a quilt square he'd been promised. And... dear God, what if Dealer Discreet had already been in Stoughton? "Kari, somebody broke into Miss Lila's house, and she ended up dead."

Kari's face slowly lost its color. "The police said the thief was after jewelry."

"Since the thief hasn't been caught, nobody really knows what he was after. When you contacted Dealer Discreet, did you actually say where the quilt square came from?"

"I said I got it from a family friend," Kari said. "That's all."

Chloe pressed her lips in a tight line. The appearance of any Laura artifact was a Huge Deal. Even rumor of such a find would cause excitement. Would Kari's letter have been enough to lead someone to Miss Lila's house, looking to see if there were any other textiles conveniently labeled "Laura Ingalls Wilder" sitting about? Far-fetched, but not impossible. In a friendly, close-knit community like Stoughton, a couple of innocuous questions in a coffee shop would lead to chats about Kari, Mom and Dad, and even their next-door neighbor Lila.

"If nothing else, we know for sure that Dealer Discreet has *your* address," Chloe reminded Kari. "If you don't show up at the Missouri homesite with quilt square in hand, it's always possible he'll end up in Wisconsin. At your farm."

Kari looked shaken. "That *must* not happen. So my idea is the best plan. I take a replica square to the homesite, hope Dealer Discreet identifies himself, and sell him the goods. Once we know who it is and see how the whole thing is handled, we can decide if we have reason to talk to the police." She looked at Chloe. "I know you and Roelke have already helped me enormously but *please*, help me do this."

Chloe didn't want her imagined thug to be waiting when Anja and Astrid got off the school bus one day. Still, the plan made her anxious. "Just—give me time to think about it."

She left the room. The motel was on a busy street, hardly scenic, but at least out here she could take more than two steps without bumping into something. By the time she'd looped the parking lot she'd organized her thoughts into a pretty impressive list of reasons to bow to her sister's wish to keep going, and not to her boyfriend's wish that she turn for home.

First, Dealer Discreet could show up in Wisconsin if Kari didn't make an appearance in Missouri with quilt square in hand.

Second, Chloe still needed to see Mary's childhood quilt on display in Missouri. That Nine Patch offered the very last chance to link the Ingalls girls' childhood with Miss Lila's quilt. Chloe's period of custody ended in a few days. The conditions in Miss Lila's will might send the quilt *anywhere*, maybe to auction. Chloe had left South Dakota believing that there was still a tiny chance that Lila's Bear Track was actually Laura's long-lost but not-burned-up childhood quilt. If Chloe didn't do everything she could to document the quilt now, answers might be lost forever.

Third, there was Alta to consider. Life had kicked her hard, but she was trying to rise up. In Chloe's opinion, Alta was doing good, important work—as a grandma and as a businesswoman. Chloe couldn't help her gain legal custody of her granddaughter, but she could help keep alive Alta's dream of turning Laura Land Tours into a successful enterprise.

Finally… back to Kari, who needed help. A small, mean part of Chloe wanted to feel put upon… but most of her actually felt gratified. She'd spent her whole childhood asking Kari for help, getting advice both solicited and not from Kari, listening with resentment as adults held Kari up as a shining example of everything good Norwegian-American girls should be. It was kind of nice to be on the other side of the equation for once.

And maybe—not to get too metaphysical or anything—but maybe that was what she was supposed to figure out on this trip. Maybe *Looking For Laura* wasn't all about finding her childhood, or even discovering what she wanted from a home. Maybe *childhood* and *home* were pretty much the same thing as *family*. Chloe had Roelke now, and he was a rock, but Kari was the only sister she had.

Chloe looped the parking lot one more time, just to be sure there were no further insights floating around the crannies of her brain. There didn't seem to be, so when she got back near the room, she veered off and went inside. Kari and Alta looked up anxiously.

"Kari, I don't like your plan," Chloe said, "but I don't have a better one."

Kari pushed her shoulders back. "On to Missouri?"

"On to Missouri," Chloe agreed, hoping like anything that she wouldn't regret it.

Alta glanced at the clock. "I need to pick up the gang soon. Time to put on my happy face." She touched Courtney's photo with a tender finger and slipped her wallet away. Alta's expression, half loving and half bleak, made Chloe want to cry.

"And I need to go find a fabric store." Kari reached for her purse. "If we're going to make this work, we need to get moving."

They discussed a few logistical details before Kari and Alta left the motel. Chloe stayed behind and fetched her fax, a concise summary of Nika's foray into Jayne Rifenberg's professional life. Bless you, Chloe told Nika silently, and headed back to the room to read in private.

Jayne had received a B.A. in American History and a Masters in Women's Studies from the University of Oregon. She'd taught at several small colleges, hopping from Oregon to Connecticut to Ohio before landing most recently in Rochester, Minnesota.

Chloe lowered the page, struck by the geography. Ohio and Minnesota, the two states where Dealer Discreet had post office boxes. Were—or had there been—two Dealers Discreet? If Jayne had been one of them, who was the other?

Nika had also found a handful of published articles. The first, "Dark Shadows from the Little House: Why Wilder's Books Should Be Banned," had been published in a now-defunct woman's magazine in 1966.

Jeez, Chloe thought. Banned? That was harsh, even for Jayne.

After that, Jayne had roused herself from muckraking long enough to produce "Central Medallion Motifs in Revolutionary War-Era Quilts" and "Resist Printing and Quilts in the 1800s," both published in respected journals. Then came "Little House, Large Doctrine: Laura Ingalls Wilder and the Libertarian Agenda." Finally, in Spring 1980, Jayne Rifenberg's "Penny Squares and Scarlet Thread: The Rise and Fall of a Popular Pastime in America" had appeared in a women's history quarterly.

Chloe put the paper aside and stared blindly at a cigarette burn in the carpet. Resist printing referred to a particular dye process, and Penny Squares were stamped embroidery patterns commonly made into quilts. Bottom line: Jayne clearly *did* have more than a passing interest in historic quilts. That was disconcerting, but it did explain why she'd been having a convivial conversation with Kim Dexheimer back in Pepin.

Jayne had also been gunning for Laura, academically speaking, for at least seventeen years. She'd come back to Laura once again for the symposium presentation, with publication of her paper to follow. Why on earth had Jayne hated the Little House books so much?

Chloe had no clue. But she really wanted to find out.

She ensconced herself back in the telephone booth outside. The operator put her through to the college in Rochester where Jayne had most recently taught. After navigating through the switchboard, Chloe finally reached the History Department receptionist.

Chloe introduced herself. "I'm wondering if I might speak with someone who knew Jayne Rifenberg well. I've been traveling with her this week, and what happened was such a shock…"

"I'm going to transfer you to the English department. Ask for Louise." The woman clicked off.

When Louise came on the line, Chloe repeated her introduction. "I didn't know Jayne well, but now…I wish I had taken the time to know her better," she said, which was not actually a lie.

"I don't think that anyone knew Jayne well," Louise said. "We struck up an acquaintance when I discovered her interest in Laura Ingalls Wilder. I asked her to speak to my American Lit classes, but honestly…she had no rapport with the students, so I didn't ask again. How did her talk at the symposium go?"

"She presented her material very well," Chloe said. Also not a lie.

Louise sighed. "I'm glad she had that chance, then."

"She seemed…unhappy. Do you know why?"

"Not in any great detail. She mentioned her miserable childhood a couple of times, and I know she was married once."

"Really?" Chloe tried and failed to picture Jayne as a beaming bride.

"I don't think it lasted long. Jayne went through life with a chip on her shoulder, you know? I would have steered clear of her altogether if…" Louise's voice trailed away.

"If?" Chloe prompted, trying to sound kind and caring, and not just curious.

"If she hadn't been so…vulnerable. Jayne had an enormous need for professional validation. Unfortunately she tried too hard, pushed to publish too fast, didn't ever connect with others. I think she came here because her contract wasn't renewed at the college where she'd been teaching. And at least once she published an article that got scathing reviews."

"Oh dear. Was it about Laura?"

"No, it was about Penny Squares, whatever they are."

"Penny Squares were pieces of muslin printed with simple designs," Chloe explained. "The pictures made it easy for children or beginners to practice embroidery stitches. They were popular in the late 1800s and early 1900s."

"Well, Jayne made a point of sharing the article when it came out, but later a letter to the editor in the same journal ripped her work to shreds," Louise said. "Someone in her department passed photocopies around."

"Ouch." Chloe was starting to regret making this phone call. It was easier to dislike Jayne Rifenberg than feel sorry for her. Or worse, to feel horrible for not trying harder in the *Be polite to Jayne* department.

Louise was saying, "The last paragraph of the letter basically said, 'Rifenberg delved into a fascinating and little-known aspect of commercial quilting, but her research was flawed. Ultimately, Rifenberg's conclusions were not worth a Penny Square.'"

Chloe winced. Harsh words for someone desperate to gain recognition and respect in the academic world. But what Louise was describing was exactly what had happened at *Looking For Laura*. Jayne had latched onto a legitimate topic—the role Laura's daughter Rose did, or did not, play in editing the Little House books—but then alienated everyone in the audience by presenting a clearly unbalanced paper.

"Please forgive me," Louise said. "I've been indiscreet. I guess that after hearing the news of Jayne's death yesterday I just needed to talk."

"May I ask just one more question? The last time I saw Jayne, she gave me an Indian Head penny just like the ones Mary and Laura received for Christmas the year they were in Kansas. Did Jayne collect Laura memorabilia, do you know?"

"Oh my, yes," Louise said. "That's how I discovered our shared interest in Laura. We both went to an auction to bid on a glass plate like the one Laura and Almanzo got from Montgomery Ward."

Chloe felt a shuddery sensation on the back of her neck. "Who won?"

"She did," Louise said. "I can't afford to spend *too* much on a hobby collection. Besides..."

"Besides...?"

"Well, when the bidding started, Jayne got this fierce look in her eyes. She was going to get it or *else*. Frankly, her intensity was a little... disturbing."

Chloe thanked Louise profusely before hanging up and sorting through what she'd heard. The personal stuff, the chip on Jayne's shoulder—that wasn't news. But the collecting? That made no sense. Why would a woman who despised Laura collect antiques related to her life? Jayne had gone out of her way to belittle Laura fans, Chloe thought, but evidently she also wanted to belong to the club.

It was sad. So was her hopscotch professional career, and the wretched review of her final quilt article. Chloe had published a few journal articles in her day, and she couldn't imagine how it would feel to have someone publicly attack her scholarship.

Heads or tails, who's going under?

Not me, Chloe thought. She plugged the phone again and called the textile library on the UW campus. She identified herself as a State Historical Society of Wisconsin curator and made a request. "I'm away from my site right now, so I need the pages faxed to me. You can bill

269

Old World Wisconsin." That would surely kick her in the butt later, but Chloe had more urgent things to worry about than Petty's hyperscrutiny of any expense with her name on it, or his subsequent tantrums.

Chloe tried calling Roelke at home—no answer. She called the EPD and learned that Roelke wasn't there either. "Please just tell him I called," Chloe told Marie, "and that my sister and I are headed to Missouri."

*Laura's heart stood still. Were wolves coming to the sheep yard? She
waited, listening, but could hear nothing but the swish of the snow
against the windows; or was that a sheep bleating?*

The First Four Years

TWENTY-FOUR

JUST BEFORE ONE O'CLOCK that afternoon, as planned, Chloe and
Kari arrived at Rocky Ridge Farm, the Laura homesite just outside of
Mansfield, Missouri. Kari had finished the replica quilt square during
the drive, and they'd tucked the original into the archival box hidden
in the trunk.

Chloe saw clear signs of a special event in the making: a maintenance crew placing rows of chairs in front of a temporary stage, volunteers preparing booths and tables for special activities. A steady
stream of cars was turning into the small parking lot across the street.
The inevitable adorable girls in prairie garb darted back and forth,
begging parents and brothers to hurry up.

As she and Kari walked up the hill to join Alta's group on the
lawn, heads turned and chatter died—not surprising, since the tour
members had been subjected to the Ellefson girls' better-than-
primetime performance in Kansas the day before. If their mission

hadn't been so important Chloe would have gladly dropped and belly-crawled back to the car.

Then Hazel Voss stepped forward. "How good to *see* you!" she exclaimed, hugging Chloe and Kari in turn. Her sincere smile lasered through the awkwardness. Henrietta Beauchamps, the Whelans, Haruka Minari, and other symposium acquaintances greeted them as well. Even Leonard Devich gave Chloe a nod that, for him, passed as friendly. She was absurdly touched. *Laura fans are good people,* she thought humbly.

Hazel linked one arm through Chloe's in a final gesture of solidarity. "I've wanted to see Rocky Ridge Farm forever, haven't you?"

"Actually, I'd never heard of it until a few weeks ago," Chloe confessed. "It's pretty, though." The white farmhouse was built on a hill, backed by woods showing the fresh green of spring foliage. Walnut and cedar trees dotted the lawn. The whole place had a Currier and Ives appeal.

Alta clapped for attention as Director Carmelina Biancardi joined them. Carmelina had clearly paused mid-errand, for she held a cardboard carton topped with a plastic bucket of crayons, but her smile was warm as ever. "Welcome to Rocky Ridge Farm! There's a lot going on here this weekend—"

"No kidding," Kari murmured.

"—so I wanted to provide a bit of orientation. As you know, Laura and Almanzo's first years of marriage were marked by one tragedy or disaster after another—"

"No kidding," Chloe murmured.

"—and they decided to leave South Dakota. Eventually they made their way here with their young daughter Rose. Laura liked this rocky ridge, and the family moved into a one-room log cabin. They arrived with almost nothing, and struggled to make a go of it. Rose said later that malnutrition caused her some lingering health problems."

Another farm, Chloe thought. And evidently, another round of misery.

"It was here in Missouri that Laura began her writing career—in part to help earn money," Carmelina continued. "After Laura's death in 1957, Rose and some family friends formed the Laura Ingalls Wilder Home Association to preserve and protect the farm and Laura's legacy. Family belongings are on display in the museum"—she pointed to a modern structure—"and docents are giving tours of the house."

Hazel sighed happily.

"We're starting our festival weekend with two very special events. Rose built her parents a small stone cottage a mile from here." Carmelina gestured vaguely at the wooded hill beyond the buildings. "It was quite modern for its day, and Rose hoped to make life more comfortable for her aging parents. The cottage was later sold, and by the time we were able to acquire it, the building needed extensive—and expensive—renovation. But at three o'clock today, you are invited to join us for the first public tour of the Rock House."

Henrietta Beauchamps leaned close. "Laura wrote some of her books there, you know," she whispered. Chloe nodded sagely.

"And I'm happy to announce a *very* special surprise." Carmelina's expression suggested a child on Christmas Eve. "We've always been proud to display Pa's fiddle in the museum, but recently we had it restored. At six thirty this evening a local musician here on the lawn is going to play some of Laura's favorite tunes on Pa's fiddle."

"Oh dear Lord," Hazel gasped. Even Chloe, preoccupied as she was, felt a tingle of awe. If Dealer Discreet showed up during the performance, he'd just have to wait.

"I'll see you all at the Rock House," Carmelina promised. Then she caught Chloe's eye and beckoned.

Are we already in trouble? Chloe wondered, before reminding herself that she had made an appointment with the director. They took a few steps away from the crowd.

"I'm looking forward to seeing your quilt," Carmelina said. "I know we said six p.m., but if I get caught up with something, there's a study room in the office building where you can wait." She cocked her head toward a small structure near the museum. "Also, a fax for you just came in." She gestured with her chin toward two papers anchored by the crayon bucket on top of the box in her arms.

Chloe felt a twinge of guilt. "I'm sorry. That's the last thing you needed today."

"No problem." Carmelina smiled before hurrying away.

Chloe glanced at the cover page. The fax, sent from the textile library at UW–Madison, could wait. She stuffed the pages into her bag and returned to the group.

"You're on your own until the Rock House tour begins," Alta was telling her charges. "We'll be here tomorrow as well, so you'll have plenty of time to explore."

Kari caught Chloe's eye and gave a small nod. They'd agreed to split up, theorizing that Dealer Discreet might feel more comfortable approaching Kari if she was by herself. Alta was also going to roam. It was possible that the dealer might not know how to recognize Kari and would want Alta to serve as go-between.

"Are you two alright?" Hazel asked, watching as Kari wandered away, snapping photos like a good tourist.

"We are," Chloe said. "And we both regret the melodrama yesterday. It was a sisters thing. But how about you? You've had an eventful week of your own."

"I have," Hazel admitted. "Now I have to figure out what my new life will look like."

"It must feel overwhelming."

"Wilbur calls me at the motels morning and night, begging me to come home." Hazel absently toed a walnut shell with one sneakered foot. "He says I can't manage without him, and I've had moments when I believe him. But you know what?" She summoned a bright little WWLD smile. "I will manage. Alta invited me to stay with her while things get worked out."

"That's lovely," Chloe said. Alta had already divorced a jerk of a husband; she'd be a source of comfort for Hazel while she divorced hers.

"Well, I want to see the house," Hazel said. "Care to join me for a tour?"

"I'm itching to see the museum," Chloe said. Kari and Alta were on the prowl for Dealer Discreet. *She* had a date with Mary Ingalls's Nine Patch quilt.

"We'll catch up later, then," Hazel promised. "After—oh, no." Beneath the purple sunbonnet, her eyes filled with dismay.

Chloe's heart slid lower in her chest as she followed Hazel's gaze and saw a familiar sedan turning into the parking lot across the road. "Is that Wilbur?"

Hazel nodded with resignation. "I guess I had better go talk with him."

"I'll walk over with you," Chloe offered. She was in no mood to put up with any crap from the likes of Wilbur Voss.

He watched them approach. Chloe could tell that he wasn't pleased to see her. Back atcha, she thought. He shifted his stance, trying to pretend that he and Hazel were alone.

"Wilbur," Hazel began, "what on earth are you doing here?"

"I came to see *you*. We need to talk. In private."

Hazel sighed. "Are you asking me, or telling me, Wilbur?"

Way to go! Chloe cheered silently.

Wilbur opened his mouth, then bit back his response. His struggle to be conciliatory would have been comical if it hadn't been so sad. "*Hazel*. I came here because I know it's important to you. I'm sorry things didn't go right in Pepin, or in Burr Oak. That was my fault. But this is the last stop on your tour. After you see the house or whatever, I'll take you home."

"No, thank you," Hazel said with polite finality, as if a broom salesman had shown up at her door.

Wilbur stared at her for a long moment. Finally he tossed Chloe a resentful look. "Do you mind?" The words seemed to squeeze between clenched teeth. "I would like to have a conversation with my wife."

Chloe looked at Hazel.

"It's all right," she said. "You go on." She patted Chloe's arm.

It should be okay, Chloe thought. Wilbur showed no sign of intoxication, and there were lots of people in the parking lot. Still, before walking away she gave Wilbur a meaningful, narrowed-eyes look: *You make trouble, I call the cops.*

Chloe retreated to a bench on the lawn, part-way up the slope so she had a clear view of the parking lot. Wilbur's appearance bothered her a lot. She didn't want him to get angry and somehow disrupt the festival. And she didn't want him to make more trouble for her friend.

Chloe didn't think that Hazel would crumble, though. And she wouldn't complain, either. Hazel never complained. Even after leaving Wilbur, Hazel had expressed no malice, no resentment, only concern for his welfare. Back in Walnut Grove, Hazel had tried to explain that Wilbur's actions just meant he cared. Cared about controlling you, Chloe thought now. Nothing had changed the opinion she'd formed of Wilbur six seconds after glimpsing him haranguing Hazel in Pepin.

Kari's accusation abruptly rewound in Chloe's brain: *Maybe if you weren't so damn sanctimonious all the time…*

O-*kay*, Chloe thought grudgingly. In his own Neanderthal way, Wilbur Voss cared about Hazel. He used to drive Hazel to her Laura Ingalls Wilder club meetings. After she left he was so upset that he got soused and made an ass of himself.

All that was well and good. But the timing of his reemergence from the ooze was bothersome. She looked back at the parking lot. Wilbur and Hazel were still talking.

Half-formed thoughts and snatches of memory danced in her brain. And a faint red flag of warning began to wave.

Chloe sat up very straight, which sometimes helped her think, and mentally replayed snippets of conversations she'd had with Hazel. Then she pulled out her notebook and jotted down the ideas as they came. Bits of evidence lined up like dominoes:

Wilbur Voss

1. *took Hazel to LIW club meetings,
   and waited in the back till she was done*

2. *works for a trucking company*

3. *got hours cut back, with subsequent loss of $$ and status*

4. *followed Hazel to Burr Oak to beg her to reconsider*

5. *seemed more upset about missing symposium
   than their marriage, according to Hazel*

6. *calls Hazel every morning and evening*

7. *showed up at Rocky Ridge today*

Chloe stared at the list. "Oh my God," she whispered. "I think Wilbur Voss is Dealer Discreet."

It all fit. Hazel had provided Wilbur access to Laura Land. After sitting in on umpteen club meetings, he probably had a very good idea what kinds of memorabilia interested Little House devotees. It would be easy for a trucker to maintain post office boxes in more than one state. His employer had reduced his hours, and his little woman had started talking about getting a job—both reasons for him to look for new avenues of income. He took Hazel's desertion so hard that he showed up blotto in Burr Oak, begging her to come back to him...but was he concerned about his marriage, or about the severed connection to Laura fans and collectors?

Chloe was particularly struck by Hazel's comment, back in De Smet, that Wilbur seemed more upset about missing the symposium than the end of their marriage. Why on earth would he care about that? Most likely, he'd figured out that *Looking For Laura* would attract an unprecedented number of fans—i.e., collectors—including one Kari Anderson, who'd written him a letter describing Laura's quilt square.

He was calling Hazel every morning and evening. Hazel, solicitous sweetie that she was, would no doubt have called *him* if he didn't beat her to it. But that might have raised suspicions, because Chloe suspected that once discharged from the hospital, he hadn't meekly gone home to Peoria. Wilbur was shadowing the Laura Land Tour group, trying to connect with Kari. And he had appeared in Mansfield right on time.

Chloe glanced toward the parking lot. *Dammit.* The sedan was still there. But at some point while she'd been scribbling, Hazel and Wilbur had disappeared.

———

Roelke entertained a fantasy of shooting Marie's radio. It was tuned to her favorite pop-schlock station, and KC and the Sunshine Band were imploring women of the world to shake-shake-shake their booties. Honestly, it was more than anyone should be asked to endure.

But Marie would be more annoyed at him than she already was. Chief Naborski too. Roelke mentally holstered his gun and tried to appear productive by looking out the window for a citizen in need.

I'll wait for ten people to pass by, he thought. If no one comes inside with a problem, I'll make the call.

No one came inside with a problem. He made the call. "Mrs. Enright? It's Officer McKenna in Eagle."

"Is something wrong?"

"No, ma'am." Roelke didn't ask for what he wanted: reassurance that after *he* had taken the infant from his mother and delivered him to strangers, the baby was going to be okay. "I was just checking in. Is Travis still in foster care?"

"He is. There is nothing new to report."

"It's just that—"

"Officer McKenna," Mrs. Enright said, in a polite but I'm-way-too-busy-for-this voice, "I suspect that wheels turn quickly in your world. Unfortunately, they often grind very slowly in mine. You did your job admirably, and I'm grateful. Now you must let me do mine." She hung up.

Roelke was painfully aware that Marie, although typing, was listening to every word. "Yes, of course," he told the dial tone. "Let us know if we can be of any further assistance."

"Baby's still in the system?" Marie asked over her shoulder.

"Yep."

Marie rolled the page from her typewriter. "I need to make a deposit at the bank, and then I'm heading home." She filed the report, retrieved her purse, and—to Roelke's profound relief—turned off the radio. "You did the best you could," she said on her way out. "Don't let it get you down."

Easy for you to say, Roelke thought. He *was* down…although it wasn't all work stuff. The situation with Chloe was driving him nuts. Last February she'd gotten into some trouble in Minneapolis, and he hadn't been there. Hadn't even *known* about it. He'd been up to his eyeballs in his own trouble in Milwaukee at the same time, but he'd felt terrible afterward.

Now he had this nagging feeling that Chloe was flirting with trouble again in Missouri. He wasn't there, he didn't know exactly what was going on, and this time he wasn't doing anything that mattered. That felt worse than terrible.

He stewed for a few minutes, pulled out a map of the Central United States, considered. If Skeet or one of the part-timers could cover for him, he could be on the road by three, maybe three thirty. Or…he could call the Palmyra airport, see if he could rent a plane. That would be a whole lot quicker.

Roelke picked up the phone, but before he could dial, the door opened. He looked up and saw young Crystal regarding him solemnly. She wore jeans and a pink top with kittens on it, and carried a schoolbag.

He put the phone back down. "Hi, Crystal. Is everything okay?"

"My parents are fighting again."

"Are they hitting each other?"

She shook her head. "No, but they're really yelling."

This, Roelke thought, is getting out of hand. "Would you like me to go talk to your parents? Maybe I can get them to stop yelling." He hoped so. It was also possible that one or both would go nuts, and he'd end up arresting Mom or Dad's sorry ass right in front of Crystal.

But Crystal shook her head. "May I do my homework here?"

"Um…sure!" Roelke cleared a space on Marie's desk, making sure nothing that shouldn't be seen by a nine-year-old was visible. "How's this?"

Crystal sat down, pulled a math workbook from her schoolbag, and carefully selected a pencil with a good eraser from a little plastic case. She found her page, leaned over, and silently mouthed the words of the first problem.

"Do you need any help?"

She glanced up, looking surprised. "No, thank you." She went back to her work.

Roelke picked up the phone again, then paused. Skeet would probably come in, but Crystal didn't know Skeet. She knew *him*. He put the receiver back in its cradle.

———

Chloe began to search the sprawling, hilly grounds. There were a lot of visual obstacles. Besides the farmhouse, museum, and office, there was a gift shop, fenced garden, small orchard, henhouse, and a modern house where, presumably, Carmelina or a caretaker lived. There were picnic grounds across the road, and the footpath that disappeared toward the Rock House. She did not see Wilbur. Or Hazel. Or Alta or Kari, for that matter. Short of screaming at the top of her lungs, which would attract all the wrong kinds of attention, there was nothing else to do.

There's no reason for panic, Chloe told herself. The Voss sedan was still in the parking lot, and Kari's Rambler too. They all had to be there someplace. Hazel was probably touring the farmhouse. If Wilbur Voss *was* Dealer Discreet, maybe he and Kari had stepped calmly into some quiet corner to conduct business. Kari would blithely sell him the fake quilt square, and Wilbur was not likely to guess that the prize was all of two hours old. He had no reason to harm Kari. All he wanted was an antique to sell at enormous profit to some wealthy Laura-smitten collector.

Chloe glanced at her watch—thirty minutes before the grand opening tour of the Rock House commenced a mile away. She hurried to the back door of the farmhouse, where a docent was ushering a tour group out through a spacious porch. There was a little mudroom to one side too, discreetly roped off to protect a number of antique tools from grasping hands. Laura used those, Chloe thought. She'd finally reached a historic home where everything in sight had belonged to Laura.

When the docent was free, Chloe got back to business. "Pardon me. Have you seen a woman maybe sixty, sixty-five years old wearing a purple sunbonnet?"

The docent considered. "I don't recall a purple sunbonnet."

"Or a woman who looks a lot like me?" Chloe didn't think Kari would have taken a tour, but it was worth checking.

"Nope, sorry. But there is one group still inside. We can take a quick peek."

Chloe followed the older woman through a kitchen and dining room, then on into Laura and Almanzo's bedroom. Chloe felt a stab of regret at the sight of two single beds. The couple that had courted so shyly and sweetly in *These Happy Golden Years* ended up sleeping apart. If Chloe had been clinging to a shred of hope that real-life Laura found a happy ending, seeing those narrow cots was the death blow.

"The other group is in the front room there," the docent whispered, gesturing.

Chloe scanned the crowd, then shook her head. "No luck," she told the docent, "but I appreciate your help."

The other woman ushered Chloe back to the screened porch off the kitchen. "Your companions are probably headed over to the Rock House. The farmhouse and museum will be closed all afternoon so everyone can enjoy the grand opening."

Outside, Chloe debated her options. If she was all wrong about Wilbur, he might be meekly tagging along after Hazel to the Rock House. Perhaps Kari had gone with the flow and walked over too. Stymied, Chloe decided to look for everyone there.

The path to the Rock House meandered over the property, skirting fields and woods, dropping and climbing through ravines. Chloe emerged from the woods near a pretty cottage perched on a rise overlooking a grand open vista of Missouri pasture. She eeled and elbowed her way through the growing throng, and ... *there*. Hazel stood a little apart from the crowd, deep in conversation with Henrietta Beauchamps.

A few minutes later Chloe spotted Alta standing with David Rice and Norma Epps. Chloe beckoned the tour leader over. "Alta, did anyone ask you about the quilt?"

She shook her head. "I had to drive here with some of my people who weren't up to the walk, but no one approached me before I left."

Chloe leaned close. "I think the dealer is Wilbur Voss."

"*Wilbur*? Why do—"

"No time to explain. Have you seen Kari since you left the main farmhouse?"

"No ... " Alta's eyes grew alarmed.

"I'll try to find her. You keep an eye on Hazel, okay?" Chloe pointed. "If Wilbur shows up, don't let her go anywhere with him."

Alta lifted her chin. "Got it."

Okay, Chloe thought as she resumed her search through the crowd. Hazel and Alta were accounted for. But where the hell was Kari?

"What would you have done if you had found the wolves?" Manly asked.

"Why, driven them away, of course. That's what I took the pitch-fork for," Laura answered. The First Four Years

TWENTY-FIVE

COMING HERE TO THE Rock House was stupid, Chloe thought. If Wilbur wanted to conduct business, wouldn't he do it near the main farmhouse while the buildings were closed and the grounds largely deserted?

But at this point, walking back might be stupid too. Kari might have jumped into the Rambler to make the short drive. The best thing to do now was linger and hope that Kari would turn up.

Chloe retreated from the crowd and pulled out her notebook. There were plenty of things that still didn't make sense—the inexplicable destruction of artifacts, the troubles plaguing Alta's tour, and, obviously, Jayne's murder. When they last talked, Roelke mentioned several things that motivated people to commit murder. She began adding his ideas to hers.

1. Revenge

Chloe nodded. She'd focused on that from the beginning, right? Jayne pissed someone off in a big way, and that someone got revenge by killing her. Maybe it was premeditated, maybe it wasn't, but it was revenge all the same.

2. Greed

That was possible too. Just how big was Jayne's collection of Laura-related antiques? How much was it worth? Who now stood to inherit it? Who else knew about it? If Jayne made a habit of bidding at public auctions, anyone might have seen her.

A little girl in neon pink shorts and an orange bonnet raced by shouting, "Mommy, Mommy! There's going to be a *spelling* bee tomorrow!"

Jolted from her thoughts, Chloe scanned the scene again. Still no Kari. She bent back over her notes.

3. Fear

It was hard to imagine anyone feeling truly threatened by Jayne's antics. Unless… *unless*, Chloe thought, Jayne was more disturbed than I realized. She'd attacked the Wilder canon over and over, and yet she'd collected relevant artifacts with, according to Louise, a fierce zeal. Jayne had seemed obsessed with Laura Ingalls Wilder. Chloe had no idea why, but it was worth considering.

Chloe thought about the impaled Charlotte doll found at the Pepin Wayside, the decapitated china shepherdess she'd seen in Burr Oak, the defaced book illustration Kari had found in Walnut Grove, and the broken bread plate in De Smet. To the best of Chloe's admittedly limited knowledge, nothing menacing or creepy had happened at the Kansas homesite.

Was that because the perpetrator of earlier evil deeds was now dead? *Had* Jayne been responsible? It was one thing to verbally attack a long-dead author; it was quite another to willfully destroy reproductions and antiques that others cherished. Whoever had done those things must really loathe Laura, Chloe thought. Or really loathe someone—or anyone—who loves Laura.

Maybe Jayne had been guilty of the destruction. But it could have been someone else. People were icebergs, showing just a bit of themselves above the surface. Look at Kari, for crying out loud. I spent a week in a car with my own sister, Chloe thought, without understanding her at all. Kari had made stupid mistakes, and when they started to close in, fear of exposure pushed her to do something desperate.

Had someone been afraid that Jayne might expose some secret? So afraid that killing her seemed necessary? Chloe stood with pen poised, trying to think what secret Jayne might have taken to her grave.

Zip, zilch, zero.

… And there was still no sign of Kari.

Chloe slapped her notebook closed and shoved it back into her bag. It crunched against paper—the fax from the textile library Carmelina had given her earlier. Chloe pulled the pages free and smoothed them out.

Jayne's ill-fated article about Penny Squares had appeared in the Spring, 1980 issue of *The Distaff Side*. Chloe had requested the Letters to the Editor pages from the next two issues. She found what she wanted in the Fall edition, and began skimming the two-column response to Jayne's conclusions about Penny Squares. Although it wasn't pleasant to read a systematic rebuttal of a dead woman's work, Chloe was hungry for *anything* that might provide new insight about Jayne. But she got to the end of the letter without finding anything meaningful.

Then Chloe read the name below the letter, and felt the air sucked from her lungs. The letter was signed by Kim Dexheimer.

Kim Dexheimer, noted quilt authority who'd been scheduled to speak about Laura Land quilts at Alta's symposium. Kim Dexheimer, who Haruka had spotted having a seemingly pleasant chat with Jayne at the Pepin Wayside. Kim Dexheimer, who'd died gasping for breath in the picnic grove where Chloe had first met Jayne.

What did that *mean*? Had Jayne tracked Kimball to Pepin? It wouldn't have been too difficult. All she'd have to do was call him, give a fake name, and ask for information regarding a Penny Square. Chloe could almost hear Jayne's false accolades: "I'd *love* to get your expert opinion, but I live in Wisconsin... Oh? You're going to be passing through Wisconsin? Why, I could easily meet you..." Haruka had said that Jayne was holding an embroidered handkerchief. It could have been a Penny Square.

Still... had Jayne truly poisoned the man? Chloe pictured Jayne, tottering about in her high heels and Saks suits. She might have been vindictive, even seriously disturbed, but it seemed likely that she would have kept her own hands clean.

If so, that meant she'd had an accomplice. All Jayne had to do was distract Kimball Dexheimer with her Penny Square while her accomplice wandered by and sprinkled a trace of ground peanuts over the victim's salad. An accomplice motivated only by whatever Jayne paid. An accomplice who, after the deed was done, shared a mighty and horrible secret with Jayne.

An accomplice who perhaps became terrified that Jayne might expose him?

And it was a him, Chloe was almost certain. And she was almost certain that Jayne the collector had formed a deadly alliance with none other than Wilbur Voss. Wilbur, in need of cash. Wilbur, probable blackmarket dealer. Wilbur, who'd been, in his own bullying way, frantic to get the hell out of Pepin that afternoon.

Wilbur, who right this very minute might be striking up a conversation with Kari.

Chloe hitched her bag onto her shoulder and began to run.

———

At the Eagle police station, Crystal worked with earnest concentration. Roelke stared out the window, tapping his thumb against the desk.

And he thought about Chloe. What he could do for her, what he couldn't. He wanted badly to head for Missouri … but honestly, nothing she'd told him justified that. He couldn't charge off every time she did something that worried him. He had to trust that she would ask for help if she needed it.

Then he thought about Angelica and Travis, and what he could and couldn't do for them. In the quiet office, forced to be still, it finally occurred to him that his recent frustration maybe came from *not* wanting to think about them. Slow shifts did nothing to keep his mind from replaying that call to Angelica's apartment over and over. When he'd worked in Milwaukee calls were perpetually stacked up, and he'd been able to forget the bad stuff. Some cops buried bad stuff in booze; his drug of choice was busyness.

But neither of those strategies worked forever. Which was why so many cops struggled with alcoholism or insomnia. Bottom line: sometimes being a cop in the Village of Eagle meant an adrenaline rush. Sometimes it didn't, and in a way that truly sucked, but … honestly, it was probably for the best.

He hadn't been able to let go of the call where he'd taken infant Travis from his mother. He'd tried hard to frame it all in terms of the baby. He'd been bugging Mrs. Enright because he needed to reassure himself that Travis was okay. Travis—so tiny, so defenseless, so warm in his hands.

But in the late-day silence, broken only by the occasional whisper of Crystal's pencil, Roelke forced himself to consider the pain he'd brought to Travis's young mother. He remembered Angelica curled on the floor of her ratty apartment, sobbing. He wondered if Travis's father had come home and exploded. He wondered if there might have been some action that would have protected Travis without devastating Angelica. He didn't come up with any answers. But at least he'd started asking the questions.

Which took his thoughts right back to Chloe. He'd borrowed *Little House in the Big Woods* from Libby, and a quick skim-through was enough to convey that young Laura trusted her parents to protect her from bad things—bears, hunger, whatever. He glanced at Crystal, wishing she had the same thing. Wishing all kids had that.

Crystal worked for an hour or so, and he drove her home. "I'll stay in the car while you go inside," he told her. "If things are scary, you come back and tell me, okay?"

"They're probably done yelling by now." Crystal opened the door and got out. "Thank you."

He waited for a good five minutes after she went inside, but she didn't come back. Finally he put the car in gear and drove away.

———

The trail back to the farmhouse seemed a whole lot longer and steeper than it had on the way to the Rock House. Chloe tried to jog, murmuring apologies as she jostled past a few stragglers. Into a ravine, back up again, winding through woods, skirting pastureland. When her burning lungs felt ready to burst she slowed to a walk, but she trotted again as soon as she was able.

When the main Rocky Ridge farmhouse finally came back into view Chloe paused at the edge of the woods, chest heaving. The gate at the bottom of the driveway had been closed. Much of the lawn below was blocked from view by one of the buildings, but it looked like the staff had successfully diverted everyone to the Rock House.

No, not everyone. Kari was pressed furtively against the back of the museum building.

Chloe's racing heartbeat zoomed to overdrive. She didn't see anyone else. But something had sent her sister into hiding. Not daring a shout, Chloe tried to send Kari a silent message: *Turn around! Signal me!*

Sisterly telepathy did not engage. Kari was peeking around the museum's far corner, toward the back of the farmhouse.

Chloe took one last glance around—still nobody else in sight. Then she raced across the grass toward the museum, shoulders instinctively hunched against a hail of bullets or something. Only a narrow strip of land separated the museum building from a wooded ravine, and her vague plan was to dive for the trees and roll if trouble erupted. But nothing happened.

As Chloe reached sanctuary behind the museum Kari whirled, eyes wide. Then she gestured frantically: *Come here.*

Chloe sidled closer. "Is it Wilbur?" she panted.

"He approached me after most of the guests had left the site," Kari hissed. "He bought the bogus square, and we each got into our cars. I figured that was that, but as I drove toward the Rock House I saw him in the rearview mirror, walking back to the farmhouse. So I parked around the bend and snuck back around—just in time to see him grab the docent and lock her in the storm shelter beneath the museum. Then he went into the farmhouse."

That was not good. "Cops," Chloe managed. "We should—"

"There's no time! He could come out any second. I'm going to hide in the screened porch. It has a back door." Kari pointed. "I can surprise him."

That plan struck Chloe as simplistic and dangerous. Surprise him—and then what? Besides, she'd seen the space, and it provided Kari only a tiny corner to hide. "Don't you dare."

"You go out on the lawn. Distract him if he comes out."

"Kari—"

But Kari had already slipped away.

Shit. Chloe ran the other way, around the museum building and back into the wide empty lawn.

Moments later, the farmhouse's back door slammed open. Through the screen Chloe saw Wilbur emerge from the kitchen. He was carrying something. That bastard's been stealing artifacts, Chloe thought.

He should have kept going, crossing the porch and exiting to the lawn. But something made him pause. He looked over his right shoulder, toward the narrow corner where Kari was presumably hiding.

"Hey!" Chloe bellowed. She launched toward the porch.

Wilbur yelped with shock as she plunged through the door. A bulging satchel slipped from his hand.

Kari charged from the other side, clutching an antique pitchfork Poseidon-like.

Wilbur froze, trapped between the two furious Ellefson girls. *"Please,* I—"

Kari thrust the fork at Wilbur's right thigh. He screamed, clutched his leg, and went down.

"Don't let him go anywhere," Kari commanded Chloe. She grabbed an old mallet from the tool display and shoved it at Chloe. "I'll go let the docent out. She'll know how to call the cops."

Chloe found herself standing over Wilbur Voss with a mallet that, for all she knew, Almanzo Wilder had last used to wallop hogs before butchering. She considered giving Wilbur a good wallop herself, on Hazel's account if nothing else.

Wilbur rocked back and forth, clutching his thigh, moaning. "She could have killed me," he sniveled, as a dribble of blood seeped through his fingers. "I'll probably get tetanus!"

"Do—not—*move*." Chloe raised the mallet. "Or I'll use this where it will *really* hurt."

He played the marching songs of Scotland and of the United States; he played the sweet old love songs and the gay dance tunes, and Laura was so happy that her throat ached. These Happy Golden Years

In all the hard times before, Pa had made music for them all. Now no one could make music for him. The Long Winter

TWENTY-SIX

ROELKE TRUDGED UP THE stairs and knocked firmly. Angelica opened the door. She looked awful—stringy hair, dark puffy shadows beneath her eyes. He thrust one foot into the room before she could slam it in his face.

"Get out of here!" she flared. "I don't have any more babies for you to steal."

It was hard not to flinch. "May I come in?"

"Hell no! Just leave me alone. You ruined my life." She glared, tears seeping from her eyes.

"I just want to talk with you."

"I have nothing to say," she snapped. But Roelke didn't move his foot. After a standoff, she let go of the door.

Roelke came inside. She dropped into a chair, and he perched on the sofa. "Here's the thing, Angelica. My first responsibility was to

Travis. I did what I had to do to protect him, and he's safe. Now I want to protect you."

"I don't need protecting."

"You might. From Travis's father, maybe even from yourself."

She shrugged, avoiding his gaze, and picked at a hole in her jeans.

"I've called Mrs. Enright several times to check up on Travis." He leaned forward, elbows on knees. "I also asked if she thought you'd be able to get him back. She said it was up to you. She told me that you're clear on what choices you need to make. Has Travis's father been here?"

"No."

"Is that his choice, or yours?"

"I told him not to come around anymore."

"If he comes back, call the cops. You have the right to feel safe. And it's absolutely essential to stay away from him if you want to get Travis back."

She shrugged. He waited. Someone in the tavern downstairs plugged the jukebox, and a throbbing bass reverberated through the floor. Roelke waited some more.

Finally Angelica nodded. "I know. I get it."

That was enough for today. Roelke stood. "Look, you made a couple of bad mistakes, but I believe that you are ready to be a good mother to Travis. I'll stop back again. If there's something I can do to help, I will."

He let himself out and jogged down the stairs, feeling…not good, but better. What he liked best about working in a small town was the chance to get to know people. Sometimes that came with a price, but in the end, it was one he was willing to pay.

———

Law enforcement officials took Wilbur Voss into custody without a struggle. Carmelina had been summoned, but the deputies' cars were gone before visitors began drifting back from the Rock House.

The next few hours blurred by. Chloe was exhausted by the time she and Kari had given their statements at the sheriff's office and a deputy drove them back to Rocky Ridge. The historic site gate was open again. The parking lot was full of cars. Visitors massed on the lawn—adults claiming seats for the evening's performance, children racing back and forth.

Kari rubbed her arms as she surveyed the scene. "This is kind of surreal."

"It is," Chloe agreed. The line for the day's last farmhouse tour stretched from the back porch. That porch looked no different than it had earlier. That was, Chloe decided, a blessing. Visitors did not need to know what *she* knew. "You were amazing, Kari. Seriously."

"Well, that guy pissed me off."

"Remember how wistfully Hazel spoke about her dream of owning something of Laura's? And here her husband was dealing in Wilder artifacts."

"I knew he was after more when he went into the house. But I'm not sure I could have stopped him if you hadn't shown up when you did."

"Yay us."

"Yay us," Kari echoed. "So … what now? It's five forty-five. I do want to stay to hear Pa's fiddle played, don't you?"

"Absolutely," Chloe said firmly. "The museum is closed, but I'm supposed to show Carmelina the quilt at six. She may not even remember our appointment after the day she's had, but I'll go find out. You want to come?"

"I think I'll stake out a peaceful bench beneath a peaceful tree. We can hear the music from there."

"Sounds good." Chloe couldn't think of any better cap to the day. She didn't know if Wilbur had confessed to any murders, but the cops had him cold on attempted robbery, and probably on some charge for locking the poor docent into the storm shelter. Presumably the cops could hold him for those lesser crimes while they investigated the deaths of Kimball Dexheimer and Jayne Rifenberg. Chloe felt as if the black cloud that had followed them all from homesite to homesite had finally blown away.

She got Miss Lila's quilt box from their car and made her way to the small office building tucked discreetly beyond the museum. A volunteer pointed her to the study room Carmelina had mentioned. It was brimming with shelves and boxes and cupboards, but tidy. Chloe put her box down on an empty table spread with clean white paper. She removed Miss Lila's quilt and regarded it with affection. Thanks to Wilbur, she'd had no chance to compare this quilt with Mary's childhood Nine Patch, but he was no longer an obstacle. Soon, she thought. Maybe, just maybe, some answers would emerge.

While she waited Chloe examined photographs of Laura, from sober adolescent to smiling elder, that hung on the walls. Then she plucked a scrapbook from a row of volumes lining a nearby shelf. Someone had typed a label: *Clippings, 1960–1965.* Chloe sat down with the treasure and leafed through, careful not to harm any of the yellowed and brittle newsprint. Most of the articles detailed progress made by the Laura Ingalls Wilder Home Association after Laura's death in 1957. It was touching to glimpse the loving and determined efforts made by a small group to ensure that Rocky Ridge Farm and its treasures would be preserved. Touching too were letters from supporters, many of them children who spoke of sending hard-earned pennies to help.

Then Chloe turned a page and found a letter, published by the local newspaper in 1963, with a different tone. *What a waste of time and money… Surely it would be better to invest in Mansfield's public schools instead of enshrining a hack…*

"Hack? You have got to be kidding me." Chloe skimmed indignantly through the twenty-year-old column of complaints.

Then she reached the signature: Jayne Devich, Portland, Oregon.

Jayne Devich? Chloe's jaw slowly dropped. She had never perceived an inkling of any long-term relationship between Jayne Rifenberg and Leonard Devich, but that was too bizarre for coincidence. Jayne *had* been married once… but no, surely not to Leonard. More likely Jayne had been born Devich, married a man named Rifenberg, and kept the surname after her divorce. Prestige-hungry Jayne had nothing in common with bumbling Leonard.

No, that wasn't true. Jayne and Leonard had shared one trait: a dislike of all things Laura.

I should have seen that, Chloe thought. But even after Jayne's death, Leonard had continued on the tour! That seemed bizarre, even if he and Jayne had not been close. Why would he…

Oh God.

Chloe put the scrapbook aside, jumped from her chair, and bolted from the office. Instinct protested and she darted back, snatched Miss Lila's quilt into her arms, and ran back outside. Where was Leonard Devich?

More visitors were gathering. Chloe urgently scanned the crowd. Where *was* he? She hurried through the chattering guests, peering this way and that. No luck.

She finally spotted Kari beneath a walnut tree. "Have you seen Leonard?"

Kari scrambled to her feet. "What's wrong?"

"Find Carmelina," Chloe said. "Or find a cop. Or find somebody who can call a cop."

"But—"

"Please! Just do it!" Still clutching her precious quilt, Chloe took off again. If she was wrong, well, so be it. But she didn't think she was. She and Kari and the police—*all* of them—had declared victory too soon.

If Wilbur killed Kimball Dexheimer, he did it for money, presumably paid by Jayne. And if Wilbur killed Jayne, he did it to protect himself—and his little sideline of selling Laura artifacts and memorabilia. But Wilbur Voss never would have destroyed antiques or valuable reproductions.

Maybe Jayne had skewered the Charlotte doll in Pepin, and decapitated the china shepherdess in Burr Oak, and scrawled *DIE LAURA DIE* on an illustration torn from *On the Banks of Plum Creek*, and deliberately smashed an antique glass bread plate identical to Laura's. But it could have been Leonard too. Besides, it was almost impossible to picture Jayne sabotaging Alta's bus. And since Hazel was on board, Wilbur surely wouldn't have done that.

But Leonard had not been on that bus. Leonard had stayed in Walnut Grove that afternoon, ostensibly to discuss his cockamamied theories about Charles Ingalls with curator David Rice. Leonard had rejoined the group at the pageant grounds.

And now, Chloe couldn't find him.

A dozen girls wearing Brownie uniforms ran toward the rows of folding chairs. "Come *on*! It's almost time!"

Lovely, Chloe thought. The performance must be about to begin. She really wanted to hear the musician play Pa's fiddle—

Oh God oh God oh *God*. Pa's fiddle.

Laura's earliest memories were of falling asleep while Pa played the fiddle. The series' lowest moment came when Pa tried to play during the Hard Winter, and couldn't. Laura told Almanzo that her family probably would not have survived without her father's music.

There was perhaps no artifact with more meaning for Wilder fans than Pa's fiddle.

Chloe ran toward the stage, heart hammering against her ribs. Visitors trying to find seats clogged the center aisle, so she cut wide. She approached the stage from the right side just as applause rippled through the crowd. It was a fine evening, and Laura fans were about to hear Pa's fiddle played right here, right now.

But the man climbing to the stage was not the local musician entrusted with this rare performance. Clutching Pa's fiddle in one hand, Leonard Devich faced the audience for his grand finale.

"Were you much scared, Laura?" Carrie asked.

   "Well, some, but all's well that ends well," Laura said.

The Long Winter

Laura thought the trouble was all over now. But that was not to be…

The First Four Years

TWENTY-SEVEN

MOST OF THE GUESTS settled expectantly with a collective murmur and rustle. Chloe, certain that Leonard was not planning to play a tune, went cold inside.

Carmelina erupted up the steps on the far side of the stage. "Who *are* you?" she demanded. "Give me that fiddle!"

"Keep away!" Leonard raised the instrument over his head. He held it by the neck, arm cocked like a baseball pitcher about to let fly.

Carmelina went still. The audience did too. No, no, *no*, Chloe moaned silently. Not Pa's fiddle!

Leonard pulled his arm back even farther, gathering force for the fatal blow.

Chloe shot forward. "Wait!"

Leonard froze, blinking down at her.

"*Please*, Leonard." Chloe wished the stage didn't give him a four-foot advantage. "Let's just talk about this, okay? You do not want to do this."

"I do," he mumbled. "I have to."

"Are you doing this for Jayne?"

He flinched. "You—you don't know anything!"

Chloe tried to sort the stray snippets of knowledge pinging frantically through her brain. What might get through to Leonard? What might prevent his final act of destruction? She inched forward and gambled. "I know she used to be called Jayne Devich. I know she had a miserable childhood. That means you did too, right?"

Leonard frowned at her. "How did you find out?"

"That doesn't matter. All that matters is that you *stop*. You don't need to go to prison, Leonard. And you don't need to hurt all these good people here today. You have every right to be angry, but not at these people. Not at all the kids here."

As if cued, a child in the front row began to cry and was instantly shushed by her mother. Leonard's upraised arm begin to tremble. The fiddle trembled too. Sunlight glinted on varnish.

"Look, I get that you loathe Laura Ingalls Wilder," Chloe tried. "I just don't know why. I really want to hear your side of things."

Very slowly, Leonard lowered his arm. Pa's fiddle dangled from his hand.

"Before we talk, why don't you give Carmelina the—"

"No!"

"Okay! Okay." Chloe licked her lips. She was acutely aware of the crowd holding its collective breath. Acutely aware of the priceless fiddle dangling from Leonard's careless hand. Acutely aware that if Leonard followed through, everyone would remember that in the end, *her* interference led to the fiddle's destruction.

Just keep trying, Chloe told herself. She craned her neck again, trying to catch his gaze. "I know you wouldn't be doing these things without good reason, but it would help if you just explain."

"Jayne turned into her," Leonard muttered.

"Into *who*?"

"Nellie Oleson."

Nellie Oleson? The tormentor Laura described so exquisitely as mean, selfish, and spiteful? The sneering little witch portrayed so perfectly in television show and pageant?

Chloe could think of only one connection. "Are you related to Nellie Oleson? Was she your..." Negotiations stalled as she struggled to do the math.

"Grandmother," Leonard mumbled.

Before Chloe could think of a suitable response, someone appeared at the far edge of the stage and began climbing the steps. Chloe tried to send a mental message: *Stop! You might set him off!*

But Hazel Voss kept going, slow but steady. "Oh, Leonard, what's all this?" she asked sadly as she crossed the stage. "I've had a horrible day, and I think you're having a horrible day too."

"Stop!" Leonard took a step backward. Carmelina, still behind him, eased one hand toward the fiddle. But Leonard saw her, and stumbled toward the stage's edge.

"Oh, *honey*," Hazel said. "All you need is a hug." She held out her arms. Leonard stared at her, motionless, as if mesmerized. She slowly closed the distance between them and managed to wrap one arm around him. "There, there."

Leonard began to cry.

Chloe saw his fingers release their death grip and go slack. As if in slow motion, the fiddle began its descent.

She lunged, arms extended, shoving Miss Lila's quilt forward. The edge of the stage met her rib cage hard. The fiddle seemed suspended in air. Chloe strained forward, queasy with fear. Please...*please*...

The fiddle plopped onto the quilt. It did not shatter. It did not even crack.

That minor miracle launched a tornado of movement and sound. Carmelina pounced, grabbed the fiddle, and disappeared with it cradled in her arms. Staff surged onto the stage, closing in on Hazel and Leonard. Visitors surged from their chairs, shouting and muttering and questioning.

Chloe stood dazed amid the frenzy. She began to tremble. It's a little late for that, she told herself, biting her tongue to suppress a giggle of hysteria.

Kari shoved through the crowd. "Chloe! Was the fiddle okay?"

"I think so."

"Are you?"

Chloe drew a shaky breath, trying to compose herself. "I think so."

"What did he *say*?"

Chloe tried to explain the final pieces of this trip's deadly puzzle to Kari—how she'd figured out that Leonard and Jayne were siblings; how Laura's portrayal of Leonard and Jayne's grandmother had made them psycho-bitter. "I'm pretty sure that Leonard, and maybe Jayne too, spent the week destroying Laura mementos. I think one of them left that '*Die Laura Die*' page for us to find."

"But *why*?"

"Maybe it was all about their own rabid dislike of Laura." Chloe shrugged helplessly. "Maybe they wanted to hurt all the people who love Laura. Maybe they knew that Alta's symposium would foster a sense of Laura community, and it was all a desperate effort to stop that."

"My God," Kari said.

Several people jostled by, shoving Chloe—and, much more importantly, Miss Lila's quilt—against the stage. "What a pretty quilt!" a visitor exclaimed.

"Chlo-eee! Kar-ee!" Henrietta Beauchamps called. She and the Whelans were pushing through the crowd.

"Listen, head them off, will you?" Chloe begged. "I need to get this quilt packaged and back in the car." It felt safe to conclude that Carmelina would definitely be too busy this evening to settle in for a quilt chat.

Besides, Chloe thought, when cops show up someone will want to take statements. Again.

Hunched protectively over the quilt, Chloe made her way back to the staff building. Excited voices were coming from Carmelina's office. Chloe headed straight to the study room. An anxious inspection revealed that the abrupt meeting of antique quilt and rough plywood stage had left a broad streak of dirt, and one bit of rust-colored fabric was torn and flapping free.

"I'm sorry," Chloe murmured sadly, easing the flap into place with a gentle finger. Still, things could have been a whole lot worse.

As she walked down the hill toward the parking lot, box in her arms, she thought about those seconds when Pa's fiddle had rested safely on this Bear Track quilt. If by slim, stray, miraculous chance Miss Lila *had* come to own Laura's childhood quilt, the two artifacts had an entwined history. The notion that she, Ingrid Chloe Ellefson, had briefly cradled *both* heirlooms in her arms was overwhelming.

As Chloe reached the road a police car approached, sirens silent but lights flashing, and turned in the main gate. A few visitors were heading for their own cars, but not many. A microphone's squeal echoed down the hill as Chloe crossed to the parking lot. Someone announced something—unintelligible at this distance, but the crowd roared with approval.

Had Carmelina actually decided to proceed with the fiddle concert? The original musician chosen to play must be okay, thank God. Chloe had been afraid to speculate how Leonard had managed to get onstage with Pa's fiddle.

Going on with the concert felt like the right decision, actually. The Ingalls family had not let adversity or disaster keep them down. And at every homesite she'd visited that week, staff and volunteers had done everything possible to help the guests who came searching for Laura—whoever *their* Laura happened to be. The visitors here wanted to hear Pa's fiddle.

Suddenly all Chloe wanted to do was forget the trip's tragedies, shocks, and disappointments. She wanted to listen to a real musician play Pa's fiddle. She wanted to be a fangirl. She wanted to bump shoulders with Kari and say stupid things like, "Oh my God! Can you believe we actually got to hear this?"

And she would do all of those things. Just as soon as she found the Rambler.

Chloe hitched up the big box, which was getting heavy, and studied the parking lot, which was not all that big. No luck. Where on earth had Kari left the car?

An ugly restroom building squatted toward the back of the lot—maybe the Rambler was behind it. Music drifted faintly down the hill as Chloe rounded the building. I'm missing the show! she moaned silently. She balanced the box on one knee for a moment to rest her arms. She still didn't see the car.

Something small, hard, and round pressed into her back, just below her right shoulder blade.

Almost everything disappeared from Chloe's awareness—the warm evening, the faint cheerful sounds of a fiddle, the knowledge that there were other people in the world.

"Do exactly what I tell you," a woman hissed. "Or I will kill you."

The only things left were the wild beating of her heart, the weight of the ungainly quilt box in her aching arms, and the pressure of that gun against Chloe's shirt.

"Do not turn around. Put the box on the ground. Very slowly."

Chloe's skin prickled. Her arms trembled. Fear sucked all moisture from her mouth. Who was *doing* this? The voice seemed almost familiar, but not quite.

The gun's pressure increased. "Do it."

On the other side of the restroom building a dad yelled at his kids to get in the car, or else. Chloe felt a touch of hysteria. Should she scream for help?... Dear God, *no*. There were children over there.

"Do—it—*now*." The woman holding the gun shoved so hard that Chloe stumbled. Momentum carried her forward. The box almost touched the ground.

Then something snapped inside Chloe, something cold and hard. She pivoted right, bringing the heavy box around in a wild swing. The box connected with flesh and bone before soaring from her arms and thudding to the ground.

Haruka Minari gasped in pain. The pistol flew from her hand.

Both women staggered for balance and lunged for the gun. They landed on gravel—clawing, kicking, rolling, gasping as blows landed, each straining to reach the pistol. Haruka was closer but Chloe was taller. She jammed one elbow into Haruka's chin and shoved forward with her toes, right hand scrabbling desperately. Finally her fingers closed around the metal barrel.

With a squawk of triumph she rolled to a sitting position and quickly reversed her grip. "Don't move," she commanded, pointing the pistol at Haruka.

Haruka put one palm against the ground and pushed herself upright.

"I *mean* it!" Chloe got to her feet. Her right hand trembled and she wrapped her left over it. She felt shaky and sick to her stomach. Command presence, she told herself. It was something Roelke talked about.

"You're not going to shoot," Haruka said contemptuously. She'd lost her mellifluous Japanese accent.

"Stay *down*!" Chloe widened her stance, still trying for that command presence thing, but Haruka was right. Chloe didn't think she had it in her to actually shoot anyone. Even if she knew how. Guns had safeties, right? Did this pistol have a safety? Was it on, or off? She had no idea.

She tried to buy time so she could come up with a better plan. "Just tell me this: did you know about the quilt all along?"

"Of course. In Pepin I tried to get the quilt without inconveniencing you. In Burr Oak I tried to get the quilt by distracting you with the museum's fire alarm."

I *knew* someone was after the quilt, Chloe thought.

Haruka slowly got to her feet, a disdainful *I dare you* expression souring her lovely features. "But this has become tedious. I'm out of time and patience." She sidestepped carefully toward the gray quilt box. "You are not capable of shooting me."

Chloe glanced wildly around for help. No one was in sight, but... *yes*. She abruptly swung her arms toward the familiar blue Volkswagen Beetle parked nearby, aimed at the closest tire, and pulled the trigger.

She'd feared that nothing would happen, so the explosion and backlash was startling. She quickly regained her balance, aimed at another tire, and fired again. For good measure she shot each rear tire twice more. She heard shouts as the shots died away.

Chloe bestowed on Haruka the special smile she reserved for people she despised. "I may not be capable of shooting you," she agreed. "But you're not going anywhere."

Mary ... could sew quilt-patches if the colors were matched for her.
By the Shores of Silver Lake

It was odd that when they were little, Mary had been the older and often bossy, but now that they were older they seemed the same age.
Little Town on the Prairie

TWENTY-EIGHT

THE NEXT MORNING, CHLOE and Kari arrived at Rocky Ridge two hours before the grounds officially opened. "Maybe we'll finally make it into the museum to see Mary's quilt this time," Kari said with a faint smile as she unlocked the Rambler's trunk.

Carmelina was waiting for them in a lovely garden area beside the museum. Norma Epps from Pepin was there, and David Rice from Walnut Grove as well. As soon as Chloe put her box down Carmelina crushed her into an embrace. "Thank you for *everything*," the site director said. "You too, Kari."

"I'm just glad everything turned out okay," Chloe said fervently. Wilbur, Leonard, and Haruka were the cops' problem now.

"I know you're anxious to see Mary's quilt," Carmelina said. "I invited the site representatives who are here for the Wilder Heritage Festival to join us. We're just waiting for Edna Jo."

Oddly enough, now that the moment of truth had come, Chloe was in no hurry to begin. For the first time she was able to draw a deep breath and simply soak the place in. This part of Missouri was reminiscent of her beloved Appalachians. The rolling hills and lovely old farmhouse were soothing. "I don't mind waiting," she told Carmelina. "The site is so peaceful now."

"Yesterday was a nightmare." Carmelina shuddered.

"Three nightmares," David observed.

Norma shook her head. "I'm still sorting it out," she admitted. "Jayne Rifenberg hired Wilbur Voss to kill Kimball Dexheimer. Then Voss killed Jayne. Voss was also a blackmarket antiques dealer."

"The police found a quilted pillow that he'd stolen from the living room in his bag," Carmelina said indignantly. She looked at Chloe. "Bear Track pattern."

Chloe felt a tingle of anticipation.

"But I still don't understand what happened with Pa's fiddle," Norma said.

"We kept Leonard and Hazel in my office until the police arrived," Carmelina said. "Leonard was docile, and Hazel got a lot of the story out of him. He and Jayne had a very rough childhood—no dad in the picture, alcoholic mother, poverty. In fourth grade Jayne got a school assignment to compile a family tree. Her mother told Jayne—perhaps with bitterness young Jayne didn't catch—that *her* mother was famous, and had been written about in books."

"So Nellie really was their grandmother," Chloe said. She'd never pictured Nellie as anything but a nasty child and teen. It seemed odd to think that the real Nellie had grown up, gotten married, and had children of her own.

"But which Nellie was it?" David asked. "Nellie, Genevieve, or Stella? The character was based on three different girls."

310

Carmelina spread her hands. "That wasn't clear, but Jayne proudly told her classmates that she was descended from the real Nellie Oleson. Maybe she thought that being famous trumped all else, but the other kids evidently tormented her and Leonard mercilessly about it. The bullying lasted for years."

"Horrible," Norma muttered. "It really twisted Jayne."

"Something odd happened soon before she died," Chloe told the others. "She was tossing a penny, and she said 'Heads or tails, who's going under?' It's a quote from *Farmer Boy*." Roelke was the one who'd made the connection, actually. Chloe had repeated the odd exchange on the phone with him the night before, and he fetched the book and read the entire passage. "It has no real meaning in the book—it's just a joke—but I keep wondering if the phrase maybe came to symbolize in Jayne's mind the enormity of the gamble she took when she hired Wilbur Voss to commit murder. Maybe she knew Voss might target her, or maybe she thought about the police catching her. Or both."

A chickadee landed on the ground nearby, then quickly flew away. Carmelina said, "Honestly, I can't even grasp how much Leonard and Jayne loathed Laura Ingalls Wilder."

"Jayne also seemed to loathe Leonard," Kari observed.

"By adulthood they had almost no contact, but both saw the notice for *Looking For Laura* and decided it was time for revenge," Carmelina told them. "I got the impression that the destruction of artifacts was Leonard's idea, but since he was traveling with Alta, he needed Jayne's help."

Chloe wondered if Jayne had come to the dugout site that morning in hopes of seeing the Ellefson sisters discover the *DIE LAURA DIE* picture she'd left there.

"After Jayne was killed the police in South Dakota must have discovered that they were siblings," Kari said. "But since Leonard had nothing to do with Jayne's death, there's no reason why any of us would have heard about that."

"The real fiddle player is okay, right?" Chloe asked.

"Yes, thank God." Carmelina nodded. "He was tuning up behind the museum when Leonard somehow overpowered him."

"What an unlikely villain," Norma said.

"And then there was Haruka Minari," Chloe said, "tailing me down to the parking lot." She would be pissed about that for a very long time. And she'd have plenty of reminders. Her dive to the gravel had left both forearms bloody. Bruises from the scuffle had blossomed on her legs, arms, and one cheek, accompanying the tender line on her ribs caused when she threw herself against the edge of the stage. It hurt to move.

"Chloe forgot I left the car parked down the road when I went after Wilbur," Kari explained.

"I chatted with Haruka during the symposium," David said. "I *never* would have guessed she was anything other than a Laura fan."

"I missed something," Chloe said, annoyed with herself. "When Kim Dexheimer was dying, Haruka was so upset that she spoke flawless English. When I heard that pretty Japanese accent later, I just figured that *I'd* been too upset to notice it in Pepin."

"The police told us they found a business card in Haruka's purse," Kari said quietly. "She was a secretary for a textile appraisal firm in New York."

"I'd written the firm about Miss Lila's quilt for insurance purposes," Chloe explained.

Kari had also gotten a quote from the same specialty appraisal firm. There were many devoted Laura fans in Japan, and Haruka probably had an eager buyer waiting for anything she could deliver.

Carmelina, David, and Norma knew nothing about the single square, so Chloe didn't mention it now. But Kari had told the detective about it. "For all we know Haruka Minari might have somehow been involved in Miss Lila's death," Kari had explained to Chloe later, back at their motel.

"I told the detective Haruka might have had a partner," Chloe had said. "Someone driving a sedan was looking in the window of your car that night we sat by Lake Pepin. And I wanted him to consider whether Haruka or, more likely, someone she knew broke into Miss Lila's house."

"Good." Kari had nodded fiercely. "We can't let that slide. If what I did comes out, it comes out."

Now Carmelina looked at her watch. "I've got a big day ahead. We'll have to go ahead without Edna Jo."

She unlocked the museum and led the others inside. "Here." She gestured to a glass case containing the Nine Patch quilt made by young Mary Ingalls.

Chloe felt a visceral bolt of recognition. Mary's quilt was *familiar*.

It wasn't just that Mary's color scheme and arrangement were very similar to the Nine Patch Chloe had begun piecing on this trip. Mary had pieced her blocks on point. She'd arranged her blacks and browns and reds exactly as Chloe had done. She'd even used a black print for sashing that was almost identical to the one Chloe had purchased back in Minnesota.

And if that wasn't enough—

"It's *beautiful*," Kari breathed. "And..." She looked at Chloe, unable to finish.

"Yes." Chloe pressed her nose against the glass. "Several of the fabrics match fabrics in Miss Lila's Bear Track quilt."

"Ooh, get it out," Norma urged. "Quickly!"

Chloe removed the box lid and they all crowded close, pointing from one quilt to the other. "There's a match . . . and there . . . that one too."

Finally David stepped back, looking stunned. "Oh my God," he said slowly. "I think we're looking at Laura's childhood quilt."

Kari grabbed Chloe's hand and squeezed. They shared a wordless look of perfect communication. This made up for *everything*.

"Oh, dear," someone said behind them. "I'm afraid not."

Chloe whirled and saw Edna Jo Poffenwiler, who'd just entered the museum.

Norma frowned. "Edna Jo, you haven't seen these two side by side yet—"

"No, but I've examined Chloe's quilt." Edna Jo shook her head sadly. "And I've read the transcript of a letter that mentions it."

Chloe couldn't find words. Things were happening too fast.

"What letter?" Norma demanded.

"We recently found some letters in the wall of Pa's House in De Smet," Edna Jo said. "Several were written over crosswise, and very difficult to read. Given Chloe's interest I told the volunteer transcribing them to contact me if she found any references to quilts. She called me this morning."

"Who wrote the letter?" Kari asked. Chloe still couldn't speak.

"It's addressed to Caroline Ingalls from one of her sisters." Edna Jo pulled a single sheet of paper from her purse, found the appropriate line, and began to read. "'Don't let Mary lament for one moment because a few drops of bleach got spilled on her Bear Track quilt. I am amazed at her ability to stitch such fine work. I so treasure the pretty beaded bracelet she sent at Christmas . . .' Well." Edna Jo folded the letter away. "That's all about the quilt. But the implication seems definitive."

Miss Lila's quilt was not made by Laura, Chloe thought. Not as a child. Not even as an adult. Her fingernails dug painfully into her palms but she couldn't unclench her fists.

"Perhaps Mary made this as a gift for Laura after the original Bear Track quilt burned in the house fire, using the oldest fabric bits Ma was able to find in their scrapbag," Edna Jo suggested. But she looked dejected.

For a long moment no one spoke. "Well," Chloe said finally. "Now we know."

"It's still an amazing find," David said. "A quilt that Mary Ingalls made!" Everyone else nodded vigorously.

Chloe knew it was still an amazing find—but it wasn't what she'd wanted so badly to find.

Kari looked at Chloe. "What do you want to do now?"

"You mustn't leave without touring the farmhouse," Carmelina said firmly. "Come on. Director's special."

Chloe didn't want to tour the farmhouse. But she also didn't want to appear rude, so she let Carmelina lock Miss Lila's quilt safely away before taking the Ellefson girls through the screened porch where they'd cornered Wilbur the day before, and on into Laura's kitchen. Unable to concentrate on Carmelina's stories, Chloe tried to nod and smile at appropriate intervals.

Then they moved on into the Wilders' narrow bedroom. "There's such sadness here," she blurted.

Carmelina looked startled. "What's that?"

Chloe's cheeks grew warm, but there was no turning back. "Well…" She gestured. "The beds. Twin beds."

"Laura and Almanzo moved back here from the Rock House, did you know? *This* was their home," Carmelina said. "They created their beautiful home here together. This is where their dreams came true. As Laura said, home is the nicest word there is."

"That's sweet," Kari murmured. She was gazing out a window. "And so, so true."

"But when Almanzo was elderly, the effects of the terrible illness he contracted soon after he and Laura married became severe," Carmelina went on earnestly. "He was often in pain, and was a very restless sleeper. I think they got these beds then, very late in life."

"Oh," Chloe said.

"After Almanzo died, Laura couldn't bear waking up in her own bed and seeing his empty. So she began sleeping in *his* bed. She didn't change a thing—even left his box of medicines right by the bed." Carmelina gestured at the wooden box still on display. "They'd shared life, been true partners, for fifty-five years. Laura must have missed him terribly."

Laura's grief and loneliness pulsed in the narrow room. Chloe's throat ached. Tears spilled down her cheeks. "Pardon me," she choked out, and hurried outside.

Kari found her on a bench beneath one of the towering walnut trees, swiping her eyes, sniffling, and searching for a tissue. Kari pulled a packet from her purse and handed it over. Chloe blew her nose.

For a long moment they sat without speaking. Finally a vivid splash of color caught Chloe's eye as Alta's Laura Land Tours bus turned into the parking lot. The day was about to officially begin at Rocky Ridge Farm.

"So," Kari said. "What would Laura do?"

Chloe smiled a watery smile. "I think Laura would say goodbye to her friends … and then she would head for home."

When the fiddle had stopped singing Laura called out softly, "What are days of auld lang syne, Pa?"

"They are the days of a long time ago, Laura," Pa said. "Go to sleep, now."

But Laura lay awake a little while, listening to Pa's fiddle softly playing and to the lonely sound of the wind in the Big Woods ...

She thought to herself, "This is now."

She was glad that the cozy house, and Pa and Ma and the firelight and the music, were now. They could not be forgotten, she thought, because now is now. It can never be a long time ago.

Little House in the Big Woods

TWENTY-NINE

"MOM'S DOING DOMESTIC DUTY at the farm today," Kari told Chloe the next morning. They'd made it as far as Springfield, Illinois the day before, and were about to hit the highway again. "I called to check on the girls while you were out getting coffee."

"Coffee and crullers," Chloe corrected her happily, plunking the bag down on the table. "Anything going on at home?"

"Miss Lila's lawyer called her and Dad in to hear about the will. The Bear Track quilt was not mentioned, so I don't know how that will be resolved."

Chloe was still coming to terms with what they'd learned about Miss Lila's quilt. *Mary*'s quilt. "I guess we'll have to wait and see."

"Miss Lila left Mom and Dad some antique china, and she left you six heirloom linen handkerchiefs with handmade lace edging. And…" Kari lifted her palms, then let them drop back into her lap. "As promised, she left me the single quilt square Laura made."

"I'm glad," Chloe said honestly as she pulled a cruller from the bag. "I've developed a theory about that square. I think that after Almanzo died Laura felt an urge to reconstruct her bridal quilt, which burned in the fire. But after making one square, she stopped. It wouldn't bring Almanzo back."

Kari nodded thoughtfully as she stirred creamer into her coffee.

"You should frame the square. Just be sure to use archival matting," Chloe couldn't help adding.

"I'm going to donate it to one of the homesites."

"That's great, but—good luck choosing!"

"I'm leaning toward the museum in Burr Oak," Kari said. "The family's time there was so sad, and they left nothing tangible behind. It just feels right."

Chloe licked a bit of glaze from one finger. "You know, almost all of the disasters that plagued our trip have been accounted for, but not the fire."

Kari frowned. "You're right. Haruka said she pulled the museum's fire alarm, but Wilbur Voss actually got burned in the tavern."

"Well, last night I read the whole Iowa section of Laura's memoir, which I only skimmed before." Chloe balled her napkin. "She wrote about a guy who died after lighting a cigar while drinking whiskey."

"That's horrid." Kari's mouth twisted. "And … a bit eerie."

"Kind of," Chloe agreed. Probably what happened to Wilbur was pure coincidence. But maybe, in ways she couldn't begin to comprehend, it wasn't.

Once the Rambler was packed, Chloe took the wheel. They drove in silence for some time before Kari said, "Chloe? I am truly sorry I ruined our trip."

Chloe snorted. "Good God, you had a lot of help. Anyway, it wasn't ruined. I'm glad we went." She nibbled her lower lip. "You know, when we were kids it seemed like everything came so easily to you."

"I always envied *you*. Your adventures." Kari stared out the window. "After high school I didn't have the courage to go any farther than UW–Madison. If I had, I might have been better prepared to marry Tryg and settle down."

"Maybe, but don't look to me for relationship advice. I make it up as I go along." Chloe changed lanes to pass a semi. "Kari, I'd like to give you a little money to help pay that credit card bill—"

"Thank you, but no," Kari said firmly. "I'm going to tell Tryg about it. We'll figure something out."

————

They reached the land of cheese by early afternoon, and Chloe's farmhouse an hour later. She grinned when she spotted Roelke's truck in the driveway. He came outside to greet them.

"That's him?" Kari asked.

"That's him."

Kari got out. Roelke extended his hand. "Hi, I'm—"

"Thank you for getting those pictures." She pulled him into a fierce hug. "*Thank* you."

"No problem," Roelke managed. "I burned them."

"Good." Kari stepped back. "And I want to see you at the farm, okay? Come meet my family."

"Sure."

Chloe took her luggage and the quilt box inside, and received a joyful greeting from her cat Olympia. She and Roelke waved as Kari headed home.

Then Roelke crushed Chloe into his arms. "When you told me about this trip, I never dreamed you'd get mixed up in murder. Jesus, Chloe! When I picture that woman pulling a gun on you—"

"I'm *fine*," she said, although his embrace made her aware of every bang and bruise.

Roelke's grip tightened.

"First I got so scared I almost peed my pants," Chloe admitted. "Then I got angry. Honestly, I think deep down I knew Haruka wouldn't shoot me. She was a wreck after Kim Dexheimer died."

He stepped back but clasped her shoulders. "You look like a battered woman."

"Thanks," she said lightly. "I need you to tell me more about that whole command presence thing. I don't have it down."

Roelke started to growl. "You should never—"

Okay, that was enough. "I am *really* glad to be back in Wisconsin."

He let her go, accepting her change of subject. "I know you just got home, but … are you game for a drive before supper?"

"Um … sure." Chloe eyed him. Something was up.

They got into his truck. "So," Roelke said as they pulled out, "did you find Laura?"

"Yes and no." Chloe propped her toes on the dash. "Actually, I seem to have found her older sister, Mary. In more ways than one."

"Yeah?"

"Not what I expected. I shouldn't have just assumed that any lingering trace of the Ingalls family would come from Laura." Chloe thought about the quilt she'd started, which so echoed Mary's. She thought about the laughter she'd heard in the Kansas prairie, and the longing she'd felt in the Ingalls House in De Smet. Maybe, deep down, Mary hadn't been *quite* as serene an adult as she'd appeared.

"Hunh."

"I believe I did find Laura twice, though. Once was in the Burr Oak Cemetery. I didn't understand it at the time, but last night I read in her memoir that she thought it was a beautiful and peaceful place, and often played there."

Roelke rubbed his jaw. "Well, hunh."

"And later, in the farmhouse where she lived with Almanzo for so many years, I'm positive I felt something of her in their bedroom." Chloe looked out the window.

"Well, maybe you'll have another chance. Will there be another symposium next year?"

"Maybe. And that would be great, but…I think I'll pass." The scholarship was important, but Chloe wanted to keep Laura as the trusted childhood friend she remembered.

Roelke squeezed her knee. His hand was warm and strong, and felt like it belonged there.

Ten minutes later he parked in front of his family farm. He turned to face her. "Chloe, I want to buy this place."

"I know, but…you said you couldn't afford it."

"Can we go sit on the porch and talk? Something has changed."

Chloe remembered Kari's advice about neutral places vs. a man's ancestral home. "Let's just talk here. What's going on?"

"I think I *can* buy the place. Because of you."

She edged closer to the door. "Roelke, *I* can't be the reason you do or don't buy this farm. Not financially, not emotionally. That's way too much pressure—"

"Hear me out." He held up one palm. "I can afford it because of something you said."

Chloe's eyebrows rose. "Me?" she asked doubtfully.

"I rented a plane one day and flew over the farm. From the air it's really striking how the property nestles up against the state forest. I remembered the fun Libby and I used to have at the springs. Then I remembered you talking about how people used to come enjoy the mineral springs around here, and how most of the springs are gone now."

"So?"

"*So*, the springs here are still flowing. I've talked with some people about the property's historical significance, and the natural habitat. Long story short, it qualifies for a preservation easement. With that, I can manage the purchase." He'd been gazing at the house, but turned to look at her. "All because you talked about the history stuff."

"Yikes." Chloe tried to figure out how she felt about that. "That's wonderful."

"You don't sound like you think it's wonderful."

"I—I'm just not sure what it *means*. For you, for me. For us."

"Chloe, I want a home," Roelke said simply. "The idea of sharing it with you makes me happy, and I'd hoped it would make you happy too. It doesn't, and that makes me sad. But it doesn't change what I want."

Chloe hugged her arms across her chest.

"I needed to decide about buying the farm for myself. It's my family heritage, my savings, my career being affected."

"Well, my career too," Chloe objected. "As long as we're a couple."

"What I *mean* is, I'm not trying to make a choice for both of us." Roelke beat the steering wheel with his thumb. "I'm ready to settle down. If you're ready to move on, I get it."

"No, I'm not ready to move on. But Roelke, I've got nothing to contribute. I've got very little in the bank, and student loans, and a crappy car, and—"

"You're worried about *money*?" Roelke looked like she'd smacked him in the face with her checkbook. "I didn't ask you about living together because—"

"Why did you ask me? It never came up before."

"Believe me, the idea didn't pop into my brain when I saw that For Sale sign."

"But things are good for us now. Why risk it? What is it you want?"

"I want you to make a quilt for our bed and plant weird heirloom vegetables in our garden. I want to hear you hum hymns while you wash dishes—"

"I don't hum hymns while I wash dishes!"

"Yeah, you do. 'For the Beauty of the Earth,' most often."

Chloe wondered what else she didn't know about herself.

"I want Olympia to sleep in a sunny window. I want to sit in a porch swing with you and watch fireflies."

Chloe stared at her knuckles. That all sounded good. In a scary kind of way.

"I want to crawl into bed with you when I come home at three a.m. after a bad shift," Roelke said. "I want to be available if *you* have a bad shift. I want life to be a little easier for you."

The back of Chloe's throat began to ache. She couldn't bear the intensity of his gaze. "I . . . um . . . I need to take a walk."

She got out of the truck, walked across the lawn, continued around the house. Her mind cataloged the back yard—overgrown garden, large barn, sheds, even an intriguing old log cabin—but she refused to personalize the place. Instead she retreated behind the barn and sat down. Leaning against the old boards, she stared into the sun-dappled greens and browns of the Kettle Moraine State Forest. Roelke's farm had more Big Woods than the Pepin homesite, now.

She considered what he'd said. It all sounded really good. But it just wasn't that simple. Was it? Was it possible to gather the pieces of their oh-so-different selves and stitch a shared life together?

Chloe sat for a long time, thinking about Roelke. What she could do for him, what she couldn't. A warbler sang from the trees. The afternoon smelled of earth and growing things. "I just don't want to screw this up," she whispered. The warbler kept on singing.

Finally she stood and started back. As she reached the house, a totally unexpected sound floated softly through the air: an acoustic guitar. She rounded the corner and slowly approached the porch. "You're playing music!"

Roelke stopped mid-strum, looking abashed. "Well, this farm can't just be a memorial. I realized I needed to think of something *I* could do here. Something to make this place new."

"Now is now," Chloe agreed.

"I had this old guitar in the closet, and brought it out here yesterday, and…it was okay."

"I'm really glad." Chloe sat down beside him on the top step. "You know, I've always thought that *Big Woods* was my favorite Little House book because it's a Wisconsin story."

"Fair enough."

"But it's also the only book where the Ingalls family felt truly rooted." She watched a robin hopping through the weeds. "Roelke, every time you and I reach a good place, I'm afraid to change anything.

I think, Why look for trouble? I've also been afraid that moving in with you, here or someplace else, would just lead to *more* changes."

He put his guitar aside and nodded.

"But life is a river, and we can't stop the current." She sucked in a deep breath. "I need to tell you something. I got pregnant while I was living in Switzerland. I lost the child, and I still grieve."

"I…*wow*." He took that in. "I'm really sorry."

"Thanks. But the thing is, I don't know if I want to get married. I don't know if I want to have kids. Are you thinking about those things?"

"Holy toboggans, no!" He looked a little panicked. "Chloe, those questions are for someday. Maybe. And what happened in the past is…well, *past*. All I can handle thinking about is right now."

"Oh. Okay." Chloe let that in. "Well, let's talk about now. What about finances? I need some money of my own."

He shrugged. "I don't care."

"This will always be your family farm."

"We can make it *our* farm."

"I need some space of my own."

"Fine by me. It's a big place."

"Oh. Okay."

"In fact…" Roelke jumped to his feet. "I have an idea. Come on."

He led her to the small cabin. "The first Roelke immigrants lived here," he told her. "How about we fix it up and turn it into your private space? For reading or sewing or rosemaling—whatever you want."

Chloe caught her breath. "Oh *Roelke*. That would be perfect."

Looking pleased, he opened the door and stepped aside. "Take a look."

Chloe stepped across the threshold—and something immediately assaulted her senses. Something dark and heavy that lingered in the shadows.

Roelke grinned at her from the doorway. For a long flustered moment she had no idea what to do or say.

Then she stepped back outside and deliberately turned away. Whatever remains in the old cabin can wait, she decided firmly. It is not my problem today.

Grabbing his hand, she towed him to the center of the yard. The farm wrapped itself around them like a warm and welcoming embrace. *Much* better.

"Roelke, my only other attempt to make a life with someone ended badly. You obviously have a whole lot more money than I do. If Ralph Petty figures out a way to fire me, I'll have to look for a new job. And…I suspect you deserve a woman who's younger and calmer than I am."

His mouth twitched toward a smile. "Nah."

"Kari thinks us living together *here* is a bad idea."

"So does Libby."

A breeze ruffled the nearby trees, and puffy clouds sailed across the sky. The moment felt full of possibility. Chloe turned and leaned back against the man she loved. I will not be ruled by fear, she thought.

Everything she'd learned and lost on the road trip to Laura Land swirled in her mind. Laura had been a child when she stitched her first Bear Track quilt. She'd been a very young woman when she took her bridal quilt to the home she'd share with Almanzo. Laura had much grief and loss ahead of her…but love and joy too. And in the end, far from where she'd expected to settle, she'd finally found what she'd been searching for.

Maybe sometimes, Chloe thought, you just have to climb onto the wagon and set off with a heart full of hope. And that was a whole lot easier with a good man on the seat beside you.

She screwed up her courage. "If the offer's still open, I would like to move into the farmhouse with you."

Roelke wrapped his arms around her. "The offer is definitely still open," he said, voice husky. He kissed her temple. "Welcome home."

1. Replica Cabin
Little House Wayside, Pepin, WI

2. Masters Hotel
Laura Ingalls Wilder Park and Museum, Burr Oak, IA

3. Dove in the Window Quilt Square
Laura Ingalls Wilder Park and Museum, Burr Oak, IA

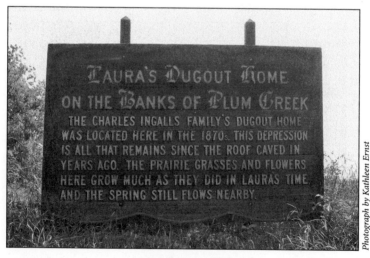

LAURA'S DUGOUT HOME
ON THE BANKS OF PLUM CREEK
THE CHARLES INGALLS FAMILY'S DUGOUT HOME
WAS LOCATED HERE IN THE 1870s. THIS DEPRESSION
IS ALL THAT REMAINS SINCE THE ROOF CAVED IN
YEARS AGO. THE PRAIRIE GRASSES AND FLOWERS
HERE GROW MUCH AS THEY DID IN LAURA'S TIME,
AND THE SPRING STILL FLOWS NEARBY.

4. Ingalls Dugout Site
Walnut Grove, MN

5. Ingalls Dugout Site and Plum Creek
Walnut Grove, MN

6. Double Nine Patch Irish Chain Quilt owned by Laura Ingalls Wilder
Laura Ingalls Wilder Museum, Walnut Grove, MN

7. Hexagonal Star or Rising Star Quilt owned by Laura Ingalls Wilder
Laura Ingalls Wilder Museum, Walnut Grove, MN

8. The Surveyors' House
Laura Ingalls Wilder Historic Homes, De Smet, SD

Photograph by Kathleen Ernst

9. Ingalls Home & Museum
Laura Ingalls Wilder Historic Homes, De Smet, SD

Photograph by Barbara Ernst

10. Replica Cabin
Little House on the Prairie Museum, Independence, KS

11. Rocky Ridge Farm, Front
Laura Ingalls Wilder Historic Home & Museum, Mansfield, MO

12. Rocky Ridge Farm, Side
Laura Ingalls Wilder Historic Home & Museum, Mansfield, MO

ACKNOWLEDGMENTS

I am grateful to the staff, volunteers, and property owners who have done so much to preserve Laura Ingalls Wilder's legacy, and to welcome visitors to each site. Special thanks to board member Mary Fayerweather, Pepin, WI; co-directors Barb Olson and Bonnie Tieskoetter, Burr Oak, IA; executive director Amy Ankrum, Walnut Grove, MN; executive director Cheryl Palmlund and assistant director Dianne Mollner, De Smet, SD; and William Anderson, author and Laura Ingalls Wilder historian. I encourage readers to visit and explore. Trips scheduled to coincide with one of the pageants or special events held at the various sites are great fun; it is also lovely to wander through on quiet days. If details of a site's history were not relevant to the story, I sometimes condensed timelines so readers could more easily picture the action.

Although my fictional tale and all primary characters are complete inventions, some aspects overlap the efforts of many. For example, in 1996, the English Department of Concordia College, St. Paul, organized what was perhaps the first conference devoted to Laura Ingalls Wilder. In more recent years the Laura Ingalls Wilder Legacy and Research Association—a nonprofit organization dedicated to the preservation and encouragement of research surrounding Laura Ingalls Wilder, Rose Wilder Lane, the Little House sites, and their legacies—has held LauraPalooza, a conference designed to bring scholars and enthusiasts together.

Chloe's presentation was inspired by a paper presented as part of the "From Little House to Historic House" panel at the 1993 Association for Living History, Farm and Agricultural Museums conference by my good friend Sally Wood, former curator of education at the Wade House Historic Site in Greenbush, WI. Finally, while writing *Death on the Prairie* I discovered the existence of Little House Site Tours, offered by an experienced guide; although I've not had contact with the company, I've heard only good things.

The Bear Track quilt Miss Lila loans to Chloe in the story is fictional. All of the other quilts mentioned in the book are real, although the letter from Rose is fictional. Of particular note, the single Dove in the Window block is displayed in Burr Oak, IA, and Mary's Nine Patch quilt is displayed in Mansfield, MO. Many quilters have speculated about Laura's handiwork on blogs and websites, and I thank them all. Very special thanks are due Linda Halpin, professional quilter, instructor, and author of *Quilting with Laura: Patterns Inspired by the Little House on the Prairie Series*. Linda generously shared her research, knowledge, and thoughts about old quilt patterns in general and Laura's work in particular. See my website for Linda's reproductions of key patterns mentioned in the book, and for links to her work.

I appreciate the law enforcement professionals who have offered suggestions and help shaping Roelke's fictional career. I am particularly grateful to Sergeant Gwen Bruckner of the Eagle Police Department, who has taught me much about police work in a small town.

Warm thanks to Tony Colin, certified airframe and powerplant mechanic for Morey Airplane Company, for his help with Roelke's flight scene, and for agreeing to appear in a cameo role.

Warm thanks to Agent Fiona Kenshole, and to everyone at Transatlantic Literary; and to Terri Bischoff, Nicole Nugent, and the entire Midnight Ink team.

I appreciate the contributions of editorial assistant Laurie Rosengren; photographer Kay Klubertanz; and artist-baker Alisha Rapp. I am indebted to the Council for Wisconsin Writers and the Shake Rag Alley Center For the Arts for providing a residency in Mineral Point,

WI; and to Katie Mead and Robert Alexander, and to Liz Rog and Daniel Rotto of Fern Hollow Cabin, for providing writing havens.

I made my own Laura Ingalls Wilder sites tour with my sister Barbara. Our travels were *nothing* like Chloe and Kari's, and I'm grateful for fond memories of our pleasant days on the road. I've always been blessed with the support of my extended family; from Scott Meeker, my husband and partner; and from my *wonderful* readers. Thank you all.

Many authors have written about Laura Ingalls Wilder's life. If you are interested in learning more I suggest starting with the work of William Anderson, John E. Miller, and Pamela Smith Hill.

ABOUT THE AUTHOR

Kathleen Ernst is an award-winning author, educator, and social historian. She has published thirty-one novels and two nonfiction books. Her books for young readers include the Caroline Abbott series for *American Girl*. Honors for her children's mysteries include Edgar and Agatha Award nominations. Kathleen worked as an Interpreter and Curator of Interpretation and Collections at Old World Wisconsin, and her time at the historic site served as inspiration for the Chloe Ellefson mysteries. *The Heirloom Murders* won the Anne Powers Fiction Book Award from the Council for Wisconsin Writers, and *The Light Keeper's Legacy* won the Lovey Award for Best Traditional Mystery from Love Is Murder. Ernst served as project director/scriptwriter for several instructional television series, one of which earned her an Emmy Award. She lives in Middleton, Wisconsin. For more information, visit her online at http://www.kathleenernst.com.

WWW.MIDNIGHTINKBOOKS.COM

From the gritty streets of New York City to sacred tombs in the Middle East, it's always midnight somewhere. Join us online at any hour for fresh new voices in mystery fiction.

At midnightinkbooks.com you'll also find our author blog, new and upcoming books, events, book club questions, excerpts, mystery resources, and more.

MIDNIGHT INK ORDERING INFORMATION

Order Online:

- Visit our website www.midnightinkbooks.com, select your books, and order them on our secure server.

Order by Phone:

- Call toll-free within the U.S. and Canada at
  1-888-NITE-INK (1-888-648-3465)
- We accept VISA, MasterCard, and American Express

Order by Mail:

Send the full price of your order (MN residents add 6.5% sales tax) in U.S. funds, plus postage & handling to:

> Midnight Ink
> 2143 Wooddale Drive
> Woodbury, MN 55125-2989

Postage & Handling:

Standard (U.S. & Canada). If your order is:
$24.99 and under, add $4.00
$25.00 and over, FREE STANDARD SHIPPING

AK, HI, PR: $16.00 for one book plus $2.00 for each additional book.

International Orders (airmail only):
$16.00 for one book plus $3.00 for each additional book

Orders are processed within 12 business days. Please allow for normal shipping time.
Postage and handling rates subject to change.